FALLING
FOR
SARAH

BOOK TWO IN THE *BODYGUARDS OF L.A. COUNTY* SERIES

CATE
BEAUMAN

DEDICATION

For my mother, Susan, for singlehandedly raising three happy, healthy, successful girls. Your strength is my inspiration.

ACKNOWLEDGMENTS

Thank you Rachelle Ayala and Aminah Grefer for your help and support.

CHAPTER ONE

September 24, 2010

SARAH JOHNSON TURNED THE KEY AND OPENED HER FRONT door. She crossed the threshold, breathing in the familiar scent of fresh-cut flowers and the hint of low tide blowing in from the Pacific. "It's so nice to be home. Welcome home, sweet baby girl." She stared at her sleeping newborn, smiling, and brushed her lips over the soft skin of the baby's forehead.

"Look out, coming through," Ethan Cooke said, loaded down with balloons and vases overflowing with cheerful blooms. "I had no idea bringing a baby home from the hospital required movers."

Sarah stepped aside, chuckling. "I know. Kylee has quite a fan club already. Let me help you with some of this stuff."

"I've got it. You gave birth yesterday, for God's sake. The nurse told you to take it easy." Ethan set the vase on the entryway table and released the balloons to the ceiling as he dropped the diaper bag from his shoulder to the floor. "Besides, Jake would kick my ass if he knew you were hauling things in."

Sarah's smile widened as she thought of her husband. "Yes, you're probably right, but I also know he would be grateful you were able to help me out. My mother wasn't expecting to run her shop today. Dana called in sick, so that was that."

Ethan moved closer to her side, staring at the baby.

7

"I'm happy you called. I wanted to come visit you ladies again last night, but things got a little crazy while I was on duty." He brushed a finger down Kylee's tiny nose. "She really is beautiful, Sarah. She looks just like you."

Sarah's blue eyes twinkled. "Thank you, but I definitely see some of Jake in her too." She wrapped her free arm around Ethan's waist. He returned her embrace, and she rested her head against his muscled shoulder. "I'm so happy right now, Ethan, so absolutely happy. Twenty-nine more days, and my family will be whole again. I can't wait to hug Jake and watch his face when he holds her for the first time. I could tell he wanted to crawl through the video conferencing equipment yesterday and touch her tiny fingers and toes." She looked down at Kylee. "No more deployments for your daddy. He'll be all ours."

"He'll be mine too." Ethan grinned, wiggling his eyebrows. "I've been waiting just as eagerly for Jake's return. It took me two years to convince him to join my firm. Now I need to get Hunter on board, and the crew will be together again."

"Getting yourselves into as much trouble as ever, I'm sure. You'll have to wait a little longer for your new security expert. He's not leaving my side for at least a week."

"I think I can live with that." Ethan kissed her forehead then started for the door. "Let me get the rest of the stuff from the truck. Then I'll set up Jake's surprise."

"Oh, I can't wait for him to see it. I've nixed the big screen TV idea for so long, I'm pretty sure he's stopped hoping for one."

"It's a beauty, all right. He'll love it. I'll have everything hooked up in no time."

"Great." Brimming with joy, Sarah kissed her

daughter again as Ethan opened the door and went outside.

Sarah took the baby to the nursery she had painstakingly painted on her own. The pale yellow stripes looked wonderful with the touches of pink scattered about the room. She put Kylee to her breast, listening to the door open and slam shut as Ethan brought their items in from his Range Rover. She smiled when she heard him rummage through the cupboards in the kitchen. If he was anything, it was always hungry.

Kylee's mouth went slack as she fell back to sleep. Sarah fastened her nursing bra and fixed her shirt. She settled Kylee against her shoulder and walked out to the kitchen while she rubbed her daughter's back, burping her.

Ethan stood in front of the open refrigerator, mumbling his excitement about her stocked shelves. He glanced up, grinned, and she itched for her camera. "Hey, I'm going to make myself a sandwich before I get started on the TV. Want one?"

"No thanks. Do you want me to make it for you?"

"Nah, you don't have to do that."

"Why don't you let me? I have another favor to ask of you. " She smiled. "The least I can do is make you something to eat."

Ethan went to the pantry, grabbing a loaf of bread. "Why don't you tell me what you need?" He pulled open a cupboard and took out a plate.

"A shower." She smiled again, nibbling at her lip.

Ethan's eyes zeroed in on Kylee, and he took a step back. "Geez, I don't know, Sarah. I've never held a baby before. What if I drop her?"

A laugh bubbled in her throat at the sheer horror in Ethan's eyes. Even after he'd helped her through hours of labor, watched her deliver Kylee, and cut the cord in Jake's honor, he'd refused to hold her.

Sarah walked to where he stood. "You're not going to drop her. Fold your arm like this." She held her arm out, bending at the elbow.

Ethan cleared his throat and followed her lead. Sarah placed Kylee in the crook of his rigid arm. He grabbed her hand when Kylee squirmed. "She's moving, she's moving. She's going to fall. Shit, Sarah, I really think this is a bad idea."

"I think it's a great idea. Trust me on this one." She adjusted the baby slightly, moving Ethan's arm closer to his body, making sure his hand held Kylee under her diapered bottom. She backed away from them, grinning at the discomfort and mild panic she read all over Ethan's face. "You're a natural. Look at you two. I need my camera."

Ethan groaned as she moved to the pile of bags outside the kitchen door and grabbed her case, pulling her Nikon D3 from the bag. She held up the camera and looked through the lens. For a test shot, she focused on Ethan's arresting face. Sharp cheekbones and straight black eyebrows accentuated long, thick eyelashes and bold gray eyes. She zoomed in on the clear gray pools surrounded by dark, smoky rings and pressed the shutter closed in rapid succession. His firm, full lips and muscular torso showcased a man perfectly comfortable with his masculinity. She tightened her focus on his big hand holding Kylee's little body and clicked away again, moving in closer, getting lost in her passion for pictures.

"Sarah, do you want that shower or not?"

She pulled the camera back, focusing on Ethan's raised brow and lips pressed firm in annoyance. "Sorry. I got a little carried away. You two make excellent subjects. The camera loves your face."

"So you've told me more times than I can count."

She placed the Nikon back in the bag and zipped it closed. "You're doing a great job with her."

He glanced down at Kylee. "I guess this is okay."

"See? I'll be quick. She just ate, so she should sleep. Here's the burp cloth, just in case she spits up." Sarah draped the cotton towel over Ethan's shoulder.

As she backed out of the kitchen, Ethan took a step forward. "Wait. Um, what if she starts to cry?"

Amused by his distress, Sarah couldn't help but smile. The man standing before her dealt with the scum of the earth every day, yet a seven-pound infant brought him to his knees. "Just jiggle your arm a little bit. She'll fall right back to sleep." She turned and walked toward the bathroom, calling over her shoulder, "Oh, and relax. Babies feel tension."

~~~~

Alone and mildly terrified, Ethan stared down at the pretty little bundle snuggled against him. Her serene face, a miniature of Sarah's, was so perfect. She smelled of baby powder and weighed next to nothing.

He began to wiggle his arm, just in case. "I guess this isn't so bad. Let's make a deal. If you keep sleeping until your mom comes back, I'll talk her and your dad into a really kickass swing set for the backyard. It'll be my present to you."

Kylee's lips made a sucking motion as she continued to sleep.

"Okay, I guess that means we have a deal."

Relaxing with more confidence, Ethan turned back to the counter, attempting to make his sandwich one-handed. He finagled the twist tie from the plastic as Kylee curled closer against him. Startled, he dropped the bread. He bent at the knees to pick up the loaf, and Kylee grunted. Seconds later, a small, wet explosion sounded in her diaper. Ethan stopped dead, still crouched. Kylee nuzzled herself against his chest and slept on.

"That couldn't be good." He stood and walked toward the bathroom, desperately hoping Sarah was finished. The radio played beyond the closed door as water sprayed into the bathtub.

The baby began to stir and fuss. He jiggled his arm from side to side, but Kylee's fussing turned into a lusty cry. Panicked, Ethan almost forgot the rules of friendship and rushed into the bathroom. With his hand on the knob, he stopped himself. *Christ, pull it together, Cooke. You've got this.*

He headed to the pale pink and yellow bedroom, glancing back at the bathroom door wistfully. "Come on, Sarah. Hurry up," he muttered.

Kylee turned a deep pink as she cried harder. Ethan stared at her mouthful of smooth, toothless gums and tiny fists curled tight as they moved about. "Okay, kid. I guess we don't have a choice here. Let's get you changed." He glanced around the cheerful room with stuffed animals piled next to a rocking chair, zeroing in on the pine changing table and the stacks of diapers and wipes lying tidy on the shelf above.

He awkwardly lay Kylee down on the soft white pad, found a package of unopened diapers and quickly scanned the directions. As Kylee continued to cry, he pulled a diaper off the shelf. "My God, look at these things. My hand's bigger than this." He located the sides with the tape, putting it down next to her, just like the picture showed. He unbuttoned her sleeper and the white onesie buttoned at her crotch. "How many layers are you wearing?" He pulled the diaper tape next, blowing out a breath. "Here goes nothing."

Ethan eased the diaper away and swore. "Jesus, this isn't right. It's black and yellow. I think we need to take you back to the hospital." He focused on the browning raisin protruding from her stomach. "And look at that thing on your belly button. It didn't look like that yesterday." Completely flustered now, he pulled a wad of wipes from the bin and knocked the diaper cream to the floor.

Kylee's short gasping cries shrilled louder.

"Shh, shh, shh, it's okay, kid. I'm trying my best here. You're all right." Ethan took the wipes, moving them over the baby's bottom. "This stuff's like cement. Man, I'd rather be in an alley with three UZIs pointed at my head."

With Kylee's tiny baby butt clean, Ethan clumsily placed the new diaper under her. He swore again when the tapes faced her stomach. Her legs moved about in her outrage, making it hard to flip the diaper around. "You're not exactly helping me out, kiddo." He adjusted the diaper and fastened the tapes.

"There." Ethan buttoned the onesie, muttering a curse when he mismatched the snaps. "Screw the pink outfit. This will have to do. You're worked up. I'm worked up." He placed his hand under Kylee's neck and head, scooping her bottom up with the other, like he saw Sarah do earlier. Kylee's cheek rested against his heart, and her cries turned to whimpers before they stopped.

"There you go, sweetheart. That was pretty awful, huh? I don't know about you, but I think I'm going to have nightmares for weeks." He walked to the rocking chair with Kylee and sat down. His big, callused palm played with the peach fuzz on her head as he moved the chair back and forth. "I think I was about to cry myself. Let's keep that between us, okay?"

"Here you are." Sarah peeked in the room with her mass of blonde hair twisted in a towel on top of her head. Her face was left unframed, showcasing big, exotic eyes, high cheekbones, and a lush Cupid's bow mouth that smiled until she zeroed in on the mess on the changing table. "I see Kylee needed a change."

"Don't even ask. It was exhausting and traumatic for both of us."

She chuckled. "Why don't I take her?"

"Oh yeah, sure, now that the hard work's done."

Sarah reached down and took Kylee, leaving behind the floral scent of her soap.

"Sarah, I don't know how to say this, but I think there's something wrong with her."

Frowning, she pulled the baby back from her shoulder, giving her the once-over. "What is it? What's wrong with her?"

"Her umbilical cord is brown and her poop's all gooey and yellow. Blackish stuff was stuck to her butt. I had a hell of a time getting it off."

Sarah's shoulders relaxed and her grin returned. "The umbilical cord is drying up and will fall off, the black stuff is meconium, and she's breastfed. Everything's perfectly normal."

As if on cue, Kylee began to cry and root around.

"How do you *know* all this stuff? You're so calm. I mean, you're always calm, but my God, she's so little and helpless."

"When you grow up with an obstetrician in your house and your mother is obsessed with children in general, you learn. I've been around babies for as long as

I can remember."

Kylee whimpered and sucked on her fist.

"Do you mind if I borrow the rocker? I think she's ready to eat again."

"I thought she just did."

"She's establishing her milk supply."

Ethan winced. "Jesus. Let me go take care of the TV for you."

Sarah sat and began to unbutton her shirt. "Thanks."

"No problem."

"Ethan?"

He stepped into the hallway and stopped.

"Your sandwich is on the counter."

He smiled. "Thanks."

~~~~

Ethan brought the sandwich and a bowl of fruit salad to the living room. He took a huge bite of turkey, avocado, and tomato then put the plate on the sturdy oak coffee table. He pulled the tape from the side of the massive box and prepared to set up Jake's new TV.

While he leafed through the instructions, Sarah's soft voice cooed to her daughter through the baby monitor. He glanced up from the booklet and around the homey living room, listening to Sarah. A flash of envy snuck up for what Jake had, surprising him. Shaking his head, Ethan looked back at the directions. Marriage and family weren't for him.

He was screwing the plasma screen onto its base when a car pulled up to the curb. "Hey, Sarah, someone's here."

"Hailey, the college girl from down the road, was planning on stopping by. She's desperate to babysit

Kylee. You can let her in," she said into the monitor.

Ethan tightened the last screw and stood. He walked by the large picture window, expecting to see the short, brown haired co-ed. Instead he watched four military men, dressed in dark green and khaki, step from a black sedan. His heart hammered against his ribs as his stomach sank. "Shit, no. Oh my God, no." He whipped his head around, making sure Sarah wasn't coming and yanked the door open, stepping outside, closing it behind him.

The men approached and Ethan stood in their path as if that would somehow change the news he knew they were here to bring. "What can I do for you?"

The group stopped in front of him. "Is this the home of Mrs. Sarah Johnson?"

"Yes, it is. Is he dead? Is Jake dead?"

"I'm sorry, sir. We need to speak with Mrs. Johnson."

Ethan saw the apology in the man's eyes, and the sudden grief knocked him back like a heavy blow. Jake had been one of his two best friends for years.

The men tried to move past him, but he blocked their way again. As much as he wanted a moment to catch his breath, he needed to protect Sarah more. "Don't take another step. I get that you can't tell me, but you're going to give me a minute to talk to her first. She just gave birth yesterday morning. This is going to crush her."

"We're here to offer any support we can, sir."

Ethan opened the door and let them in before him. "Please, sit down. I'll go get Sarah." He walked from the room and started down the hall to the nursery.

Stopping outside the room, Ethan fisted his hands at his side and took a deep breath. Memories flashed through his mind, one after the other, and he braced his hands on the wall. He took another deep breath, trying to steel himself for what had quickly become the hardest moment of his life. He was about to watch Sarah's life fall apart.

He stepped into Kylee's room and stopped. Sarah had taken her hair from the towel. Wet ropes of smooth gold rested on her shoulders. Her eyes were closed while Kylee suckled at her breast. If this were a picture, it would be titled 'Beautiful Serenity.' He was about to destroy it. He took another breath, walked to Sarah's side and knelt down, taking her hand.

Sarah's eyes flew open, staring into his. "You startled me." A smile played across her lips before it faded. "What's wrong?" She sat up straight, breaking Kylee's latch with her finger.

Ethan tightened his grip on her hand, willing her to take all the strength he could give. "Sarah, there are some men waiting for you in the living room. They're Marines."

Sarah's fingers clutched his like a vise before they went lax. The bright, bold blue of her eyes dimmed. "Oh, okay," she said dully. She stood, covering her breast and pulled Kylee close, automatically burping her.

Ethan draped his arm around her shoulders, walking with her and the baby to the living room. The men stood as they entered, and the officer stepped forward.

"Mrs. Johnson, I'm Commander Michael Driggs. I'm here to regretfully inform you that your husband, Gunnery Sergeant Jake Johnson, was killed in action today at 6:34 p.m., Afghanistan time. The United States Marine Corps is truly sorry for your loss and is proud of the service your husband provided our country."

Sarah stared at the commander for several seconds before she slowly sat down on the couch.

Ethan sat beside her.

"Jake's gone?" She spoke, her voice barely a whisper. "He can't be. He hasn't held Kylee yet. He's coming home in twenty-nine days to hold Kylee. He watched me give birth yesterday. He said he was coming home in four weeks."

Sarah's face paled with grief. Ethan swore he heard her heart shatter while the commander spoke. Her bubbly vibrancy had been replaced with fragility. He was afraid that if he touched her, she would break into a million pieces.

Ethan glanced at the man who now sat on the other side of Sarah. "Sir, Gunnery Sergeant Hunter Phillips is in Jake's company. Is there any word on his welfare? He and Jake are—" he closed his eyes on a fresh wave of pain "—were my childhood friends. Hunter is also very close to Sarah."

"Gunnery Sergeant Phillips was wounded in action. He was shot in the shoulder. He's out of surgery and is resting comfortably." Commander Driggs looked at Sarah again. "Sergeant Phillips tried desperately to save your husband, Mrs. Johnson. Is there anyone we can call for you at this time?"

She shook her head. "I don't know. I can't think." She looked at Ethan, lost. "I can't think right now. I don't want to do this. I want to be alone."

He couldn't stand to see her like this. He put his arm around her, pulling her close, pressing his forehead to her hair. "Okay, you don't have to. I'll take care of everything. Go lay down."

The men stood when she took the baby and walked from the room.

"I'm sorry, Commander, gentlemen, but I'm going to have to ask you to leave. Do you have a card or a number I can take from you? I'll have Sarah's father call you as soon as I get a hold of him."

"Of course, sir."

Ethan took the card and walked them to the door, shutting it behind them. He went to the small desk, found Sarah's parents' number programmed into the phone, and called.

~~~~

Sarah lay Kylee in her crib and covered her with a light blanket. Her daughter slept soundly in the center of the mattress, unaware that their lives were forever changed. She stared at the photograph of Jake hanging on the wall above the crib. She had taken the picture the day before he left to finish his deployment, before they were aware they'd made Kylee. His big, cheesy grin and smiling brown eyes filled the frame. *Oh God, Jake. You're gone. How can you be gone? I need you. I can't do this by myself.*

The dredges of shocked disbelief were melting away, and panic and dread quickly took their place. How was she going to live without him? Sarah glanced down at Kylee again, as a thought circled through her mind. It brought such crushing pain she could hardly breathe. They would never meet. Jake would never touch the daughter he had helped create. Kylee would be robbed of ever knowing her father's love.

Jake's deep, infectious laugh echoed in her head and Sarah buckled. She would never hear it again. He would never kiss her or hold her again. Her breath shuddered in and out.

Ethan's hands rested on her shoulders, and she flinched. He turned her toward him. She stared into his eyes, saw the grief settled there, and a tear rolled down her cheek. "Tell me this isn't real, Ethan. Please tell me this isn't real," she said on a sob.

He pulled her into his arms, holding her tight. "Come here." He picked her up and sat with her in the rocking chair. Her long legs hung over the side, just skimming the floor as the chair swayed back and forth. Ethan cradled her close to his chest.

Finding comfort in the arms of her friend, Sarah wept as Ethan's hand ran through her damp hair. "He's really gone. I can't believe he's really gone."

He lifted her chin as he spoke, choking on his own sorrow. "I'm making a promise to you right now, Sarah. You'll never be alone through this. I'll be here for you every step of the way, for as long as you need me."

"I'll always need you."

"Then I'll always be here." He rested her head against his chest again as their tears fell, mixing together on the hands they held clutched together.

CHAPTER TWO

February 2013

THE OCEAN BREEZE BLEW THROUGH HER HAIR, AS SHE FRAMED the couple in the lens of her Nikon. The gorgeous man, blond and tan, stood ankle deep in the waves, smiling down at the dark-haired beauty.

Sarah tightened her focus as the sun sank along the horizon, casting hues of pink and purple throughout the sky, creating a glorious backdrop. When the foam crashed around the couple's legs, drops of water flew high in the air, and she knew she had her shot. She pressed the shutter button, capturing the moment. "What a picture you two make. You're fantastic!"

Morgan looked in Sarah's direction and smiled. Sarah pressed the button again as Morgan's shiny brown hair flew around her face, accentuating the vivid green of her eyes.

"Let's do a couple more. Both of you walk from the surf. Hunter, when I tell you, pick Morgan up and stroll along the beach." She caught Hunter's eye roll through the lens and Morgan's quick jab to his ribs.

"Be a sport, Hunter. These pictures will be special memories for the two of you."

He blew out a long suffering breath. "I stopped being a good sport two hours ago. This is the last one. I'm hungry."

"Whine, whine, whine," Morgan said as she smiled, drilling her finger into her fiancé's muscled stomach. "If you're a good boy and do what Sarah says, you can be my date for our rehearsal dinner."

Sarah grinned. "Let's finish this. I'm losing the light."

Morgan and Hunter joined hands and began walking along the wet sand, just missing the surf. After several steps, Hunter picked Morgan up and continued on. Sarah zoomed in on the four footprints that became two, blurring the couple walking off in the distance. She glimpsed the photo she made on her digital screen and beamed. The effect was just what she'd wanted. This would be her gift to them, the perfect symbolism of marriage—two lives becoming one.

Sarah looked up from the camera, and happiness filled her heart. Hunter still held Morgan in his arms. He said something and she laughed. Her hand brushed his cheek as she answered, and he grinned.

She had feared this day would never come for her friend. After Jake's death, Hunter had closed himself off to happiness, blaming himself for something that had never been his fault. A month on duty in the mountains of Yellowstone, protecting Morgan, had taken care of that. He'd lost his heart while they'd dodged gunfire and run from corrupt government officials. Now, in less than twenty-four hours, Morgan and Hunter would be married.

"Are we finished here?" Hunter said as he set Morgan down.

"Yes, the torture is officially over." Sarah smiled.

Morgan enveloped Sarah in a hug. "We really do appreciate you doing this for us."

Sarah hugged back. "I'm happy to."

Hunter moved in, giving Sarah a quick kiss on the forehead. "Yes, we do. Thank you."

"You're welcome."

Morgan glanced at her watch. "We're cutting it a little close. We need to get home and change before we head over to the resort. Do you want to ride with us, Sarah?"

"No, I have to pack a few of Kylee's things yet and make sure Hailey can still join us tomorrow. Are you sure you want us staying with you tonight? You need a good night's sleep."

"Of course I do. Hunter will be with Ethan. I want my Matron of Honor and flower girl with me."

"Then we'll be there." Sarah shouldered her camera bag, and they made their way to their cars. She unlocked her blue sedan and got in. "I'll see you in a bit."

~~~~

Sarah ran toward the enormous gazebo with Kylee in her arms—a tricky feat in heels. "We're here. We're here. I'm so sorry we're late," she said to no one in particular as she climbed the steps to the center.

A boisterous crowd of fifty milled about, and she relaxed. It was clear there was no hurry here. Hunter, clad in a white button-down and black slacks, spoke to the officiant while Morgan, stunning in her simple, sleeveless cocktail dress—the same bold green as her eyes—chatted with her parents and Hunter's mother.

"I guess we're not so late after all." Sarah settled Kylee on her hip and smoothed her pink thigh-length dress. "Let's go tell Uncle Hunter we're ready whenever he is." She took a step forward and stopped, captivated by the spectacular view. The full moon, rising high, cast a glow upon thousands of flowers surrounding the gazebo. Sarah walked to the edge, caught up in the beauty. The distant thunder of the Pacific hundreds of feet below added to the magic. "Oh, sweetheart, it's amazing."

Kylee's blue eyes brightened. "I want to pick the fwowers."

"We can't, honey." She watched her daughter's smile dim. "They don't belong to us. We can pick flowers at home."

"O-tay." Kylee gasped, and let out a sudden squeal of delight as she held out her arms.

Sarah jumped and turned as Ethan, handsome in charcoal slacks and a white polo, swooped forward, grabbing Kylee from Sarah, resting her on his hip. "Hey there, kiddo." He kissed her chubby cheek. "Don't you look pretty tonight."

"Dis is my new dress," Kylee preened, tugging none too gently on the delicate, pale blue silk.

"You look like a princess. A pretty princess should have a flower." He walked with her to the side of the gazebo and leaned over, picking a creamy white carnation.

Kylee's blonde pigtails bounced in her excitement as she took the stem from Ethan's fingers. "Look, Mama, my pretty fwower. I'm a princess."

Sarah smiled at Kylee, then Ethan. "Yes, I see. What do you say to Ethan?"

"Tank you."

"You're welcome." Ethan bent his head close to Kylee's and whispered in her ear. Her head bobbed up and down as she smiled. Ethan bent forward again and picked another carnation. This time he walked to Sarah and handed it to her.

She grinned, touched by his sweetness. "Well, aren't you two thoughtful." She brushed her lips against Kylee's cheek. "Thank you." Her grin widened when Ethan tapped his own cheek. Sarah brushed his next, chuckling.

"Thank you, as well."

"Beautiful ladies deserve beautiful flowers, right, kiddo?"

Kylee wrapped her arms around the back of his neck. "Right."

Sarah took his hand. "This is the perfect night for their rehearsal. I hope the weather..." She stopped as a tall, voluptuous woman dressed to kill slid up next to Ethan. Her beautifully manicured finger ran down his muscled arm.

"Ethan, darling, I've been looking for you," she purred in her European accent.

"I had to come see my favorite kiddo." He let go of Sarah's hand to gently tug on one of Kylee's golden pigtails.

"Yes, of course." The black-haired beauty glanced at the toddler and waved in dismissal. "I thought we might go mingle and get a glass of champagne." The exotic woman in red looked Sarah up and down. "Are you not going to introduce me to your friend?"

"Sorry. Nicolette, this is Sarah Johnson and her daughter, Kylee."

Sarah extended her hand, smiling, trying to be gracious. "It's nice to meet you, Nicolette."

Nicolette barely touched her fingers. "You're name is familiar to me. Do you model or act?"

Sarah laughed. "Neither. I'm a photographer."

Nicolette's eyes narrowed. "Ah, yes, Sarah Johnson, 'Photographer to the Stars.' This is why I have heard of you. I read your magazine, 'Celebrity.'"

"I freelance for them when a client requests it."

"How nice, but I do not like you photographers. You are all so pushy." She scrutinized Sarah's face. "You are an attractive woman. Perhaps you should try standing in front of the camera sometime. This is where the hard work starts, no?"

"Put away the claws, Nicky," Ethan said with a tinge of warning.

More than finished with their conversation, Sarah took Kylee from Ethan. "If you'll excuse us, Hunter and Morgan are probably wondering where we are." She met Ethan's gaze for a heartbeat, turned and left.

She *definitely* didn't like that woman. Nicolette was incredibly rude, but that wasn't the problem. In her business, beautiful, ill-mannered women were part of the package. It was Nicolette's eyes. In the depths of their chocolate brown perfection, she'd seen a streak of viciousness. Couldn't Ethan see it, or was he too caught up in her long black hair and French accent?

As they walked toward the stairs, Kylee began to fuss. "I want Ethan."

"We'll see him later." She kissed Kylee's forehead. "He's busy right now."

Morgan snagged Sarah's arm as she passed. "There you are. I think we're ready to start. I need to find Ethan, and we should be good to go." Morgan beamed at Kylee. "Hi, sweetie."

Kylee turned her face into Sarah's neck and sniffled.

"What's the matter with my beautiful flower girl?"

Sarah took a deep breath and smiled, determined to be cheerful. This was Morgan's night. "She's a little upset that I pulled her away from Ethan. We just saw him over at the other end of the gazebo."

Sarah followed Morgan's gaze as she scanned the room. "Oh, there he is. Hunter's waving him over. Kylee, honey, we're going to see Ethan right now."

Kylee picked up her head and wiped her eyes. "O-tay."

Sarah watched Ethan make his way toward Hunter, with Nicolette clinging to his arm.

"So, Ethan brought his flavor of the month I see." Morgan draped her arm around Sarah's waist as they skirted through the crowd. "Hunter says she's a big-time model in France. She's the spokesperson for some exclusive fragrance. Apparently Ethan met her last month when he was over at his Paris branch. I'm assuming that since we haven't been introduced, this one isn't serious. Although none of them are."

"I just had the pleasure of meeting her. I wasn't impressed." Sarah winced when her words came out with more heat than she intended.

Morgan stopped. "Wow, she made quite an impression. I've never heard you say a negative word about anyone, even when they deserve it."

Sarah shrugged. She couldn't figure out why she was letting the situation bother her so much. Ethan was free to date whomever he chose. "She rubbed me the wrong way, that's all."

"Do you want me to have Hunter talk to Ethan?"

Horrified by the thought, Sarah's eyes grew saucer-wide as she clutched Morgan's arm. "Good God, no. Please don't do that."

"I want you to be comfortable. You're my friend. " Morgan's eyes began to heat. "She's not."

"It's fine. This night is about you and Hunter. Please, let's just concentrate on the two of you." She smiled as Morgan stared at her for another moment.

"Okay, but I want you to tell me if you change your mind."

Not on your life. "Will do."

After the guests wandered off for champagne and appetizers, the wedding party practiced for the following day. Hunter and Ethan stood, waiting in the gazebo.

"Kylee, I want you to walk to Auntie Morgan's mommy and wait for me, okay?"

"O-tay, Mama." Kylee made her way down the imaginary aisle, holding her empty basket. Instead of stopping and standing with Ilene Taylor, she kept going. Sarah stepped forward, but stopped when Ethan shook his head and scooped her up.

Sarah started down the aisle next, glancing at Nicolette leaning against the wooden banister. Her temper flashed as the woman's eyes narrowed in Kylee's direction. Standing in her designated space, she took a deep breath. Nicolette wasn't worth all this.

Sarah snapped to attention when Morgan called her name. Everyone was looking at her. "Yes? I'm sorry."

"Now that we've finished with the run-through, you and Ethan are supposed to walk down the aisle for Hunter and me. It's bad luck if we do before tomorrow."

"Yes, yes, of course." She moved toward the would-be aisle where Ethan waited, still holding Kylee. She put her arm through his and walked with him.

He nudged her gently in the side. "Where were you back there? Morgan called your name three times."

She met his gaze as the heat of embarrassment stained her cheeks. "I had something on my mind."

"I hope you're more focused tomorrow." He smiled. "I don't want to have to come drag you from your spot." He nudged her again, giving her a wink.

Uncharacteristically irritated, she didn't smile back. "I assure you, Morgan will be my main focus tomorrow, as she should've been tonight." When they stopped at the entrance of the gazebo, she removed her arm from Ethan's and made a grab for Kylee.

He turned to the side so she couldn't take her. "I was

kidding. What's wrong?"

"Nothing. It's getting late. I have to get Kylee her supper." She moved forward, trying to take Kylee again.

Ethan evaded her for the second time, sending Kylee into giggles with the motion. "You're upset because Kylee needs to eat? Try again."

"I'm not upset about anything. I really don't want to get into this right now." She glanced over as Nicolette made a beeline in their direction. She wanted to avoid another encounter with her as badly as she wanted to avoid the plague. "Your date's looking for you. Now may I please have my daughter?" She moved forward, plucking Kylee from Ethan's arms, not missing the surprise in his eyes.

"Sarah?"

She walked down the steps as quickly as her heels allowed. Ethan called after her again. She ignored him as she made her way to the function room. She would get Kylee her meal and head back to the bridal suite as soon as possible.

~~~~

Ethan's gaze roamed over the guests crowding the elegant function room. A massive buffet ran the length of one wall where people busily helped themselves to a variety of top-notch dishes. He spotted Sarah and Kylee sitting alone at a small table in the corner. Kylee took a bite of grilled cheese, followed by a heaping spoonful of applesauce. Sarah pushed salmon and rice around on her plate then set her fork down, wiping a glob of apple from Kylee's cheek.

He studied her, puzzled. In all the years they'd known each other, she'd never looked at him with such disdain as she did earlier, and she'd never spoken to him with such heat.

He caught her eye in the dim, candlelit room and started toward her just as Nicolette made her way back from the ladies' room. He watched Sarah's gaze wander to his date before she turned her attention back to her daughter.

"Let's get something to eat, darling."

Ethan glanced at Sarah once more. He would have to talk to her later. He focused on Nicolette's stunning face. "Good idea. I'm starving."

He sat down to lobster tail and filet mignon while Nicolette nibbled on her miserly salad and talked to one of Morgan's friends from D.C. Ethan looked over his shoulder, surprised to see the corner table empty. Sarah had to pass him to get to her suite, unless she left through the door leading to the shore. She knew better than to walk the beach alone after dark. Staying at a luxury hotel didn't negate the possibility of the criminal element lurking in the shadows along the water.

Uneasy, he took his napkin from his lap. "I'll be back in a minute," he said to Nicolette, who barely paid him any attention.

He moved to the picture windows overlooking the beach and spotted Sarah's blonde hair whipping in the wind as she walked toward the waves with Kylee. "Damn it, what is she doing?"

Cutting through the crowd, Ethan headed for the stairwell. He took the steps two at a time. The ocean breeze rushed across his face as he opened the door.

Walking in the direction Sarah had taken, he found her high heels in the sand. His heartbeat bumped up a notch and he tensed as he scanned the dark, unable to find her.

In the distance her pink dress billowed around her thighs, and Ethan's shoulders relaxed. She held Kylee close, pointing to the stars. A loose strand of silky blonde hair escaped from behind her ear, and she swiped it back. His breath backed up in his throat as the moonlight kissed her face, accentuating her beauty. He ached for her, yearning to be a part of the picture she and Kylee made. Caught off-guard, Ethan tried to ignore his unwanted and habitual reaction of late and moved forward.

As he got closer, Sarah's soft voice melded with Kylee's and the rush of waves while they sang Twinkle, Twinkle, Little Star. When their song ended, Kylee clapped and Sarah smiled. "Okay, little miss, it's time to say goodnight to the stars."

Kylee yawned. "I not tired, Mama."

"You're not, huh? Well, it's still time for a bath and a snuggle with Mr. Ruff. Auntie Morgan doesn't want a sleepy flower girl in her wedding tomorrow." Sarah turned and gasped, stumbling back. "My God, Ethan, you scared me half to death."

"Ethan!" Kylee wiggled to get down.

"No, honey. I don't want you getting dirty. It's time for bed."

Kylee's lip wobbled, and her eyes filled. "I want Ethan."

Unable to resist Kylee's tears, Ethan took Kylee in his arms. She snuggled her head on his shoulder as he began to walk. "It's a little late for you to be out on the beach by yourself, don't you think?"

"Kylee's restless tonight," Sarah said stiffly. "I was hoping the fresh air would help her settle. We were just heading in for a bath and bed."

"No one would've been able to hear you if you

needed help out here."

"We aren't that far from the restaurant or our room, Ethan. Everything turned out fine." She bent down to pick up the shoes she left behind.

"You could've come and gotten me. I would've come with you."

"I didn't need you to come with me, and that would've been rude. You're here with a date."

Her inflection changed on the word 'date.' He stopped walking and captured her arm when they approached the door to her beachside suite. "Is that why you're upset? Because I brought a date?"

"Don't be ridiculous." She turned away, swiping her keycard in the slot. The light flashed green, and she twisted the knob. "You're rarely without one. Why would it suddenly bother me? It's really getting late. I should take Kylee and say goodnight."

Surprised by her scoffing tone, Ethan took her arm again. "What's wrong with you? Why are you acting like this?"

"It's been a long day. I'm tired." She held out her hands for Kylee. "Come on, sweetheart. It's time for your bath."

Ethan had seen Sarah tired before, exhausted, and she never failed to be anything but sweet.

"No, Mama, Ethan."

"Ethan has to get back to the party, and you have to go to bed." Sarah wrapped her hands around Kylee's waist to take her.

Kylee wrapped her arms around his neck, resting her head on his shoulder again. "Ethan read to me."

He stared down into pleading, sleepy blue eyes and his heart melted. "Jesus, Sarah, how can you say no to that? It's just one book."

Sarah let out a quiet sigh. "One book." She stepped through the door, letting him in the spacious room. Light blue knick-knacks accented bright yellow walls. Pale green furnishings gave the room a tropical paradise feel.

"Bath time first, Kylee." Sarah took Kylee and walked to the bathroom, filling the tub.

While a reenergized Kylee sang and splashed in the water, Ethan stood by the window, staring out at ocean waves kissing the sandy shore. Sarah's voice chimed in to Itsy Bitsy Spider, making him smile. His smile disappeared as he thought of the way she'd looked at him. Her eyes had been full of disdain. He'd always played by his own rules, caring little for what others thought, but the mockery in her voice tonight bothered him. Something was eating at her. He wasn't leaving until they figured everything out. Sarah was a vital part of his life. That wasn't going to change.

Kylee ran from the bathroom wrapped in a towel. "I ready for my story."

"You look like you're missing something to me, kiddo. Where're your PJs?"

"Over der." Kylee pointed to the pink polka dot pajama-set lying on the bed. "I have to det dressed. I tan do it myself."

He smiled. "Well, go for it then. I'll get your book and wait in the other room. Call me if you need help."

"O-tay." Her angelic face beamed up at him, and for a flash, he saw Jake's smile.

Sadness warred with the comfort that a piece of him was still here.

Minutes later, Kylee crawled into Ethan's lap, soft and warm, smelling of baby shampoo. She nestled herself against him, hugging Mr. Ruff, the stuffed brown dog he'd bought her at a toy store in Germany the year before.

Ethan covered Kylee with the small patchwork quilt Jake's mother had made for her second birthday, and settled against the couch.

She looked up at him. "Mama be out soon. She getting her bath too."

As Kylee spoke, the spray hit the tub behind the closed bathroom door. Ethan knew Sarah was avoiding him. He could wait. He was patient when it suited him. "Let's read this story, Sleepy Marie."

She put her hands on his cheeks. "I not Seepy Marie. I Kylee."

Her eyes were so solemn as they stared into his; he couldn't help but grin. "Okay, Sleepy Kylee, let's read this story."

Ethan opened to the first page, and she rested her head against his chest again. By the time he made it to the third page, the water in the bathroom shut off, and Kylee's eyes drooped. He continued on until Sarah stood in the doorway, wrapped in her pale blue robe.

She stepped further into the room, bringing along her floral scent. The hem of her robe brushed her knees as she walked. "Kylee's asleep."

"Yeah, I know. I don't think she made it past the tea party."

A small smile touched her lips. "She usually doesn't. Why don't I take her so you can get back? Thanks for reading with her."

The formality was back in her voice. Ethan arched his eyebrows. "How about you sit down and tell me why you're treating me like a stranger."

"That's silly, Ethan."

He dealt with dishonesty everyday in his business. Sarah was far from an artist of deception. "I was ridiculous a few minutes ago, and now I'm silly."

"No, of course you're not." She sat on the edge of the loveseat, her hands clasped. "I'm sorry if I've hurt your feelings."

"I don't bruise easy." He held her gaze, waiting as she wiggled her foot double-time, a nervous habit he recognized.

"I don't like Nicolette," she said hastily. She bit her lip and stood. "I'm sorry. That was incredibly rude."

So that was the problem. Ethan got to his feet with Kylee. "Where would you like me to lay her down?"

Her eyes met his again, full of apology, before she glanced away. "I'll take her."

"I've got her. Which bedroom, Sarah?"

"The bedroom to the left."

He walked with Kylee snuggled in his arms. Sarah hurried ahead of him, dimming the light in the room and pulled back the covers on the queen sized mattress. He lay Kylee down and Sarah covered her. She brushed her lips over her daughter's forehead, placing two pillows next to the edge of the bed to keep her from falling. Ethan stared down at her sweet little face, running his finger down her nose.

Sarah stood by the door and walked out when he turned.

He followed her to the sitting area and snagged her hand. "Hey, let me apologize for earlier. I didn't know Nicolette's comments bothered you so much. You're an amazing photographer."

She hesitated then wrapped her arms around him in a hug. Ethan returned the embrace and relaxed.

"Let's just forget the whole thing." Sarah eased back, staring up at him. "I was oversensitive. I'm sure Nicolette's a lovely woman."

A smile ghosted Ethan's lips. "You never were a very good fibber, Sarah."

The troubled look was back as she tried to break away, but Ethan held her tight.

"She's very beautiful, Ethan, and it doesn't matter what I think as long as you're happy."

He was happy now that everything was okay between them. "I'm happy enough."

Her brows furrowed. "I don't want you to be 'happy enough.' That's not good enough. You deserve more than that."

Over the years, he'd become very content with 'happy enough,' but lately he'd been restless for more.

Sarah smoothed his shirt and tie, smiling. "You should get back, Ethan. I'm sure Nicolette's concerned."

He doubted it but nodded. "We're good here?"

"Yes, absolutely. I'm sorry again—"

"Don't be." He smiled and kissed her, instantly recognizing his mistake when his lips met hers. His fingers curled tight against the cotton of her robe as her exotic flavor left his head swimming. He remembered why he'd avoided the habitual gesture over the last several weeks as her floral scent surrounded him and he stared into her kind eyes. It was all he could do to stop himself from moving in again, from deepening the kiss and ruining one of the most important friendships he had. He stepped back.

Sarah's smile vanished as she searched his face. "Are you okay?"

He tried for a casual smile. "Yeah. It's just getting late. I need to go find Hunter." He needed to get away from her.

Sarah's brows furrowed as she walked him to the door. Her hand touched his when he turned the knob, and he jumped back.

"Ethan, what's wrong?"

"Nothing. Good night. Lock up after me." He smiled absently and stepped through the door, concerned by the direction his thoughts kept taking.

CHAPTER THREE

SARAH WATCHED HUNTER KISS HIS BRIDE, AS THE SUN SANK along the horizon. A tear rolled down her cheek as she thought of Jake, of how he should've been there to share Hunter's moment, but that would never be. Even after two years, she still missed him as if she'd lost him yesterday. She still expected him to walk through her front door. At moments like this, when the lack of his presence was so apparent, the black hole of grief threatened to swallow her whole. But Jake wouldn't have wanted that on Hunter and Morgan's special day, so she tried desperately to push the pain away.

Sarah glanced from the grinning couple now facing their clapping guests, and met Ethan's stare. He questioned her with a subtle lift of his brow. Was she okay? She swiped at her tear and smiled, giving him a quick nod. He smiled back, a gesture of support, of understanding, and she instantly steadied.

Focusing on her duties, Sarah knelt forward in her fitted, off-the-shoulder dress and adjusted Morgan's silk train before she and Hunter made their way down the white carpeted aisle of the gazebo. Candlelight, creamy calla lilies, and maroon roses gave the elegant space a fairytale feel.

As Sarah straightened, Ethan stepped up next to her, offering his elbow, and she looped her arm with his.

"Are you ready to get this party started?" he asked, still studying her, still checking.

She smiled again. "You bet."

Ethan clasped his hand with hers, holding tight, winking, and off they went, following behind the bride and groom. Sarah rested her head against his muscled shoulder for the briefest of seconds, offering her silent thanks. What would she do without Ethan, her rock, her constant source of comfort?

~~~~

Waiters bustled about, placing dessert before each guest. Music pumped from speakers with the festivities well underway. Sarah's foot moved in time with the beat as she sat next to Kylee, pretty in her tiered organza gown.

"Little bites, Kylee. I don't want you to choke."

"I not choke, Mama." Kylee scooped up another forkful of vanilla cake and butter cream frosting.

Hailey, Kylee's babysitter, sat on Kylee's other side.

"Hailey, don't look now, but one of the guys at table twenty has been looking your way most of the evening."

With a bite of cake halfway to her mouth, Hailey froze. "Oh my God, you're kidding. Is he hot?"

Sarah grinned, glancing from the pretty, honey-eyed part-time nanny to the college-aged man. "He's certainly cute enough. You've been wonderful with Kylee all day, and I appreciate your willingness to spend the night with her at my mother's. Why don't you take some time for yourself? Go ask him if he wants to dance."

Hailey gripped her hand. "Oh, I couldn't do that. What if he says no? What if Morgan needs you?"

Sarah glanced in the happy brides direction. "Morgan's mingling with her guests. I think everything's under control for the moment. Go on, Hailey, go have some fun. I can pretty much guarantee Mr. Tall, Dark, and Handsome won't say 'no.'"

"You're the best." Hailey looked down at her watch. "I'll be back in an hour. Your mom should be here by then."

"Don't worry about the time. If I really need you, which I won't, I'll come find you."

"Okay." With a final hug, Hailey departed as the next song began to play.

Kylee's bottom wiggled in her seat.

"Kylee, would you like to dance before Grandma comes?"

Kylee grinned, her eyes bright with excitement. "Ooh, yes. Let's dance."

Sarah pushed her chair back from the table and helped Kylee down from her booster seat. She guided her through the crowd, and they edged their way on the floor. Sarah let her little party animal twist and spin to the upbeat music.

As the song wound down, the DJ announced Morgan and her father's first dance. Stanley held Morgan close while they moved about the room, laughing and talking. As the last notes drifted through the speakers, Stanley dipped his daughter and everyone clapped.

The DJ invited daddies and daughters to take the floor next. Sarah's light mood plummeted as her sweet-faced little girl smiled up at her.

"I want to dance again, Mama."

Sarah brushed a soft blonde curl back from Kylee's forehead. How did she explain that this was a special moment only for little girls and their fathers? Although Kylee remained blissfully unaware, Sarah's heart broke for what her child would never have.

"You can dance again soon. Let's go to the bathroom and make ourselves pretty before the fast songs start.

You can put on some of my lip gloss if you want."

"O-tay." Kylee clapped.

Sarah turned toward the lobby, stopping short as Ethan stood before them.

"I want to take Kylee out to dance."

Sarah's eyes watered as they stared into Ethan's. "Ethan, I—" Emotions choked her, leaving her unable to finish. How did she thank him for such a kind gesture?

Ethan stepped closer, skimming his fingers along her cheek. "Let me take Kylee out to dance."

Sarah pressed the warmth of his palm to her face, holding him close a moment longer. She nodded over the lump in her throat and set Kylee on her feet. Ethan took her hand as he guided her to the dance floor, never taking his gaze from Sarah's.

She wished for her camera, wanting to capture every detail of this sweet moment in pictures. Ethan wore his white button-down, rolled halfway up his muscled forearms. His maroon necktie, loosened hours before, matched the ribbons woven through the ringlets curled into Kylee's hair. Ethan's big hands swallowed Kylee's as he moved her in slow circles, talking to her while she smiled up at him. Kylee said something, and he grinned.

The dim chandelier light accentuated his broad shoulders and arresting face, sending Sarah's pulse racing as a wave of heat coursed through her system. Surprised by her reaction, she averted her gaze to the floor. Ethan's striking looks were nothing new, so why was she suddenly affected?

She glanced up again, studying her best friend. She was being silly, that was all. Ethan was her pal. She'd gotten caught up in the emotions of the day, in the moment of tenderness between him and her daughter.

When the dance ended, Ethan picked Kylee up,

kissed her, and headed back. "Special delivery for one Sarah Johnson." He tossed Kylee high, making her laugh and caught her, placing her in Sarah's arms.

Sarah shook off her foolishness and beamed. "This *is* a special delivery indeed. Can I keep her?"

"I don't know. Can she keep you, kiddo?"

"Yes, Mama tan teep me." Kylee's eyes widened. "Gamma's here. Bye, Mama." She wiggled down and ran. Kylee blew her a kiss when Sarah's mother picked her up.

Hailey wandered over, holding two overnight bags and a piece of paper with a number on it. She glanced toward the college boy, back at Sarah and wiggled her brows.

Sarah chuckled as the DJ asked the wedding party to join the bride and groom on the dance floor.

Ethan grabbed her hand. "We're being paged."

"I want to say goodbye to Kylee first."

"I'll come with you, and then we dance."

Sarah stared down at Ethan's hand, remembering her earlier reaction to a simple smile. "I don't know. I should get the gifts together, so I can bring them over to Morgan and Hunter's house after the reception's over."

"You haven't danced at all tonight, and the DJ's calling us. The best man and Matron of Honor should give it a whirl at least once."

Stuck, she conceded. "Just one dance. Give me a minute." She broke contact with Ethan and walked to her mother, enveloping her in a hug. "Hi, Mom. Thanks so much for helping me out. I don't know how I would've been able to do this without you and Hailey. As it is, I'm going to have to make two trips with all of the presents. That would've been difficult with Kylee in tow, and I didn't want to leave Hailey home alone with the crimes being reported in the area, even with my security system."

Her mother frowned and tsked. "I'm always happy to help out, but what about you? It'll be late by the time this party's over."

"I'll be helping her out, Janice," Ethan said from behind Sarah.

"Bless your heart, Ethan. Well, you have yourselves some fun. I know I'm going to." She nuzzled Kylee close and turned to leave.

"Wait. I didn't say goodbye." Sarah moved forward, kissing Kylee. "Bye, sweet girl. I'll see you first thing in the morning."

"Bye, Mama. I gonna play with Gamma and Gampy and Hailey." With that, they turned to leave again.

"Call if you need anything," Sarah said, but Hailey, her mother, and Kylee were chatting it up as they left the ballroom. "Well, I guess I've been forgotten."

"Let's go have fun, then." Ethan took her hand and pulled her to the dance floor. The thumping beat had the wedding party dancing to the hoots and hollers of the crowd. Ethan tugged her against him as they both found their rhythm.

Hunter cut in. "Scram, Cooke." With Ethan out of the way, he wrapped Sarah in a hug. "What an awesome day. Thanks for all your help."

"You're absolutely welcome. I'm so happy for you, Hunter. Be happy."

"I am." Hunter's eyes changed, softening. "Even though I'm married now, I'll never forget my promise, Sarah. You and Kylee still mean everything to me."

Sarah blinked back tears, as she brushed her hand down his cheek. "Oh, honey, I know that."

"Are you going to be okay while Morgan and I are in Italy?"

She took his hand and squeezed. "Promise me something."

"Anything."

"Enjoy your honeymoon with your wife. Don't worry about me and Kylee. We'll be fine. Ethan's never far away. Have fun." She kissed him. "I love you. Now go dance with Morgan." She hugged him again and let him go.

The music changed, slowing down. Usher's smooth voice crooned through the speakers. Sarah walked to the deck, stepping from the noisy ballroom, breathing in the salty air. She rested her arm against the cool metal of the railing and pulled off her heels, letting out a deep sigh as she closed her eyes. The day had played with her emotions, bringing so many highs and lows.

"There you are." Ethan leaned on the rail next to her. "I turned around for a second, and you were gone."

She kept her eyes closed. "The song was over, and I have so much to do, but I needed fresh air first."

He brushed his fingers over her naked shoulder. "You're upset."

Sarah shook her head. "No, I'm not."

He took her chin in his hand until she met his gaze.

"Mostly I'm not," she amended. "I've been thinking of Jake a lot the past couple of days, especially today, but you already know that." She let out a deep breath. "I wish he could've been here with all of us."

Ethan pulled her close, locking his arms around her waist. "Let's dance." He moved her in a circle, and she clasped her hands at the back of his neck. "I thought of him a lot too. I think we all did."

"I go for long stretches where I'm able to find peace with the way things are, but then there are days like today when I don't know how I'll get through the rest of my life without him."

"I think that's pretty normal, Sarah. Tomorrow will be better." He kissed her forehead. "And if it's not, you call me, and I'll be right there."

Hadn't he always been? She stared into Ethan's eyes for a long time before she smiled. "Jake would've gotten a kick out of Kylee in her pretty dress." She laughed. "And the way her little butt wiggled on the dance floor."

He grinned. "She sure can move."

"I need to get her lessons. I think she would love dance class."

As they circled around, she glanced into the ballroom, spotting Morgan and Hunter. "They look spectacular together, don't they?"

Ethan turned his head. "Yeah, they do." He turned back and Sarah met his stare as he nestled her more truly against him. Ethan's hard chest brushed her breasts as his gaze wandered to her lips. Her heart thundered as she wondered what it would be like to feel his mouth pressed against hers in passion instead of the typical casual meeting of lips?

Sarah tried to pull away as guilt swamped her. What was she doing? Where was this coming from? Moments before she'd yearned for Jake, now she was thinking of Ethan in a way she never had before. "I should probably get back inside and check in with Morgan. They'll be leaving soon. She'll need help getting out of her dress."

Forks clinked against glasses, and a cheer went up when Hunter laid a hungry kiss on Morgan's lips.

Ethan chuckled, never loosening his grip. "I think Morgan's busy right now."

Sarah stared at Ethan again—her *friend*, she reminded herself. They'd been through so much over the years. *You're being foolish.*

Smiling, Ethan shook his head. The gesture was so casual, so Ethan. She admonished herself again for being silly, and the weight of her guilt subsided.

Forks clinked once more. This time Morgan bent Hunter back in a kiss.

Sarah's laugh mingled with Ethan's. They grinned at each other, and everything was all right.

The song ended and rolled into the next.

"Thanks for the dance." She hugged him and moved through the doors to the ballroom. "Are you coming?"

"I'll be in in a few minutes."

Sarah walked to the bathroom, thinking about her dance with Ethan. The easy feelings she'd left the balcony with were quickly vanishing as butterflies invaded her stomach and doubts snuck through. No matter how she tried to convince herself that things were status quo, she couldn't shake the feeling that something had changed. He'd looked at her...differently somehow. Had his thoughts veered in the same directions as hers? No, of course not.

Fed up with herself, Sarah blew out a frustrated huff and pulled open the door. She stepped in front of the mirror, examining her flushed cheeks and pulse hammering away in her throat. Taking a deep breath, she smoothed the fitted waist of her maroon dress and pulled the gloss from her small purse. As she rubbed the clear liquid together on her lips, Nicolette stepped from one of the stalls. Calling on her manners, Sarah smiled. "Hello, Nicolette. Are you enjoying your evening?"

"Not as much you seem to be."

Her tone was unfriendly, but Sarah ignored it. She opened her purse, putting the tube back in her bag and turned for the door. "See you around."

"You surprise me, Sarah."

Sarah paused with her hand hovering over the handle. "Oh, why's that?"

"You come across as virginal, yet you've been all over both the groom and my date tonight."

Sarah whirled. "Excuse me?"

"Are you not ashamed of yourself? Allowing Ethan to dance with your daughter as if he were the child's father? This is pathetic."

She felt the blood drain from her face. "Ethan and Kylee are very close."

"Ethan and Kylee are close, eh? Is it not Ethan and Kylee's mother that are very close? Do you walk on the beach and dance in the moonlight with many men, Sarah? Do you think I do not know what you do? If you think I will not be watching, think again."

Sarah's hand trembled as she pulled the door open and left Nicolette casually powdering her nose. She made her way through the mobs of people to the small room where Morgan and Hunter's gifts were stacked on and under a table. Shutting herself in, she threw the lock in place and sat in a chair as she took a deep breath.

Nicolette's words ran through her mind as she thought of the way Ethan held her while they'd danced and the way he'd stared into her eyes. *Had* something changed between them? Did she rely on him too much when it came to Kylee? She didn't know.

She glanced at the digital clock hanging on the wall and swore. Morgan would be looking for her. The limo was due to arrive in less than half an hour. She rushed to the suite, opening the door to the cheerful yellow room as Ilene, Morgan's mother, was unzipping Morgan's dress. Taking a deep breath, Sarah moved forward to help. "I'm so sorry. I'm running behind. What can I do?"

Morgan frowned in the mirror. "Are you all right,

Sarah? You're pale."

She glimpsed her white cheeks and cursed herself, smiling at Morgan's reflection. "Oh, I'm fine, absolutely fine. It's been an amazing day. You're such a beautiful bride. What will you and Hunter do first when you get to the resort?"

"Sleep for twenty-four hours and then...we'll see." Her green eyes glittered with mischief as she grinned into the mirror. Morgan met her mother's gaze and winced. "Sorry, Mom."

"Morgan, do you really think I don't know that you and Hunter have sex? Perhaps while you're in Italy you can start working on my first grandbaby."

"We're just going to practice, at least for a little while." Morgan pulled on creamy white slacks and a maroon colored top.

"Some girls have all the luck," Sarah breathed wistfully, smiling.

Morgan and Ilene chuckled.

A knock interrupted their girl talk. Sarah opened the door to Ethan standing before her. He'd changed into jeans and a black long sleeve shirt that accentuated his broad chest. "Limo's here. Is Morgan ready?"

"Give us five minutes." Nicolette's words plagued her mind, and she felt uncustomarily awkward in front of one of her closest friends. "We'll be out in five minutes."

"I'm going to time you. Everyone's waiting with their bubbles."

"Start your watch," she said as she closed the door again.

Morgan stood in front of her, fresh and beautiful. "I think I'm ready. Thank you so much for helping me. It's been such a special day."

Sarah pulled Morgan into a hug. "You're absolutely

welcome. I couldn't be happier for you. I'll take care of everything on this end. Have a great time. We'll get together for lunch when you get back."

"I'm looking forward to it. I know Ethan's timing us, and we have three minutes left. Go put on comfortable clothes and come see me off."

"I can wait."

"No, you can't. I can hear your feet screaming for help."

Sarah nibbled her lip and smiled. "Okay. I'll be quick." She grabbed her overnight bag and ran to the bathroom, stepping out of her pumps and sighed. Reaching behind her back, she pulled down her zipper then tugged off her stockings and garter belt and slid into comfy jeans and a pale blue sweater. "Much better," she sighed again, taking an extra second to add a bit of blush to her cheeks. Her time with Morgan and Ilene had soothed her, ironing out most of the rough spots after her confrontation with Nicolette.

Ten minutes later, Morgan and Hunter's white stretch limo drove down the long drive of the resort to bubbles and cheers. When the car was out of sight, Sarah went back to the suite she and Morgan had shared and gathered all of their things. With an armful, she retrieved her sedan from the parking lot and pulled up to the walkway the resort manager told her she could use to load Morgan and Hunter's gifts.

She took the steps two at a time to the small room she'd locked herself in not even an hour ago and began organizing boxes and bags, trying to figure out how she could manage it all in one trip. As she approached the door, loaded down with large packages, Ethan moved forward. "Let me get those." He took the boxes from her, and their hands brushed. "I said I would help you with all of this."

Nicolette stood behind him with her pencil-thin brow raised.

"I've got it, Ethan. You should take your date and go." Sarah pulled the boxes back and made her way down the stairs. As she approached her car, she spotted Ethan's Rover parked behind her. "Damn it."

He came down behind her with an armful while Nicolette swung a small gift bag between two fingers. Sarah clenched her jaw as her temper began to stretch. Out of patience, she walked over to Ethan as he placed cheerfully wrapped presents in his trunk. It was time for him to be on his way with the witch. She wasn't about to spend the next half hour fending off Nicolette's nasty looks. "Ethan, I said I've got this. I don't need any help. Just take Nicolette and go."

Ethan stopped with a package halfway in the trunk and stared.

"I'm serious. Please, just go. There isn't as much as I thought," she lied. "I can get it all in one trip." With that, she turned and made her way up for another pile.

Just as she was about to pick up the next stack, she was whirled around.

"What was that?" Ethan's gray eyes snapped with temper. "I said I would help you."

"Maybe I don't want it. No matter what anyone thinks around here, I'm perfectly capable of taking care of myself. This is my responsibility as Morgan's Matron of Honor, so I've got it."

"What are you talking about? I never said you couldn't take care of yourself. If it wasn't the middle of the night, I'd let you have at it, but I'm not about to leave you alone to deal with this when there's a fucking rapist running around the Palisades. He's attacked three women within a ten mile radius of your house."

A chill ran down Sarah's spine, as she thought of how far back Hunter and Morgan's home sat from the road, but Nicolette's words still stung. "Then I'll leave them in my car and take them over in the morning."

He snagged her arm as she turned toward the table. "Goddamn, Sarah. What's gotten into you? You've had more mood swings in the last twenty-four hours than...ever."

"I don't know, okay? But I want you to leave me alone. I—"

"Ethan, darling." Nicolette stood in the doorway. "This is taking entirely too long. Are you ready?"

"No," he said with heat.

Nicolette's full lip turned in a pout. "Fine. I will just go."

Ethan scrubbed his hands over his face as Nicolette stalked off. "Son of a bitch. Sarah, don't you dare leave. Nicky," he called as he went after his supermodel.

Incredibly confused and on the verge of tears, Sarah picked up the packages and took them to her vehicle. She came back with her third round, watching Ethan kiss Nicolette before opening a cab door for her. Surprised by the hurt, Sarah turned, more determined than ever to have the damn gifts situated by the time Ethan came back.

She almost succeeded. Only when she was bringing down the last stack of gifts did Ethan begin to climb the stairs. Sarah passed him without glancing in his direction.

She got in her car, turned the ignition over and drove off before he could reach the room and figure out it had been locked. When she was home she would pull into the garage, arm the security system Hunter and Ethan had installed years ago, and soak in a long bath. She wasn't going to emerge from the fragrant bubbles until she could think straight again.

Merging onto Highway 1, she rolled down the windows, savoring the cool ocean breeze blowing through her hair. For the first time in several hours, her shoulders began to relax. Within minutes, Ethan drove up beside her and rolled down his passenger side window. Her eyes met his in the reflection of a street lamp before she looked back at the road. The deep gray of his sparked with fury, and her shoulders coiled tight. She'd seen him angry before, but this was a whole different level of pissed.

Nicolette's words played like a mantra through her mind, and she lifted her chin, rolled up her window, and pressed her accelerator to the floor. A smile touched her lips when she pulled ahead, leaving Ethan in her dust. Ethan Cooke could go to hell.

CHAPTER FOUR

ETHAN'S BLOOD ALL BUT BOILED BY THE TIME HE PULLED INTO Sarah's drive. He would've been there twenty minutes ago if he hadn't gotten stuck behind a caravan of tractor trailers. He pressed 'send' on his cell phone—again—listening to Sarah's line ring and go to voicemail. The lights blazed bright in her house, so she wasn't in bed. Any fear that harm had come to her ended as he watched her silhouette pass one of the large picture windows in her living room.

Ethan got out of his Rover, slamming the door in frustration and walked up the lighted path to the entrance, ringing the bell. When she didn't answer, he pounded. "Come on, Sarah, open the door." The side of his fist hit glossy wood once more. "Screw this."

It was time they talked. In the past twenty-four hours, Sarah had become a mystery. Their calm, steady friendship had all but vanished. He thought of the moment on the deck when he'd held her close and their eyes met. He'd had to fight the urge to kiss her. She'd tried to pull away, but not before he saw the flash of confused curiosity. Something had changed.

He took his phone from his pocket and dialed his office switchboard.

"Ethan Cooke Security, this is Mia."

"Hey, Mia, it's Ethan. I need an override number for 555 Seacoast Drive, Pacific Palisades."

"I'll need your identification number, Mr. Cooke."

"884-echo-1-alpha-bravo."

"Thank you, Mr. Cooke. Would you like me to override the system for you?"

"Yes, please." The red light blinked twice before flashing green through the sheer curtain on Sarah's front door.

"You should be all set, Mr. Cooke."

"Yes, thank you. Re-arm the panel in thirty seconds, please."

"Yes, Mr. Cooke."

"Have a good night, Mia."

"Thank you, Mr. Cooke."

He hung up, slid his spare key in the door, and walked into Sarah's house, waiting for the double beep and blink of the red light on the panel before moving toward the sounds coming from the kitchen.

Ethan lost the train of his rant when he stopped in the doorway. The floral scent of Sarah surrounded him, knotting his stomach with desire. She moved about in a pale pink, spaghetti strapped nightshirt that skimmed the top of her firm thighs. Strands of hair escaped the loose bun piled high on her head. She hummed along with the radio, as she placed a teabag in a mug and filled it.

Clearing his throat, Ethan stepped forward, and Sarah whirled on a muffled scream. He caught her fist in his palm before it made contact with his face. The momentum sent him back a step, slamming him against the refrigerator. Sarah collided into his chest, and he grabbed her hips, steadying her.

"Jesus, Ethan, you scared me to death. What are you doing here?"

He moved his hands up, skimming her slim waist beneath soft, cotton fabric before he let her go. "We need to talk, and you wouldn't answer your phone or the damn door."

"I don't want to talk. That's *why* I didn't answer my phone or the damn door."

Silence filled the room as her mutinous eyes stared into his. Her cheeks were flushed with rare temper, and he *wanted* her. He ground his teeth and turned away, fiddling with a chunky letter 'A' on the refrigerator.

With a miffed huff, Sarah stormed off toward her bedroom.

Ethan shut his eyes and rested his forehead against the cool white of the new appliance. What was he *doing*?

Her footsteps headed back in his direction, and he turned as she tied the pale blue robe she wore the night before. "How did you get in here anyway? I locked the door and armed my system."

"It helps when you have a key and own the security company protecting you. I called and had your system deactivated until I got inside." Choosing to embellish his story, he continued, "Since you wouldn't respond to any of my attempts, I figured you might be in trouble."

She narrowed her eyes. "That's pathetic, Ethan. You knew I was perfectly fine."

"No, I didn't. You haven't been fine for the last two days. One minute you're happy, the next you're sad. Then you're hugging me, and the next you're angry. I can't keep up."

"I'm allowed to be off on occasion. You don't get to own the title of 'Brood King.'"

"See, like that. You've been taking pot shots at me all weekend. What the hell is up?"

"I don't *know*. I really don't." She tried to push past him, but he moved to stand in her way. "Move, Ethan."

"Not until we figure this out. In a matter of two days, everything's changed. Somehow, something's different between us, and I don't like it."

"Do you think I don't know that? That's why I want you to go away. I need to *think*. I can't *think* when you won't give me five blessed seconds." She started past him, and he put his hands on her shoulders.

"What do you—" His cell began to ring. "Son of a bitch." He yanked the phone from his pocket as Sarah turned and gripped the edge of the countertop. "Ethan Cooke," he snapped into the receiver.

"Ethan, where are you?"

"Nicky." He closed his eyes. "This isn't a good time." He didn't miss the hiss of breath Sarah blew out before she whirled and left the room. "Hold on," he said. He swore under his breath when Sarah kept walking down the hall toward her bedroom.

"Okay," Nicolette said.

"No, not you." He ran a hand through his hair. "Nicky, I'm going to have to call you back."

"You keep me waiting and waiting, darling."

"I know. I'm sorry. Maybe we should take a rain check for tonight."

"Non, I will wait for you."

He wasn't interested in her waiting. "No, Nicky—" The phone beeped; she'd disconnected. "God fucking damn it."

Ethan shoved the phone in his pocket and walked to Sarah's bedroom. The room was dark, but for two candles flickering in the windows. The French doors to her small outside sitting area were open to the salty breeze pouring in. He stepped on the polished, smooth stones of the patio and stared at the moon descending into morning.

"I thought you left," Sarah said without any heat as she looked at the sky.

56

He didn't say anything as she glided back and forth on the wicker swing. As she swung forward, the front of her robe lifted slightly, giving him a peek at smooth thigh. He let out a long sigh, determined to get them back on an even keel. "Are you going to bite my head off if I sit with you?"

"No." She didn't look at him.

He sat next to her, and they might as well have been strangers. The calm, easy feelings of friendship were absent as tension built again when neither of them spoke. He didn't know what to say. The distance between them was so new, so strange; he wasn't sure how to fix it. Perhaps that was where they needed to start. "Sarah, what's happening here?" He waited so long for her answer, he thought she wouldn't.

"I've asked myself the same question a thousand times, and I don't know." She looked at him then.

"I'm not leaving here until we do. You're too important to me."

A smile touched her lips, and he put his arm around her shoulders, needing to touch her.

They lapsed into silence again.

"Do I depend on you too much when it comes to Kylee? I've had some time to think, and I wonder if I've been selfish. Kylee's my daughter, my responsibility. I don't ever want you thinking I don't know that."

Shocked to the core, he sat up straight. "Where the hell is this coming from? I love her like crazy. When I help you with Kylee, it's because I want to and enjoy doing so."

He heard her small sigh and moved closer, looking her in the eye. "Is that what all of this about?"

"Some of it, yes."

"Well, this isn't so hard to fix after all." Relaxing, he

pulled her to him until her cheek rested against his shoulder. "I don't ever want you thinking those bullshit thoughts again. We've been through too much together."

She relaxed against him, and her foot began to rock the swing again. "You've always been here, so I never thought about it until Nicolette said..." Her eyes widened, and she stopped, trying to pull away.

He tightened his arm around her, trapping her as his voice grew cold. "Until Nicolette said what?"

She moved to get up again, but he held her still. "It was nothing, Ethan. She saw us dancing on the deck and it upset her. I can't blame her really..."

"What did she say, Sarah?"

"I don't think she appreciated you dancing with Kylee or me tonight. That's all."

There was more to it, but he knew she wouldn't say. "I don't care what Nicolette appreciates."

She put her hand on his cheek. "I don't want to be the cause of problems between the two of you."

Her exotic eyes pleaded with his and thoughts of Nicolette vanished as he became aware of her firm breasts pressed against his side and her breath teasing his lips. He glanced at her full mouth, wanting to taste, needing to see if the feelings that had constantly disturbed and confused him over the last several months meant anything.

Risking everything, he moved forward, never taking his eyes from hers as his mouth brushed hers. He saw a flash of surprise on her face before it vanished into something else. When she didn't push him away, he moved in again, adding more pressure. Sarah's fingers curled into the shoulder of his shirt, as her eyes closed and her lips parted. Slowly, gently, his tongue sought hers, gliding, tangling.

Ethan turned his body, pulling her closer, until they were thigh to thigh and her breasts were crushed against his chest. A quiet moan escaped her throat, and a wave of need staggered him. He moved his hands to her cheeks, changing the angle of the kiss, deepening it, and dove in again, wanting more of her surrender.

The wail of sirens barely registered as Sarah's arms came around the back of his neck, and he nibbled her full bottom lip. With his hands still on her cheeks, he eased away slightly. His pulse pounded in time with hers as he skimmed his thumb over her jaw, staring into blue eyes gone electric.

So, this is what had changed. This is what they could bring each other. What he'd been feeling wasn't all one-sided. Unable to help himself, Ethan took her lips again. He couldn't get enough of her sweet taste. Tongues met once, twice, and their mouths grew hungry before he rested his forehead against hers. "Sarah—"

Several sirens wailed, flying past the house, stopping close by. The flash of lights reflected in the night sky. An ambulance came to a halt, and both stood.

"I-I wonder what's going on?"

Ethan's heart thundered, thinking of their kiss, and he asked himself the same thing. "I'm not sure."

They walked down the hall and out the front door. Five houses down, the police and paramedics rushed around while an officer began blocking off the scene with yellow tape.

"My God, Ethan, that house is right next to Hailey's. Someone just bought the place—moved in a couple of weeks ago—a woman. I haven't had a chance to introduce myself yet. I hope she's okay."

He wrapped his arm around her waist. "Let's go back inside. I'll make some calls and see what I can find out."

Ten minutes later, he joined Sarah by the big picture window as the paramedics brought her neighbor out on a stretcher. The blonde woman, covered with a white blanket, cried. Her hand gripped a female officer's, as they put her in the back of the ambulance.

"That poor woman. I wonder what's happened."

"She was raped, Sarah."

She grabbed his hand, clutching. "Oh my God."

"They're saying the bastard went in through the back of the house. I'm not leaving you by yourself tonight. You're coming with me, or I'm sleeping on your couch."

Eyes huge, nodding, Sarah glanced from the window back to him. "Will you stay here?"

"Yeah."

"Let me get some blankets and a pillow."

Sarah walked off, and Ethan stared at the house surrounded by cruisers. It had been so close, *too* close. It could've been Sarah. What if he hadn't come by?

"Here you go."

He turned.

"You should be warm enough. If not, you know where I keep the extras." She set the blankets and pillow on the couch cushion, licking her lips as she took a step back. "Thanks for staying."

He could still taste her. "You're welcome. Go get some sleep."

"I'm not sure I'll be able to."

He wouldn't be sleeping tonight. There was too much to think about. A lot had happened in the last half hour. "You're safe. That's why I'm here."

"Okay. Good night." Her shy eyes met his before she looked down and turned.

Sarah walked away and he wanted to call her back and hold her once more, but he stopped himself. They both needed time to think about the unexpected turn their lives had just taken.

CHAPTER FIVE

SARAH TOSSED AND TURNED UNTIL DAWN WITH SO MANY things on her mind. Fear filled her as she thought of how close the rape had been to her house. Had she been letting herself into her own home when the rapist had been letting himself into her neighbor's?

She shuddered at the thought and sat up, unable to lie in bed any longer and glanced at her bedside table. Jake's smile filled the photograph she kept close by. She picked up the brushed nickel frame, nibbling her lip as guilt consumed her. Ethan had kissed her, and she'd done nothing to stop him. *What was I thinking? How could I do that to you, Jake?* She skimmed her finger along her husband's cheek, put his picture back, and stood.

Sarah walked to the window, touching the wedding rings she wore on a necklace. Her fingers tightened on the gold and diamonds as she thought of firm lips capturing hers and strong arms holding her close. Tears of shame filled her eyes, spilling over, when she realized the lips and arms she craved weren't those of her husband's. Stepping back, she dashed at her cheeks. What was she going to do? How was she going to handle this?

The stereo, turned down low, played in the living room, and she knew Ethan didn't sleep either. Letting out a deep breath, she pulled on jeans and a baggy black sweatshirt then headed down the hall. She stopped in the doorway, watching Ethan, dressed in gray sweat shorts, complete a set of push-ups. He blew out fast puffs of breath as his triceps flexed and bunched with the up-and-down motion. When he finished, he pushed himself up to standing with an efficient hop and met her gaze. Sweat dribbled down his sculpted pectorals to the darkened waistband slung low on his muscled hips.

Had she truly believed she was unaffected by his looks? She had seen him without his shirt before—several times—but as her gaze traveled up sculpted abs and over broad shoulders, stopping on his lips, Sarah thought of the way his mouth had sought hers, and a swift kick of heat scorched her system. She cleared her throat, willing the memory away. "Good morning."

"Morning." Ethan picked up the glass of water on the coffee table and guzzled, his eyes never leaving hers.

"Did you sleep well?" Sarah gripped her fingers together until her knuckles whitened.

"No." He glanced at her hands as he set the empty glass down.

"Oh." She relaxed her grip, moving her arms to her sides. "Was the couch uncomfortable? Let me make you some coffee." Having all she could take of the awkward small talk, Sarah started toward the kitchen.

"Stop it."

"Stop what?" She turned, swiping a strand of hair behind her ear.

"Stop acting like that." He clipped off each word.

His clenched jaw and rigid stance told her a storm brewed beneath his pretense of calm. "Like *what*?"

Before she could blink, Ethan stepped forward, taking her arms. "Like last night was a mistake."

Nerves stretched thin and she snapped. "It was!" Sarah closed her eyes as a flash of hurt moved through his, and he let her go.

She pressed her lips together, holding back tears as she met Ethan's unreadable gaze. "What about Jake? We had no right, Ethan."

"We had every right," he erupted, spinning away and back again.

"He's my husband." She pressed unsteady fingers to her temple, trying to find a way to make him understand.

"I loved Jake like my brother, Sarah, but he's gone. You have a right to move on, to be happy."

"I was happy with the way things were. You shouldn't've kissed me."

His hand snaked out, grabbing her arm, pulling her against him. "You kissed me right back, Sarah. You can't tell me you didn't feel anything." The intensity of his stare dared her to deny the truth.

Her heart pounded as she put her palms to his sweaty chest, desperately fighting the need to press her mouth to his. "Ethan, please."

"You tell me I'm wrong, goddammit." He cupped the back of her neck, pulling her face closer, until his lips feathered against hers with each word he spoke. "You tell me that what I felt, that what we made each other feel, was just a figment of my imagination, and we'll end this right now." He ran his hands through her hair as his breath shuddered out, mingling with hers.

She clutched his forearms, fighting her need to close her eyes and give in to what they both wanted—but she couldn't. She couldn't do this to Jake. "Ethan—"

He held her face in his hands. "Tell me, Sarah."

She shook her head as the first tear fell. "Ethan—"

"No. You tell me you didn't feel anything."

Another tear followed. "I can't. You're right, but it can't happen again."

He let her go.

She took his hand, terrified she was losing one of the best people in her life. "Let's forget this whole thing, Ethan. Let's go back to the way things were three days ago, when you were my best friend."

He dropped her hand, staring at her. "Do you really think it's that easy? There's something here, Sarah. There's something between us."

"No." She needed to deny what she already knew. "We're just friends. That's all we'll ever be."

He held her gaze as he picked up his shirt and duffel bag. "I'll call Austin to come keep an eye on the house until you're ready to go get Kylee. I'll have someone do drive-bys at night until they catch the bastard. If you want an agent to stay with you, tell Austin and he'll set it up." He walked to the door and opened it.

She rushed forward. "Ethan, please don't go like this."

"I've gotta get out of here." Without a look back, he was gone.

Sarah watched Ethan dig his phone from his bag as he walked to the Rover. Tears poured down her cheeks, as her hand tightened on the doorknob. She wanted to go out and make him come back, but she stopped herself. He wouldn't listen to her right now, and she needed time to think, to try to sort out this mess and fix it—somehow. She clutched her sick stomach, already knowing nothing would ever be the same between them.

Ethan sat in his SUV until a sleek red sports convertible pulled into the drive. The driver rolled down his window. Ethan exchanged words with Austin Casey, one of his best close protection agents, then drove down the road and out of her life, she feared.

Austin walked toward the house, and Sarah swiped at her wet cheeks, trying for a smile as she opened the door.

His smile faded when his dark green eyes met hers. "Hey, Sarah, you okay?"

She dashed away another tear. "Hi, Austin. Yes, I'm fine. Thanks for coming. Come on in. I'll get you some coffee."

"Don't go to any trouble for me. Would you rather I stay outside? I can keep an eye on things from here. It's no big deal."

"No, no, please." She opened the door wider to accommodate his linebacker size. "Can I make you something to eat? I haven't had breakfast yet myself." The thought of eating made her stomach quiver, but it was early, and Austin's sleepy eyes told her Ethan had gotten him out of bed.

"I don't want to put you out."

"You're not. What can I get you? I've got eggs and turkey bacon."

He smiled. "Sounds great."

Relieved to be busy, Sarah dashed around the kitchen, making Austin's meal. She poured a cup of coffee, setting the steaming mug in front of him. His eggs, bacon, and toast followed shortly after.

He sniffed with reverence. "This smells amazing. I haven't had anything good to eat in a week."

Wanting to think about anything but Ethan, she sat with a piece of toast and a cup of tea. "Why's that?"

"I was on duty. Surveillance usually equals fast food and little sleep, but it's part of the deal."

"It's not all glamorous, huh?" She smiled then sipped her tea.

Austin, handsome and sweet, smiled back. "Not even close."

"Well, I won't keep you long this morning. I'll head

out to get Kylee in the next hour or so. She'll be pretty upset I'm so early—so will my mother—but I think a day at the beach should take care of that. My schedule's clear today, so we might as well take advantage of this warm front."

"It's no trouble, Sarah. Take your time. I'll be back at sundown to keep an eye on things."

"I have to admit it's a comfort knowing you won't be far. Having a serial rapist running around the Palisades is scary. Knowing someone was violated five houses down is terrifying. Thank God Hailey wasn't home."

"The story's been all over the news this morning. They're saying a light blue poker chip was found on the woman's bedside table. This is the fourth rape with the same M.O. The media's officially calling the bastard the 'Blue Chip Rapist.'"

"That's horrible."

Disgust hardened Austin's kind eyes. "Yeah, it is."

~~~~

Sarah sat in her beach chair, snapping pictures with her Nikon, capturing the moment while Kylee filled colorful buckets with sand wearing her pink and white striped sun hat.

"Play with me now, Mama." Kylee beamed.

Sarah hit the shutter button before letting the camera hang by its neck strap. "Are you ready to make the castle?"

"Yes."

"Let me put my camera away." She put the camera in its bag and moved closer to her daughter. Kylee's small hands patted the sand down in the buckets as Sarah did. Her daughter's cheerful chatter soothed her, as the sound of waves crashed against the shore. The salty scent of the sea whipped along the breeze, giving her the energy she'd lacked for most of the day.

Her argument with Ethan still weighed heavily on her mind. The hard look he'd seared her with and lack of inflection in his voice as he left troubled her. He'd sounded so final when he'd spoken of security and Austin handling it for her—as if he had no intention of coming back. Tears threatened again.

"Mama." Kylee's soft, sandy hand shook her leg. "Mama!"

Sarah blinked behind her sunglasses, forcing herself back in the moment. "Yes, honey."

"Look!"

The lopsided pile of sand, perilously close to crumbling, glistened in the sunshine.

Kylee clapped and grinned.

Infected by her daughter's delight, Sarah grinned back. "What a beautiful castle you've made. I need to take a picture of you next to it." She dashed forward, concerned that Kylee's creation would fall apart before she captured the moment. "Sit next to it. That's a girl. Now give me your best smile."

She snapped the picture and looked down at the screen. "Perfect."

"Dis castle is our house, Mama. I the princess and you are the tween."

"That sounds very special." Sarah smiled as she played with Kylee's ponytail.

"And Ethan is the ting."

Sarah's hand stopped halfway through Kylee's hair and her smile vanished.

Kylee frowned. "Dat's nice too, Mama."

Sarah forced another smile. "Yes, it is." She wanted a

change of subject. "Let's get some ice cream from the stand. We can walk by the water while we eat, but then we have to go home."

Kylee scrambled to her feet. "I want strawbewy."

Hand in hand, they walked to the stand.

~~~~

He sat in the car, peering through his binoculars, looking for the next one. Power still surged through his body, even hours after he'd played with his newest conquest. Each time he took what he wanted, he felt stronger, more invincible.

His latest playmate had been strong. She'd given him a hell of a fight, and he'd really, really liked it. A smile spread across his face as he remembered how she'd struggled and screamed. When he'd slapped her—hard—and then again just for the fun of it—she'd finally shut the hell up. He knew he'd won when she lay on her bed, whimpering as he'd used her the way women were meant to be used.

He had to do it again, and it had to be tonight. His bitch of the evening would have to be another strong one, someone who thought they were better than Ezekiel M. Denmire—until he was in them, then they always wanted a piece of him. He had to tell them to moan or he'd kill them, but that was beside the point.

Zeke stopped reminiscing and grew hard when the long-legged blonde passed his vision. Her sleek body, covered in a black bikini top and jade green sarong, were just what he was looking for. He groaned as her tongue darted out, swiping ice cream from her cone. She smiled down at a little girl in a pink striped hat and knew she was the one. Oh no, not the one for tonight, but *the* one, the ultimate conquest. The bright blue of her eyes told him so. He'd waited, so patiently, for her to come.

Her face was perfect, the shiny gold of her hair magnificent. He focused on her taut breasts just spilling from her top before his gaze wandered over her toned, narrow torso. Firm thighs peaked through the slit of vivid fabric with every step she took, and he slid his hand over himself, working himself into a frenzy.

He wasn't ready for her, not yet. He still had plenty of practicing to do. Women who looked like her never noticed men like him. They thought they were perfect, and deserved to be punished. Oh, and she would be punished just for being beautiful.

His binoculars stayed pressed to his face until the blonde beauty packed her things up and headed for her car. She and the little brat she tugged along made two trips, but that was fine and dandy; he had more time to watch.

When she put the girl in her seat, then buckled herself in, he started his car and followed behind her dark blue sedan. She pulled into a driveway, and he laughed hysterically, appreciating the awesome irony of her proximity to his last victim. He continued past 555 Seacoast Drive, knowing he would be back very soon—and often—but he had work to do tonight.

CHAPTER SIX

SARAH UNLOCKED HER DOOR AND DASHED FOR THE RINGING phone. "Yes, hello?"

"Sarah, it's Lisa. I have a last minute request and really need your help."

"What's up?"

"Tatiana Livingston had her baby yesterday. She wants you, and only you, to come photograph her. They would be our cover shot for this week's edition. Tomorrow night's deadline. I'll give you more than top dollar."

Sarah armed her alarm, as she listened to the editor in chief of *Celebrity* Magazine ramble on in her grainy smoker's voice about America's favorite movie star.

"Tatiana figures she can head off some of the paparazzi if we get her picture first. She and Kevin are staying in Park City, Utah."

"Utah? Lisa—"

"I know. It's short notice, but we want this. For Christ's sake, this is the biggest thing since man walked on the moon. We'll have a limo pick you up within the hour. A private jet will be waiting at LAX."

"What about Kylee?"

"Bring her. Bring an entourage for all I care. Just say you'll do this."

"I need to call my neighbor to see if she's available to come help me." Thinking of Hailey's dismal financial state, a shrewd glimmer came to Sarah's eye. "I think she has plans tonight and tomorrow for that matter, but I'm sure I can convince her to change them if the magazine is willing to pay her for her time as well." Between what she would give her herself and what *Celebrity* would fork over to secure this once-in-a-lifetime opportunity, Hailey might be able to get back to school full-time.

"Done. Be ready in an hour, and she can have anything she wants."

"I'd be happy to help you out, Lisa." Sarah hung up and turned to Kylee, sitting on the couch, feeding Mr. Ruff with a bottle. "Guess what?"

"What?"

"We're going on an airplane, and I'm pretty sure I've not only paid for your entire college education, but your wedding, too, with this job."

"Ooh, a wedding like Unke Hunte. Auntie Morgan is so bootiful."

"Yes, she is. I need to call Hailey, and we have to pack. Go get Mr. Ruff's bag ready, okay?"

"O-tay." Kylee scrambled down from the couch with her stuffed dog in hand.

~~~~

With a super excited Hailey on her way over and Kylee happily packing most of her toy box into a large pink and purple bag, Sarah hurried about, grabbing her camera equipment. When she was sure she had everything she needed, she hustled down to Kylee's room to pack a suitcase, then her own.

She brought the heavy bags to the entryway in the living room, stopping cold as she zeroed in on one of the numerous photographs decorating her living room wall. Jake, Hunter, and Ethan stood together with beer bottles in hand, grinning at a backyard BBQ so long ago.

She looked three frames over and stared at her own grinning face nestled against Ethan's as she held sonogram pictures up for the camera while Ethan stood behind her, wrapping his arms around her enormous belly, pointing at the mound with one hand. They'd sent the picture to Jake, along with pictures of the fetus, when they knew for sure she was carrying a girl.

Ethan had gone with her that day when her mother had called, too ill to make it. He'd held her hand as the technician told her she was having a girl and grinned, giving her a kiss on the forehead. Ethan had been there all along, every step of the way. She thought back to the night she'd waddled out to the couch where Ethan had slept during the last month of her pregnancy.

"Ethan, Ethan, wake up. I think my water broke."

He shot up from the cushions, sleepy-eyed. "What?"

"My water broke." A contraction squeezed her insides in a vise grip, causing her to gasp. "Oh, God, it's definitely time."

He stood, wrapping his arms around her as she rested her forehead against his naked shoulder. "It's okay, Sarah. Slow breaths in and out, just like we practiced in class," he said as he ran his hands up and down the back of her t-shirt.

She clutched his biceps, fighting to stay calm against the vulnerability such pain brought with it. "We have to call my parents and the hospital. We have to call Jake's commander, so they can get the video cameras ready over there. I don't want him to miss this."

"Shh," he whispered next to her ear as he continued to rub her back. "I'm going to take care of everything."

As the pain ceased, she stood again, sniffling.

He took her chin in his hand and stared into her eyes. "I want you to think about taking care of yourself and the baby. I'll handle the rest. I'll be here every step of the way, just like I promised you and Jake."

His confidence reassured her, and she smiled. "I know." Her smile vanished as the deep ache spread through her womb again, hardening her stomach. "Another one already."

Ethan checked his watch, pulling her close again. She pressed her head to his warm chest, listening to his heart slam against his ribs despite his soothing words, as they worked through the next contraction.

Kylee dropped her bag at Sarah's feet with an enormous thud, jarring her from her memories.

"I ready, Mama."

Sarah struggled to focus on the present. "I see. Where's Mr. Ruff?"

Kylee covered her mouth as she gasped. "He's on my bid dirl bed."

"Go get him. We need to leave."

Kylee ran down the hall as Sarah glanced at the pictures once more and turned away. She needed to get out of here. For the next forty-eight hours, she would be so busy with her daughter and Hollywood's Box Office Queen she wouldn't have time to think of anyone or anything else.

Ten minutes later, the limo driver stowed their bags as Kylee and Hailey climbed in the huge back seat.

Sarah dialed Ethan's number as she locked her front door. Her heart thundered when it continued to ring. Ethan's voice told her he'd get back to her. Disappointment warred with relief as she was sent to voicemail.

"Ethan? Um, it's Sarah. I wanted to let you know that Austin has the next couple of nights off. I'm taking Kylee and Hailey with me to Utah on a last-minute photo shoot. We'll be back Tuesday night."

She nibbled her lip as she fiddled with the keys in her hands. "I-I want to... I need..." She closed her eyes, frustrated, when she couldn't find the words that were so important. "I'm so sorry for everything, Ethan. I've hurt you, and I'm just so sorry." She paused then hung up, taking a deep, steadying breath as she walked to the limo. There was nothing she could do to fix anything now.

~~~~

Ethan sat behind his desk, staring out at the Los Angeles skyline. His cell began to vibrate among the paperwork scattered on the glossy oak. He picked it up as Sarah's number appeared on the readout. His thumb hovered over the 'talk' button before he set the phone back down. He couldn't talk to her right now. Hurt and anger had battled for first place throughout the day, leaving him cloaked in misery.

The missed call alert beeped and the message light flashed red. He tried to ignore the incessant blink by shoving the phone in the leather holster on his belt—and succeeded for about thirty seconds. "Well, fuck me," he said as he yanked his phone back out, knowing he was sunk.

He walked to the massive windows showcasing the lights of the city, watching the sun set. Sarah's voice filled his ear as he listened to her message and the pain radiating in each word. He fisted his hand against the glass, resting his forehead on it, realizing she hurt as much as he did.

Ethan added confusion to his mixed bag of emotions and closed his eyes, remembering the way she tasted when her tongue met his, the way her soft skin felt pressed against him as she moaned and brought her arms around his neck. He'd thought of little else all day. How could they go back to the way things were after a moment like that? How would they look at each other and pretend it never happened?

Ethan let out a sigh, knowing they couldn't. So where did that leave them?

Exactly where they were.

Their argument played through his mind, and he swore. He'd been caught completely off guard by her reaction after she'd been so responsive last night. She'd seemed a little shy as she went off to bed, but he hadn't expected her to be sorry after sharing something that meant so much to him. When Sarah stared at him with regret in her eyes, she'd hurt him in a way no one ever had. If he'd been even slightly prepared, he would have dealt with things differently—or at least he would've tried.

He understood the guilt she felt. He'd had to contend with it himself over the last several months, but at the end of the day, he truly believed Jake would want Sarah to be happy. Sarah had grieved and struggled to keep going for much of the first year after Jake died. She'd found comfort and peace in Kylee and in her work, and her life had slowly smoothed out from there.

It was okay for her to move on. Sarah could regret what happened between them all she wanted, but she hadn't been able to deny that she'd been just as caught up in him as he'd been in her, especially when she'd been on the verge of surrendering again this morning. He saw the need in her eyes and heard it in her strained voice.

"Knock, knock." Austin stuck his head in the office.

Ethan turned. "Hey, man."

"I'm heading over to Sarah's place. Here's the report on the surveillance detail for the Williamson Case." Austin put a thick stack of paper on Ethan's desk.

"Thanks. We'll meet tomorrow, nine a.m., and go over everything. We also need to discuss next week's premiere. With Hunter gone, we'll both be putting in some overtime. I want an update on background checks on the staff at the Wyman. We'll have to start staging routes for Tatiana Livingston's limo. They're already buzzing about this being an Oscar-caliber performance, so it's going to be a mess."

"Okay. See you at nine." Austin started through the door.

"You're off the hook with Sarah until Tuesday night. She went to Utah."

Austin paused and stepped back in, making himself at home in a black leather chair. "She didn't mention anything about it this morning."

"I got a call just before you came in."

"Is she okay?"

Ethan's head snapped up, his eyes meeting Austin's. "Why?"

"She was crying when I got to the door this morning."

His jaw clenched. "How was she when you left?"

"Fine, I guess. She made me breakfast, saying she wanted to eat, but she just played with the toast on her plate. We chatted a bit before she went to get Kylee. She said she was going to take Kylee to the beach for the afternoon."

Ethan nodded. "Go home and get some rest. You look like hell."

"I'm planning on it."

Austin left and Ethan sat down. He opened the

report on his desk, trying to concentrate on his work, but stared at the print on paper. He hated when Sarah cried. He hated even more that he'd been the reason for her tears.

Knowing there was nothing he could do to fix things for the time being, Ethan scrubbed his hands over his face and forced himself to focus on the words in front of him.

Moments later, Nicolette stood in the doorway, trailing her exotic scent with her. "Darling."

Ethan automatically closed the classified report and leaned back in his chair. Apparently he wouldn't be getting to Austin's report anytime soon. "Nicky."

"You stood me up." She pouted, playing with the silver necklace resting above her lush, golden cleavage.

"I told you it wasn't a good time."

"I waited for you."

"You shouldn't have."

She shut the door and turned the lock before walking to his desk. Her sleeveless red top and short black skirt fit like a second skin over her glorious body. She sat in his lap and made herself at home, playing with his tie. "I had plans for you last night, darling." Her bright red fingernail traced his lips, and he couldn't help but respond.

"Very naughty plans." She smiled wickedly. "Perhaps you will take me to dinner first, and we will go back to my hotel. Or I can show you right here." She moved, straddling him, as she pulled his mouth to hers and rocked, grinding herself against him.

He felt nothing. *What the hell's wrong with me?* He knew exactly, but tried to deny Sarah had a monopoly on his emotions. *"We're friends, Ethan. That's all we'll ever be."*

The hurt and helpless anger came back full throttle, and Ethan deepened Nicolette's kiss, grabbing her ass, clutching her more truly against him.

She eased away. "We will play now, then." Her fingers wandered to his belt.

He wasn't thinking straight, and he knew it. "Dinner first." He stood, bringing her with him, dropping her to her feet.

"A quick dinner." She smiled, touching her tongue to her top lip.

He ruthlessly shoved the soft lips and blue eyes of another to the back of his mind. She didn't want him. Trying to find his enthusiasm for Nicolette, he smiled back, pulling her against him. "Let's try room service."

~~~~

Zeke left the way he came in—through the open window at the back of the house. He chuckled as he checked his fly and adjusted himself, tugging his black hood in place. He cut through several backyards, daring someone to spot him and call the cops.

Fucking-*A*, this was too easy. The stupid bitch asked for it. An unlocked window was an open invitation as far as he was concerned. The lovely *ladies* of the Palisades needed to be more careful with a rapist on the loose. He covered his mouth, suppressing a snort of laughter as he circled back down a block to where he left his car.

This one didn't even bother to play hard to get, which had been a disappointment, but it wasn't a complete waste. After all, part of the fun was getting into the house without waking them first. Most of the pleasure came from watching them open their eyes. The fear alone was enough to make him cum. He was getting hard just thinking of it.

And this one had been afraid, all right—fucking terrified. He'd watched her eyes blink open and grow huge when she saw him standing over her. Her gasp had been priceless. But then she just laid there—whimpering and crying like the big fucking pussy she was. She didn't bother to try and fight, which pissed him off. Even when he raised the stakes by tying her up and telling her he was going to kill her, she still only lay there, so he'd punched her and finished himself off with a little extra mean. She deserved it. She'd been desert dry. How could he practice with a dud like that?

He'd worked hard to find her too. He'd gone to the gym for this one, sitting across the street at the bus stop for hours, waiting for just the right one to walk past the big windows of Robertson's Racquetball and Fitness Club. When the blonde stepped on the elliptical and began to move, he knew she would be the one. She was pretty enough, but she was no Sarah Johnson.

Zeke got in his car, driving past his latest bitch's house, blowing her a kiss as he sneered. He made his way down three blocks to Sarah's, taking the blue rose from a container. He'd worked for years, hybridizing his roses, perfecting this very color. The soft blue, a shade hinting with touches of cornflower and periwinkle, matched Sarah's eyes perfectly. He'd stared at the picture he found of her on Google Images and knew it was fate. She'd stood next to a dumbass movie star at some red carpet deal, but who cared about that?

He eased up to the curb, just feet from the house of the whore he nailed the night before and got out. The upscale neighborhood was dark and quiet, but he pulled the black hood over his hair, just in case as he walked to Sarah's front yard, looking behind him once, before he made his way to her door. He kissed the delicate flower petals with relish and laid the blossom against wood. "For you, my beautiful Sarah." He stared at the house for several seconds, fantasizing about how he would enter it when he was ready. Then he strolled back to his car and drove off.

~~~~

Ethan pulled into Sarah's drive and shut off the engine. The light she left on in the entryway cast shadows around the front as he stared at the darkened living room window, wondering why he came. He rubbed his fingers over his forehead, blowing out a long breath. He couldn't stop thinking about her.

During dinner with Nicolette, he'd been consumed by Sarah and the moments they'd shared over the past six years—their hug before she walked down the aisle to Jake; laughing together while they strolled along the beach; Sarah running into his office, throwing herself into his arms, glowing with the news of her pregnancy; him resting a cool cloth on her neck while she sat pale and sick in her bathroom during the rough first trimester; her eyes full of shocked wonder when she took his hand, holding his palm against her belly as the life inside her womb kicked for the first time.

Their lives were so wrapped up in each other's. How were they going to get things back to the way they were? What if they couldn't? His stomach jittered with the thought.

While he toyed with the two-potato crusted salmon on his plate, Nicolette had gone on about her newest fragrance campaign. He'd lost the thread of their conversation as he remembered pressing his mouth to

Sarah's and the yield of her soft lips against his, then he thought of her apology for their *mistake*. Hurt bubbled to the surface, colliding with frustrated anger, and he'd become determined to show himself that he didn't need Sarah, that it didn't matter.

He'd shoved his chair back from their small table overlooking the city, interrupting Nicolette midsentence and scooped her up, kissing her the way he wished he were kissing Sarah. With each new thought of the woman he desperately wanted but couldn't have, he tried harder to push Sarah out of his mind by falling to the bed with Nicky. He yanked her shirt over her head, pressing his face against her neck and remembered the way Sarah's eyes had stared into his the moment before he'd changed everything. The instant of forced passion died as quickly as it burned, and he pulled away from Nicolette, standing, telling her it was over. She'd given him a slap for his trouble, which still stung.

Running his tongue around the inside of his cheek, Ethan started his vehicle. There was no use being here tonight. He shifted into reverse and glanced at the house as he eased out of the drive. The flower lying in the shadows caught his eye, and he stopped, shifting the Rover back into first and parked again.

He frowned as he stepped from the vehicle, scanning the yard as he walked to the entryway and stood in the dim light, staring at the blue rose resting against the door. He looked around, searching for a note, but couldn't find one. *Odd.*

He leaned forward to pick up the rose but stopped mid-reach. Although it was just a flower, he didn't like it. Crouching down, he examined the fresh petals. Who brought a flower to a woman's home after dark? No, he definitely didn't like it—unless someone made a mistake and left it at the wrong door.

Ethan walked to the Rover, grabbing a napkin from a fast food bag then went back to Sarah's door, picking up the rose by the stem. He scrutinized the bud, turning it from side to side. The thorns had been removed, leaving the shoot smooth. It would've taken time to do that. If someone put in the effort to dethorn a rose, they would want the flower seen by the right person. Even if they'd gone to a florist, they still wouldn't want to waste a flower at the wrong address. This had been deliberately placed here.

With nowhere to put the flower, he dumped the rest of the contents from the fast food bag on the seat and set the stem inside.

On alert, Ethan took his gun from the lockbox under his seat and walked the perimeter of Sarah's house. Everything looked the way it should. He got in his vehicle and put the pistol away, staring at the spot where the rose had been before he drove off.

When he made it to the stop sign at the end of Sarah's quiet street, several emergency vehicles flew past. *What the hell is going on around here?* He turned right, away from the chaos, toward home.

Chapter Seven

Sarah held baby Ryan in her arms after the photo shoot. "He's perfect, Tatiana, just perfect." She moved her cheek over his soft newborn forehead and smiled.

"I know. I'm in love."

Sarah sat next to the redheaded beauty on the deep green couch they'd used for the photos. "Treasure this time; it goes so fast."

Tatiana smiled, playing with the pleats in her flowing white night dress. "You can count on it. After the premiere next week, Kevin and I plan to bring Ryan back here for the next several months. I'm finished with movies until next fall."

"America will be waiting for you, whenever you decide you're ready to return." She handed Ryan to Tatiana, recognizing the eager look in the new mother's eyes.

Ryan began to fuss and root, and Tatiana settled him at her breast. "You're planning on coming next week, right? I would love to have you there. I've put you on the security clearance list for the after-event."

"Sounds fun." It sounded like a nightmare. Premieres were always such a hassle. The screaming fans alone were overwhelming, even if they weren't screaming for her. The press and security were so tight. It suffocated her.

The majority of her clients were Hollywood A-listers. As a result, premieres and red carpet events were part of the job description. She loathed that aspect of her career.

Being home with Kylee would always beat the circus of Tinsel Town.

Tatiana laughed. "You're a terrible liar, Sarah."

Sarah smiled. "I'll be there." She glanced at her watch. "I really have to get back to the hotel. The limo will be by to pick us up in a couple of hours."

Tatiana stood as Sarah did. "Make sure you bring Kylee next time."

"She and Hailey are playing at the indoor water park. It's quite impressive. I won't be shocked if I have to go down and drag her up to our room myself." She hugged Tatiana. "Enjoy your precious boy." She stroked a finger over Ryan's cheek.

"I certainly will. I'll see you next week."

Sarah grimaced.

Tatiana laughed. "If I have to suffer, so do you."

~~~~

In the week since the photo shoot, *Celebrity* Magazine flew off the shelves faster than it could be printed. Sarah's usually hectic schedule turned chaotic shortly thereafter. She juggled her time between shoots, proofing, and Kylee, which left barely a moment for anything else. It was only when she lay in bed, before exhaustion took her under, that she thought of Ethan. He never called her back. She hadn't seen him since the morning of their argument.

Sarah stood in front of her bathroom mirror, securing the last pin into the shiny, loose curls piled on her head. Wispy trendils pulled at random, framed her face.

"Sarah, you look amazing," Hailey said as she bent forward, applying clear gloss to Kylee's puckered lips.

Sarah met Hailey's gaze in the mirror and smiled. "Thanks." She turned from side to side, examining the full effect of her hair and makeup. "I'm ready for my dress. Will you help me, so I don't mess up my curls?"

"Of course." Hailey plucked Kylee from the bathroom counter and set her on her feet.

Sarah took the black spaghetti strap evening dress from the bag and pulled it over her head with Hailey's help. She smoothed the fitted satin against her waist as Kylee and Hailey stared in silence. "Do you think it's too much?" She stood in front of the three-way, full-length mirror, turning. "My entire back is exposed."

"Mama, you so pretty."

She brushed a hand over Kylee's pigtail. "Thank you, honey."

"Seriously, Sarah, Tatiana has nothing on you tonight. You're stunning." Hailey fixed a wisp of Sarah's hair as she spoke.

"That's very kind of you. Hopefully people will ask where I got this dress so I can plug my mother's shop. I have to go." She walked over to her jewelry box, selecting the square-cut diamond earrings her parents gave her for Christmas and fastened them in place. Picking up her perfume bottle, she misted the flowery scent into the air and walked into it.

"Me too, Mama."

"Okay, but close your eyes and hold your breath." Sarah sprayed the wildflower scent again.

Kylee walked into the mist, giggling.

Sarah knelt down to Kylee's level and nuzzled her neck, making Kylee laugh. "You smell beautiful. You be a good girl for Hailey tonight." She kissed Kylee's slippery lips and stood, looking at Hailey. "I'll be back as soon as humanly possible, I promise. Arm the system when I leave and don't open the door for anyone. Austin's working the premiere tonight, but another one of Ethan's men, Jackson, will be in the area. He'll be doing drive-bys every twenty minutes or so. If you even think you need him, hit the panic button on the panel and call the police."

"You're freaking me out, Sarah."

Sarah touched Hailey's arm. "I'm sorry. The crime going on around here is pretty scary. The last ra—" She stopped herself, glancing at Kylee. "The last couple of incidents happened three blocks away. That's worth freaking out about. Do you want me to call my mother? You can take the car and go to Malibu. Dad is doing rounds at the hospital tonight. You know my mom would love to have you both."

"No, we'll be fine."

Sarah hugged Hailey. "You know where the keys are if you change your mind. See you in a bit. I think the limo's here."

~~~~

Sarah stepped from the limo into the pandemonium of screaming fans and camera bulbs flashing. Looking down, she walked ahead, following the high-heeled feet in front of her as someone called her name. She glanced up into more flashbulbs and scanned the frenzied crowd as someone shouted to her again. She spotted Tatiana, waving, as the star stood in front of a massive banner showcasing the title of her new movie, *Final Hour*.

Sarah waved back, making her way through the chaos, finally reaching the redheaded stunner and was enveloped in a hug. She returned the embrace, smiling— until she looked over Tatiana's shoulder. Ethan, handsome in his tuxedo, stood to the side. He was all business as he spoke into his earpiece. Although he wore sunglasses, she knew he focused on her.

Tatiana eased back. "You look beautiful, Sarah."

Sarah tore her gaze from Ethan, struggling to keep up with the conversation as her heart pounded. "Thank you. So do you." She focused on Tatiana's form-fitted gown, the forest green accentuating her shiny mane of hair. "It's hard to believe you gave birth last week."

"My nutritionist has been evil." Tatiana rolled her eyes, bending close to Sarah's ear. "So, are we having fun yet?"

She glanced at Ethan again, feeling the waves of tension radiating from his body. "Uh, not so much."

"Tatiana, we should keep moving," Ethan said. "The fans are getting pretty restless."

"Okay. Sarah, you can walk with me." Tatiana waved and stopped to sign an occasional autograph as they moved past throngs of reporters and fans kept back by metal blockades while Ethan stayed glued to her side.

"Tatiana, how's Ryan? Where's Kevin? Is he meeting you inside?" journalists shouted, reaching their microphones over the large barriers.

Mobs of eager fans shoved at the barricades, breaking through. Ethan pulled Tatiana back, yelling into his invisible mike as he put an arm around her shoulder. He snagged Sarah, enveloping her against his other side. Within seconds, people were everywhere—screaming and crying, shoving papers and pens in their faces. Somehow, Ethan kept them moving toward the door.

From out of nowhere, Austin's linebacker frame plowed through the crowd, taking Tatiana from Ethan's hold as fans pushed and shoved, growing more frantic. Austin shoved back, yelling for people to move out of his way, as he hurried Tatiana into the safety of the Wyman.

Within seconds, Sarah and Ethan were swallowed by the masses. Ethan continued to holler into his mike as people thrust pen and paper at Sarah. She put her arm up defensively, shielding her face while her other arm held firm around Ethan's waist, her hand clutching at his jacket. Did they realize she was just a damn photographer?

"Put your head down, Sarah, and keep walking," Ethan shouted close to her ear.

She could barely hear him over the din of chaos. His death grip tightened around her waist as he carried more than guided her, using his shoulder to propel them through. Finally they approached the door, and Austin opened it, pulling Sarah in by her arm.

Tatiana moved forward, gripping Sarah in a hug when Ethan turned to help Austin and five of his men, along with several police officers, shove people away from the entrance.

"My God, Sarah, that was awful."

Sarah's heart galloped as she tried to catch her breath. "Yes, it was." She eased back from the trembling star. "And no, I'm not having fun yet."

Tatiana's eyes brimmed with tears as she attempted a smile.

Sarah took Tatiana's hand and led her to the bathroom. She hugged her friend again when the door closed behind them. "Are you okay, honey?"

"I'll be fine." Tatiana brushed a tear away with unsteady fingers. "I'm a little shaken up. That has only happened once before, and it was just as scary. I love my fans, and they love me, but they get so crazy. I think they would love me to death without my security." She let out a laugh strained with nerves.

Sarah took two cloths from the toiletries stocked in the luxury restroom and ran them under cold water. She wrung the excess from the soft, white cotton, handing one to Tatiana. "Let's both take a deep breath." She dabbed the blessed cool against the back of her neck.

Tatiana did the same as the star took deep, steadying breaths.

"Does it ever get to be too much? Do you ever get sick of constantly being followed and watched?" She wouldn't be able to stand it.

"Yes, all the time now that Ryan is here. I used to love the attention when my career started taking off, but now..." Tatiana shrugged, shaking her head. "My baby will never want for anything but a normal life." Regret filled her eyes. "I'll never be able to give my son that."

Sarah took her hand. "You and Kevin are wonderful parents. You'll find a way to make it work. I'm glad you're taking some time for just the three of you."

Tatiana gave her hand a gentle squeeze. "Me too. I'm counting down the hours until I can hold my baby." She glanced down at her chest. "So are my boobs. They're so full they hurt."

Nerves eased, and they both chuckled.

After several minutes of light conversation, Tatiana fixed her makeup and smiled. "I'm good now. I need to get to the party. Everyone's waiting. Are you ready?"

"Go ahead. I want to call and check on Kylee and Hailey real quick."

Tatiana hugged her again. "Thanks for everything, Sarah."

"Anytime, honey. I know I missed the movie portion, but from what I hear, I look forward to photographing you with your newest Oscar."

Tatiana laughed as she opened the door. The bubbly

sound faded as the door closed behind her.

Alone, Sarah took her phone from her bag. She stopped dialing when someone knocked on the outside door.

Ethan stuck his head in, scanning the room before he stepped in the rest of the way. He'd removed his sunglasses and his earpiece dangled at the collar of his shirt. "Hey. I just wanted to be sure you're okay."

Sarah's heart beat wildly as a myriad of emotions flooded her—happiness, longing, confusion. She dropped the phone back in her bag and walked forward. "Yes, I'm fine. Thank you for helping me. That was pretty scary."

"It got out of control fast."

Tension filled the room when that appeared to be the extent of their conversation. Sarah played with the zipper on her purse as she searched Ethan's face, her eyes pausing on his firm, full lips before meeting his gaze. "Ethan, I know this isn't the time, but I want to apologize again for—"

"I don't need an apology." Temper snapped into his voice.

She hesitated then took his hand. "I hate that things are like this between us. I miss you."

His grip tightened on hers fingers as he looked away.

She nibbled her lip. "Kylee misses you too. She's been asking for you. Why don't you come over—"

"I can't do this, Sarah." He dropped her hand. "You want things to be the way they were. They're not the same. I have feelings for you."

She wanted to wrap her arms around him, so she turned away from the heat of his gaze and closed her eyes. "I don't know what you want me to say. I told you I can only be your friend."

The fabric of Ethan's jacket brushed her naked back

91

as his breath feathered against her neck, heating her skin. She glanced up, her gaze meeting his in the mirror, her photographer's eye recognizing the picture they made. There was no denying they were stunning together.

Ethan took her hands at her sides, lacing his fingers with hers. He kissed her neck once, sending shivers down her spine as gray eyes burned into blue. "I have feelings for you, Sarah," he repeated, his teeth grazing her ear. "You feel something too. I see it every time you look at me."

A tear slid down her cheek. "I can't do this, Ethan."

He turned her toward him, and their breath mingled. His calloused fingertips traced gentle circles along her back as he pulled her closer. "Sarah," he whispered.

She moved forward, captivated, wrapping her arms around his waist, ready to give into her needs and his. Her necklace brushed his shirt, and her wedding rings pressed against her skin like a shock, reminding her that this was wrong. She pulled back, shaking her head. "No, Ethan, I'm sorry."

"Goddammit, Sarah. Why are you doing this?" He walked to the door, yanked it open, and left her staring after him.

Sarah leaned back against the marble countertop as guilt and confusion careened through her system. She covered her face with her hands as she fought to keep her breath steady and tears at bay. She didn't know what to do. As her feelings changed, she dishonored Jake's memory and caused Ethan pain.

Turning again to the mirror, she stared into her own sad blue eyes. Everything was such a mess. She had no desire to be here any longer. If she could get out of this place without being mobbed again, she would go home to her baby and friend, but she didn't dare try.

Stuck, she had no choice but to make the best of it. She pulled her phone from her purse and cursed the time. Her limo wouldn't be back for two hours. Ethan would be in the ballroom, but she could easily avoid him. The elegant function space was massive. It would be best to keep her distance until she could find some sort of handle on the direction her life was taking.

She sent Hailey a text instead of calling. Kylee would be in bed. *Is everything okay?*

Moments later, her phone vibrated. *A-okay here. Kylee is asleep. Ogle at least one hottie for me. I'll expect a detailed report.*

Sarah smiled and relaxed fractionally. She was so lucky to have Hailey, not only for Kylee but for herself. *I'll see what I can do. Be home later.*

Steadier, Sarah stuffed her phone back in her evening bag. She stood taller and fixed a wisp of hair at her temple, walking from the bathroom, ready to grin and bear the next couple of hours.

~~~~

Ethan stood in the corner of the ballroom not far from Tatiana, scanning the guests and doorways, constantly on the alert. He glanced toward the entrance just as Sarah walked through and clenched his jaw. Her beauty was so potent, it stunned.

The dress she wore accentuated her long, slender body. With every step she took, her smooth, sleek leg snuck from the slit in the black fabric, and he wanted her.

Her floral scent still clung to his jacket, torturing him. The torment was only worse as he remembered the way she'd wrapped her arms around him only moments ago, staring into his eyes. She'd been seconds away from giving him everything he needed, everything he'd craved over the last week since he'd seen her.

Ethan came to attention when one of Hollywood's most sought after men walked up to Sarah, giving her a hug and kiss on the cheek. She smiled as she spoke to him, nodding as he took her hand, and they strolled to the dance floor. He ground his teeth, watching Brand Larson and Sarah move together effortlessly. Her laugh carried across the room when the muscled blond said something close to her ear, and Ethan stepped forward before he remembered he was on duty.

Not even two weeks ago, he and Sarah had been as casually comfortable with each other. Regret ate at him, as he feared he'd ruined everything. He thought of their dance at Morgan and Hunter's wedding and the way they'd looked into each other's eyes. Had things changed already? Would they have ended up here eventually anyway? He didn't know.

He tore his gaze from Brand's hand on Sarah's naked lower back and focused on the door, watching people enter and exit while the chatter between his team of men buzzed in his ear. The song ended, rolling into the next, and Ethan flicked a glance in Sarah's direction. She hugged Brand once more and made her way to the bar, ordering water with lemon then turned, pausing with the glass halfway to her mouth. Her eyes met his, holding, before she pivoted away and walked toward a group of women.

Two hours later, Ethan moved to yet another location, standing in the background not far from Tatiana, struggling to focus on his job as his gaze wandered to Sarah—again. He couldn't help but smile when she discreetly pulled her phone from her purse, sneaking another peak at the time. She hated these events.

She made her way in his direction, stopping next to Tatiana. Tatiana grinned and wrapped her in a hug. Tatiana eased back, and her brows furrowed as she said something to Sarah, who shook her head.

He couldn't hear their conversation, but Sarah was close enough for him to get a good look at her. She smiled as she spoke, but it didn't reach her eyes. She glanced in his direction, her eyes full of misery and hurt, before she turned and walked from the room. He wanted to go after her, but they would solve nothing surrounded by a thousand people, so he stayed where he was.

"Austin, everything's all set here. Make sure Sarah gets home safely." He said into his mike.

"You got it, boss."

~~~~

Zeke sat in his car two houses down from Sarah's with binoculars at the ready, waiting for her return. She'd been gone for *hours*, and he was getting pissed. It was after midnight, for Christ's sake. He had to work tomorrow.

His hand flexed and bunched at his side as he worked himself into a rage. Was it too much to ask for her to get her ass home? He left her something, didn't he? They always fucking *wanted* something. Here he'd gone and gotten her a present, and she couldn't even hurry back to find it. *Some bitches are so inconsiderate.*

The flowers were going to wilt at this rate. He'd brought her two—a symbol of sorts. Zeke figured by the time he left her half a dozen, he would be ready, especially if his practice sessions went as well as tonight's. He'd discovered a neat little bonus he definitely wanted to explore further. If he liked it as much as he had this evening, he might add it to his repertoire to spice things up a bit.

The whore he chose had breezed by while he'd been stopped at a traffic light earlier in the afternoon. It'd been fate, just like the day at the beach when he found Sarah. His 'lady' of the evening's hair was darker blonde, almost too dark, but he couldn't let trivial things like that stop his progress. Her eyes had been blue and that was what mattered. Their eyes had to be blue, like Margaret's.

Fury spewed through his black heart as he thought of the woman who'd never given him a second glance, even after he'd sworn his undying love—but that didn't matter anymore, because he had Sarah. She was hotter than Margaret by a mile.

He wondered if Sarah would like the new twist he'd added in the bedroom. He'd let this bitch fight, and *boy* did she fight. In fact, she almost overpowered him at one point, but when he grabbed her by the throat and squeezed until her legs kicked and her arms thrashed, he'd cum in his jeans from the power.

She'd settled right down, gagging and coughing when he removed his hands. When he knew he had her full concentration, he'd forced her to play with him until he'd been good and hard and ready to go again, then he'd plunged into her until she cried out.

She didn't exactly cry out in ecstasy the way the others always did, but it had worked. He'd put his hand on her throat and applied pressure until she gasped and her eyes had gone huge. He'd seen fireworks while he filled his condom.

Fuck yeah, he couldn't wait to do it again.

He definitely had plans for the next one, wherever she happened to be. He wasn't sure if she would like the new game, but who the fuck cared. He sure as hell would.

The black limo pulled in Sarah's drive, and she got out.

Zeke pressed the binoculars close, whistling as the beam of headlights accentuated her slender build and the creamy skin of her back. "Hot *damn*, I can't wait to get my dick in you." He reached for the door handle. Perhaps it wouldn't be so bad if he got a little closer. Maybe he could rub one out by her bedroom window while she changed.

Shaking his head, he put his hand back on the binoculars. Good things came to those who waited, and he'd waited a very long time. Besides, he could rub one out in the comfort of his own bed while he *thought* about her getting undressed—just for him.

The limo pulled away, and Sarah walked to the door, bending down to pick up the flowers. A thrill coursed through his veins when she put them to her nose and smiled. Instantly, he was in love—a love more powerful, more all-consuming than he'd ever felt for Margaret. "Oh, Sarah, it's going to be perfect. You wait and see."

Zeke started his car and drove off as visions of just how it would be began to take shape.

CHAPTER EIGHT

AUSTIN PULLED INTO THE DRIVE AND KNOCKED ON SARAH'S door. She answered holding blue roses. He zeroed in on the flowers, immediately remembering what Ethan had told him about the one he'd found a week ago.

"Hey, Sarah, where'd you get the roses?"

She beamed down at the delicate blooms. "They were at the front door. I think Kylee and Hailey left them for me. I'll have to thank them in the morning."

It didn't feel right. Unsure of how to handle it, Austin gave her a small smile. "Uh, can I use your bathroom?"

"Of course, go right ahead."

"Arm the panel, okay?"

"I always do."

Austin shut the bathroom door and twisted the lock as he took his cellphone from his pocket and dialed the office number, careful not to move around too much in the small, feminine half-bath. Within seconds, dispatch patched him through to Ethan's earpiece. "Cooke, it's Casey."

"I can hardly hear you. Speak up."

"I can't. Listen harder. I'm in Sarah's bathroom."

"Austin, if you called to talk while you're on the shitter..."

The laughter of six men on duty bounced through Austin's phone.

"Screw you, Cooke. I didn't call to joke around. There were two more flowers at Sarah's door. She thinks they're from Hailey and Kylee, but I don't."

Any remaining chuckles died away.

"What color and type?" Ethan's voice tightened with tension.

"Blue roses."

"Don't leave until I get there. I'll have Michaels come cover me here. It'll probably be a good half hour before I can get up to the house."

"What am I supposed to tell her? She's going to want me to leave so she can go to bed."

"Tell her I told you to stay. I'll be there as soon as I can."

"But—" Ethan disconnected. "Shit." Austin put the phone away and followed the dim light to the kitchen, focusing on the roses in a glass budvase on the counter.

Sarah sat at the table, wrapped in her pale blue robe, with a cup of tea. Her eyes, usually so vibrant, were dull and sad as she stared off at something.

He wondered if it had anything to do with earlier in the evening. The boss man had been in the bathroom with her for several minutes. When Ethan yanked the door open and stalked away, he'd looked just as unhappy as Sarah did now. Interesting. He'd been curious as to why Ethan tensed up every time Sarah's name came up in conversation, and why he'd been handling her security instead of Ethan himself.

Austin cleared his throat and Sarah glanced up. A small smile touched her lips. "Thanks for coming all this way to check on us."

"Hey, no problem." Desperate for an excuse to stay, he honed in on the steaming mug she held between her hands and shuddered. *How does anyone drink that stuff?* "Would it be any trouble if I made myself a cup of tea? It helps me relax. I'm sure you want to get to bed. I can let myself out when I'm finished."

"Not at all. Make yourself at home. I always have such a hard time winding down after an event. I'll get it for you."

"If it's no trouble."

"None."

In no time, tea and a plate of double chocolate chip cookies were set in front of him. He bit into the moist center of gooey chocolate as Hailey walked into the room dressed in vivid pink pajama pants covered in maniacally grinning bunnies, her ponytail bobbing with each step.

Austin glanced at her small perky breasts accentuated in her white, spaghetti strapped top while she yawned and stretched. "Hey, guys. Did you have fun?"

Flitters of desire sparked to life as he met her friendly honey brown eyes. He stared down at the table as guilt drowned any remaining embers. She was a college kid, for Christ's sake.

"If you consider almost getting trampled to death and spending the night listening to actors and actresses talk about their craft fun, then yes, I think we both had the best time of our lives. Not to mention the hour-long ride through traffic." Sarah grinned at Austin, then Hailey.

"Well, I can't wait to hear all about it, especially the trampled part, unless you spoke to any really hot actors. I'll want to hear about that first." Hailey took a glass from the cupboard and filled it with water. "Pretty flowers. Please tell me they're from a Hollywood hunk and he'll be picking you up for dinner tomorrow night."

Sarah frowned. "I thought they were from you and Kylee."

Hailey sat down at the table. "Nope."

"Well, then, I don't know."

"I didn't even know blue roses existed—and look how they match your eyes. That's pretty cool."

Sarah's frown deepened. "Yes, I guess they do, but where did they come from?"

"Maybe you have a secret admirer." Hailey winked. "You did look hot tonight."

Austin took a sip of the wretched tea, trying not to squirm. Headlights hit the window, and he got to his feet, relieved. "I think that's Ethan. I'll go check."

"Ethan?" Sarah stood, following him to the front door. "Austin, why is Ethan here?"

"I'm pretty sure it's him. Let me go check. Stay inside." Like a rat abandoning a sinking ship, he sent her a sheepish smile and closed the door.

~~~~

Puzzled and slightly miffed, Sarah went back to the kitchen.

"Sarah, why are Ethan *and* Austin here? I haven't seen Ethan around here in days, which is really weird, now that I think of it."

"He's been busy," Sarah said quickly as she walked over to the vase. The pleasure of receiving flowers dimmed, leaving her uneasy. Who had they come from? She turned again, staring at Austin's mug all but untouched and the empty plate of cookies, realizing she'd been had.

Ethan and Austin walked in, and their conversation stopped.

Ethan zeroed in on the roses before he met her gaze.

Trickles of unease tensed her stomach as she watched the hard light come into his eyes. "What's going on?"

"Have a seat and I'll tell you."

The cool slap of his voice raised her hackles. "Can I get anyone anything first? Austin, can I freshen your tea? I know how much you enjoy a good cup."

Austin winced. "Sorry, Sarah. I wanted Ethan here before we started."

"Just sit down, Sarah, so we can get this over with," Ethan snapped.

Hailey's eyes popped wide and slid toward Austin's.

"Don't you talk to me like that. This is *my* house." She yanked a chair back and sat down.

"Um, I'm going to bed, or maybe I should just go home. Would you mind walking me, Austin?"

Sarah pinched the bridge of her nose and blew out a breath. "Please don't, Hailey. It's well past midnight. I'd feel better if you stayed."

"Okay, then. Good night." She gave Sarah's hand a squeeze before she left.

Austin's phone rang. He pulled the cell from his pocket and looked at the readout. "I need to take this. It's Michaels." He left the room.

Ethan unbuttoned his sleeves and rolled them past his elbows before he sat across from her. "I'm putting one of my men on the house permanently. It'll probably be Austin."

She laced her fingers together, squeezing as the trickles of dread returned. "Why?"

"At this point it's precautionary."

"Is this because of the flowers?"

"Yeah, some of it." He stared at her for several seconds.

"Are you going to tell me anything more or just let me sit here half sick?"

"I came by the night you left for Utah to check things out. I found a flower on your doorstep."

Her stomach clutched as alarm bells rang. "Why are you just telling me about this?"

"I'd made Austin aware of it. It might not be anything, but something doesn't feel right. I didn't want to scare you."

"But you do now?"

"No, I don't. I want you to be careful. As I said before, this is just a precaution. There's nothing to worry about at this point, but it seems odd for someone to leave flowers like this. With all of the rapes in the area, I think it would be better to have Austin here until they catch the guy—at least at night."

"Thank you."

"Don't worry about it."

His eyes, like his voice, lacked any of their familiar comfort. She was so scared. The flowers creeped her out, but the fear came from sitting across from this cool, professional stranger who used to be her best friend. Was this it? Was this the end of their road? Ethan's clenched jaw and tense shoulders told her it might be. She wanted to fix this more than she wanted her next breath. She reached for his hand. "Ethan, I—"

He leaned back in his chair and moved his hand from her reach, looking away.

She pulled her hand back as pain slashed like a knife. "I'd like to pay him for his time."

He flicked her a glance. "It's been taken care of."

"By who? You? That isn't necessary."

"Just leave it alone. This was my idea."

"You're not paying for Austin to stay here. I'm more than capable—"

"Forget it. Things don't always get to be your way."

Ethan stood and walked out.

She sat in her chair long after Ethan had gone, thinking of his lips capturing hers and the glide of his tongue against hers in the moonlight. One kiss had changed everything, had ruined everything.

~~~~

Sarah nodded at Kylee, giving her the go-ahead to press the doorbell. Kylee stabbed her little finger against the chrome button with enthusiasm.

Hunter, tan and relaxed in bare feet, jeans, and a navy blue polo, opened the door and grinned.

"Unke Hunte," Kylee squealed.

He took Kylee from Sarah and gave her a big hug. "How's my baby girl?"

"I not a baby dirl. I a big dirl now."

"Okay, how's my big girl?"

"Dood."

"I missed you. Are you ready for a birthday party?"

"Yes." She squirmed to get down. "I go say hi to Auntie Morgan."

Hunter set Kylee down, tapping her bottom, and she ran off. He yanked Sarah into a bear hug. "Hey, you. Happy birthday."

She returned his embrace. "Thanks. You look wonderful, Hunter. Did you two have fun?"

"Absolutely. Morgan took an insane number of pictures, which should make you happy."

She grinned. "You bet. I can't wait to see them—all of them."

"Make sure I'm not here that day," he said with a pained look.

Morgan stepped from the kitchen in jeans and a

cream-colored sweater, holding a smiling Kylee. "Happy birthday, Sarah."

Sarah walked over, giving her a huge hug, clinging a little too tightly. She hadn't realized how much she'd missed her friends. "Thank you. I hope you had a great time, but I'm so glad you're home."

Morgan eased back, frowning. "I'm glad we're home too. What's the matter?"

"Nothing, not a thing." *Everything.* "I'm just ready for that lunch date we talked about before you left."

"I need to get into the office over the next couple of days. How about this weekend?"

"Perfect. My weekend is strangely blank—which almost never happens—but I'll take it. I could use a breather."

Morgan glanced at Hunter and put Kylee down. "Kylee, we have a present for you in the living room. Would you like to open it?"

"Yes!"

"Go with Uncle Hunter, and he'll get it for you. Sarah, why don't you come with me while I finish making dinner," she said as she walked back to the large kitchen.

Sarah followed Morgan into the spacious room decorated with oak cabinetry and dark green granite. The room felt homey, with plants and no-nonsense cooking gadgets placed about the sunny space. Morgan's homemade pasta sauce wafted through the air. "It smells great in here. I can't wait to eat."

"Good. I made enough for an army. Would you like a glass of wine?"

"Sure. I'll take white."

Morgan poured the buttery golden liquid into crystal glasses. "Ethan called a few minutes ago. He might not be able to make it. He said something came up at work."

"Oh, okay." This would be the first time he'd missed her birthday in six years. Considering the circumstances, it shouldn't have stung, but it did. "We'll save him a piece of cake." She took the glass Morgan handed her and tried a smile.

Morgan stared and Sarah glanced down, scrutinizing the flecks of color in the smooth granite. Afraid her friend had seen too much, she attempted to move the conversation to more distracting topics. "So, tell me about the honeymoon. What did you guys do while you were in Italy, besides practice, of course?" This time she smiled fully when her gaze met Morgan's.

"What's going on, Sarah?"

Her smile vanished as she let out a long sigh, knowing she'd failed to fool Morgan. "I'm a little stressed out. I'm sure you've heard about the roses at my door. I thought maybe someone made a mistake and left them at the wrong house, but it definitely wasn't. We found three more the other day—with a note this time. It said, 'For you, my lovely Sarah.'" She shuddered. "Now the police are involved. They're trying to trace the paper and ink the person used, but I don't think they've gotten anywhere yet."

"I'm so sorry, honey. Hunter told me on the flight home yesterday. Ethan didn't say anything to him until we got to the airport. He didn't want us worrying. Hunter would've been at your place this morning, but he knew you had a shoot. I didn't want to bring it up and spoil your night."

"I won't let it, but I am scared. The note wasn't threatening, but it is all at the same time. If someone's interested, why don't they call me like a normal person would? But that's the scary part; I don't think this person's healthy."

"You and Kylee can stay with us. You know you're always welcome."

"I appreciate it, but you're newly married. You can't have spontaneous sex on the kitchen table—or wherever else you want, for that matter—if you're worried about your friend and her two-year-old walking through the door at anytime. Besides, Austin's keeping an eye on things."

"He's a nice man—comes off as very gentle."

"He really is."

The kitchen timer beeped, and Morgan turned, pulling a huge dish of lasagna, bubbling with cheese from the oven.

"Morgan, that looks and smells amazing. What can I do to help?"

"Grab the salad from the fridge. We're just about ready. Would you tell Kylee and Hunter? I need to get the bread."

"Sure." She walked through the beautiful dining area, running her finger over the dark wood of the china cabinet on her way to the living room. "Kylee, Hunter, supper's—"

Ethan sat on the floor with Kylee in his lap. She clutched a new doll in her hands while he read her a book from the pile Morgan and Hunter kept on hand. He stopped reading and glanced up.

"Look at my new baby, Mama!" Kylee kissed the olive skinned beauty before she scrambled out of Ethan's lap.

Sarah knelt down next to her daughter. "She's very pretty. What's her name?"

"Baby."

Sarah smiled. "Of course."

"Is everyone com—" Morgan stepped in the room. "Oh, Ethan, you made it." She beamed. "Great."

He stood and gave her a hug. "Welcome back."

"Thanks. Dinner's ready." She glanced at him, then at Sarah. "Kylee, do you want to help me find Uncle Hunter?"

"He in his office."

"Let's go get him." She took Kylee's hand and they left the room. "Do you like your pretty baby?"

Kylee's chatter followed them down the hall.

Ethan shoved his hands in his jean pockets and rocked back on his heels. "Happy birthday."

"Thank you. I'm glad you were able to come." Sarah didn't know what to say as they stared at each other. "We should probably go eat." She turned toward the door.

"Sarah, wait." He snagged her wrist. "If this makes you uncomfortable, I can leave."

"No." She put her hand on his arm. "I want you to stay."

"Then let's eat." He smiled.

Sarah took two steps before he yanked her around and pulled her into a hug. She closed her eyes and wrapped her arms around his waist, holding on, breathing him in while she nestled her head against his shoulder. For the first time in two weeks, everything felt right.

"I miss you." He kissed her hair, an old gesture that soothed.

She wrapped her arms tighter. "I've missed you too." She eased back just enough to look him in the eye, unwilling to let him go. "Ethan, I don't know what to do."

He rested his forehead against hers. "That makes two of us."

"Everything's so messed up."

"Can we have dinner and try to figure this out? I don't want to lose you. You're too important."

"Ethan," she whispered, undone, framing his face. "I'd like that very much, but I'm pretty booked up this week. How about Saturday?"

"You've got it." He smiled, hugging her close once more before they wandered toward the aroma of Morgan's fabulous lasagna.

~~~~

After lasagna, cake, and conversation, Sarah took the envelope Morgan handed her.

"This is something from all of us. Happy birthday."

Sarah peeked across the room at Kylee sleeping on the couch, snuggled under a blanket, then opened the card and gasped. "Oh, this is too much." She stared at her smiling friends. "I don't know what to say."

"'Thanks' will do," Hunter said.

She glanced down at the brochure for the exclusive resort and four plane tickets made out to herself, Hunter, Morgan and Ethan, then stood and hugged each of them. "Thank you so much. I'm so excited. A weekend away."

She looked at the white roses in the center of the table and her excitement dimmed. What about Kylee? She'd never been away from her for more than one night. She couldn't leave her right now. Some weirdo was sending her flowers and her house was being guarded.

Hunter took her hand as she sat back down. "Hey, this is supposed to be fun. You don't turn twenty-eight every day."

"I'm sorry. It is, but I can't go this weekend. I can't leave Kylee right now, not with everything that's going on."

"Kylee's not the target, Sarah." Ethan met her gaze across the table. "You are."

"Jesus, Cooke," Hunter said with disgust.

"I didn't get to finish." He stood and walked around the table, resting his hands on her tensed shoulders. "We booked this a couple months ago, before all this started. Your mom's planning to take Kylee. Hailey's going to help out. Now that there's a need, Austin's assigned to go with them. He's one of the best men I have. He won't let anything happen to Kylee or anyone else."

Morgan took the seat next to Sarah. "If you're really uncomfortable, we can change the dates. It's not that big of a deal."

Hunter squeezed her hand again. "The only reason we didn't change the dates ourselves is because this could be a good thing. If Kylee's away somewhere safe and so are you, we can run surveillance and see if we can figure out what the hell's going on. Once the guy figures out you're not there, he might relax a little and make a mistake. Our cameras would pick it up."

"You're sure Kylee will be safe?" Doubt trickled through in Sarah's words.

Ethan knelt down eye to eye, taking her chin in his hand. "Nobody loves her more than the four people in this room. We wouldn't suggest it otherwise."

Staring into Ethan's eyes, trusting what he said, she nodded. "Okay then, let's go."

CHAPTER NINE

THE SATURDAY MIDMORNING FLIGHT FROM L.A. TOOK LESS than an hour. By late afternoon, Sarah lay in a lounge chair by the private pool, sipping an iced tea heavy on the lemon. "You were so right. I really needed this."

Morgan rolled to her back. "I couldn't agree more. You were pretty stressed the other night."

Sarah grinned. "Stress? What stress?"

"I've enjoyed watching you decompress over the last six hours. By the time we leave, you'll be a whole new woman."

"Oh, I hope so. You might have to hide my phone though. I've already called my parents three times. My mother didn't sound particularly happy with me when we hung up. I was told that if I call again before Kylee's bedtime, she'll disconnect the phones."

"Kylee's fine, Sarah. Try not to worry."

Hunter came from one of the three adjoining suites dressed in trunks as Ethan closed the slider on the other.

Sarah's gaze trailed down Ethan's naked, muscular chest, and she blew out a quiet breath. She pushed her sunglasses up the bridge of her nose, afraid he'd seen her. She tried for a casual smile. "Did you enjoy your golf game?"

"Not as much as I'm going to enjoy this." He and Hunter grinned at each other before Ethan scooped her up.

She only had time for a quick breath before he cannon balled into the water with her in his arms. Sarah surfaced, choking and wrapped her arms around his neck, trying not to drown in the twelve-foot depths. When she had her breath back she glared into Ethan's grinning face as her sunglasses floated by. "You jerk. I didn't want to get wet. We're supposed to go to dinner in less than an hour."

He grinned again. "You'll dry."

A drop of water glistened on his bottom lip in the setting sun, and she fought the urge to move in and capture it with her tongue. Surprised by her own thoughts, she was suddenly conscious of her breasts pressed against his chest in her skimpy pink bikini top as Ethan's powerful arms moved back and forth, treading water. Their legs, slippery from the water, tangled together as they kicked to stay afloat.

Sarah's mind flashed to the moonlit night when his eyes stared into hers moments before he took her mouth. What would it be like to lay under him, to feel the weight of his smooth, muscled body covering hers? Desire churned, and she pulled away. *Dear God, what is wrong with me?*

Swimming for her sunglasses, she struggled to clear her head. As she made a grab, Ethan's hand snaked up from under the water, snatching them first.

"Damn it, Ethan."

Hunter roared with laughter as he sat in the chair next to Morgan.

Ethan surfaced, grinning. "If you want these, you'll have to come get them."

"He's a dangerous man," Morgan said, smiling. "Go show him what girls are made of."

Determined to do just that, Sarah dove under the water and came up for air, knowing Ethan would be ready for her. She reached for her glasses as he held them above his head, and she maneuvered around him, grabbing the waistband at the back of his shorts and yanked up—hard.

His swear was drowned out by Morgan's long peal of laughter.

Hunter fell off his chair, hysterical. "Christ, Cooke, if you could've seen your face," he said in between fits of mirth.

Still chuckling, Morgan grabbed Hunter's hand, helping him up. "She showed you, didn't she, Ethan? We're going to get ready for dinner. We'll meet you two in half an hour."

Sarah gave Morgan a triumphant grin as she swam to the side and hiked herself up, using the cement lip, but was quickly pulled back into shoulder-deep water.

"That wasn't very nice," Ethan said as he turned her toward him.

"You deserved it." A giggle escaped before she could prevent it.

He grinned. "I probably did."

"No, you definitely did." She started to laugh.

"I guess you want these back." Ethan unfolded the glasses and rested the lenses on top of her head.

"Thank you. Now, we need to get out or we're going to be late."

"I think we can spare another couple of minutes."

Sarah recognized the hungry look in his eyes and knew she should pull back but didn't, couldn't. Her heart pounded and heat curled deep in her belly as he clutched her waist, moving her more truly against him. His mouth met hers, barely touching, and she closed her eyes, no longer able to deny her need for him.

He traced his tongue over her bottom lip and tugged with his teeth, sending a shiver down her spine. He captured her lips again with more heat and slid his tongue against hers, changing the angle, going deeper.

Sarah wrapped her arms around his neck, bringing her breasts against him as he skimmed his fingertips up and down her waist, sending rockets of need—long dead—soaring through her system. Caught up, she ran her fingers through his wet hair, tugging him closer, pressing his mouth more firmly to hers.

He groaned, framing her face with his hands as his tongue dove once, twice more, before he eased back, his breathing ragged. "God, Sarah, please don't tell me that can't happen again."

She rested her palms against his shoulders, catching her own breath, wanting him like she hadn't wanted in a long time. "This isn't exactly figuring things out. We still haven't talked this through."

"Sarah—"

"I don't want to be a tease, Ethan, but I need time. This is so new. It has to be right for both of us, for Kylee too."

He brushed her hair back from her face. "You can have all the time you need. I just want to be with you."

She wanted to give him everything he asked for, but thought of their tension-filled conversation at her kitchen table not that long ago. "What if this doesn't work? Look how rocky the last few weeks have been for us. We're too much a part of each other's lives. You mean too much to me to risk it."

"You mean too much to me not to try. Let's take things a day at a time and see where we end up."

Sarah stared into his eyes and realized they could never go back to where they'd been. They had to move forward. "Okay." She rested her forehead against his chest, wrestling with the weight of her decision. There was so much at stake.

Ethan slipped a finger under her chin, and she met his gaze. "One day at a time, Sarah." He kissed her again, and they got out of the pool.

~~~~

Morgan pulled the poolside door open, gasped, and closed it again, quickly, quietly. She would get her cover-up later. She moved to the large glass window and parted the curtain—just a hair—to confirm what she thought she just saw: Ethan and Sarah in one hell of a lip lock. *Oh, shit.*

A lot of things made sense now. The undercurrents between the two had been different the last few times they'd all been together. She'd thought it was the stress of the situation back home, but this new development was certainly more...interesting.

Ethan and Sarah had the potential to be a great couple, she could see it, but they also had the ability to damage a friendship few people could say they had. Ethan wasn't known for his long-term relationships, and that's what Sarah would want, would need. She was still struggling to move past the life she'd shared with Jake, and Ethan would have to know she could love him enough to be the only one.

Morgan peeked once more before she closed the curtain. She would watch and hope for the best, but she was also going to worry for the both of them. They meant the world to her and Hunter. She winced when she thought of how her husband would take the news that his two best friends were...involved. That was another mess they were all going to have to sort through. She would have to find a way to tell him.

"Did you get your cover thing?"

Morgan turned quickly. "Uh, not yet."

Hunter stood by the bathroom in a blue shirt and khaki shorts. "What are you waiting for?"

Inspiration struck. "For you." She walked toward him, a smile spreading across her lips, as she unbuttoned her blouse and let it fall to the floor.

He grabbed her around the waist. "Right now?"

She skimmed her finger over his lips. "Right this second."

"We should call the restaurant and tell them we're going to be late."

She nibbled at his jaw as she unbuckled his belt. "I don't think we need to do that. I think we can make quick work of this. It'll be like an appetizer. We'll get to the entrée later, when we get back."

He grazed her ear with his teeth then stared into her eyes. "What about dessert?"

She smiled. "You're so ambitious."

~~~~

Ethan sat on the wooden bench close to the connecting suites, waiting. The sound of waves rushing the shore a short distance away kept him company. Sarah opened her door, smiled, and his mouth watered. Her hair, still damp from her shower, hung loose at her shoulders. The deep blue backless top she wore complemented snug white pants, showing off her excellent figure.

"I thought I was running behind. I'm glad I'm not last." She sat on the bench next to him.

He breathed in her floral perfume and wanted her. "You look amazing."

She smiled again. "Thanks. You look pretty great yourself."

Ethan glanced at his watch. "They said thirty minutes, right? We're coming up on forty-five."

"They're running a little behind." Mischief twinkled in her eyes. "I'm sure they'll be out soon."

"Maybe I should give a knock and make sure everything's okay."

She raised her brow. "Don't be dense, Ethan."

"What's that—"

Morgan and Hunter's door opened. Rosy cheeked, Morgan licked her lips as she smoothed down her skirt and stepped from the room. Hunter shut the door and swiped an arm over his sweaty forehead then took his wife's hand. "Sorry we're late."

Sarah stood, biting her cheek. "Not a problem."

"Let's go eat. I'm starved," Hunter said.

Catching on quickly, Ethan grinned and winked at Sarah. "I bet. You missed a couple buttons there, Phillips."

Sarah elbowed him as Morgan and Hunter stopped in their tracks, both glancing at Hunter's shirt.

"Just kidding. So, I wonder what's good to eat around here." He rested his hand against the small of Sarah's back as he pulled the door open to the restaurant.

"You're a real bastard, Cooke," Hunter said as he walked in after Sarah and Morgan.

The maître d' smiled. "Good evening, ladies and gentlemen."

"Good evening. We have reservations. Cooke. Four of us."

"Ah, yes. We saved a lovely spot for you out on our deck. Please follow Maura to your table."

"Thank you."

Surrounded by candlelight and the sounds of ocean surf, Ethan watched Sarah while the breeze played with her hair and she took a sip of her pinot noir. Her tongue swiped her top lip as she set her glass down. When the wind pushed at her hair again, she brushed it behind her shoulder, laughing at something Hunter said. He wanted her like he'd never wanted another.

Sarah was worried about messing up what they had, and he couldn't blame her after the shaky three weeks they'd had since he kissed her. Despite it all, he didn't share her concerns. The tension and arguments of the past few days had been road bumps. There were bound to be some. At the end of the day, what they had meant too much to screw up.

Spending his life with someone had never been in his plans. He'd never believed in a lifetime with one person, but then, he'd had terrible role models. When his feelings for Sarah changed, he started to think permanent, which had shocked the hell out of him.

They could move as slow as she needed, because they'd get where he wanted them eventually. Now that he had her, he wasn't letting her go.

She glanced at him, smiled fully, and his heart melted as he smiled back. His phone vibrated against his hip, and his light mood fell away, knowing Sarah had another flower at her door. "Excuse me for a minute." He met Hunter's gaze and walked off, dialing Collin Michaels's cell number on the way through the lobby.

"Michaels."

"It's Cooke."

"I picked up some activity at Sarah's house."

"What do you have?"

"Not much. The guy must know the house is wired. You can see someone put a rose on the step but he's careful. He's completely covered from head to toe in black, and he's hunched, making it impossible to get a height and build on him. He peeked into a couple of windows, but he's masked. By the time I called the cops and got over there myself, he was gone. The note, same style as the others, said, 'I count the days until we meet.'"

Rage rushed through Ethan's veins. "Have you contacted Austin?"

"Yeah. Everything's quiet."

"I want you to replay the video until you find me something we can use."

"I'm on it. There was another rape tonight, Ethan. He killed this one—strangled her to death."

"Why are you telling me this?" He already knew. He'd come to the same conclusion himself, but the thought made him so ill, he had to hear Collin confirm his worst fear.

"I can't help but notice that every time Sarah gets a flower, the 'Blue Chip Rapist' assaults someone first. I talked to the cops, and they didn't like it."

"I don't like it either. Put another guard on Kylee, but make it discreet. I don't want Hailey or Sarah's mother panicking. I'll be back on Monday. Call me if you come up with anything."

"Will do. Ethan, I don't think he's figured out she's not home yet."

"He will soon enough." He closed his phone.

Hunter stood next to him.

"The fucker left another rose."

"I gathered that. What did Michaels get on the video?"

"Not a goddamn thing. This guy's smart, Hunter. The boys downtown are starting to think there might be a connection between this and the rapes. I know there is.

He killed his victim tonight, Phillips. When we get back, Austin will cover her full-time, 'round the clock."

"If Morgan and I didn't have to go to D.C. for more interviews over that fucking mine, I'd do it myself. Why can't you?"

"Because I'm too close to this. I want to find the bastard and kill him. That means I'm not thinking clearly. I won't risk her."

"Austin and most of the team will be assisting the secret service detail for the next two weeks. You can't pull him from that, or any of them for that matter."

"We'll figure something out. I don't want to tell her about this. She's finally relaxing."

"I agree. There's going to be hell to pay, though. If we're not telling Sarah, I'm not telling Morgan."

"Let's let them enjoy the weekend. They can hang us by our balls on Monday."

~~~~

After saying goodnight to Morgan and Hunter, Ethan and Sarah took the steps to the shore. He wrapped his arm around her shoulders, breathing in her shampoo. She locked her hands around his waist as they walked barefoot in the sand still warm from the sun.

Sarah let out a long sigh. "What an amazing day. Everything's been wonderful—the rooms, the food, and my friends, of course. What a perfect birthday present. After the spa tomorrow morning, I might have to call and have you carry me back to the room. I'll be a puddle of relaxed mush."

Ethan looked into calm blue eyes and smiled. The call an hour ago wasn't going to ruin their weekend. She was safe here, and they were alone. Roses and rapists could wait until Monday. He kissed her hair. "I think that could be arranged."

"Let's go back and sit out by the pool. We can look at the stars and wait for one to fall."

"I can definitely get behind that." He didn't care what they did as long as he was with her.

They wandered back down the beach and picked up their shoes at the bottom of the steps. Sarah took her keycard from her purse as they approached her room. "Come on in. I'm going to put my pajamas on if you don't mind. Then we can bring a blanket out with us and sit in the big hammock."

"Yeah, sure. Take your time." Ethan wandered around the suite after Sarah went in the bathroom and closed the door. He opened the glass slider, breathing in the ocean air as he stared into the sky, watching the stars wink. This was just what they needed: a quiet evening to just be.

He took the fleece blanket from the couch and stepped outside, lighting the fireplace tucked in the corner of the large patio closest to his suite and pulled the two-person hammock closer to the flames. He eyed the flimsy bunk, giving it a testing wiggle before he lay back on the dark blue and white striped fabric, surprised at how steady it was. Resting his head against the navy pillow, he stared at the rush of waves beyond the pool.

"You look comfy," she said.

He turned his head, and his thoughts disintegrated as she stood in the doorway in her peach cotton camisole and matching pajama pants that were simple and sexy. She'd pulled her hair back in a ponytail, leaving her neck and shoulders unframed.

She smiled. "Can I join you?"

He couldn't stop staring. "Why did it take me six

years to realize you're the most beautiful woman I've ever seen?"

Her smile disappeared as her hand moved to her hair in a self-conscious gesture. "I-I don't know what to say to that."

"There's nothing to say. It's the truth." His need to be with her consumed him. He sat up, intending to go to her, but stopped. She'd asked him for time, and he would give it to her. When she was ready, she would let him know. He held out his hand. "Come keep me company." Playing it casual cost him, but he was determined to do this right.

She laced her fingers with his and sat next to him on the hammock. They lay back, and the swing rocked wildly.

"Yikes." Sarah's eyes grew wide as she gasped and clutched at Ethan's shirt.

"Shit," Ethan said at the same time. His arm wrapped around her waist as he kicked his leg and other hand over the side to keep them from toppling.

When the hammock settled, Ethan moved his leg back, crossing it over the other, and pulled Sarah against him, chuckling. "Well, that was a moment."

Laughing, she moved her head to look down at him and sent the hammock swinging again. "Oh, *crap,* Ethan," she squealed.

Despite his best efforts, the taut fabric dumped them over. Ethan landed on his back with a thud as Sarah crashed against his chest.

"Oh, oh my God, are you okay?" Sarah attempted to sit up but had to duck as the hammock swung in their direction.

Ethan's hand shot up and caught the swing, steadying it. "Yeah, I'm fine."

"Did you hit your head?"

"No."

"That's good." She looked away. Seconds later, she snorted out a laugh. "I'm sorry." She covered her mouth as another fit of laughter escaped.

He grinned up at her. "So, you think this is pretty funny, huh?"

"I'm afraid so." She let out a full-throated hoot as she got to her feet and extended a hand. "The least I can do is help you up."

He reached out to take it, and she collapsed forward, hands on her knees, fighting to catch her breath. "Oh, oh, that was so funny. If your eyes got even half as big in the pool when I gave you that wedgie..." She swiped at her cheeks, brushing away happy tears.

He stood, enjoying Sarah's mood. He couldn't remember the last time he heard her laugh like this. "You know what they say about payback, right?" He started toward her and she sobered up, walking backward.

"Ethan, I don't want to go for a swim, and you better not even *think* about returning the wedgie favor."

He grinned, wiggling his brows. "I think you should be afraid, Sarah—very, very afraid."

"Ethan," she said in her warning tone as she glanced behind her quickly when she banged into the wicker couch. "I'm serious."

"Oh, so am I." He lunged forward, making a grab for her, and she pivoted toward her room. He snagged her arm and pulled her body over his shoulder in a fireman carry. "I'm pretty sure you're at my mercy." He spun her in two fast circles as she laughed.

"Yeah, until I lose my dinner all over your backside."

Thoroughly enjoying himself, he stopped. "You bring up a good point." He walked to her room. "You do realize you're in the perfect position for an ultimate wedgie, right?"

"You wouldn't *dare*." She pounded against his back. "Ethan, don't you dare."

"There's really only one way out of this." He tugged up gently on the elastic of her pants with his opposite hand.

"Damn it, Ethan." She tried to bite his back, but he moved her out of position.

Inspiration struck as he remembered his childhood fights with his sister. "I'll give you a choice—the wedgie, or you have to call me King Ethan for the rest of the night."

She stopped struggling. "*King* Ethan? You've got to be kidding."

He tugged on her pants again. "It's your choice, Sarah. I'll give you to the count of three. One, two, th—"

"Okay, *okay*, King Ethan, put me down."

He set her on her feet and grinned as she glared at him. This wasn't exactly what he'd had in mind for their evening, but it worked. "So, what should we do now? Don't say lie on the hammock."

Her glare dissolved into a smile. "No, I think once was enough."

"I can order champagne, and we can sit on the *couch* by the fire." He took her face in his hands as he emphasized couch. "Stargazing still isn't out of the question."

"You're a real sport." She kissed him quick, and he let her go with the contact, stepping back. He needed her with a desperation he could hardly handle.

Her smile disappeared as she stared into his eyes. "Ethan," she murmured, taking a step forward, stopping toe to toe with her palms resting against his cheeks. "I want to kiss you first this time."

He wrapped his hands around her wrists. "I don't think that's a good idea right now." He wanted this, but he wanted her more.

"I do." She moved in hesitantly, and her lips warmed against his.

Unable to fight any longer, Ethan took her face in his hands and plundered, savoring her sweet flavor. Her fingers moved to his hips, hanging on the waist of his slacks, then her hands slid under his shirt, slowly moving up his back, her cool skin tracing circles over his, making him shiver.

He ran kisses down her neck and over her shoulders, before he met her gaze. His need for her was staggering. "I have to touch you, Sarah. When you want to stop, we can, but please let me touch you."

Eyes dark, cheeks flushed, she nodded.

Ethan took her hand as he led her to the bed. He pulled the tie from her hair and watched her golden locks cascade to her shoulders, surrounding him in the scent of her flowery shampoo. He ran his hands through her silky tresses and kissed her softly, sensing her nerves. He moved his mouth to her cheekbones, feathering kisses along her skin. Her breath shuddered out, and she closed her eyes as he traced her earlobe with his tongue. He wandered back to the soft skin where neck meets shoulder and nibbled.

She tipped her head back in surrender.

He wanted to give her more and watch as he gave her everything. He moved his hands down her waist and under her cotton top, skimming his fingers along hot skin, wandering up until fingertips met naked breasts.

She snagged her bottom lip with her teeth and moaned when he brushed his palms over taut nipples.

He crushed his mouth to hers, frenzied, ready to explode.

She unbuttoned his shirt, parting it, and her mouth left his, wandering. Lips and tongue moved across his chest, driving him mad.

"Sarah," he whispered as he lifted the camisole over her head and pulled her against him, wrapping his arms around her, reveling in the feel of her pale, firm breasts pressed to his skin. He took her mouth again, devouring.

He tugged her pajama bottoms down, leaving a swatch of frilly peach lace behind. "My God, Sarah." He tugged on her lip with his teeth, fighting the need to free himself and take what they both wanted.

He sat on the edge of the bed and pulled her into his arms. Long, smooth legs wrapped around him as she pulled his shirt free, tossing it to the floor.

"I want to taste you." He didn't give her a chance to respond. His mouth was at her breast, flicking, tracing, suckling, then the other, until she gasped and clutched at his shoulders.

She snagged his ear, her breath heaving as she said his name: "Ethan, Ethan, Ethan."

He lifted her arms above her head, running his hands up, capturing her fingers between his, his eyes burning into hers. "Be with me, Sarah. Will you be with me?"

"Yes." She captured his mouth.

He collapsed back, taking her with him, setting her hands free as he slid his beneath her panties, grabbing at the smooth, firm skin of her ass, pulling her against him, heat to heat.

She let loose a long, throaty purr as she fumbled with his belt. "I want you, Ethan."

He reversed their positions, more than ready, yanking at the skimpy patch of her underwear and she stiffened. He stopped, his breath heaving. "What is it? What's wrong? Am I being too rough?"

"No. No, it's not that. My phone's ringing." She yanked her panties back up and scrambled from the bed, grabbing her cellphone on the nightstand. "It's my mother."

Instantly tense, he waited for his own phone to ring.

"Mom, is everything okay?" Sarah closed her eyes and let out a long breath. "She did? Oh, poor thing. Yes, put her on." She glanced over, mouthing 'nightmare.'

He breathed his own sigh of relief and sat back as Sarah soothed her daughter, standing in nothing but panties by the bed. Knowing they were finished for tonight, he got up and put a blanket around her shoulders.

She smiled at him and continued to talk to Kylee.

When she hung up, Sarah gripped her hands together. "I feel so guilty right now. Kylee had her first nightmare, and I wasn't there."

Ethan took her hand, pulling her until she sat on the bed next to him. He wrapped his arms around her and nuzzled her neck. "It won't be her last, and she's fine now, right?"

"Yes, but I should've been there."

"What was the nightmare about?"

"Mr. Ruff got eaten by Goldie, Hailey's fish."

"That's some pretty serious stuff," Ethan said solemnly.

"Yes, it is. Goldie grew pointy teeth and ate him all up."

"Traumatic." He bit his cheek, trying not to smile.

She took his chin in her hand. "You're laughing."

"No." A grin split his lips. "I'm sorry, Sarah. I just see this little goldfish swimming around, and then, wham, he opens his mouth full of shark teeth and poor, unsuspecting Mr. Ruff gets it."

Sarah's smile turned into a laugh as she hugged him then kissed him.

He brushed his fingers through her hair. "I should probably say goodnight. If you don't go to bed, you're going to sleep through your massage tomorrow instead of enjoying it."

"Are you sure?"

He knew what she was offering, and it was tempting, but he didn't want to make love to Sarah for the first time with her guilty and worrying about Kylee. "Yeah."

"I'm not tired." She took his hand. "We can watch a movie."

The purple smudges under her eyes told him different. He reached under the pillows and pulled back the covers then bent down, grabbing her pajama top from the floor and handed it to her. "Call me when you're finished tomorrow, and we'll do something."

She grabbed the remote from the bedside table and flipped through the channels. "Oh look, one of those action flicks you like. Stay and watch it with me."

"You don't like action movies."

"This one isn't so bad." She winced as a building blew up on screen and a gunman lost an arm.

His brow arched. "Sarah, what's up?"

"I feel silly admitting this, but I've been pretty creeped out at night."

If only she knew the direction the case was taking. "That's not silly, Sarah. I would be concerned if you weren't."

"It's been such a comfort having Austin around..."

"Do you want me to stay?"

"Yes," she said immediately.

Ethan smiled. "Do you want a second to think about that?"

She smiled back. "No."

"All you had to do was ask."

"I'm asking for tomorrow night then too. Will you stay here with me tomorrow night?"

"Absolutely."

Sarah pulled her top on and crawled under the covers as Ethan slid out of his slacks and got in on his side, turning off the light. The moonlight filtered through the curtains, illuminating the bed. He rested against the pillow, turning his head to look at her.

She smiled. "Thanks."

"Get some sleep."

She hesitated then slid over.

He lifted his arm, inviting her.

She snuggled close, resting her cheek against his shoulder, wrapping her arm around his waist and looked up, kissing him. "Night, King Ethan."

He chuckled and kissed her hair, content with where they were going. "This is good, Sarah. I think this is going to be good."

CHAPTER TEN

THE SUN'S RAYS HAD REPLACED MOONLIGHT WHEN SARAH opened her eyes again. She looked at Ethan sleeping on his stomach with his arm hooked around her waist, pinning her to the mattress, and she smiled. She'd snuggled against him during the night, struggling with guilt. This was the first time she'd lay in a man's arms since Jake.

She couldn't deny her want for Ethan—on so many levels. When his eyes had burned into hers, she'd been ready to give him what she never planned to share again. Her body had burst into a flame of need as he touched her. It had been so long since she'd felt that kind of desire. Her experience with Ethan was so different from what she'd had with Jake. Jake had always been sweet where Ethan was...intense.

She was eager for the heat and to see where they would go. Ethan was right, things were good between them—they always had been.

Sarah moved her hand to her necklace and the ring Jake placed on her finger years before. She wanted to believe—no, *needed* to believe—he would be okay with this. She stared at Ethan's handsome face, no less arresting in sleep, and brushed her fingers through his hair. He was a good man—tough, but with so many soft spots. He'd always been so gentle and patient with Kylee, taking on a role in her life not many men would. He'd been there for both of them, just as he promised, and she'd never had to ask.

Ethan had come with her, holding her hand and the baby, when Kylee received her first series of immunizations. When Kylee spiked her first fever, he'd rushed right over, concerned. He'd stayed so many times, helping her through the endless nights of teething, taking turns walking a fussy baby up and down the hall.

When Kylee vomited all over his brand new Armani on a visit to his office, he never batted an eye. Or the day in the park when she toddled up to him, arms open for a hug, calling him 'Dada,' he'd hugged her and smiled, never mentioning it.

It crossed her mind on occasion that Kylee had always been more Ethan's than Jake's. Jake didn't get the chance to be a part of Kylee. He'd been back in Afghanistan before the pregnancy test turned blue. It had been Ethan who'd been there every second after conception. He'd been her comfort during the wonder and agony of birth with Jake watching from thousands of miles away. They'd both been great.

"Oh, oh, here comes another one. I have to push."

"Then go ahead and push," Ethan said next to her ear as she leaned her back against his chest, her hands gripping his.

"Come on, Sarah, you can do it," Jake said from the laptop screen the hospital staff set up beside the bed.

Pain radiated through her rock-hard stomach as she bore down against the need to free her baby. Groaning loudly, she gave it her all, clutching Ethan's fingers, listening to his quiet encouragement while Jake cheered her on. She took a breath and pushed again, unable to stop. "It burns, it burns so much," she cried.

"It's almost over, Sarah. You're almost there," Ethan said with excitement. "Look in the mirror. You can see the top of her head. Touch her, Sarah. That's what you're working for."

She panted through the pain and reached down, touching her baby's hair. "My baby."

"Yes, your baby." He grinned at her when she glanced up, breathing fast and deep.

Her mother held the camera close. "Jake, do you see your daughter?"

"Yes. Oh, my God, Sarah. Come on, honey, you can do this. She's coming."

"I need to—" She couldn't finish her thought through the overwhelming power to try again. She wanted to stop and somehow avoid the pain, but her body knew what to do. Ethan clutched her closer as she tensed up, crying out as Kylee's head was born.

"Breathe, Sarah. Breathe," he encouraged, his voice calm. "She's almost here. She's almost here."

She heard Jake and her mother in the background, but focused on Ethan's strong hands locked with hers and his murmurs of confidence against her ear. He was her beacon of calm.

With her next push, Kylee was born. Reaching forward, she grabbed her baby, pulling her to her chest as Kylee screamed out her protest. "She's here, Jake, she's here."

"She's perfect, honey."

She grinned into her husband's awestruck eyes as Ethan brushed his fingers over her daughter's back, his hand bigger than most of Kylee's tiny body. She glanced up into Ethan's swimming gray eyes as he sniffed.

"You did it, Sarah. She's amazing."

"Yes, she is. Thank you, Ethan, for everything. I wouldn't have gotten through this without you."

He kissed her forehead before she turned back to her baby girl and Jake, still resting her body against Ethan's.

Sarah smiled, remembering the best moment of her life. She glanced at Ethan once more then turned her head, looking at the bedside clock. She had fifteen minutes to get over to the spa. Wiggling out from under his arm, she dressed.

While she brushed her hair, Sarah stared at her necklace in the mirror. She reached behind, feeling for the clasp and freed it. The ring swung back and forth on the chain. "It's time, Jake. I hope you can understand. I need for you to understand. I love you. I'll always love you, but I have to give this a try." She kissed the diamond ring given to her in love, accepted in love and placed it in her small jewelry case, tucking it deep in her makeup bag.

She opened the door, looking back at Ethan still asleep, and left.

~~~~

After three blissfully relaxing treatments, Sarah and Morgan wandered back toward their rooms, stopping off at the small, complimentary breakfast buffet.

"We need to make this an annual event, but next year I'm paying my own way," Sarah said as she scooped fresh fruit from a large serving bowl.

"You tipped the ladies for our services today."

"Which was a drop in the bucket compared to the price of the treatments."

They sat at a table overlooking the rocky cliffs.

Morgan popped a glossy green grape in her mouth. "Did you enjoy yourself?"

She grinned. "How could I not?"

"Then don't worry about it." Morgan pushed her chair closer to Sarah's. "So, now that I have you all to myself, I'll expect some details."

Sarah frowned. "We had the same treatments."

"When I left my room this morning, a sleepy-eyed Ethan was leaving yours—without a shirt on. He didn't have much to say."

Sarah chewed her bite of sweet strawberry, stalling. Morgan's pretty green eyes never left hers.

"He stayed with me last night. This creepy rose business gets to me after dark."

Morgan raised her brow. "Austin stays with you too. Do you kiss him the way I saw you kissing Ethan in the pool?"

Because Morgan smiled, her question didn't sting. "You saw that, huh?"

"It was hard to miss. I'm just glad it was me and not Hunter."

Sarah winced, thinking of what a messy scene that would've been. "We're not sneaking around. This is all so new. It just sort of happened. One night we were fighting—right after your wedding, in fact—and the next, he was kissing me. It took me by complete surprise."

Morgan sipped at her water with a twinkle in her eye. "So how was it?"

Sarah laughed. "Pretty darn great."

"And the sex? I have my ideas about the sex. You can't look like that man and not be good at it."

"We haven't gotten that far." She leaned in closer, whispering, heart pounding with the thrill of the memory. "But we came pretty close. It felt so good to be *touched* like that. He definitely knows all the right places, and we were just getting started. My mom called. Kylee had a nightmare. Things pretty much fizzled from there."

Morgan's brows shot up. "Really. Well, I'll expect

details, lots and lots of details, when you two decide to finish things up."

Sarah smiled again, but it faded when she thought of her wedding ring. "Is this okay, Morgan? What I'm doing? What I'm feeling? Am I letting Jake down? Because I feel like I am. I took off my ring this morning for the first time in over five and a half years. It feels like I'm betraying him."

Morgan took her hand. "Did he love you, Sarah, really love you?"

"Yes, of course."

"Then wouldn't he want you to be happy? Wouldn't he want to know that you and Kylee are well loved and provided for? Isn't that what love is all about?"

Touched by Morgan's words, Sarah's eyes filled. "Yes, I guess so. You're right. I never thought about it like that."

"All kidding aside with the sex—make sure you take your time, honey. This is a big adjustment for you both."

Worry took over again. "What about Hunter? He, Jake, and Ethan were so close. How do you think he's going to take this?"

"You let me worry about that. Ultimately, he wants you happy. He loves you so much. He might need a little time, but he'll come around."

"Excuse me," a deep voice said.

Sarah put her hand to her brow, shielding her eyes from the sun. "Yes?"

"Sarah, is that you?"

The man moved forward, blocking the blazing glare. "Neil Harris?" She stood, grinning. "How are you?"

"I'm okay. I'm sorry if I'm interrupting."

"No, no, not at all. Neil, this is my good friend Morgan Phillips. Neil and his wife, Tracey, went to USC with me."

Morgan held out her hand and shook. "It's nice to meet you. Let me leave you two to catch up. I'll see you back at the rooms later." She gave Sarah a quick hug.

"It was nice meeting you, Morgan," Neil said as Morgan walked off.

"You too."

Sarah looked around and over Neil's shoulder. "So, where's Tracey? I would love to see her. It seems like so long."

Neil's eyes watered. "She-she passed away, Sarah."

"Oh my God." She took his hand. "I'm so incredibly sorry. Come, sit down."

"I'd rather walk. Would you like to walk with me on the beach?"

"Of course." Still holding his hand, they made their way to the water.

~~~~

Where was she? She'd finished her massage two hours ago. Ethan knocked on Morgan and Hunter's suite as worry set in.

Morgan opened the door dressed in jeans and a t-shirt.

"Hey, is Sarah with you?"

Morgan frowned. "No. She's not back yet? She ran into an old friend from college. I left her at the little breakfast bar quite awhile ago." She shrugged. "She's probably still catching up."

"Okay. I'll see you at dinner." He started up the path leading to the buffet. Hopefully she was there, safe and sound, reliving her glory days. With everything going on, they would have to talk about her letting him know where she was going to be, so he wouldn't worry.

Sarah's blonde hair caught his eye, and he did a double-take as she sat in the sand—hand-in-hand—with a tall, thin man. Ethan stopped in his tracks. His initial shock turned to confusion. Who the hell was this guy?

By the time Ethan made it to the beach steps, Sarah and the mystery man stood. She held him in a long embrace, kissing his cheek as she took something he handed her and stuffed it in her pocket. The man started walking away, and Sarah rushed toward him again, hugging him.

A punch of disbelief hit Ethan hard. He tried to shake it off. *There has to be an explanation*, he reminded himself as he turned and walked to his room, letting the scene play back through his mind, but he thought of his parents and their farce of a marriage riddled with lies and infidelity.

Shaking his head, he struggled to push it away. Sarah wasn't like that. They were building something here. But she'd looked pretty damn cozy. He tried to deny it again, especially after last night, but seeds of doubt began to bloom.

Moments later, he heard a gentle knock and yanked his door open. Beautiful, windblown, and flushed, Sarah smiled. Betrayal, sharp, stabbed at him, and he armored himself against the pain.

"Hey." She walked in.

Ethan shut the door behind her. "How was the massage?"

"Wonderful. Everything was perfect. I had an amazing time."

He met her gaze. "I bet."

She stepped closer, her bright smile fading. "What's wrong?"

"Oh, not much really. I spent the night with the woman I thought I was building a relationship with, only to find her holding hands and kissing another man."

Confusion filled her eyes. "What are you talking about?"

So she was going to deny it. "Give me a break, Sarah. Me last night, him this morning. You're spreading yourself a little thin, don't you think?"

She gasped. "What a filthy thing to say."

"From where I'm standing, you deserve it."

"Are you talking about Neil? I went to college with Neil."

"I went to college with several women too, but the only person I'm putting my hands on right now is you."

Her eyes grew wide before they narrowed to slits. "How dare you." She tried to walk past him, but he blocked the door. "Get out of the way."

He didn't move.

She whirled, starting toward the sliding glass.

He grabbed her arm, turning her to face him, wanting her to explain and deny what he'd just seen, but she only looked at him with hurt filling her kind, blue eyes.

He fought against the tug of guilt and the need to pull her close and let the whole thing go, but he thought of his parents again, and anger pushed him on. "I think we're done here, Sarah. You should probably ask Neil to keep you company tonight, don't you think?"

She stared at him a moment longer then left without another word, closing the door behind her with a quiet click.

~~~~

Sarah let herself into her room and sat on the bed. Confused and outrageously hurt, she rested her face in her hands. What just happened? Ethan's eyes had been so cold and mean and his words so final. He'd never looked at her that way before, as if she were vile and cheap. She hadn't done anything wrong.

Poor Neil had needed her. Her long-ago photography partner grieved as she had after she lost Jake. Who knew better how quickly a life changed when violent and unexpected death took everything away?

Poor Tracey. She'd been so sweet and kind. Two tractor trailers and a foggy California night ended her life too soon. Heartache for Neil and Tracey warred with the shock of Ethan's behavior.

Clearly Ethan saw her hug Neil, but it had been so innocent. Memories, grief, and understanding filled her two hours with a long-ago friend—nothing more. She would let Ethan cool off before she tried to explain, but it stung that he didn't trust her.

She lay back against her pillow, listening to the waves, smelling Ethan's aftershave clinging to the soft cotton, and fell asleep.

An hour later, Sarah woke with a start, glancing at the clock. "Shoot." Springing from the bed, she rushed to the bathroom. What a time to fall asleep. She had to find Ethan. She freshened her makeup and brushed her hair. They were going to fix this misunderstanding and get on with the rest of their weekend.

She left her room and knocked on his door, but he didn't answer. Blowing out a frustrated sigh, she walked away, strolling to the small tiki bar a hundred yards from their suites. She made her way to the seats farthest from the large jellybean-shaped pool open to all the resort's guests and placed her purse down, taking a stool.

"What can I get for you, pretty lady?"

She tried a smile when the older man with the jovial face approached from behind the bar.

"I think I'll take a lemonade for now, please."

"Coming right up." Moments later he set the pale yellow liquid in front of her. "Here you go, ma'am."

"Thank you."

"I'm Clyde." He took her hand and kissed her knuckles in a gallant gesture.

A warm smile lit her face. "Sarah."

"That's what I was waiting for, Sarah with the sad eyes."

She glanced down. Was she that easy to read?

"So, what brings you to 'The Cliffs?'"

"A weekend getaway with friends."

He frowned, looking at the seats next to her. "Some friends."

She grinned, charmed. This man reminded her of her grandfather. "I'm meeting them later for dinner." She glanced at the couples enjoying themselves in the pool and the few snuggled up close along the long bar, more determined than ever to make things right with Ethan. There was still a lot of fun to be had in this small piece of paradise.

"Clyde, I missed lunch. Can I see a menu please?"

"Certainly, Sarah."

"Thank you."

She sipped her drink and decided on a half turkey sandwich with a cup of black bean soup. She looked up at the couple she hadn't noticed before and stared. Ethan sat next to a tanned, bikini-clad goddess with streaming black hair. They clinked glasses as she said something, making him smile.

The lemonade turned bitter on her tongue, and her

stomach clutched as a thousand waves of betrayal washed through her while she watched in disbelief. Did she mean so little that she didn't even get a chance to explain before he moved on? If it was really this easy for him, he'd never felt anything for her in the first place. After everything they'd been through, how could he do this?

Ethan looked over, meeting her gaze. The goddess said something, but he stared. When the black-haired beauty tapped his shoulder, he glanced back at her, smiling.

Reaching blindly in her wallet, Sarah pulled out a bill and set it on the smooth wood of the bar.

"You okay, Sarah with the sad eyes?"

"No, Clyde, I'm really not. If you'll excuse me." She stood, whirling and knocked her glass to the ground with a crash. "I'm so sorry." She hurried off, never looking back.

"Wait, Sarah. You left me a fifty," Clyde shouted. "That's too much."

Sarah continued on, walking quickly to her room. She had to get out of here. Unlocking her door, she went to the resort phone and pressed zero for the operator.

"Front desk."

"Yes, this is Sarah Johnson in the Triple Suites. I'll be checking out early. Could you please have a cab waiting for me up front—as soon as possible?"

"Of course, Ms. Johnson. Will the rest of your party be departing as well?"

"No, just me. Can I also get the number for the local airport? They run flights to L.A. frequently, correct?"

"Yes, ma'am, every half-hour or so on the weekends. If you're in a rush, I'll keep the cab here that just pulled up, and I would be happy to call the airport myself. I'll put a hold on their next available flight."

"Perfect. I'll be up in a couple of minutes." She dashed around the room, throwing her belongings in the suitcase. When she was sure she had everything from the bedroom and bath, she sat down at the small table and wrote a note:

Morgan and Hunter,

Thank you very much for such a special weekend. I had to go home. I couldn't stand to be away from my baby for another second. I'll call Austin when I land in L.A., so don't you dare worry about me. Stay and have fun.

Love you,
Sarah

She folded the note and grabbed her purse and suitcase. As she walked past Morgan and Hunter's room, she slid the white paper under the door, then handed in her key and took the taxi to the airport.

In her rush to be gone, she hurried to the counter, paying for her overpriced ticket before dialing Austin's number. If she called now, he'd be home with Kylee and Hailey when she got there.

"Casey."

"Austin, it's Sarah."

"Kylee's fine."

She smiled. "I'm sure she is. I'm coming home."

"*Now?*"

"I'm waiting for my plane to take off. I should be boarding in about ten minutes. It's an hour-long flight. I figure by the time I get a cab and sit in traffic, the three of you could be there, easy."

"We're at the zoo. If we go see the elephants first, we should still be home by the time you get in."

She couldn't wait to be with Kylee. She needed the simple comfort of her little girl. "That sounds like the best thing I've heard all day."

"See you in a bit."

"Okay." Sarah turned off her phone and put it away as the desk attendant of the small, bustling airport called for flight 22 to Los Angeles.

Minutes later she stowed her bag and sat down, buckling herself in. After the safety spiel, the full twenty-passenger plane taxied down the runway and took off. Sarah stared out the window, watching the ocean take over her view. With sixty minutes of down-time, she had no choice but to think about her situation with Ethan.

Why couldn't they get this right? Why did he start something if it meant little more than nothing? Even as she thought it, she didn't believe it. Last night meant something. Last night meant *everything*.

She played with the zipper on her purse, remembering the fun on the patio and the way he'd looked at her, captivated, as they'd been on the verge of making love. Did she imagine it? She shook her head. No, it wasn't possible to imagine the feelings they shared. There was no way to fake that kind of intensity and intimacy.

So why? Why did he want to hurt her? Maybe this just wasn't meant to be. Tears flooded her eyes, and her view of the vibrant blue water blurred. She'd been ready to try, to give it her all, but maybe this was for the best. It was better to get out now before she got in any deeper. Once she'd really relaxed and let herself feel, she'd realized she felt strong and deep.

Where did they go from here, and why did she have to keep asking herself that? Because they weren't meant to be. There was no question this time, just fact.

Emptiness mixed with a void of depression. Could they move past this? Perhaps, but maybe not. She'd be sorry if they couldn't, but this wasn't how she would greet her daughter at the door.

Determined to put the pain away for now, Sarah took the magazine from the pocket in front of her and forced Ethan from her mind. She had a daughter to get home to. That was all she was going to let matter for now.

CHAPTER ELEVEN

ETHAN SAT AT THE BAR, DESPERATELY TRYING TO ENJOY AMY'S company. It was Amy, right? He thought of Sarah instead and sipped at his beer, attempting to muster up the enthusiasm to continue his 'conversation' with the beautiful but empty-headed woman at his side. His phone vibrated in his pocket, and he looked at the readout. "I really need to take this. I'll be right back."

"Okay."

Ethan walked to the other side of the pool as he answered, "Cooke."

"I can't reach Sarah."

He didn't like the tension in Austin's voice. "Is Kylee okay?"

"Yeah, she and Hailey are with me, but we're stuck in a massive traffic jam. We aren't going to be back in time to meet her."

"Meet who? What the hell are you talking about, Casey?"

"Sarah called about ten minutes ago. She was boarding a plane to come home. I thought you knew. I planned to meet her at the house, but I don't see us getting out of here anytime soon. Her phone must be turned off. I can't tell her not to go home."

Ethan's heart stopped on a wave of fear. He sprinted toward the room for his wallet and keys. "Send Michaels or Matthews or fucking *somebody* over until I can get there."

"There isn't anybody. They're either on duty or

145

meeting with the Secret Service today. The World Leaders Conference is next week, Ethan. With the other crew in Europe for that training, we're shorthanded. I called the cops before I called you. They said they would send a car over to check things out before she gets there."

"Well, that's something." But he wouldn't relax until he saw her safe for himself. "I'm heading for the airport now."

He grabbed his keys and wallet and closed his door as Hunter stormed out of his suite, holding a white piece of paper. "She left."

"I know. Casey just called. I'm on my way. He's stuck in traffic, and everyone's on fucking duty." Ethan kept going, yelling over his shoulder, not stopping until he got in the lobby.

The gray-haired attendant smiled. "Good afterno-"

"I need a cab. Now."

Her smile dimmed. "Let me call you one, sir."

"No, I don't have time to wait." He was losing precious seconds. "Do you have a car here?"

The older lady only stared.

He read her nametag. "Lil, I'll give you a thousand dollars right now if you let me take your car to the airport."

She frowned, her mouth hanging open. "You must be out of your mind."

He pulled out his wallet and threw a wad of one-hundred dollar bills on the desk, then showed her his bodyguard and security badges. "I need your help, ma'am. My friend's life is in serious danger. I have to get to her."

She pressed her lips together.

He could tell she was teetering. "Sarah, the pretty

blonde who left here about half an hour ago, she's the person in danger. Please, ma'am."

She sighed and took out her keys. "Janet, cover me." She met Ethan's stare. "I'm coming with you."

"Fine, but I'm driving. Where are you parked?"

"Just out front. It's the Oldsmobile."

Ethan ran to the car, gritting his teeth while he waited for Lil to limp to the passenger side.

She shut her door, and he peeled out of the lot. She squealed, "Slow down, young man."

Ethan glanced over. "I'm sorry. I can't." He had to get to Sarah.

The ten-minute drive took five. When Ethan came to a screeching halt, Lil hit him with her purse. "You're insane, absolutely insane."

He ran from the car up to the front desk. "I need a ticket to L.A. for the next available flight."

"You're in luck. We have one seat left. Let's hurry though. They're boarding now."

"Perfect."

Fifteen minutes later, Ethan was in the air, seething inside, full of self-loathing, knowing this was his fault. Sarah wouldn't have left if he'd stuck to his plan of walking the beach instead of going to the pool. He remembered how she'd looked when their eyes met across the long bar. Surprise had quickly turned to shocked hurt. At the time it brought a quick moment of pleasure, before her glass crashed to the ground and she hurried off.

He pressed his head back against the seat and closed his eyes. Fuck, why was he such an asshole? Why couldn't he have let her explain? There was little doubt in his mind that she would've had a simple explanation.

Somewhere during his boring exchange with... What

the hell was her name? Who cared? Somewhere during their conversation—if he wanted to call it that—he'd realized he'd been completely wrong. He'd been about to excuse himself from the bar and apologize when he got the call from Austin.

Sarah would never hurt him; not on purpose; not the way he'd hurt her. If anything happened to her... He fisted his hands in his lap. No, he couldn't let himself believe that anything would. The cops would be there.

~~~~

Sarah frowned when the taxi pulled into her driveway. Austin's car wasn't there. "Where is he?"

The cabbie looked in his rearview mirror. "Do you want me to wait?"

"Yes, please." A few short weeks ago, she never would've been afraid to stand alone outside her own home in the dark. She scanned her yard, the darkened windows, the light burning bright in her front entrance, and zeroed in on her door, relieved when she didn't see blue roses waiting for her.

She spotted the police cruiser sitting down the road in the stream of the street lamp and smiled. "You know what? I think I'm all set."

"You sure?"

"I am." She slipped the cabbie an extra ten.

"Thanks, lady."

She pulled her suitcase out of the cab and walked to the door as the yellow car drove away. She let herself in the house and turned on a light, arming the panel, checking it three times. Because the cop was just down the street, she relaxed a little, but she would feel better when Austin arrived.

She glanced at her watch. He would be pulling up with Hailey and her baby any minute. Spooked by the silence, Sarah turned on the stereo. A jumpy Top-40 beat burst from the speakers, and she sang along.

She'd shower, then dig through the fridge to find something to make for everyone—or maybe they would just order out for pizza. She checked the panel on her way back through the living room, reassured by the red light blinking and stepped into the bathroom, locked the door and turned on the water. Because the music was drowned out by the spray, she switched on the small radio she kept on the shelf above the sink. Undressed, she pulled her hair into a bun and stepped into the heat and steam, hoping to drown away her troubles.

~~~~

It was fate, he was sure of it. She was home alone— finally. Zeke waited behind the pink rose bush close to the officer's body as the cab pulled away. The fucking pig should've stayed in the car.

Lights blinked on throughout the house, and he scooted closer to the window, watching Sarah turn on the stereo and move her hips in time with the beat as she sang along. He stared at her beautiful body as she teased him with her dance, enjoying the private show. Oh, the things he planned to *do* to her. She gave a little shimmy and wandered off to another room.

It was tradition to leave her flowers after he'd helped himself to a whore bitch, but traditions, like rules, were made to be broken—and he really liked to break them.

Maybe he would just scratch his plans and have her right now. After all, she'd disappointed him and made him angry. His beautiful Sarah wasn't perfect anymore.

She'd turned out to be a whore bitch too. She went away overnight but didn't bring her brat and the man and woman who were *always* fucking there. Sarah's prince charming had driven up in his fancy Rover and took her off somewhere.

Well where the fuck was he now?

Zeke walked to the door and jiggled the knob, but it held firm, locked, of course. Peeking through the sheer curtain on the door, he stared at the red light flashing on the home security keypad—his opponent for the next couple of minutes. He grinned, delighted with the challenge.

The system would put him to the test, but he could beat it. It was going to be close, which made it all the more exciting. He gloved up, cut a circle in the glass, and reached in, untwisting the lock. Stepping inside, Zeke smiled and closed his eyes, savoring the scent of Sarah. The house smelled as pretty as she was, like valley flowers. Yes, indeed this was fate.

With the thirty seconds he knew he had, he jammed the cellular alarm system with the small device he'd made at home. See, it paid to be fucking brilliant. The red light still blinked, but he only chuckled. God, this was fun. The sneaky bastards thought they could outmaneuver him by installing multiple systems. He ran outside to the phone lines close to the body he left behind and took out his Swiss Army knife, waiting until he had two seconds to spare then severed the wire.

Jogging back, he snickered. The lights on the panel were dark. The fuckers had nothing on him. Oh, how the kids had laughed all those years, calling him 'Zeke the Geek'—but who was laughing now? He was about to have everything he ever wanted.

He couldn't hear Sarah as he moved into the living

room with the volume of the stereo so high, but it made it like a game of cat and mouse. He loved a good game. Forgetting himself, he swore. The flowers. He almost forgot the flowers. He left again, quickly gathering the precious blue roses he'd brought along.

Finally ready to begin, he closed the door and held the bouquet in front of him, proud that he would hand them to her face to face. After all, he'd grown them just for her. He roamed the house, touching things he knew she'd touched. If only he could take off his gloves. He started down the hallway, listening to her beautiful voice singing along with the radio as water ran behind the closed door. His own angel. He grew rock hard, imagining her wet and naked and all the glorious things they would do together It would be his honor to be her angel too—her angel of death.

Gripping the bouquet tighter, he struggled to keep his hands off his dick, needing relief from his own fantasies, which were about to become his reality. He settled his hand on the knob as a phone rang in some distant room. What the *fuck*? He just cut the line, didn't he?

Moving away from the bathroom, he followed the incessant shrill that pissed him off with every step. He'd made a mistake, and he *never* made mistakes. It was all Sarah's fault. If she hadn't danced around like a little bitch in heat, he wouldn't have missed the other line.

He found the phone in Sarah's spacious studio among the lights and other photographer's equipment filling the orderly space while dozens of pictures hung on her walls, most of which were of her daughter.

"Thank you for calling Sarah Johnson Photography. I'm sorry I missed your call. Please leave a name and number, and I'll get back to you as soon as I can."

"Sarah, it's Ethan. Goddammit, please pick up the phone. Please. I'm about three minutes out, five at the most. I'll be right there." The phone clicked off, and the dial tone filled the office.

Zeke's heart pounded. "I'm going to fucking kill you, *Ethan*. You won't ruin this for me." Spit flew from his mouth as he spoke, shaking with rage. "Oh, yes, Ethan, you'll have to die."

~~~~

Time slowed to a crawl on the drive from the airport. Ethan maneuvered around cars like a madman on a racetrack. He punched in his buddy's number on the police force and relaxed, fractionally, when Tucker told him an officer had been sent to Sarah's house.

As he exited the freeway his phone rang, and the same friend told him the officer wasn't responding to dispatch. Ethan pressed his foot to the floor, caring very little that he was well over the speed limit.

He tried Sarah's main line over and over, but she didn't answer. When the rapid busy signal pulsed in his ear, he knew the fucker had gotten past the alarm and into the house. His heart pounded, and his fingers jittered against the steering wheel as terror tore at his soul. He couldn't lose her.

He gave her business line a try next, fighting to stay in control of his racing mind. It continued to ring, and he left a message after the tone. If the bastard had Sarah, he might not hurt her if he knew he didn't have enough time. He pressed on the tiny latch well under his seat and grabbed his gun.

Tires screeched as he whipped around the corner of Seacoast Drive and pulled into Sarah's driveway. He put the Rover in neutral and tugged on the emergency break, bringing the vehicle to a jerking stop. Three police cars descended on the house as he shoved his door open and sprinted into her house through the wide open door. Music pumped from the speakers as he shouted her name over and over instead of entering silently. "Sarah! Sarah!" He scanned several rooms and crashed through her bedroom door.

She whirled on a piercing scream.

He moved forward, yanking her robe-clad body against him, his heart jack hammering and his body shaking. He pulled her back again, brushing trembling fingers through her hair. "Oh, God, Sarah. Oh, thank God."

"What are you doing besides scaring me half to death?" She tried to shove away. "I left a note with Morgan and Hunter telling them to go ahead and stay— that meant you too. Austin should be here any minute."

He couldn't let her go. "Just let me hold on for another second." He kissed her hair.

"Stop it." She pulled free. "You don't get to walk in here and act like you weren't incredibly cruel. You've hurt me. I'm very angry with—"

"Freeze!" Two policemen entered the room with guns drawn, and Sarah screamed again.

Instinct kicked in and Ethan whirled, pulling his gun from his waistband, pointing at the officers before it registered who they were.

"Drop your weapon and get on the ground, now!" an officer yelled.

Ethan let his gun fall from his hand, laced his fingers behind his head, and dropped to the floor. It would really ruin his day if they put a bullet in his chest. "I'm Ethan Cooke, CEO of Ethan Cooke Security. Your dispatch knew I was on my way. My ID is in my wallet—back left pocket."

One of the officers moved behind him, grabbing his wallet while the other continued to hold him at gunpoint. The man spoke to dispatch, and seconds later, the cop helped Ethan off the floor, handing him back his gun. "Sorry about that."

"I would've done the same thing."

Arms crossed, Sarah looked at each of the men. "What is going *on* around here? Why would you call the police? There's already a cop out front. I made arrangements with Austin to meet me here. I'm being cautious, Ethan. I have no intention of taking any risks."

"Ms. Johnson, your security system was disabled. When we arrived, Mr. Cooke ran through an open door."

Her knuckles whitened as her eyes grew wide with terror. "He was here? That man was here?"

"We believe so."

"Officer down! Officer down! 555 Seacoast Drive," the radio belched, "I need an ambulance, immediately."

The policemen ran from Sarah's room, and she followed.

Ethan caught her three steps into the hallway. "Throw on some clothes first, Sarah."

She dashed back in the bedroom, tossing her robe to the floor.

He turned away from the spectacular view of her stunning naked body as she snapped a bra in place and yanked a t-shirt over her head.

"I need to see, Ethan. I need to help."

He met her eyes and nodded as she buttoned her jeans, and they hurried outside.

Three officers surrounded a uniformed man lying on the ground. His bloodied, purple face swelled as they watched. "Pulse is thready. Hang on there, Steve. Help is coming."

"That poor man." Sarah struggled against Ethan. "Let me go help them, damn it!" She tried to yank free.

He held her close. "The best thing we can do is stay out of the way."

"At least let me get him a blanket." Sarah dashed toward the house, and he followed. She grabbed the soft, creamy afghan from her couch and ran back outside, handing off the blanket to one of the officers, then stepped back.

The ambulance arrived moments later, backing into her yard. As the paramedics jumped from the cab, a crime scene unit pulled up. An officer cordoned off her driveway and yard with yellow tape. More officers went into Sarah's home.

Sarah covered her mouth with her trembling hand.

Ethan wrapped an arm around her stiff shoulders. "Let's see if we can get some of your stuff, and we'll get you out of here."

"Okay." She glanced back at the wounded officer, shaking her head. "I need to check on Kylee."

"Kylee's fine. Austin has her. Let's go." He tugged on her hand.

They moved forward as a man in jeans and a t-shirt walked toward them. Plain clothes, Ethan knew.

"Ms. Johnson? I'm Detective Chris Allen. I need to ask you some questions."

"Yes, yes, of course."

A crime scene cop wearing vinyl marker boots and gloves stuck his head out the door. "Detective, you're going to want to see this."

See what? What had that asshole done?

Moments later, Ethan stepped away from Sarah as

the detective walked back. "I want to know what's going on."

"This is official police business, Mr.—"

"Cooke. Ethan Cooke, of Ethan Cooke Security. I'm in charge of Ms. Johnson's protection. I've kept in contact with Detective Tucker Campbell during this entire investigation. You can tell me now, or I'll call him and find out myself. I can't keep Ms. Johnson safe if I don't know what's coming at her."

The cop's eyes cooled. "A bouquet of flowers was found on the kitchen table—five blue roses wrapped with a white ribbon. The card attached read 'Soon, whore bitch, very, very soon' in bold red ink.

"Oh my God." Sarah's voice trembled as the color drained from her face and she gripped her hands together. "That monster was in my home? He got into my *house*? I know my system was disabled, but I didn't realize he'd actually made it in." She shuddered. "I was in the shower just before Ethan barged in."

Ethan took her shoulders. "Sarah—"

She broke free, running to Hunter as he stepped up to the officer guarding the scene, showing his ID, and ducked under the tape. She wrapped herself in his arms and stabbed Ethan in the heart.

They walked back with Hunter still holding her close, moving out of the way as the ambulance pulled away with its lights flashing and siren screaming.

"Let's get her out of here, Cooke," Hunter said, stopping in front of him.

"I have questions for Ms. Johnson."

Hunter flicked a glance at the man standing next to Ethan. "You can ask them at my house or tomorrow. I'll leave it up to you." Dismissing the detective, Hunter spoke to Ethan. "Austin picked us up at the airport for a fucking tight squeeze of a ride home. He dropped me off and took Morgan, Hailey, and Kylee to the house. I want us back ASAP." He glanced at Sarah. "You'll stay with Morgan and me until we have to leave for D.C. next week."

She freed herself of his hold. "Absolutely not. I'm not about to put you and Morgan in any danger. You didn't see the officer they wheeled out of my backyard." Her voice broke. "He was here to help me, and now he might die."

Hunter brushed his thumb across her cheek, catching a tear.

She sniffled, shaking her head. "I'm all right, Hunter. I want you to reconsider. I couldn't live with myself if this sicko hurt Morgan because of me."

Ethan watched her struggle to keep herself together while Hunter hugged her. He should've been doing that, always had. He wanted to take her and Kylee home with him, but he didn't think she would be open to that right now.

Needing to touch her, Ethan ran his finger down her arm. "Austin and Hunter are going to cover you, Kylee, and Morgan. It's the safest option at this point."

Sarah met his gaze and nodded. "Okay. Can we get out of here?"

~~~~

Late that night, Ethan sat at Hunter's dining room table with a cup of cold coffee at his elbow. They both stared at the surveillance footage from the cameras at Sarah's house, watching the cop on tape wander around her yard, shining his flashlight among the bushes set back from her patio by the bedroom. Out of nowhere, he fell to the ground statue stiff.

"The fucker fucking tased him," Hunter said as he rewound the disc, letting the video play back in slow-motion.

"There." Ethan pointed to the flash of explosion when the taser dart left the gun.

Hunter hit a button, letting the disk play at regular speed as the policeman lay stiff. A masked man dressed in black came into video range, smashing the officer over the head with one of Sarah's small concrete planters.

Ethan winced. "Goddamn."

The man in black followed the first hit with a second blow, followed by several punches with vinyl-gloved hands. He kicked the officer once in the stomach, twice in the kidneys then dragged him back to the shrubbery. The man then crouched by the bushes and waited.

Ethan pushed fast forward on the laptop. Fifteen minutes of video time flashed by before he stopped it again as Sarah stepped from the taxi, pulling her suitcase with her. She unlocked the door, shutting it behind her.

Camera four caught a movement and took over, showing the man in black walk along the side of the house until he crouched in front of the living room window.

"He must be watching her," Hunter said, flexing his fingers.

Ethan boiled with rage, disgusted by the fucker who invaded Sarah's privacy. Minutes later, the sick bastard went to the door, put on a fresh pair of gloves, and cut through the glass, letting himself in.

"Why the fuck didn't the alarm go off?" Hunter stood.

"He must've jammed it."

They both watched the masked invader run out of

the house and back before running out again. He came back with his bouquet of roses and entered the house, shutting the door once he stepped inside.

Ethan couldn't take any more. The fear of what could've been sent his stomach into a churning fit of nausea. He stopped the CD and stood. "I need a break."

"I'll get more coffee."

He walked to the massive sliders showcasing the bright lights of Los Angeles in the distance. He'd almost been too late. He'd almost lost Sarah.

Hunter stepped back into the room, carrying two steaming cups. "Ready to finish this?"

"No. It makes me sick." Ethan glanced at the city before he blew out a breath. He had to sit back down and watch the rest. They might miss something if they stopped where they were.

He took his seat and the mug Hunter handed him. "Thanks." He set it on the table. His system couldn't handle another shot of caffeine. "Let's get this over with."

Hunter pressed 'play.' Nothing happened for several minutes until the masked man stormed out the door, leaving it wide opened.

"What the hell? Why'd he leave?"

"He must've gotten my message. I called her office line. It was the only one he missed."

They both came to attention when Ethan's Rover sped into the driveway. He sprinted forward, gun in hand, rushing through the door as if his life depended on it. It had. If the bastard had hurt her...

"Jesus, Cooke, what the hell was that?" They exchanged a heated glance. "What if he'd had her?"

He'd thought of that a million times on the drive over to Hunter's. His breach in protocol could've cost her her life. "Back off. I fucked up. I already know it." *In more ways than one.*

The two L.A.P.D. officers hurried in just moments later, while others walked the perimeter of the house. They scrambled forward when they found their fallen man.

Ethan shut the lid on the laptop. "That's it. We both know the rest." He sipped at the coffee gone cool and winced. "He's escalating and becoming careless. It's only a matter of time before they get him." He had to believe it.

Hunter looked at him. "He's also getting more erratic. Austin or I will be on her at all times. Whoever isn't with her will be with Kylee if they're separated for any reason. Morgan's finally speaking to me again, now that I've properly groveled for not telling her about the incident that occurred while we were at the resort, so we've talked. She'll work from home until we have to leave for D.C. next week."

"I don't think it would hurt to have Hailey stay with you too. She spends a lot of time with Sarah. Not only will she be good company, but she's a potential target. His anger toward Sarah seems to be increasing, making it more likely he'll try for someone close to her, just to hurt her." Ethan rested his weary head in his hands on the table. "If he can't get to her, he'll find other ways to bring her pain. Ultimately, that's what he wants to do." He met Hunter's gaze again. "If Sarah's parents weren't leaving Saturday, I'd want us to put someone on them. The cops are on it, but I'd like someone closer."

"That's the problem. There isn't anyone. We're stretched thin. I think we have to look at taking on new hires, Ethan. The business is only growing."

"I've already thought of that. I just haven't had the chance to talk to you about it. That doesn't help us now.

We've got three-quarters of our men contracted for the World Leaders Conference next week and all but two on private duty. Most of our guys overseas will be here covering diplomats, so that pretty much leaves me. I'll take Sarah and Kylee until the Conference is over or until the bastard is caught, whichever comes first. I can orchestrate the puppet show from my home office." He pulled back from the table. "I'm going to head out."

"Later." Hunter stood, taking the cups to the kitchen.

Ethan walked toward the door but veered to the right and up the steps to the room he knew Sarah was staying in. He needed to be sure she was okay. He stood outside her doorway as the hall light blazed bright, illuminating the darkened room. Sarah lay next to Kylee, holding her close. She moved enough so that he knew she didn't sleep. Just as he was about to poke his head in, Sarah spoke. "Austin?"

"Yeah?"

Ethan followed the voice, spotting his bodyguard lying on a cot across the room.

"Don't leave tonight, okay?"

"I'm not going anywhere."

"I'm scared. I feel like I can't admit that to anyone else, so I'll tell you. I'm so damn afraid."

Ethan fisted his hands at his side as her voice vibrated with fear.

"I'm not going to let anything happen to you or Kylee, Sarah. Neither is anyone else. Try to get some sleep."

Ethan turned and walked back downstairs. Had things changed so much between them? Was this what was left? He needed her right now as much as he wished she needed him. If he hadn't screwed everything up, they'd be lying in each other's arms at the resort.

He'd been stupid, jealous, and had hurt her because of his own insecurities. He wanted it all back.

The conversation she'd had with Austin should've been something they shared together. They always had. As much as he wanted more for them, maybe friendship would have to be enough. Having her in his life was what mattered. Going backwards would be better than losing it all.

CHAPTER TWELVE

THREE DAYS LATER, AUSTIN PULLED AWAY FROM MORGAN and Hunter's house. Sarah held Kylee up to the window so she could wave.

"Bye-bye, Austin."

"Did you see that? He waved back."

"Yes." Kylee squirmed to get down. "I go play with Auntie Morgan now."

Sarah held her tight. "Not right now, Kylee. Auntie Morgan is busy with her work. You can see her later."

Kylee smiled. "I go play with Ethan and Hailey."

Sarah nuzzled Kylee's neck. "Have fun. I'll be in in just a minute." She set Kylee on her feet, and her daughter ran to the living room. She turned back to the window, staring out at the bright, beautiful day before she cringed and moved away, fearful of who might be watching. She bumped into a solid wall of muscle and spun around, gasping. "Oh, Ethan, you scared me."

He grabbed hold of her arms, steadying her, then let her go. "Sorry. You okay?"

A fleeting smile crossed her lips. "Yeah, I'm fine. Thanks." This was the first they'd spoken since the night of the break-in. She'd heard the door open and Ethan's voice greet Kylee, Hunter, and Hailey ten minutes ago, when she'd been upstairs, quickly folding a load of laundry. By the times she'd come downstairs, Ethan had wandered into the other room and Austin had been leaving.

Sarah stared into eyes she knew as well as her own,

wanting to hold on to the anger from the day at the resort, but it didn't seem to matter anymore.

Ethan shoved his hands in his pockets and cleared his throat. "Can we talk?"

She glanced toward the living room, hating the thought of being away from her daughter, even a few feet.

"She's okay, Sarah. Hunter's with her."

"It's that obvious, huh?"

He smiled. "No, I just know you."

Hunter growled and Kylee screamed in delight, and her deep belly laugh echoed through the house.

"How about a walk?" Ethan gestured toward the door.

Sarah hesitated then Kylee laughed again. Kylee would be fine without her for a few minutes, and she'd allowed Morgan and Hunter's home to become her fortress. Every moment she was afraid, the man who stalked her won. She nodded. "Okay, let's talk."

"Phillips, Sarah and I are going for a walk. I have my phone on me."

"All right," Hunter called back before he growled and sent Kylee into another fit of screams.

Sarah grabbed her sunglasses from her purse. They stepped outside into the warmth, and she sighed, feeling instantly lighter. "This was a good idea."

"Fresh air makes all the difference."

She knew Ethan scanned the area under his sunglasses as they walked; she tried to ignore it.

"So, how are you holding up?" He brushed her arm with his fingers.

She shrugged. "Pretty well, I guess."

"Good. That's good."

They stepped apart when two young boys soared

past on their bikes and closed the gap again as youthful laughter faded.

Ethan blew out a breath. "Sarah, I'm sorry about the other day, really sorry."

She glanced at his profile. "It's water under the bridge."

He stopped and took her hand. "It's not. I was way out of line, *way* out there. I said things—implied things that were so far off base..." He shook his head, tightening his grip against hers. "My assumptions were knee-jerk. There isn't anyone I trust more than you. I want you to know that."

Any residual hurt washed away with his words. Sarah touched his cheek. "Ethan—"

"You're my best friend," he interrupted, "and I think we've taken a wrong turn by trying to be something more."

"Oh." Her stomach sank and she dropped her hand away. This wasn't how she'd anticipated their conversation going. The sharp slap of shock left her speechless. Although she'd been hurt and angry, she'd fully expected them to work things out and move along with their relationship. While she lay awake during the endless nights, staring at the ceiling of the guestroom, she'd found solace in thoughts of Ethan and their night away. She'd realized the extent of her want for him, her *need* for him. One argument didn't have to be the end.

"I need you in my life," he went on. "If the only way to keep you there is by going back to where we were before, I'm okay with that."

"But—"

"Let's leave it here, Sarah. It's better like this."

Confusion joined the gamut of her swirling emotions. Was this his polite way of telling her he wasn't attracted to her after all? Unable to deal with any more rollercoaster rides in her life, she reluctantly resolved to find peace with this new turn of events. "Then I'm okay with it too." She was glad she wore her sunglasses, or he would've seen the lie.

Ethan pulled her into a hug, holding her tight against him. "I've missed us, Sarah. It's been too long since we've been easy with each other."

"Yeah, it has."

This wasn't what she wanted. Finding her courage, she eased back to tell him so, but he smiled at her, looking more relaxed than he had in days. This was what *he* wanted.

Ethan took her hand as they turned at the end of the street and started back toward the house. He stopped in front of the mailbox as they approached the pale green cedar shingles and white trimmed porches of Hunter and Morgan's charming home, pulling letters and junk mail free. He handed over the stack as they stepped inside and locked the door behind them.

Sarah leafed through the pile. "Lisa said she would be sending the swimsuit edition contract here." Spotting *Celebrity* Magazine's letterhead, she grabbed the envelope. "Here it is. I'll be right back." She walked upstairs to the room she and Kylee shared, frowning as she studied the package, surprised by its light weight. The contract was usually an inch thick.

She tore the envelope open, pulling papers free. Crisp brown rose petals fell to the floor, and she stared, confused, before it finally clicked. Heart pounding, legs buckling, she sat on the edge of the bed, eyes locked on the mess. With trembling fingers, she picked up the newspaper clipping at the top of the small pile and looked down at a picture of herself. The shot had been taken the night of the break-in. She sat in the backseat of Ethan's Rover as he drove away from her home. Hunter's arm draped her shoulder. The caption read 'Celebrity Favorite Under Attack.' Ethan and Hunter's heads were colored over with dark red marker.

She grabbed the next clipping, and her breath came in shuddering gasps as memories rushed back, bringing with them staggering pain. Tears stung her eyes as she read, 'The Price of War,' remembering the firestorm the photo had caused when a reporter froze her grief in a moment that would last forever.

She sat in a chair close to Jake's draped casket while Hunter, in his dress blues and arm in a sling, rested his hand against her shoulder. Ethan flanked her left side, gripping her hand in his while he held her infant daughter in his free arm. She clutched the American flag folded tightly in a triangle as tears drenched her face. The photographer had captured her agony for all of California to see. This clip had 'Widow Whore Bitch' scrawled across it in the same angry red.

The plain white backing of another photograph glared up at her. Unable to stop herself, she picked it up and flipped it over. A long, keening moan escaped her throat as horror shuddered through her. Kylee's smiling face stared back at her. It was a picture from the day they'd spent at the beach building sandcastles. 'Isn't she lovely?' was followed by a vicious looking smiley face. *Not my baby. Not Kylee.*

Pulsing with anger, Sarah rushed to her feet, her breath heaving as she threw the vulgar clippings and photograph, watching as they sailed to the floor. She fought the urge to clear off the dresser as helpless rage consumed her. Kylee's picture landed face up, and the fury vanished as quickly as it invaded.

Defeated, shattered, Sarah staggered back to the bed, collapsing against the mattress, fighting for each gulp of air. A tear fell, followed by another as a sob escaped her lips. Eyes wide, she covered her mouth with an unsteady hand, trying to hold the next back, but she couldn't stop it.

Bright, hot fear left her body shuddering as disgust curdled her stomach. She lay on the bed, burying her face against her pillow, and began to weep wildly.

"Lisa must've sent you two... Sarah?" The bedroom door closed and the mattress sagged as Ethan sat at her side. "Hey, hey, hey," he said gently, pulling her up to sitting.

She wanted to say so many things, to tell him she was sick and terrified, but could only shake her head as he nestled her in his strong arms.

He lay them down, his body cocooning hers, and her sobs were lost against his chest. "I can't... I can't take this anymore."

"Shh," he whispered next to her ear, stroking her hair.

"Oh, God, Ethan. He took pictures of Kylee," she choked out.

He kissed the top of her head, bringing her closer.

"Not my baby. Not Kylee. I don't know what to *do*. I don't know how to make him go away. I want him to go the hell away."

"I know. I know you do."

She held on to him, absorbing the warmth of his body, finding comfort in his murmurs of reassurance.

Several minutes passed as she cried herself dry, purging herself of the helpless grief that had threatened to suffocate her over the last few days. Weighty exhaustion slid into its place as she stared into Ethan's gaze and her lids drooped. "He found me already," she said sleepily.

"Yeah."

"I have to get Kylee out of here. She's not safe. He sent me stuff. It's on the floor."

"I saw. I'll take care of it. We're going to figure this out. Let's talk about it in a little while." He skimmed his thumb against her skin, drying her tears. "I know you're upset. You have every right to be, but I want you to try to rest."

She shook her head. "No. I'm fine."

"Turn it off, Sarah. You need to sleep. Hunter has Kylee right now, and I have you. Getting some rest will only make things better."

Ethan's gentle voice hypnotized her, and Sarah's eyes slid closed. She was in danger, her daughter was in danger, but she was drowning in a sea of fatigue. She struggled with her heavy lids. She'd hardly closed them in three days. When she fought them open, she looked into Ethan's smoky gray pools as the familiar scent of his aftershave and his big hands moving in gentle circles over her back brought comfort.

"Go to sleep, Sarah," he whispered. "I won't let you go." He snuggled her closer, pressing firm lips against her forehead.

She blinked once, twice more before her world went black.

~~~~

Ethan slid his fingers through Sarah's soft hair as he stared into her tear-stained face, fighting to keep his body relaxed as his fury raged. His capacity for violence was at its peak. Sarah's breathing was just now steadying out after she'd cried as he'd only seen her do once before. If the fucker was lucky, the cops would find him before he did. The bastard was going to pay for every drop that had run down Sarah's cheeks.

A light knock sounded at the door.

Ethan turned his head. "Yeah."

Hunter peeked in and frowned. "Is everything—" He shoved the door wide as he walked to the mess on the floor. "What the fuck is this shit?"

"Keep it down," Ethan said with a calm he didn't feel. "She's finally asleep."

Hunter glanced at Sarah, then at the hardwood. "She found this?"

"She thought it was the contract for the swimsuit edition. She was almost hysterical, Phillips. I'm going to kill him."

Hunter crouched down by the petals and paper. "Jesus, he's been busy. The envelope is from *Celebrity*. He had to get into the newsroom to get this. And these newspaper clippings... The one about Jake is original print. He would've had to buy this from a collector." Jaw clenched, Hunter stood, staring hard at the floor. "He's not going to stop until he has her."

Ethan cradled Sarah closer as fear mixed with the fury. "He'll die first."

Hunter met his gaze, holding it. "I'll get some gloves and get this out of here." He left the room.

~~~~

Sarah's eyes flew open, staring into Ethan's as he draped his arm around her while she curled into him.

He smiled. "Welcome back."

"Thanks."

She tried to sit up. "I need to get up."

He held her in place. "Stay for a couple of minutes. You only slept for an hour."

"That's better than last night." She hadn't slept well since the last time he held her like this at the resort.

Ethan skimmed his knuckles against her jaw. "You can't keep this up, Sarah. You're going to make yourself sick."

"I can't help it. I know Austin's sleeping on the other side of the room, and Hunter's just down the hall, but once the sun goes down, my imagination gets the better of me." Her eyes darted to the window. "I feel like I'm being watched constantly, like he can see me, even when the curtains are closed."

Ethan brushed her hair back from her cheek. "You have every right to be afraid, but we're not going to let anything happen to you. That bastard can send you mail and leave flowers wherever the hell he wants, but he can't get to you." He tapped the tip of her nose. "Remember that when your imagination starts to take off."

She smiled because she knew that's what he needed. She'd known him too long to miss the anger brewing underneath the surface of his calm. "I worry about you, Austin, and Hunter too. He scribbled over your faces with red marker. He wants to hurt you. Look what he did to that poor policeman." She could still see the man's swollen, disfigured face. "I called the hospital to find out how he is, but they won't say anything."

"My friend on the force said he's been downgraded from critical care to serious condition. He's going to need a couple of surgeries and some rehabilitation, but they expect him to make a full recovery."

"Well, thank God for that. I feel responsible for his

injuries."

Ethan sat up, pulling her along with him. "You're absolutely *not*. There's only one person who is, and they're going to catch him, Sarah."

She fiddled with the edge of the covers, still edgy with nerves. "What am I going to do in the meantime? I need to do something besides worry, or I think I might go crazy."

"Get back to work. Call Lisa and tell her you're ready. I'll be covering you and Kylee for the next two weeks while Austin's busy and Morgan and Hunter are gone. We can get your stuff from the office and set it up at my house."

Her gaze flew to his. "We're not going back to my house?"

He shook his head. "The security's better on my property. I set your home up to deal with burglars and typical, everyday threats. This situation goes way beyond that."

Restless, Sarah moved to stand, but stopped when she remembered. She glanced down at the floor, bracing herself, expecting to see dried rose petals, pictures, and newsprint scrawled with red marker. "They're gone."

"Hunter came to check on you a while ago. He took everything away. The police stopped by and picked it up."

Sarah thought of Kylee's photo, of her sweet, innocent face marred by evil. "I'm scared for Kylee, Ethan. I'm so scared for her." It was time to ask the question she'd been avoiding. "Should I send her away with my parents until this is settled?" It broke her heart to think of being so far from Kylee, but her safety came first.

Ethan blew out a long breath and took her hand. "As

much as I want to say no, I have to say yes. The person doing this is escalating. He's becoming more erratic, more dangerous."

There was an edge to Ethan's voice. He was hiding something. "What else?"

"Let's leave it at that."

"Just tell me. I can handle it. What choice do I have?" She walked over to the window, pulled the curtain back, letting the sunshine in, and immediately stepped away, feeling like eyes were on her. She covered her face with her hands, determined not to let fear and frustration break her again.

The bed gave a slight squeak as Ethan stood. His arms came around her, holding her in a hug. "Sarah, I don't want you worrying about all the details. We have this under control."

She pushed away, temper straining. "Don't you get it, Ethan? I have no control—over *anything*. I'm a mess right now. I recognize that, but I also have to know what's going on in my own life. At this point I don't hold any of the cards. You, Hunter, Austin, and that lunatic have them all. I can't live like this." She paced away.

"I'm just trying to protect you."

Sarah stopped, closing her eyes with a weary sigh. "I know you are." She walked to Ethan, touching her fingers to his shoulder, giving him a small smile. "I'm sorry."

"Don't apologize. I know this is hard."

Understanding filled his voice, his eyes, and her heart melted. He was everything she needed. Sarah brushed his cheek as she closed the distance, pressing her lips to his. His mouth instantly heated against hers, and she deepened the kiss, running her palms down his muscled chest and back up, wrapping her arms around his neck.

He grabbed her wrists in a vise grip, pushing her away. "Friends, Sarah. Remember?"

She nodded and looked down, struggling with hurt. "Right."

He turned away as a quiet tap sounded at the door.

"Come in," Sarah said, welcoming the distraction.

Hailey stuck her head in the room. "Am I interrupting?"

Sarah smiled. "No. In fact, I need to talk to you. Give me ten minutes?"

"Sure." Hailey closed the door again.

Sarah picked up her cellphone from the side table, too embarrassed to look at Ethan. "I need to call my parents and find out if they're willing to take Kylee to Europe—Hailey too, if she's willing to go."

"I think that's a good idea. I'll inform Jackson Matthews that he's going to accompany them, just as a precaution."

"What about Austin?"

"He has to stay here. He's been in charge of the details for the World Conference security. Matthews is good. He used to be a cop."

"Okay."

CHAPTER THIRTEEN

ETHAN DROVE NORTH ON THE 405, SLIDING SARAH A GLANCE under his sunglasses. She hadn't said a word since they'd dropped Kylee, Hailey, and her parents off at the airport. He'd watched her struggle to hold back tears when Kylee waved, smiling in Hailey's arms, as they went through security. She'd waved back until they disappeared into the busy Saturday crowd. "Your stuff should be at my house by now."

"Hmm?" She looked away from the window.

"Your office equipment will be all set up when we get home."

A smile ghosted her mouth. "That's good."

Ethan took his hand from the steering wheel and snagged hers. "It's only two weeks, Sarah. She's going to have a blast."

Her lips quivered and she sniffled as her eyes filled. "I know." She shook her head. "I'm sorry. I'm going to miss her so much. I already do. Two weeks will feel like forever. I only lasted one night at the resort."

"Yeah, but you would've lasted two if I hadn't been an asshole. You were having fun."

"Ethan, stop." She squeezed his hand. "Water under the bridge, remember?"

He could still see the way she'd looked at him at the tiki bar, her eyes full of shock and hurt. It continued to bother him. "Right. Are you still up for going to my parents' party tonight?" He wasn't. He was never up for spending an evening in the company of his mother and father.

"Of course. It's been forever since I've seen Wren. I can't wait."

The one highlight of the evening—his baby sister. Barely a year separated them, but she would always be his baby sister. He imagined she was dreading this evening's event as well, but they were both expected to be there.

Nobody put on a show like Grant and Rene Cooke, the dedicated chief of staff and L.A.'s top plastic surgeon. They'd been dedicated to everyone but their children. Patients, boardroom meetings, and marital indiscretions had always taken priority for the lovely Mr. and Mrs. Cooke. He and Wren had grown up in the care of nannies and governesses, barely registering a blip on their parents' radar.

If the parties weren't good for drumming up business—for himself and his sister's interior design firm—Ethan would've told them to go fuck themselves a long time ago. "I know she's looking forward to seeing you too." He stopped at the wrought iron security gate in front of his house and punched in the code he'd selected for the week. The gate slid back, receding into the twelve-foot brick wall surrounding his property, and he drove through. He watched in his rearview mirror until the gate locked shut then continued down the long drive through the heavy tree cover concealing the front of his house.

Pulling around the circle, Ethan stopped in front of the rambling glass, brick, and wood structure he called home. When Ethan Cooke Security had gone international, he'd decided to celebrate by purchasing a home. He and Sarah had scoured the Palisades for two weeks before they found it. When Jake and Hunter had returned from a month-long mission, they'd had a huge housewarming party in an empty five-bedroom, six-bath house. Four and a half years later, the house was anything but empty. Wren had had her way with the place, accenting his home in various shades of tan, cream, and blue. The casual, masculine undertones fit him perfectly.

He opened the front door, and Bear and Reece met him and Sarah in the entryway, tails wagging. Ethan gave them both an enthusiastic rubdown. "Hey there, fellas."

The enormous bullmastiffs rubbed up against Sarah next, almost knocking her down with their excitement. Ethan gave a lightning fast hand command, and the dogs sat like perfect gentlemen.

Laughing, Sarah bent close for kisses. "How are my babies? Have you been good boys?" Her hands moved over saggy jowls as she spoke. "Have you snacked on any bad guys lately?"

"No, they've had the month off. We'll use them at the conference, though." Ethan loved watching her with his dogs. Most criminals wept with fear when Bear and Reece came running, but Sarah adored them. The feeling was mutual.

"Okay, men." He snapped and pointed to the living room. Both dogs immediately went on their merry way.

"Hey, I wasn't finished playing with them."

"There's plenty of time for that. I want to show you where I've set you up."

They wandered through the huge living room and down a long hall, stopping at the room across from Ethan's office. "I thought you'd be comfortable in here." He'd transformed the sitting area into a relaxing office space. He would be able to see her from his desk. For protection purposes, it was ideal; for his sanity, probably not. It would be hard to have her so close and not be able to touch her.

She smiled. "Ethan, this is absolutely perfect. Thank you."

"No problem." He took her hand, pulling her from the makeshift office and up the curved staircase to the bedrooms. He'd struggled with which room to give her. He'd wanted her in his, but that wasn't an option, so he opted for the room next door instead. The balcony overlooking the Pacific connected his room and hers.

"I can't believe I'll be waking up to this view every morning." She pulled the massive glass doors fitted with security-grade glass open and stepped outside. The ocean breeze played with her hair and molded her navy blue v-neck against her breasts. "I know I say this every time, but it's absolutely sensational. My camera and I will be very busy out here."

"It's yours to enjoy." He couldn't count the number of times he'd imagined her right here over the past six months.

She walked up to him, smiling, and gave him a long hug. "Thank you so much. I think I might actually get some sleep tonight." She pulled away, settling her hands on the railing. He'd seen the sorrow in her eyes before she turned.

He boxed her against the polished wood and placed his hands next to hers on the rail, resting his chin on her head. Golden whips of hair flew up, tickling his cheeks. "What is it?"

"I keep thinking of Kylee. Do you think she's bored? It's such a long flight to London."

"I think she's charmed the flight attendants already and is enjoying one of the several hundred movies or books you packed for her. She should be set for at least a year."

Sarah moved her chin up, meeting his gaze, and smiled. "You're such an exaggerator."

Wanting to keep the light in her eyes, he grinned and nuzzled her neck. "Am not." His hand snaked up, grabbing her halfway up the ribcage—a secret ticklish spot he knew she had.

Sarah screeched out a surprised laugh as she turned and tried to shove him away. One handed, Ethan grabbed her by the wrists and pulled her arms high over her head. His free hand made a threatening motion to go back to the forbidden spot.

Still laughing, she dodged his hand the best she could. "Ethan, don't you dare! This isn't fair. You're stronger than me!"

Enjoying himself thoroughly, his grin turned devilish. "I know."

The tinkle of dog tags on collars joined the laughter on the balcony. Ethan turned to Bear and Reece, tongues hanging, tails wagging. "I've got her, boys. Now, what should I do with her?" He turned in time to see perfect white teeth aiming for his shoulder. "Hey, that's dirty."

Flushed, eyes glowing with fun, Sarah grinned and wiggled her brows. "I know."

Brow raised, he smiled. "Truce?"

She nodded. "Absolutely."

He let her wrists go, weary of the mischievous light in her eyes as he backed his way to the door. When she stood leaning and relaxed against the rail, he turned. "We should probably get ready to—"

Sarah let out a loud whoop as she ran toward him, and he staggered forward when the weight of her body landed on his back before he found his balance. "Jesus, Sarah."

She wrapped her legs around his waist. "Didn't they teach you to never turn your back on an opponent at your fancy bodyguard school?" She stuck her hand in his armpit, and he let out a yelp of laughter.

"Knock it off, Sarah. I thought we made a truce."

"I crossed my fingers. Karma's a bitch, Cooke."

He wandered into her room, stopped at the bed, and turned. Falling backwards like a toppling tree, he smushed her into the California King.

"Get up," she said, laughing, shoving at his back. "You're smothering me."

He flipped his body so that he lay intimately between her legs. "Karma's a bitch, Johnson."

"Okay, truce, truce." She wiggled her hands in front of his face. "See, no crossed fingers."

"I accept."

Her body molded perfectly to his as her breasts rose and fell against his chest, and the playful light left her eyes as they looked into his. Hesitantly, her fingers moved to play with the hair at his neck, sending shockwaves down his spine.

Aching with want, his hand clutched the navy blue spread as he reminded himself they could only be friends and freed himself of her before he made another mistake. "We should get ready to go to my parents.'"

Still lying where he'd left her, Sarah stared at him for several seconds before she got up, went into the bathroom, and closed the door.

~~~~

The lights blazed bright at the Cooke estate. Three hundred rich bastards milled in and around the grounds, wasting precious oxygen as far as Zeke was concerned.

Several of the asshole guests graced his TV screen when he chose to watch it, but he wasn't impressed.

He stood in the back corner of the ballroom dressed in the fucking penguin suit he'd stolen from the idiot he'd taken care of three miles down the road, fantasizing about what he'd like to do to several of the 'ladies' flaunting their stuff. When their titties hung out of skin-tight dresses, they were always surprised when they got what they deserved, what they asked for. Sluts, every one of them.

Speaking of, where in the hell was *his* slut? She was supposed to be here. He gritted out a smile when a man came to take a flute of champagne from his tray. He glanced up and, like magic, she appeared through the door across the room. The short, powder blue dress she wore hung on her body by two thin spaghetti straps, stopping mid-thigh. The front dipped low, showing off a hint of cleavage. Strappy, ice-pick heels put her at eye level with the fucking hotshot bodyguard who was never far away.

Zeke's eyes narrowed to slits when the dick in the charcoal gray suit placed his hand on the small of her naked back and spoke close to her ear. His blood boiled as the smile on her face spread to a grin. Her shiny hair, loose and curling, brushed his cheek when she turned her head to say something back. Her 'bodyguard' smiled into her eyes. Zeke would bet his life they were fucking. They were going to pay. Sarah belonged to *him*.

He moved from the corner of the room, making his way forward, his gaze never leaving his whore bitch. Giddy that he'd fooled them all, he stood next to her, breathing in her summer garden scent. All he had to do was extend his hand and he could touch her—all that soft, smooth skin. He bunched his hand into a fist at his side, afraid he'd do it. "Champagne?"

The asshole moved forward and took two flutes. "Thanks." He turned, gave one to Sarah, and put his hand on the small of her back again, and they walked off.

Oh, he couldn't wait to deal with Master Ethan Cooke. The remaining glasses on his tray moved ever so slightly as he trembled with rage. Perhaps tonight was finally going to be the night. Moving back to his corner, he watched and waited for just the right time.

~~~~

Sarah smiled at Ethan as they danced together on the outside balcony, surrounded by the scent of flowers, moving in a slow circle among numerous other couples. "I know you weren't super excited about coming here tonight, but you have to admit, it's been pretty fun."

His brow rose. "It's been bearable."

"Stop with all the enthusiasm, Ethan. I can hardly take it."

He grinned.

"Now that's a look I rarely see," Wren Cooke said, sliding up next to Sarah. "My big brother's actually smiling."

Sarah stepped out of Ethan's arms and into his sister's, giving her a hug. "Wren, you're absolutely stunning. I love that color on you, and the cut."

"What, this old thing?" She winked, fingering the fabric of her deep red halter dress. "Thanks. I actually picked it up at your mother's boutique." She moved forward, kissing her brother's cheek. "Beat anybody up lately, bodyguard?"

"That's close protection agent to you."

Identical grins beamed back at each other. Wren was

the petite, female version of Ethan.

She turned to Sarah again. "How's the squirt? I haven't seen her in ages. You two should come by and visit."

"Kylee's good. She went to Europe with my parents for a couple of weeks." And she already missed her like crazy.

"Lucky little girl. She's a globe trotter, and she's two."

Put that way, Sarah smiled and relaxed a little. "Yes, I guess she is."

Thunder rolled in the distance as lightning lit the sky, and Wren's gaze wandered to the heavens. "It looks like we're in for a little rain. I don't think the weather gods checked with Mother. She's not going to be pleased." She rolled her eyes and smiled.

Sarah's gaze darted past the lights of the party into the dark edges of the well-tended lawn. She couldn't shake the feeling that she was being watched. She stared hard into the shadows, trying to find the direction of her discomfort. The tinkle of laughter from a group of guests snapped her back as she stepped closer to Ethan and his arm came around her waist. Feeling silly, she focused on the thread of sibling banter he and his sister spewed back and forth.

A waiter walked by again with champagne. Wren took a glass, handing it to Sarah, and took two more for herself and Ethan. "Thanks." She sipped at the golden wine as the man strolled away. "So, did you check out Mom's hot new lover?"

Sarah's eyes popped wide as her champagne flute stopped halfway to her mouth.

Ethan choked on the liquid bubbles. "Jesus, Wren."

"It's the personal trainer she's been working with. He's been sending her puppy eyes all night. And I'm pretty sure Dad's banging his new secretary. It's so clichéd. You would think that with all their practice at the big game of infidelity, they'd try to be more original." She gave a good-humored shrug and took another sip from her glass.

"You're really sick, Wren. Doesn't it bother you, even a little, that our parents have never been faithful to each other? That they act like two dogs in heat?"

"No. Why should it? They're adults. If they choose to continue with their farce of a marriage, there's nothing I can do about it. And quite frankly, I just don't care, so I might as well find the fun in it." She kissed Ethan's cheek again and hugged Sarah. "See you two later." She walked off.

"I always feel like I've been through a whirlwind after spending time with your sister."

"Imagine growing up with her," Ethan said, his voice tight.

Sarah took his hand. His clenched jaw told her his light mood was gone. "You know, I think your sister has a very healthy attitude about the way things are between your parents. Their behavior isn't a reflection of who you are."

A flash of doubt moved through his eyes just as a rustle in the garden caught both their attention. His hand tightened on hers when his mother and an athletic looking man kissed before walking into the large shed and closed the door.

Sarah looked away from the building, meeting his steely stare. "Ethan—"

Lightning flashed bright in the sky, followed by a blast of thunder. She shuddered, certain she and Ethan were not alone. "I want to go back inside."

"What do you say we call it a night? Let's get the hell

out of here." Ethan took the champagne flute from her hand and placed his and hers on a patio table. He wrapped an arm around her shoulders, and they walked into the comfort and light of the ballroom.

Sarah glanced behind her one last time, out into the dark as rain began to fall in sheets. She turned back to the music and laughter filling the room, admonishing herself for being silly and overly paranoid. There wasn't anyone here tonight that wanted to hurt her. Stalkers didn't hang out at five-thousand-dollar-a-plate charity events, did they? "I need to use the restroom before we go."

Ethan followed behind as Sarah headed down the hallway.

She stopped, more at ease, smiling. "You don't have to come with me."

"Yes, I do. I'll stand outside the door." The line was four-people deep. "Follow me. You can use the bathroom in the other wing." He took her hand as they turned down another long hall, and the noise of the party grew distant.

"Do they give out maps when guests stay here?"

Ethan smiled, but it didn't reach his weary eyes. "They didn't when I was a kid. To the best of my knowledge, everyone made it out alive."

She stopped and turned to him. "Do you want to talk about it?"

"No."

She nodded, knowing him well. He'd talk about the scene with his mother and her newest lover if and when he was ready. If she didn't push, he'd open up eventually. "Can I say one thing?"

He blew out a breath and smiled a little wider. "You're going to anyway, aren't you?"

She smiled back. "Yes."

"Well, go ahead then."

Sarah brushed her fingers over his cheek. "You're nothing like them, Ethan. Nothing." Eye to eye in her heels, she touched her lips to his.

He grabbed her hips. "Sarah," he said against her mouth.

She pressed her lips to his again, wanting to feel him, needing to give comfort.

Hesitating, he groaned, meeting her mouth with fever, diving deep, playing tongue against tongue. He gripped her hips tighter as he nipped her bottom lip with his teeth, sending rockets of need coursing through her body.

Thunder crashed and he pushed her away. "Damn it, Sarah."

Confused, frustrated, she moved forward again. "Why are you angry? I want to kiss you. I want you to kiss me."

"No." He paced away and back to stand in front of her. "This isn't going to happen. We're friends, only friends. I'm not interested in anything more."

Flashes of the night at the resort ran through her mind, and the way he kissed her just now told a different story. "I don't believe that. You're the one who changed things in the first place."

"Well, now I'm changing them back."

Sarah walked to the bathroom and slammed the door. She moved to the sink, watching the rain pour through the reflection in the mirror as lightning brightened the sky. Resting her hands on the countertop, she closed her eyes. Was she wrong? It'd been so long since she had dated. She had no idea how to play the game, but this wasn't a game. She wanted Ethan, but he said he didn't want her. She sighed out a weary breath. Her instincts, although rusty, told her he did. Why was he doing this?

She turned on the water, taking a cloth from the ornate silver rack. She dampened the soft fabric, glancing in the mirror again and froze. A man's tuxedoed silhouette filled the window behind her as he stood, holding a blue rose in his hand.

Her breath rushed in and out as she tried to scream, but the strangled sound wouldn't leave her throat. She whirled, staggering to the door, struggling with the handle, never taking her eyes from the man's.

In the next spark of light, he stepped forward, slamming a paper to the window. The crack of his gloved hand against the glass echoed like a gun blast. The red marker ran like blood in the rain. She made out the words, 'Now Bitch' as she frantically yanked at the knob.

Ethan ripped the door open, and she fell against him, trying to catch her breath.

He pulled her against him. "What's wrong? What is it?"

"He-he's out there." Her whole body trembled as she pointed to the window.

There was no one there.

"He was wearing a mask. It was him. I know it was him." She gasped for air, clutching at Ethan's jacket. "Get me out of here, Ethan. I can't be here anymore." Her legs buckled as she tried to move forward.

Ethan picked her up and brought her to another room. He sat with her in a chair.

It was too quiet. Sarah's ragged breathing and the rain pounding on the roof filled the room. She needed people and bright light. Her eyes darted from window to window, certain the man still watched. She curled against Ethan as he gripped her tight in his lap. "He's still watching me. I can feel it. He's laughing while he watches me."

"Okay, Sarah. It's okay. I'm here. He won't touch you." Rage edged his voice as he picked her up and hurried up a flight of stairs, bringing her to an office and set her on a couch in the dark. He closed the curtains before turning on a light.

Blinking rapidly, she looked up as Ethan made a call.

"Tucker, it's Ethan Cooke. I have Sarah with me at my parents' house. He was here."

CHAPTER FOURTEEN

IT WAS WELL AFTER MIDNIGHT BY THE TIME SARAH WALKED into Ethan's guest bedroom. She froze two steps in, staring at the massive glass doors exposed to the dark and pouring rain. The pleasure and comfort the view had given her hours before no longer existed. Fear that the man with the black mask and white latex gloves stood on the other side consumed her.

Heart pounding and braced to run, she stepped back, gripping the doorjamb, never taking her eyes from the door, fighting the need to flee. She made herself stop and breathe as her chest constricted with short, rapid breaths, making it hard to steady herself. She had to settle down. Closing her eyes, she took air in through her nose and let it out through her mouth, consciously loosening her grip on the glossy wood before she opened her eyes.

Calmer, Sarah moved forward again, telling herself he wasn't there—couldn't be. She paused mid-step. Wasn't that what she'd thought at Ethan's parents' house? Turning to retreat, she stopped when the familiar jingle of Bear and Reece's collars moved down the long hallway toward her bedroom.

The dogs entered the darkened space, and she relaxed. Even if the man was standing outside, waiting for her, they wouldn't let him hurt her. With all the courage she could muster, she made her way to the windows, never stopping to enjoy the city lights reflecting off the water in the distance. She snapped the navy blue fabric over the thick glass and flicked on the lamp on the bedside table.

Sighing, too tired to change, she pulled off her heels and sat on the floor. The dogs joined her, resting on each side of her outstretched legs. She settled her head against the dark beige wall and ran her hands through soft fur, listening to their steady panting. Sarah closed her eyes and rehashed her interview with the detective, trying to remember if she'd forgotten any major details. Her mind shot her back to the reflection in the mirror, and she shuddered.

"Sarah?"

She flinched and looked up.

Ethan stood in her doorway. His tie had long since been removed and his sleeves rolled to his elbows. "Are you going to bed?"

She shook her head. "I'm not ready yet."

He walked in and sat on her bed. "You're exhausted."

"I know, but I can't stop seeing that man. It was dark and he wore a ski mask, but I saw his eyes, Ethan. He's crazy and he won't stop until he has me."

Ethan stood, signaling for the dogs to move. They got up and lay down outside the door as he sat next to her. His cologne and warm hand over hers eased the tension along her shoulder blades.

"I'm not going to try to tell you this isn't a dangerous situation. It is. But he's not going to get to you, Sarah." Ethan's fingers tightened on hers until she looked at him. "I promise you he's not going to get to you." His gray eyes, hard and intense, stared deep into hers.

She nodded, needing to believe him. "I hate that I'm so afraid. It gives him more power than he deserves." She glanced at the curtains. "I don't know how long it's going to be before I can stand in front of a window at night and not see his eyes and that horrible blue rose."

Ethan pulled her to her feet and walked to the massive panes of glass, yanking the curtain back.

Sarah tried to step away.

His hand tightened on hers, moving her until she stood in front of him. "You aren't going to be afraid in my home." Their reflections stared back at her as rain poured and puddled on the balcony. Ethan wrapped his arms around her waist. "He's not here, Sarah. There's no way for him to climb the cliffs."

Sparks of need tingled along her skin as his lips brushed her ear with each word.

"You're safe. The security system is absolutely solid with several backups—not to mention Reece and Bear. Nothing's going to happen to you."

Sarah rested her head against his shoulder, finding peace for the first time in hours.

He reached over and turned off the lamp. The blurry lights of the city twinkled in the rain.

She covered his hands with hers, and their fingers laced. "It really is beautiful."

They stood in silence for several minutes until Ethan finally spoke. "It's been a long night. I'm going to let you get some sleep. I'll be in my room if you need me." He stepped back and she turned.

"Okay."

"See you in the morning," he said, his voice strained.

Sarah moistened her lips, staring into gray eyes gone black in the dim light. "Ethan," she whispered as she rested her hand on his chest, his heart pounding against her palm.

His jaw clenched as he reached up, grabbing her wrist.

She needed to be with him, needed to be lost in him.

He wanted her. She was sure of it. It was there for her to see. Stepping forward, closing the distance, she brushed his lips with hers. "Don't say no." She moved in again, her gaze never leaving his as her mouth touched his.

Ethan's hand held her in a vise grip before he surrendered, yanking her against him, his tongue diving deep.

Jitters of anticipation flittered in her stomach as a hungry groan escaped his throat. She wrapped her arms around his neck, ready for what he would bring.

He moved his hands along the waist of her dress, down to her hips, and back up as he captured her mouth with a nip of teeth. He freed the barrette from her hair and tugged until her head fell back.

Lips and tongue assaulted her neck as a rise of heat flashed through her system. She wanted the flames, wanted to burn. As he moved to her collarbone, Sarah unbuttoned his shirt, pulling it free of his slacks. Her fingers traced his muscled skin, making him quiver.

He yanked the white button-down from his arms, tossing it to the floor. His gaze stayed on hers, his eyes intense, promising more, while he flicked the spaghetti straps from her shoulders, and her dress pooled at her feet. His mouth followed the path the soft fabric took, torturously slow as he left a trail of warm, open-mouthed kisses against the swells of her breasts, sending shivers along her skin.

He pulled her backless bra free and she lost her breath, reeling, as he nibbled and licked her nipples in equal measure. Helpless whimpers escaped her as she clutched at his shoulders, drowning in the moment of pleasure.

Ethan took her mouth again, walking her backwards. Her thighs met mattress, and he laid her back, joining her on the bed, pressing her to the navy blue comforter with his weight. Tongues tangled and teeth grazed as her sensitized skin rubbed against the heat of his chest. She wanted more, craving everything.

On a snappy whip of power, she ran her hands over his muscled biceps and back, eager to feel him, eager to touch as he touched her. She reached for his belt, ready.

He grabbed her hand as his breath heaved. "Not yet." He skimmed his mouth along the valley of her breasts, against her ribcage, nibbling at her hips, setting her aflame. Her breath shuddered in and out as he stared into her eyes, sending her a wolfish grin as he pulled her white panties down her legs.

"Ethan." God, she needed him, couldn't stand to wait a second longer. But he rained kisses over her calves, her thighs. "Ethan," she whimpered as he whispered his palms along her skin, brushing two fingers over her, tracing as she rocked against his hand, her body reaching for release, straining.

He pressed, rubbing in gentle circles, sending waves of sensation through her core until she felt the clutch and cried out, erupting. He sunk his fingers deep, and she shuddered, trying to catch her breath before his rhythmic motion sent her flying again.

Crawling forward, he straddled her hips and pulled off his shoes, throwing them to the floor. She traced him through his slacks, playing her palm against him. He closed his eyes on a hiss of breath and fisted his hands at his sides. "God, Sarah."

She fiddled with his belt buckle, unbuttoned, unzipped, freeing him from his boxers. Cool fingers caressed hot, hard skin and she gripped him, moving, making his stomach muscles shudder.

Ethan moved fast, his mouth taking hers as he pulled

off his pants, his boxers, his socks, and nestled himself between her legs. He hovered over her as their gazes locked.

She brushed a hand through his short hair and smiled.

He smiled back, slowly, as he captured her lips tenderly and stole her heart. He skimmed her cheek, caressing her skin with his knuckles. "I've been waiting, Sarah, waiting for this. I've wanted you for so long."

Undone by his sweetness, Sarah pulled his mouth to hers as he entered her slowly. She shuddered as pleasure careened through her center, and she stroked her fingers along his back as her hips moved with him, rocking to the lazy pace he set. With every gentle thrust, she sighed then moaned, clutching around him, going over.

He nuzzled her neck and grazed her jaw before he stared into her eyes shuddering, groaning, following her over the edge.

~~~~

Ethan stared down at Sarah as she trembled and gasped for air. He'd never seen anything as beautiful as Sarah lost in passion. Cheeks flushed, blue eyes glowing, she continued to trace her fingers along his spine. He'd wanted her here, just like this, for so long.

She smiled. "I'm glad you didn't say no."

He smiled back and kissed the tip of her nose. "I couldn't have." He rolled from her body to his back.

She yanked the covers up, pulling them to her chin.

Surprised, Ethan looked at her. "Cold or shy?"

"Cold."

He got under the blankets and tugged her against him.

She nestled into his side and closed her eyes on a yawn. "No offense, but I'm about to be the one who orgasms, rolls over, and falls asleep. That's supposed to be your job."

He chuckled and rubbed the smooth skin of her arm. "Go ahead and get some rest."

"Don't leave me, okay? The last time I slept well, you were with me."

"I'm not going anywhere." He glanced down when Sarah didn't respond. She was already out. He continued to move his hand along her arm as he studied her stunning face finally relaxed in sleep, thinking of what they'd brought each other.

He'd been foolish to think they could go backwards, that he could keep things the same by ignoring the last few weeks. From the moment his lips met hers in the moonlight, he'd known this was where they would end up. He'd changed things, and there was nowhere to go but forward, there was nowhere he wanted to go but forward. She was everything he convinced himself he could never have. So now that he had her, why was he worried? Why did he want to push her away?

He thought back to the party and his mother walking to the garden shed with her latest lover, of Wren's casual shrug at their parents' constant indiscretions, wondering if he was capable of anything more than what he'd watched all his life. Sarah said he was nothing like them, but could he be sure?

Looking back on his track record with relationships, he'd hardly done better. He had never cheated on a lover, but he'd never stuck with one long enough to see where it would go. He wasn't made that way. 'Fast and fun and no one gets hurt' had always been his motto, but that wouldn't be enough for Sarah. He didn't want that for her. He didn't want that for himself, but when it came down to it, was he able to give her anything more? Could he spend night after night with the same woman, building a life with her? If it was Sarah, he wanted to believe so, but what if he couldn't?

Staring up at the ceiling, he thought back to the tiki bar, remembering the hurt that moved into her blue eyes. He'd done that. Each time they tried to be something more than friends, he hurt her. Would that be all he could give her? He was very afraid it was.

~~~~

The warm sun on her skin blazed bright through the open windows. Well rested for the first time in too long, Sarah stretched and smiled, feeling the soft cotton sheets against her naked body. Her smile turned to a satisfied smirk as well used muscles protested. She finally opened her eyes, glancing to her side and frowned. He was gone. "Ethan?" Sitting up, Sarah swung her legs over the bed and almost stepped on the dogs. "Morning, guys. Where's your dad?"

Tails thumped when she bent to give them each a rub. She focused on the bedside clock, and her eyes widened at the time. "Eleven-twenty? No wonder." Less concerned now, she moved into the bathroom and reached for her robe.

Walking down the stairs, she knotted the blue tie in place, winding her way toward Ethan's office. She stood in the doorway as he talked on the phone, bare-chested in workout shorts. Her heart beat faster and her stomach curled tight as she studied his spectacular face, watching his lips and tongue curve around words while he spoke fluent Italian. Dark stubble covered his jaw, lending a sharp look to his already rawboned cheeks. He ran a hand through his black hair and glanced up, holding up a finger.

"Io vi richiamera. Grazie." He hung up.

She stepped into the room. "I love listening to you speak in one of your many languages. It sounds so exotic. It's very sexy." She expected a smile, but he only stared at her. Suddenly self-conscious, she brushed a strand of hair behind her ear. "Am I interrupting?"

"No, I'm just checking in with the foreign branches."

"Oh." Why was this so awkward after what they'd shared last night? Unable to read his eyes, she walked toward him.

He closed a file on the desk and stood. "Did you get yourself something to eat? You must be hungry."

She stopped in front of him and smiled, running her finger over the stubble on his jaw. "I'm hungry, but not for food."

He pulled her finger from his face, placing her hand in his as he blew out a breath. "Now's not a good time. I have a lot of work to do."

Sarah tugged her hand from his, recognizing his irritated tone. "Sorry. I'll let you get back to it then."

He sat down without saying anything further.

She got to the door and turned.

He closed his file again. "

Are we back here already, Ethan?"

He glanced at his watch then looked at her. "Where's that?"

"That's what I want to know."

"Look, I'm expecting a call from Milan in ten minutes. Let's talk later."

Perilously close to tears, she nodded and walked off. Halfway down the hall, she stopped, needing to know one thing, although she feared she already did. She made her way back to his office, staring as Ethan sat with his elbows on his desk and his forehead in his hands. "Do you regret last night?"

His gaze snapped up to hers, and the apology was there for her to see.

Shaking her head, she turned and hurried up the stairs to her room and straight for the bathroom. She twisted the knob for the shower and untied her robe as tears fell down her cheeks. What had happened? How could last night have been a mistake when it meant everything to her? She took a step toward the spray, gasping as Ethan whirled her around. "Why?" she demanded as anger replaced hurt. "Why did you do this? Why did you start all of this if you don't even want me?"

"Don't *want* you? You're all I want, all I've *ever* wanted." He backed her against the granite countertop, crushing his mouth to hers.

Confused, undone, but wanting, she pulled him to her.

He moved back, taking her face in his hands, brushing tears away with his thumbs. "I can't stop thinking about you, Sarah. I've tried everything, but I can't get you out of my mind." He grabbed her at the waist, sitting her on the edge of the counter, nestling himself between her legs. In a flash of a second, his shorts were on the floor and he pushed himself into her.

Sensations careened through her body, and she cried out at flashpoint. Her gaze met his as he took her mouth again. Her gasps intertwined with his ragged breaths as she grabbed his shoulders and wrapped her legs around his waist. He pounded into her, never taking his eyes from hers. When she built and crested on a long moan, he gripped her hips and groaned.

In the echoes of their heavy breathing, they stared at each other.

"Damn it." He pulled away and yanked up his shorts. "Don't you see? This doesn't work."

She shook her head. "What?"

"I can't think straight around you. Every time I look at you, I want you."

She hopped down from the counter on wobbly legs. "The feeling's mutual."

"No, okay? No." He emphasized with his hand as he paced. "I had time to think after you fell asleep. I can't do this to you, Sarah. I'm not made for what you need."

She shook her head, her frustration growing. "I can't keep up with you. 'Let's be more, Sarah.' 'No, let's be friends.' 'I want you, Sarah.' 'Never mind, Sarah.' Which one *is* it?"

He stopped pacing. "The first—no, the third. Fuck! All of them." He walked back and forth again. "What if I can't be faithful to you? What if I can't give you the long haul?"

She grabbed his arm, and he stopped. "I thought we were taking things a day at a time? Where has all of this come from?" She remembered his mother and her newest lover. "Is this about last night, about your parents?"

"Yes. I come from that."

"I've known you for years, Ethan. You're not like them."

"How do you know? You know my track record. I've never dated anyone for more than three months. I'm a lousy gamble, Sarah. You and Kylee need more than that."

Her voice gentled. "Yes, we do, but I'm willing to bet on you."

"The odds aren't in your favor." He sat on the chair in the corner of the room with his head in his hands.

"Why is this bothering you so much all of a sudden? I know you've never been pleased with the situation, but this is really eating at you."

He looked at the floor. "There was never you. There's never been anyone important enough to worry about messing up."

Sarah stared at the miserable man in the corner so desperately afraid to hurt her, and her heart melted. "I love you."

His gaze flew to hers as he dropped his hands. "God, don't say that."

A glimmer of hope shone in his weary eyes, and everything was all right. She walked to him, kneeling on the floor, taking his face in her hands. "I love you, Ethan."

He rested his forehead on hers. "I love you too."

She smiled and kissed him.

He eased back. "I need to sort this out, Sarah. Let me figure this out so it's good for us, for all three of us."

"Okay."

CHAPTER FIFTEEN

ETHAN WATCHED SARAH FROM HIS OFFICE WINDOW AS SHE played with Bear and Reece in the front yard. Pretty in a light pink t-shirt and jeans, she tossed a toy for the dogs to chase. They each held an end of the bright yellow rubber—covered in drool, no doubt—and brought it back. After each pursuit, they fell at her feet. She bent forward, ponytail bouncing, and rubbed their canine bellies into ecstasy.

He turned from the happy scene on the lawn, looking at his desk, clenching his jaw as he stared at copies of the letters Sarah had received during the week-and-a-half she'd been living with him. Each note, written in blood-red ink, was more vulgar than the last, promising her in one sickening way or another the ultimate pleasure before her death. It appeared to both him and the police that her stalker escalated each day she spent behind the protective walls of his estate.

The perpetrator no longer bothered to hide that he was the 'Blue Chip Rapist.' He raped and murdered a woman every day, sending L.A. County into a panic, putting the police force on high alert.

Sarah remained unaware of what went on outside his home, blissfully ignorant to the fact that every woman murdered was a replacement for her. Kylee was due back in seventy-two hours, and he had no idea how to tell Sarah that it would be best if she continued to stay away. She'd marked the last eleven days off on her calendar with Kylee's arrival date circled in pink and purple with a big happy face. He wanted Kylee home as much as she did, so they would have to find a way.

Perhaps Hunter and Morgan would be willing to move in for a while when they arrived back on Saturday. He imagined Hailey should come along too. It would be a full house, but everyone at risk would be under one roof, making protection easier for him and his associates.

Ethan glanced outside again just in time to see Sarah and the dogs heading in. He closed the file as the front door shut. Paws and footsteps made their way down the hall toward his office.

Sarah knocked on the doorframe and poked her head in, the scent of the sea and wildflowers following her into the room. Cheeks rosy from fresh air and exercise accentuated the bright blue of her eyes. She smiled and staggered him with her beauty. "Hey, I need to call Lisa down at *Celebrity*. Then I'll make us some lunch if you want. I've been starved all day."

"You don't have to wait on me, Sarah."

She walked to his desk. "Making you a sandwich isn't exactly butler service." Her hand snagged his, pulling him toward the door.

"What are you doing? I thought you were going to call Lisa."

"It can wait. I feel like I haven't seen you in ages, and we live in the same house."

Ethan had been careful to give himself plenty of space. After their discussion last week, he'd needed it. She loved him. Her declaration thrilled and terrified him in equal measure. His feelings for her were so big, so all consuming, they overwhelmed and shook him to the core. Sarah had been more relaxed and easy in the eleven days since she'd told him while he'd become more uptight and concerned. The stakes were high. He couldn't mess this up.

Sarah tugged again, heading backward down the hall. "Let's see... I can do sandwiches, pasta and shrimp salad, or we can heat up the chicken from last night." The phone in her office started ringing, and she paused.

He caught her around the waist, almost bumping into her, and his hand flew up to the wall before they slammed into it. "How about you go get that, and I'll heat up the chicken from last night."

"I'll be quick." Sarah dashed off toward her office.

~~~~

Lunging across the desk, Sarah grabbed the phone. "Sarah Johnson."

"Sarah, it's Jarrod down at *Celebrity*."

"Hey, Jarrod." She sat in her plush office chair and began doodling on a piece of scrap paper. "I was just about to call Lisa. I need to schedule a time to come in and check on details for the big photo shoot coming up."

"Good luck with that one. Things have been busy with the special edition we're attempting to put together for Monday. It's been hell around here trying to get bios on all the victims. He's killing them faster than we can come up with copy."

She frowned and stopped drawing the antennae on her smiling butterfly. "What are you talking about?"

"You know, 'The Blue Chip Rapist.' That's why I'm calling, actually. I'm hoping you can provide me with an insider statement—colleague to colleague. One of my sources close to the investigation revealed there may be a correlation between your case and the recent attacks on the women of L.A. County."

The pencil fell from her numb hand. "What?"

"My source tells me you continue to receive threats mailed to both your home address and the address of..." Papers rustled in the background "...Ethan Cooke. Can you confirm this? Is Ethan Cooke Security in charge of your personal protection at this time?"

Jarrod's voice buzzed in her ear as he continued on. Her heart pounded and her hands trembled as she hung up. Turning in her chair to her computer, she typed in the web address for the *L.A. Times.* The page loaded instantly, and she stared at fourteen blonde haired, blue-eyed faces similar to her own. The headline read, 'L.A. County Crisis: Victim Count Continues to Rise.' "Oh, my God." Sick to her stomach, she pushed back from the desk, almost knocking over the chair.

Her breath rushed in and out as she hurried into Ethan's office. He had to have the notes Jarrod spoke of. With hands that shook, she opened file folder after file folder, shoving them off the desk until the photocopies of blood red ink on cardstock stopped her dead. Her legs buckled at the thickness of the stack and she sat before she fell.

One by one, she picked up the paper and read. 'With their last breath I think of you;' 'She was almost perfect, but she wasn't you;' 'When they scream, I call out your name.' She flipped to the next sheet and stared. 'I'll never stop until I have you.' Sarah stood, knowing that was the absolute truth. He would keep killing until he had her.

For almost two weeks she'd closed out the world, pretending the ugliness in her life didn't exist. While she'd sat back in her cocoon, fourteen women had paid. She ran from Ethan's office, up to her room, grabbing her purse and took off for the driveway. There had to be something she could do.

~~~~

Ethan carried two steaming plates of chicken, peppers, and brown rice down the hall and stopped when the front door slammed. Frowning, he walked into his office, staring at the mess covering the floor, spotting the file open on his desk and copies of cardstock lying in two piles. "Shit! Fuck!" He turned to go find Sarah and watched her run past the window with car keys in hand. "Sarah!" Plates fell with a crash as he took off through the house at a sprint. He whipped the door open as she stepped from grass to concrete. "Sarah, stop!"

She glanced behind but kept going.

"Hey!" He accelerated forward, catching her by the arm as she made it to the blue sedan.

"Let me go!" She struggled against him.

"That's enough."

"They're dying!" She whirled and pushed him. "They're dying because of me!"

He grabbed her wrists, shocked by the venom spewing. "They're dying because of *him*." He held on tighter as she fought to free herself from his grip.

"No! Have you seen their pictures? There are so many pictures. Why didn't you tell me?" She shoved at him again as tears poured down her cheeks.

"Stop it!" He pulled her body to his, immobilizing her, standing nose to nose as he gave her a shake. "What good would it have done? There's nothing you can do to stop this, Sarah, absolutely nothing."

"How do I deal with this, knowing that each time he takes a woman away from her child or husband, mother or father, it's because he couldn't get to me?" Sobbing, she fell to her knees.

He knelt down in front of her, staring into

devastated eyes, taking her chin between his fingers, desperate to make her understand. "You keep reminding yourself that you're just a madman's excuse to do what he would've done anyway. If it wasn't you, Sarah, it would've been someone else. I can promise you that."

Weeping, she shook her head. "I want this to be over."

"I know." He pulled her close in a hug, kissing her hair. "I know."

She wrapped her arms around his waist. "I miss my baby, Ethan. I need her here with me."

His heart ached from the agony echoing in her voice, in each racking sob. "Just a couple more days, and we'll all be together again."

"Oh, that sounds so good. I'm counting on it."

He held on to her as she soaked his shirt with tears, until her weeping turned to deep shuddering breath. He closed his eyes, wishing he could make it all go away.

Several minutes later, Sarah moved her head, staring into his eyes. "Kylee will be safe here, right?"

Her eyes were red rimmed and swollen, her face blotchy and wet with tears, and he couldn't have loved her more. "You'll both be as safe as I can possibly make you." He kissed her lips and wrinkled his nose. "You're salty."

She gave him a watery laugh.

He smiled before it disappeared. "Where were you going?"

She glanced down then met his gaze again. "To the police station. I wanted to see if there was something I could do to help."

"Going off alone won't help anyone. You staying safe and giving them one less person to worry about will. That's all you can do. Please don't try anything like that again." He took her face in his hands. "You scared me."

She closed her eyes, nestling into his hold. "I'm sorry."

He helped her to her feet. "Are you feeling any better?"

Her lip wobbled. "Not really. Fourteen women are still dead. Unless they catch him soon, there's bound to be more."

There would be more, Ethan had no doubt. "We'll keep hoping they get him." Unless he got to him first. Either option worked for him. He wrapped his arm around Sarah's waist, pulling her close and changed the subject, wanting her to think of happier things, normal, everyday things. "Let's go back inside and find something to eat. I'm willing to bet Bear and Reece made quick work of the meal I left all over the floor."

She chuckled, resting her head on his shoulder

"There should be enough chicken if we want to try again," he said against her hair.

"Sounds good to me. Then I have a big mess to clean up in your office."

"We'll save that fun for later. Let's get out of here for a while. We should probably hit the grocery store. My house is about to be invaded."

"Invaded? Kylee and Hailey don't eat that much."

"Morgan and Hunter will be joining us too, and you can bet Austin will wheedle his way into a meal here and there."

Sarah's brow rose. "I guess we do need to get to the store." She kissed his cheek as they stepped inside and shut the door.

~~~~

Zeke followed behind the Rover at a distance. After completing a thorough search of Ethan Cooke's background, he discovered he had an extremely worthy opponent. His adversary had quite the resume—expert in computer forensics, fifth-degree black belt, close protection training at the best facilities in the world. Blah, blah, blah. Even with all that fancy shit, he wasn't worried. It just upped the ante. Master Cooke had to have a weakness. He'd find it and use it to his advantage. That's what he did best.

He pulled into the fast food parking lot across from the grocery store, watching the bastard look around before he got out of his fancy, rich-boy SUV. He walked to Sarah's side and opened her door. She stepped out, and Zeke smiled. It had been *days* since he'd gotten a glimpse of her. She was amazing—perfect in her snug denim jeans and pink t-shirt.

Zeke's smile disappeared as Ethan's well-muscled arm went around her shoulders, pulling her close. Sarah grinned as she wrapped her arm around his waist, hooking her finger through one of the belt loops in his jeans.

"No! You little *bitch!*" He slammed fisted hands against the steering wheel as torrents of breath steamed in and out of his mouth. Oh, she was going to pay for that. "Just wait, Sarah. You just wait." He started the car and crossed over to the grocer's parking lot, parking right next to the Rover, struggling to find his calm through the rage. He closed his eyes and thought of all the painful ways to pay Ethan back for touching what was his. He checked the mirror to be sure he looked like every other Average Joe, got out, and grabbed a cart from the corral.

He moved swiftly into the store, throwing items into his cart at random as he kept an eye on Sarah, careful to go down the same aisles only on occasion. He stopped in the cereal aisle, feet from her and pulled a box of oatmeal from the shelf, pointing at the label as if he were reading the nutritional facts. Turning slightly, he watched her out of the corner of his eye.

Her brow wrinkled. "What's that?"

Ethan smiled, holding a bright red box in his hand. "Cereal for Kylee."

"I don't think so. There's nothing but sugar and chemicals in that."

"Oh, come on, Sarah. She'll love it."

"Absolutely not. She can have oatmeal or Cheerios."

"Absolutely not," Ethan mimicked in an uncomplimentary voice.

Sarah snagged his ear, grinning. "Put those back and grab me a box of Cheerios, Cooke."

He moved in close and nipped her lip. "I love it when you're bossy, Johnson."

They stared at each other, chuckling before Ethan switched out the cereal then snuck his thumb in the back pocket of Sarah's jeans as they moved down the aisle, disappearing into the next.

Zeke crushed the side of the box he held, fighting the urge to clear everything from the shelf. *Slut! Fucking slut!* Oh, he couldn't wait to get his hands on her. He would show her what happened to ho-bags who couldn't keep their legs closed. It was time to finish this. He had the taser in his trunk. If he took Dick Face out, he could grab Sarah and teach her a lesson she wouldn't soon forget—but then she'd be dead, so it wouldn't matter much anyway.

Working out his plan, he walked away from his cart, making his way toward the parking lot. He stopped at the automatic doors and bit the inside of his cheek, drawing blood as Sarah and Ethan placed groceries on the belt while they spoke to the fucking tank of a man, Austin Casey, who usually stood guard over her. Zeke had done his homework on that dildo too.

It's ruined! It's all ruined! There was no doubt in his mind he was smarter and stronger than both muscled-freaks put together, but he couldn't tase them at the same time. They were all going to have to die. He glanced back at Sarah once more and left, dreaming of revenge. He slammed his car door and drove to the fast food parking lot for the second time, waiting for Sarah, Ethan, and the giant to load up the Rover, cursing them. When the fancy red sports convertible took a left and Ethan turned right, Zeke started his car. A movement in his rearview mirror made him stop.

A tiny blonde dressed in a black uniform pulled an overflowing trash barrel toward the back of the restaurant into the shadows of dusk. A smile ghosted his mouth as his pecker grew hard. Change of plans.

He backed into the alley next to the massive dumpster, careful to hide his vehicle from the view of the drive-through and got out, opening his trunk, grabbing his supplies, then moved through the back fence silently. The stench of rotting trash mixed with the tinge of cigarette smoke curling in the air.

The blonde took another drag, and he moved forward, pulling the taser's trigger. The woman let out a muffled scream and fell to the ground, stiff from the current coursing through her body. "This is your lucky day, bitch." He bent forward, pummeling his fist into her face, imagining it was Sarah's. Adrenaline soared as he whipped down his jeans. He'd never done it like this before. Anyone could walk out here and catch him. He yanked down her black pants, rubbered-up, and slammed himself into her as she began to stir. Her eyes flew open and he smiled down. "You make a noise and you're dead." He picked up the wire he'd brought along and wrapped it around her neck. "Oh, wait, you're dead anyway."

He pulled while she desperately clawed at her neck. He no longer saw the woman fighting for her life, but Sarah in her pink t-shirt. "This is what happens when you spread your legs, whore. Why did you let him touch you? I'm the only one who's allowed to touch you." Through his blinding rage, he came.

The blonde no longer moved. Her eyes, blank and opened wide, stared into nothing.

"That wasn't half bad." He gave her ass a slap as he removed the bloodied rubber from himself, keeping it in his hand. He wouldn't be leaving any DNA behind. He tugged up his pants, grabbed his taser, and went back to his car. As he pulled away from the alley, he thought of Sarah.

CHAPTER SIXTEEN

THE GROCERIES HAD LONG SINCE BEEN PUT AWAY AND THE mess in the office cleaned. Ethan sat on the deck in the warm ocean breeze, watching the flicker of candlelight play over Sarah's face. The smooth, jazzy sounds of John Mayer played through the stereo as she dipped lobster tail in butter and brought the dripping morsel to his lips. He pulled the tips of her fingers in his mouth along with the meat, sucking, staring into her eyes.

She smiled. "I can't feed you another bite if you don't give me my fingers back."

"Your turn." He plucked a bright red strawberry from a bowl, holding it to her lips.

She bit in and rolled her eyes. "Mmm, good."

"The whole meal's amazing. You did a great job, Sarah."

"It was the least I could do after trashing your office." She stacked plates and stood.

"Uh, uh." He placed a hand over hers, halting her movements. "We'll get this later."

"But I made dessert."

"Later," he repeated, standing, pulling her with him to the center of the floor. "Right now, I want to dance with you in the moonlight."

"A perfect end to a perfect evening." Her hair and pale green sundress billowed in the wind as she settled her arms around his neck.

"We're just getting started," he promised, breathing in Sarah's summer scent as he held her around the waist, skimming her jaw with his lips. "I like being with you like this." He rained kisses along her neck. "Just the two of us." He brushed his mouth against her shoulders. "With our own private view of the ocean and city lights."

"Mmm." Her fingers played over his skin, tensing.

He met her gaze as a dozen candles reflected in her eyes and her beauty staggered. Wanting nothing more than to be with her, he covered her mouth with a tender brush of his lips.

She stopped the gentle massage against the back of his neck as her tongue met his.

He took her face in his hands, deepening the kiss, while they swayed in a lazy circle. Their mouths grew hungry as he walked her back to the sturdy rail of the balcony, pressing her against it. He nibbled her bottom lip as he cupped her breasts through fabric.

Her breathing grew unsteady as her mouth met his once more then moved to his neck, his ear, tracing her tongue along his lobe, sending a shiver of need down his spine.

Craving to feel her against his hands, he tugged on her strapless top and flicked the clasp on her bra, exposing her breasts. He feathered caresses against her nipples, circling, watching them pebble as she closed her eyes, letting her head fall back.

"Ethan," she murmured on a husky whisper.

His mouth replaced fingers, and she moaned, running her hands through his hair.

Greedy fingers traveled down to the hem of his shirt and pulled up. He held his arms high as she removed his black t-shirt, letting it fall where they stood. Her palms roamed over his muscled shoulders and back while she left open-mouthed kisses along his skin.

He clenched his jaw as his need grew, wanting to

taste her and watch her come undone. He knelt before her, trailing fingers up smooth thighs, snagging her panties. Giving a tug, the swatch of lace landed at her ankles. He hiked her dress high, grabbed her ass, jerking her forward, pressing his mouth against her and she gasped.

She gripped the railing as his tongue stroked and circled with light flicks until she trembled. Throaty purrs escaped her throat and her hips rocked as he assaulted her system with steadier pressure before his fingers dove deep.

She clutched his hair as he quickened his rhythm then she stiffened, her legs buckling as she throbbed, pulsing against him, crying out.

Ethan locked his arm around her, holding her in place as he continued, relentless with teeth, tongue, and fingers, ready to explode as her gasps and moans grew wild and desperate, while he watched her be consumed by wave after wave of ecstasy.

She gripped his shoulders, breathless, and he made his way up her slender body, her breasts brushing his chest, her eyes glazed with passion, driving him mad. He had to be inside her.

Sarah unsnapped his jeans and pulled at the zipper. Before she could do more, he boosted her up and her legs wrapped around his waist. Their lips met, devouring, as he walked toward his bedroom. He would have her in his bed where she belonged.

He turned, landing on the mattress with her straddling him. Their tongues danced as he moved his hips, helping her free him of his pants. He pulled her dress over her head, and she stared into his eyes as she sat back, taking him deep.

His rush of breath mingled with her gasp as she

began to move slowly. Wet and warm, Sarah rocked against him while moonlight washed over her skin from the skylights, casting her in an ethereal glow. He laced their fingers, watching her climb. Her stomach muscles quivered on each ragged breath as she pulled him deeper with each movement. Her hands clutched against his as she arched and closed her eyes, tensing on a stunned cry.

Lost in her, captivated, Ethan could only stare.

Sarah smiled, her gaze meeting his as she moved, rocking, sliding, up and down. She bent forward, her breasts brushing against him, her lips capturing his.

He took her face, needing to tell her. "I love you, Sarah. God, do I love you."

Before she could speak, he rolled, reversing their positions, unable to handle her achingly slow loving. He set a fevered pace, and she clutched at his hips while he stared into blue eyes glowing in the moonlight and fisted his hands in her mass of blonde hair. He struggled for each gasp of air, ready, holding on, waiting for her.

Her breath came faster, mingling with his as she worked herself to the top. She tensed on her way over, her eyes never leaving his. Their mouths met, swallowing each other's moans as he filled her.

~~~~

Four days later, chaos reigned at the Cooke house. Kylee screamed with delight as Bear and Reece lay on their backs, tails wagging against the grass while she petted them. Hunter and Ethan spoke as the grill heated for a barbeque. Hailey and Morgan set the table on the lower deck while Sarah hurried around the kitchen, trying to prepare food for the army of people now living in Ethan's home.

Ethan swung through the door. "I'll be in to grab the chicken and steaks in about ten minutes. Does that work for you?"

Giving the potato salad a final stir, she glanced up. "Yeah, that's fine. After I take care of the watermelon, things should be good in here."

He winked and grinned then stepped back out.

She smiled, completely happy. Her baby was home, friends that meant everything surrounded her, and she was desperately in love. After the night on the deck, they'd spent their last two days of quiet wrapped up in each other.

Ethan had relaxed, becoming more comfortable with his feelings. He hadn't said he loved her since their night of candlelight and lobster tail, but she didn't need the words. She *knew* how he felt. Snagging her lip between her teeth, she smiled again, remembering his gray eyes staring into hers while he told her, sending jittery waves of pleasure coursing through her belly. Shaking her head, focusing on the moment, she got back to work, balling the melon for the fruit salad she'd made.

Ethan strolled in. "Yum, watermelon." He grabbed for a piece, and she slapped his hand.

"You'll have to wait for dinner."

He snagged her around the waist and nuzzled her neck. "What if we share?"

Grinning, she plucked up a pink ball and turned in his arms, biting the piece in half, popping the rest in his mouth. "Don't tell Kylee. I told her she had to wait."

"I'm not sure if I can do that. I do take bribes though." He closed his eyes, puckered up.

She chuckled and met his lips. His tongue darted into her mouth, sweet from the fruit. What started in play soon turned hungry. The melon baller fell to the floor with a clatter as she moved her palms over his back jean pockets.

His hand snaked up to capture her breast.

"Hey, what's the hold... What the fuck?"

Sarah and Ethan jumped apart as Hunter stood in the doorway.

"Cooke, what are you fucking doing?"

Ethan's smoldering eyes meet Hunter's. "I'm kissing Sarah."

Hunter looked at her next. "Sarah?"

Guilty for the surprise and hurt she saw on his face, she started toward him. "I'm sorry, Hunter."

Ethan whirled her around. "Don't you say you're sorry. We have nothing to be sorry for."

Morgan and Hailey rushed into the kitchen, and Morgan clutched Hunter's arm. "What's going on in here?"

"I came in to ask about the food and found Ethan with his hands all over Sarah and his tongue down her throat."

Ethan took a step forward. "That's enough."

"It's hardly enough, you asshole. How could you do this to Jake? It's always about the pussy with you."

Gasps echoed before Ethan dove forward, punching Hunter on the jaw. They landed on the floor, swearing, rolling, blocking punches as fast as they threw them. Two well-muscled bodies slammed into the counter. Potato salad crashed against marble tiles, and the dogs came running. Hair up and teeth bared, they growled.

"Hold!" Ethan shouted at them.

Bear and Reece continued to threaten but didn't lunge forward.

Kylee followed the mastiffs into the room and began to cry. "Ethan! Unke Hunte!"

217

Hailey picked her up and left.

Heart pounding and horrified, Sarah moved into the thick of things, pulling at whoever's shirt she could grab. "Stop this! Stop right now! You've just scared Kylee!"

Hunter landed a blow to Ethan's mouth before Ethan rammed Hunter's head against the floor.

Morgan walked forward with a massive bowl of cold water and poured it on top of the grappling men. They broke apart, eyeing each other, gasping.

Morgan crouched close to Hunter. "What is your *problem*? What are you *thinking*?"

"He was—"

She held up a hand. "I don't want to hear it. I don't even want to look at you right now. You clean yourself up and stay out of my face." She stormed out of the room.

Hunter got up, shook his head at Sarah, and went after his wife.

Sarah stared down at Ethan as he wiped blood from his puffing lip. "Are you okay?"

He sat up. "Yeah, I'm fine."

She walked toward the freezer. "Let me get you some ice."

"No. I need to check on Kylee and make sure she's not afraid of me."

She grabbed his arm as he started passed her. "I'll talk to Hunter, Ethan. I should've talked to him about this weeks ago."

"I'll take care of it. I want to change and clean up my lip before I see Kylee." He didn't look at her as he walked away.

Sarah rushed out to the porch where Hailey held Kylee as Ethan left. "I'm so sorry, Hailey."

"It's okay. I think she's okay too. She's just a little

shaken up."

Sarah took Kylee from Hailey's arms. "Hi, baby."

Kylee hugged her tight.

"Why don't we go upstairs and read with Mr. Ruff."

Kylee nodded. "O-tay, Mama."

Sarah walked up the stairs with her daughter, trying to figure out how to fix this mess she helped make. She set Kylee down in the guest room, now crowded with toys and books. The day before Kylee came home, she and Ethan gathered and boxed most of her things. When they'd returned to Ethan's, he'd surprised her by clearing out a spare room, telling her he would be turning the space into a playroom with Wren's help. "What should we read, honey?"

Kylee walked to her bag, grabbing *Fuzzy Wuzzy Goes to the Park*. "Dis one."

Sarah smiled. "Bring it on over." She pulled Kylee onto the bed and rested her back on the pillows, snuggling Kylee against her.

"Knock, knock." Ethan stood in the doorway, his eyes guarded.

"Ethan!" Kylee scrambled down, running with her arms out.

He scooped her up and hugged her close. "Hi, kiddo."

Kylee pulled back, touching her little fingers to the raw wound on his swollen lip. "Boo-boo. I kiss it." She puckered tiny lips, pressing them against his. She smiled at him. "All better."

He hugged her tight again, closing his eyes for an instant. "Thank you. It feels much better." His gaze met Sarah's, and she held out her hand.

He walked toward the bed still holding Kylee and clasped his fingers with hers.

Sarah smiled up at him and relaxed. "Come read with us."

He let go of her. "I should probably—"

"Sit down and read with us," she interrupted.

"Ethan, read Fuzzy Wuzzy to me."

"Okay." He held Sarah's gaze for another moment then sat on the bed.

They settled back against the pillows, holding Kylee between them. He took her hand again, and Sarah closed her eyes when his lips brushed her forehead. She laced her fingers with his and rested her head on his shoulder.

He wrapped his arm around Kylee while she held the book in her hands, settling her head against his chest.

Savoring the moment, Sarah smiled, listening to Ethan's deep voice add expression to the words, delighting her daughter.

Minutes later, Hunter appeared in the doorway, a bruise blooming on his jaw. Her eyes locked with his before his gaze traveled over the three of them, settling on her fingers still twined with Ethan's. "There's a call from Europe. It's urgent."

Ethan's fingers tensed on hers. "I have to take this."

"Of course. Go."

"Unke Hunte!" Kylee scrambled out of her and Ethan's hold and ran to Hunter.

Ethan brushed past Hunter as Hunter knelt down to Kylee's level. "Hi, baby girl."

"I a big girl, Unke Hunte."

He grinned. "Yes, you are. I keep forgetting."

Kylee pressed her fingers into his knotted purple bruise and he winced. "You boo-boo too."

Hunter traced the welt before he looked up at Sarah. "Yeah, I have a boo-boo."

"I kiss and make it better, just like Ethan." She

puckered up and kissed his jaw. "All better. I feed Mr. Ruff now." She walked over to the stuffed dog and sat on the floor with the pretend bottle.

Hunter stood, rocking on his heels. "Hey."

Sarah patted the bed. "Come sit down."

Running tongue over teeth, he sat, staring at her.

They began to speak at the same time.

"Please, Hunter, let me."

"Okay, shoot."

"I'm so sorry I didn't tell you about Ethan and me. I certainly should have."

"I'll admit I never saw this one coming."

She looked down, picking at the navy blue comforter. "You think I'm letting Jake down."

"No, I don't." He blew out a breath. "Jake loved you. I know he would want you to be happy."

Eyes watering, she glanced up. "I'm the happiest I've been since he's been gone. I will always love him, Hunter. He'll always be a part of my heart."

He brushed away the tear rolling down her cheek. "I made him a promise, Sarah. I hope you'll let me keep it. I'm connected to you and Kylee."

Overwhelmed by his sweetness, she hugged him and sighed when his arms came around her.

"Ethan is as much my brother as Jake was. I only want the best for both of you."

She brushed his jaw, touching the purple bump gently as she stared into bold blue eyes. "I'm so lucky to have you. I love you so much."

He touched her lips. "I love you too."

"And me too." Kylee stood at his knee.

Sarah chuckled when Hunter bent to her level and gave Kylee a noisy kiss on the cheek. "And you too, big girl."

He stood. "I really have to get downstairs."

"We'll see you in a bit."

~~~~

Ethan hung up as Hunter walked in his office. "David Enzo was shot critically. I have to go to Italy."

Hunter raked a hand through his hair. "Shit. What happened? I'm a little out of the loop."

"He's been providing close protection for Fabiano International's CEO, Nico Fabiano. Apparently Nico discovered major discrepancies in numerous accounts about a month ago. Someone didn't like it. An attempt was made on him an hour ago. David took a bullet to the chest. It missed his heart by millimeters."

"Jesus. What about Nico?"

"He's fine." Ethan stacked files into a briefcase. "I'm heading over now. Tino's covering Fabiano at our safe house until I can get there. I'm hoping you can handle anything Mrs. Enzo will need long distance. She's a mess, understandably."

"Yeah, of course. Why are you going over? Why can't you send someone from one of the European branches?"

"Because I'm the computer geek. If I get into Fabiano's systems, I can get to the bottom of this faster."

"What about Sarah?"

On guard, Ethan stared into Hunter's disapproving gaze. "That's a loaded question, isn't it? We'll have to save personal business for later." Glancing down, he zipped his laptop into its case. "I called Austin. He'll be here in fifteen minutes. You two are going to have to cover her until I get back. I'm hoping I can get this wrapped up in the next couple of weeks."

Hunter walked over and opened the file on his desk,

picking up copied cardstock. "His notes are fucking sick."

"Yeah, they are." Ethan blew out a long breath. "I think he followed Sarah and me to the grocery store the other night, the night the girl was killed behind the restaurant. I talked to Tucker down at the Cop Shop. The timeframe fits. The note sent the next day said, 'I watched him touch you and now you'll pay.' I'm the only person who's been touching her, and that's the only place he could've seen us." He turned to the window, hating that he was about to leave Sarah. "The thing that concerns me most is I never spotted a tail. He knows what he's doing."

"Maybe you weren't paying close enough attention."

Anger burned in his gut, slow and hot. His fist clenched at his side as he turned back to face Hunter. "You may not approve of what's going on between Sarah and me, but don't ever question how I do my fucking job."

Hunter sat in one of the leather chairs opposite the desk. They eyed each other as tension choked the room, until Hunter finally spoke." Let's get this out of the way right now so we can move on. I'll tell you, just like I told Sarah—all I want is what's best for both of you. As much as I love you, man, as much as I think of you as my brother, I'll be honest and say I'm not sure you're what's best for her."

Hunter's words wounded. "Fuck you."

Hunter held up a hand. "Let me finish. She's not like the other women that float in and out of your life. Sarah needs someone who's gonna stick. She's happy. You make her happy. As long as that continues, I wish you two nothing but the best." His eyes hardened. "But if you have any doubts, Cooke, you better figure them out now, before this goes any further, because if you hurt her, I'll break every fucking bone in your body."

They continued to stare at each other as Austin walked in. "Hey."

Neither responded.

"What's going on? Is everything okay with Sarah?"

Ethan glanced at Austin. "Sarah's fine. Thanks for coming so quickly. As I said on the phone, I'll be out of the country for the next couple of weeks—less, I hope. You and Hunter are in charge. Sarah has several photo shoots and meetings coming up, which means we're on red alert. This guy is smart. He knows what he's doing, and he's become extremely volatile. Every day he goes without seeing her appears to make him more unstable. I want a two-man team on her when she leaves the house. Pull Matthews to come stay here with Morgan, Hailey, and Kylee when Sarah goes out."

"Maybe we should just pull Matthews and have him stay here," Austin said as he took the seat next to Hunter.

Hunter shook his head. "I don't think that's necessary. If he could get in, he would've already."

Ethan nodded. "I agree. With the two of you and the dogs, no one's getting to anyone here on the grounds, but outside's a different story. I want you to watch yourselves as well. The profiler I spoke to says anyone seen with Sarah is perceived as an enemy, especially people who are actively trying to keep him from her. The last three victims he's killed, including the girl behind the restaurant, have almost been decapitated. He's sick, escalated, and extremely dangerous." He glanced down at his watch. "I really need to go."

"Don't worry, boss. She'll be safe with Phillips and me."

"I'm counting on it." He looked at Hunter one last time and left the room.

~~~~

Sarah stood next to Ethan's Rover as he shut his trunk and walked to the driver's side. "You be careful over there. I'm going to worry about you." She didn't want him to leave.

He opened the door. "I'll be perfectly fine. I want you to take care of yourself. Stay close to Austin and Hunter when you're not at the house."

"They'll be my shadows." She smiled, wrapping him in a hug.

He held her tight. "I have go, Sarah. I'll miss my flight."

She eased back, keeping her arms around his waist. "I'm going miss you."

"I'll hurry home." He brushed his lips over hers.

She stared into his eyes and worried. Something was different.

All thoughts vanished when he took her face in his hands and pulled her into a kiss. His tongue sought hers, and she held on, reeling, treasuring their last moment until he came home.

As quickly as it began, he pulled away. "I'll see you in a week or two."

"Okay. I-I'll see you then." She hesitated, stopping herself from telling him she loved him. Despite the warm kiss, he seemed distant, as if he'd taken a step back.

Ethan got in his Rover and drove around the circle, giving her a wave. He stopped, hollering out the window, "I'll call when I can."

"Okay."

She watched him until the taillights disappeared down the long drive. Nibbling her lip, Sarah walked toward the front door. What had changed? Everything had seemed fine—normal—while they'd read together with Kylee. He was probably worried about his agent. He'd call her when he could. Everything would be just fine, she tried to tell herself, but in her depths, she couldn't make herself believe it.

~~~~

Ethan waited at the gate with twenty minutes to spare, thinking of Sarah, wanting to stay. If the situation he was walking into wasn't as volatile as the one she faced now, he would've packed her and Kylee up and brought them.

His conversation with Hunter continued to bother him. Was he really wrong for her? Could he stick and be what she needed him to be? He thought of the way they'd been together, of the way it felt when he was with her, and believed he could.

Perhaps the time away would be a good thing. It would give him a chance to clear his head and think everything through. He needed to be sure he was making the best choice for Sarah and himself.

They announced the boarding for his flight, and he turned from the window overlooking the tarmac and stopped. His father and newest mistress strolled to their gate across from his, hand-in-hand. "Son of a bitch. You've got to be fucking kidding me," he muttered. He almost walked to the line forming at the jetway but moved forward instead. What the hell? He'd give Wren's casual approach to their parents' lifestyle a try.

His father's eyes widened and conversation halted when Ethan stopped in front of him. The stunning brunette turned.

"Dad."

"Ethan, what are you doing here?"

He held up his briefcase and carryon. "I have business overseas. And who's this?"

His father's eyes glinted. "Ethan, this is Jessica. Jessica, my son, Ethan."

The brown-eyed beauty smiled invitingly. "Nice to meet you, Ethan."

I'll bet. "So, how's Mom? Does she know you're off to—" he glanced at the departing flight screen—"Milan, or is she too busy with the personal trainer?"

His father gripped his arm, pulling him aside. "What the hell are you doing?"

"What the hell are *you* doing?" Ethan pulled away when his father yanked on his arm again. "You're going to want to let go of me."

He dropped his hand. "Why are you doing this, trying to embarrass me in front of Jessica?"

Ethan scoffed in disgust. "You embarrass yourself. Did you see the look she gave me? She'd just as soon fuck me as you."

His father's cheeks reddened as his fist curled. "That'll be enough." He started to walk away.

"Let me ask you something first. I think you owe me an answer."

Grant blew out a weary breath. "What?"

"Why do you and Mom do this? Why don't you call it quits? In all the years I lived under your roof, on the few occasions Wren and I actually saw the two of you, there wasn't even a pretense of a marriage. So why?"

"Because it works." He shrugged. "We have an image to uphold, and it's easier on the accountants if we stay together."

Ethan pivoted away, revolted.

"We're Cookes, Ethan."

He stopped and turned. "What does that have to do with anything?"

"We're just not marriage material. Never have been, never will be."

Ethan walked toward his gate without looking back, fearful that his father was right.

CHAPTER SEVENTEEN

"SARAH, WAKE UP."

Foggy with sleep, Sarah blinked in the dark as Hunter rubbed her arm. "What is it?"

"You and Kylee need to come with me—right now."

The urgency in his voice cleared away any dredges of fatigue as she focused on Bear and Reece's vicious barking in the distance. She reached over, pulling Kylee into her arms as her heart thundered and she stared up at Hunter. "He's here, isn't he?"

"Just come on." He took her hand, pulling her to her feet, keeping her close.

They walked down the stairs and down the hall. As they passed Ethan's office, she noticed the flashing red lights on the large screen attached to the wall—the security panel for the house. "Oh, God, he *is* here. Where are Morgan and Hailey? Where's Austin?"

"Austin and the dogs are out on a perimeter search. Morgan and Hailey are waiting for us."

Her gaze darted left and right as they passed through the darkened rooms, convinced that the man with the black mask and crazy eyes would jump out at any second.

Hunter stopped in front of the downstairs bathroom closest to Ethan's gym and knocked on the door three times. "It's me, Morgan."

The doorknob rattled as Morgan twisted the lock. When they stepped in, Morgan threw her arms around her. "Oh, thank goodness."

"I want all of you behind the shower wall," Hunter said, locking the door again.

Hailey, already sitting where Hunter asked, gave Sarah a weak smile. "I have a nice big towel we can cover Kylee with. It's super soft."

"Thanks, honey." She sat against the granite wall of the massive walk-through shower, clutching Kylee close. "I'm sorry I've gotten you into this mess."

Hailey gave her knee a squeeze. "This isn't your fault, and I'm safer here with you than I am on my own." She handed over the creamy white bath towel, big enough to cover all three of them.

Sarah tucked it around her sleeping daughter as she looked at Morgan. "What's going on, exactly?"

"You need to whisper or stop talking," Hunter said, pressing an earpiece into place. "I have to be able to hear Austin."

"Sorry." Sarah watched as Hunter murmured into his mike, spreading out a blueprint, using the dim glow of a nightlight to read it by. All traces of the loving friend she'd known for years were gone. The serious man with deadly eyes sitting on the opposite side of the room was in full work mode.

Morgan whispered, "Someone tried to deactivate the alarm at the front gate, and a sensor went off on the west wall. The cops are on their way. Austin and Hunter are in charge until they get here."

Flashes of the police officer laying beaten and unconscious in her yard played through Sarah's mind. "What if he hurts Austin?"

Morgan took her hand. "Austin's going to be fine. Bear and Reece won't let anything happen to him."

"Austin? Austin?" Hunter pressed on his earpiece as he spoke into his mike again. "Austin, do you copy?"

Seconds passed, but Hunter didn't speak. He pulled a gun from the waistband of his shorts, sliding the rack.

Oh, God, not Austin. He hurt Austin. Sarah struggled to keep her breathing steady as nausea roiled in her stomach. She pulled Kylee closer, instinctively rocking, and exchanged a glance with Morgan.

Hailey slid up to Sarah's side, gripping her arm with unsteady fingers.

"Austin, answer me, damn it."

A shadow moved past the door and Hunter stood. He pressed his finger to his mouth as he leaned against the wall closest to the door, taking the position of gun against chest like Sarah had seen in so many cop shows.

Concentrating on bringing air in through her nose and out through her mouth, Sarah braced against her own trembling, fearful she would wake Kylee.

Footsteps and paws approached moments later, stopping. "Green light, Phillips."

Hunter uncocked the gun, swearing as he yanked the door open. "What the fuck, Austin? I radioed you several times."

"I figured as much, but something jammed the signal. The cops are here combing the shit out of this place—inside too. I was hoping you weren't going to get trigger happy and start shooting."

Hunter's brow rose as Austin smiled. "We'll stay in here until we get the all clear." He opened the door wider, letting Austin and the dogs in. Bear and Reece, still on full alert, paced the spacious room until Austin gave them a command: "Relax." They lay down immediately, ears still perked, panting.

Several minutes later, Detective Tucker Campbell stepped into the bathroom. "There's no one here. The house is tight and secure; so are the grounds. Ethan has a very impressive setup. He puts our SuperMax facilities to shame."

Hunter grinned. "That's Ethan. He doesn't mess around."

"Can I speak to you for a moment?"

Hunter and Austin followed him into the hall. After a whispered exchange, they returned.

"Morgan, we're going to move to the bedroom across from Ethan's room. Hailey, you're going to sleep in the room Sarah's in now. Sarah, we're going to have you and Kylee stay in Ethan's."

Sarah stood with Kylee, looking at Hunter. "What about Austin? Why is everyone moving around?"

"Austin's going to stay downstairs with the dogs. We'll all sleep better if we're close, and Austin can keep an eye on the monitors."

"Do they think that man tried to get in?"

Austin and Hunter exchanged a glance before Hunter spoke. "They don't believe his intention was to come over the wall, especially after he activated the flood lights by setting off the sensor."

Sarah shifted Kylee in her arms and leaned against the counter. "Why then?"

"Mind games. He wants you to feel like he can get to you anywhere."

Closing her eyes, she shuddered. Wasn't it only a matter of time?

Austin moved to her side. "He can't, Sarah—not here, and he knows it. You're still safe here. Don't give him the satisfaction of worrying about it for one second."

"I'll try." But she would. Her stalker would never stop until he had what he wanted. The notes she had read said as much. The madness she'd seen staring back at her through the window left no doubt.

Kylee stirred, and Sarah rocked, kissing her forehead. "Shh," she whispered, "go back to sleep, honey." Kylee settled and slept on.

Sarah glanced at her friends, concentrating on the fierce look in Hunter's eyes, at the concern in Morgan and Hailey's, and quiet encouragement in Austin's. They were all here for her, because of her. There was nothing she could do to change the situation, and she was ultimately as safe as anyone could make her. Struggling to shove her terrorizing thoughts away, she tried to ignore the clutch of fear in her stomach as she concentrated on keeping the tremors that wanted to rack her body at bay. The dull throb of a headache was slowly hammering at her temples. She suddenly craved her bed and the quiet, wanting the oblivion of sleep, hopeful that for even just a little while, she could pretend this wasn't happening.

An hour later, after both Hailey and Morgan were settled in their new rooms, Sarah lay awake, listening to the sounds of the house. When the wood of the floor snapped, she jumped and her heart rate accelerated. Bear and Reece wandered in, laying down on the plush rug close to the side of the bed, and she took a deep breath. "Decided you would sleep upstairs after all, boys?"

They looked up, tails giving halfhearted thumps before they rested their heads.

She smiled, trying to relax, concentrating on the distant, rhythmic crash of waves. The sounds of water rushing over rocks and the scent of Ethan's aftershave against the pillows soothed her. It was as if he were here with her. Longing for his arms to wrap around her, to feel the comfort only he could bring, she snuggled into the covers and thought of Ethan's gray eyes staring into hers as she drifted off.

~~~~

Adrenaline still pumped through Hunter's veins as he sat across from Austin in Ethan's office. Sipping his coffee, he picked up the disk Detective Campbell slipped him. "Ethan should be on the ground by now. We'll have to give him a call and let him know what happened."

"He's not going to like it."

"No, he's not, but at least it's a controlled situation. I would've liked to have gotten a picture of the roses left at the gate and on top of the wall. Hopefully Campbell can hook us up with those too." He slipped the DVD into the drive on his laptop. "Let's see what's on this bad boy."

Austin walked around the desk, taking a seat, as the grocery store surveillance, dated four nights ago, loaded on the screen. "What are we looking for, exactly?"

"Anything that seems off. Ethan thinks the bastard followed them. They were there around the time that girl was murdered behind the restaurant. She was only seventeen, for Christ's sake. Campbell said the boys downtown saw a few interesting details, but they're not sharing. We'll have to find them for ourselves."

"I bumped into them at the checkout counter—ran out of T.P." Austin pointed to the screen as Sarah and Ethan entered the store. "There they are."

Hunter watched Ethan and Sarah walk through the aisles, conversing as they added items to their cart. They stopped in the cereal aisle, and Ethan picked up a red box, pausing. He and Sarah exchanged words then Sarah grabbed his ear. Hunter narrowed his eyes when Ethan pulled her close, said something, and nibbled her lip. She eased back, and they both smiled.

Hunter stopped the video, hit a few buttons and

zoomed in, tightening up on the frame. He stared at Ethan and Sarah, grinning at each other, and knew he'd been wrong. In all the years he'd known Ethan, he couldn't remember seeing that content look in his eyes before. He was in love with her. "Well, son of a bitch," he muttered.

"What is it?"

He glanced up at Austin's puzzled expression. "Did you know about this? About Ethan and Sarah?"

Austin stood, diverting his gaze. "No. I'd noticed undercurrents, but I've never seen them together like they are here. I mean, they've always been close, but..."

Hunter stared at their happy faces again then zoomed out and started the video. Hunter and Austin both inched closer to the screen as Sarah and Ethan walked down the aisle with Ethan's finger in Sarah's back pocket.

"Stop. Go back, go back. That guy there." Austin pointed at the top left corner of the monitor.

"I saw it too." He rewound the footage and zoomed in on the man who kept his face hidden under a black cap. The bill of his hat followed Sarah and Ethan's direction, as if he tracked their movements. They turned into the next aisle, and the man crushed the box he held in his hands.

Hunter felt the skitter along his shoulder blades and clutch in his gut. "That's him, Austin, right there."

They played with the video for an hour, zooming in from different angles. Even with Ethan's state-of-the art equipment, they couldn't get a make on the face. They followed his track through the rest of the store, where he paused at the sliding doors.

"There we are. When I saw Ethan and Sarah with their cart full, I offered to help load the Rover." Austin huffed out a breath and stood. "Damn. He was right there and we were completely oblivious."

"We won't be next time. Let's call Ethan."

Chapter Eighteen

Sarah woke in the dim light of dawn, exhausted. She'd met each day with dragging fatigue since Ethan left—it was as if he'd taken her energy with him. For two weeks, she'd struggled to keep up with Kylee and the demands of her job. Her work hours had been brutal with the swimsuit edition photo shoot only fourteen days away.

The six weeks leading up to the shoot were always hectic and tiring, but she couldn't remember ever feeling like this.

She sat up and closed her eyes, breathing through a wave of dizziness. When she opened them again, the room no longer spun. She looked down at Kylee and smiled. Angelic and peaceful in sleep, her little girl snuggled with Mr. Ruff among the soft blankets.

Sarah kissed her finger and touched Kylee's nose before she stood to begin her battle with the day.

She slipped off her robe and turned on the shower, catching a glimpse of herself in the mirror. She stopped, staring at her pale face in the reflection and sighed. "I don't have time for this. I really don't." She had a full day of test shots to contend with. Out of patience with her lack of energy, she stepped into the warm spray, letting the jets of water sluice over her body.

While she lathered shampoo through her hair, she thought of Ethan. What was he doing? Was he safe? Why hadn't he called? She remembered their goodbye and the distance she'd felt from him and worried. Had he changed his mind? She tipped her head back, rinsing the suds away, thinking of the way he'd stared into her eyes as he told her he loved her. Shaking her head, she smiled, scolding herself for being silly. He would call when he could. He was busy.

Shower finished and dressed in comfy jeans and a blue t-shirt, she wandered downstairs, passing Ethan's office on the way to the kitchen. She heard Austin's voice and stopped.

"That's awesome, boss. So it's all wrapped up."

"Great. You'll be back soon, then."

"Oh, well, yeah, that makes sense. I heard Sarah moving around upstairs. Do you want me to—"

"Okay. I'll talk to you later."

Sarah struggled against tears as realization struck. Austin came out of Ethan's office every morning at this time. She stepped into the room, giving him a small smile. "Good morning."

His gaze darted to the phone before he met hers and stood. "Hey, Sarah." Frowning, he walked to her, taking her arm. "Are you okay? Why don't you sit down? You look like hell."

"I'm fine—just tired. Was that Ethan?"

He dropped his hand from her arm. "Uh, yeah."

"It sounds like he's well."

He walked back to the desk, rubbing his fingers over his chin. "Appears to be."

"Does he call here every morning?" She hated putting Austin in this position, but she had to know.

He glanced down at his watch. "Hunter should be down any minute. We're going to have to leave pretty soon."

Heart pounding, her stomach clenched. "Austin?"

Blowing out a breath, he looked up. "He calls to check in."

"Okay." Sarah nodded as her heart broke. He'd called every day for two weeks and hadn't spoken to her. "Well, I'm going to finish getting ready."

"He's been really busy, Sarah."

She heard the apology in his voice. "Yeah, I know." She turned, walked to the kitchen, and out the door, standing on the lower balcony, staring at the ocean lapping against the cliffs in the distance. The salty breeze rushed up to meet her, blowing her damp hair dry. She gripped the railing as the seagulls screeched and dove toward the waves. Why did he tell her he loved her? Why did he give her words he didn't mean?

She'd been a fool to have given her heart so freely and to have let herself believe. A few nights of passion and easy feelings between longtime friends didn't equate to the dreams she'd let herself weave. Wasn't she responsible for her own pain when she'd known all along Ethan had never been sure? He'd made his choice, and it wasn't her. A tear escaped as she rubbed at her chest, trying to stop the ache that settled there.

"Mama?"

She dashed at her cheek and turned, smiling. Kylee, sleepy eyed and beautiful, stared up with open arms. Bending forward, Sarah scooped her up, breathing in the baby shampoo scent of her daughter, nuzzling her soft, warm neck. "Hi, sweet girl. Did you have a good sleep?"

"Yes. Mr. Ruff did too."

"I'm so glad."

A strong gust blew off the water, twisting and tangling Kylee's blonde hair with hers. Kylee's eyes widened as she laughed. "Windy!"

"Very." Pushing despair away, she hugged her little girl close and stared out at the cliffs again. She had a child to raise and a business to run. If she learned anything after Jake died, it was that life went on, and she'd had to go with it. Ethan had been there to help her pick up the pieces, he'd been there all along, but he wouldn't be here now. Life had brought her full circle. She'd let herself love again—and lost again. She ignored the swift kick of grief. It was time to keep going, time to open a new chapter.

Determined to begin, she smiled at Kylee. "Are you and Mr. Ruff ready for breakfast?"

"Yes. I very hungry."

"We should go eat."

~~~~

Ethan replied to a thank-you e-mail from Niko Fabiano while he sat at his gate, waiting to board a flight for Germany. The job had gone smoother than expected. After poring through computerized records for a week and a half, he found the connection linking Niko's brother, Giovanni, to the misappropriation of millions of dollars in funds. From that point, the authorities had become involved, and Giovanni's plan to take over as CEO—by any means necessary—came crashing down.

Interviews with the police, meetings with his top men at the Italian branch, and frequent trips to visit his injured agent kept him occupied over the last few days. Through the chaos of his days and nights, he'd thought of Sarah—hadn't been able to stop.

The conversation with his father played through Ethan's mind, as it had each day, each hour, while he had been away. The Cookes weren't marriage material; never had been, never would be. If that were true, what did he have to offer Sarah?

How did a marriage end up the way his parents' had?

Would he wake up one morning after starting a life with her and decide he couldn't do it anymore? Would he look at Sarah across a room ten years down the road and suddenly feel nothing? He couldn't stand the thought. He loved her too much for that. His desperate love for Sarah wasn't the problem. The fear that he would ultimately let her down was.

He tapped at his keyboard, bringing up the grocery store surveillance Austin sent over two weeks ago, watching himself and Sarah move through the aisles like any other couple. When he pulled her close and nibbled her lip, he froze the frame, zooming in. Gray eyes smiled into blue, and he wanted that moment back, that moment when everything was perfectly right and he was sure.

He zoomed in again and Sarah's stunning face filled the screen. His stomach clutched as need for her staggered and consumed him. He slammed his laptop closed in defense and gathered his things as his flight was called. He'd made the right choice to exchange his ticket for a one-way flight to Germany. He couldn't go back to California, not yet. He couldn't go home until his head was clear and he could move past the want, the need, and make a decision that would be best for both of them.

Things were still under control at home. Sarah was safe in the care of his two best men. He would take the time he needed and check on his European branches while he did.

CHAPTER NINETEEN

"TURN TO YOUR LEFT A LITTLE, GABRIELLA. PERFECT. HEAD UP into the wind. Awesome." Sarah pressed the shutter button continuously, catching the Brazilian stunner's every move in the beach sand. Gabriella's black hair swirled by her face as the sun caught her translucent brown eyes while she smiled. And there it was—*Celebrity*'s cover picture for the swimsuit edition.

Sarah let the Nikon strap rest around her neck as she took a deep breath. Lunch wasn't agreeing with her. "Take twenty, everyone. When you come back, Gabriella, let's try the white bikini. I think it's going to be striking with your golden skin and the deep blue of the water."

Gabriella stepped forward. "Sarah, are you okay? You are looking unwell."

Heat coursed through her body and her mouth began to water. She was going to be sick. "Yes, I'm fine." Bolting for the trailer, she made it just in time. She flushed away her sickness and glanced up as Hunter stood in the door, holding out a bottle of water.

"Feel better?"

No. She took the bottle, pressing the cool plastic against her forehead. "Yes. I think I got too hot. The sun's blazing out there."

"Maybe we should call it a day."

"Absolutely not. I'm already behind schedule." She'd been horribly ill that morning, causing her to be late to the set. "I just need another second, then I'll be good to go."

Hunter stared, stepping back.

Alone, she closed her eyes and rested her head against the wall of the pretty trailer. She uncapped the water and sipped as she stood on unsteady legs. She stared at herself in the mirror. Dark under eyes and pale cheeks told her what she'd tried to deny. "Austin? Hunter?"

Austin appeared and he frowned. "Jeez, Sarah, you really look sick. Maybe we should go to the emergency room."

"If I don't feel better by tomorrow, I'll make an appointment with my doctor. Can you send Melanie in here?"

"Sure. Are you going to cancel the rest of the day?"

"No."

"Sarah—"

"Please, Austin. I just need Melanie."

Moments later, Sarah's long-time friend and part-time assistant came into the bathroom. "Oh, honey. You should lie down."

"I'm okay. Can you close the door?

"Sure." Melanie swung the door shut as she sat on the lip of the tub. "Do you want me to talk to Lisa?"

Drained of energy, Sarah collapsed to the lid of the toilet. "No. I need a big favor, and I need it to stay between you and me. Only you and me, Melanie."

"All right. You know you can trust me."

"Yes, I do. Will you go to the store for me? I can't get to one without my entourage, and I really want to keep my suspicions to myself for a while yet."

"Your suspicions?" Melanie's eyes widened, and she stood. "Oh my goodness. Of course. There's a drug store down the road. I'll be right back." She started for the door, stopped and turned, wrapping Sarah in a hug.

Sarah held on, taking the comfort of a friend. "Thank you. I'm going to get back to work. If you'll just stuff it in my purse."

Disappointment filled her friend's brandy colored eyes. "Oh, I thought you could do it now."

Smiling, Sarah stood. "Waiting a few more hours isn't going to change anything."

"Will you call me?"

"Sure."

~~~~

While Sarah took pictures of the goddess in her white bikini, Austin stood by the trailer, dialing Ethan's number.

"Cooke."

"It's Austin."

"Is everything okay?"

"The coast has been clear. We're still getting the notes. In fact, Matthews called about two hours ago saying he intercepted another package. This one had an earring with a blue stone in its center; the same color as the roses. The police came by and took it. The detective says the earring belonged to one of the victims."

"Jesus. Did Matthews photograph everything?"

"Of course." Austin watched Sarah stop, take a deep breath and clutch at a chair as she sipped her water. "Ethan, when do you think you'll be back? You've been gone for a month."

"I haven't been to the Paris branch yet. I'll be home after that. You two've been handling it. Why?"

"Sarah's sick, man. She's been sick."

"What do you mean?"

Raking his fingers through his hair, Austin felt a tug

of war between giving Sarah her privacy and letting his boss know that the woman he was seeing was ill. "I didn't say anything at first because I thought maybe she just had the flu, but Hailey and I talked. We think the stress is really getting to her. I checked in on her last night. She was asleep with Kylee by seven. I can't remember the last time I've seen her eat a real meal, and she threw up on set about a half-hour ago. If she weren't talking and breathing, I'd swear she was a ghost. She's so pale."

"How long has this been going on?"

"Pretty much since you left—the exhaustion anyway. The rest started a couple of weeks ago."

"You didn't think it would be important to tell me before now?"

"Like I said, I—"

"I'll be on the first flight back. Keep this between you and Hunter."

"Okay, but—"

"That's the way I want it." Ethan's tone left no room for argument.

"I'll see you when you get back."

~~~~

When the lights were dim and the house finally quiet, Sarah pulled the covers from her legs, got out of bed, and tiptoed to the bathroom. She took her purse from the gray marbled countertop and dug to the bottom, pulling the rectangular box free. Despite the situation, she couldn't help but smile. Melanie had scrawled 'Good Luck' on a post-it and stuck it to the package.

Her hands shook as she fumbled with the plastic wrapper. She pulled the pregnancy test free and stared at it while nerves twisted her already sensitive stomach. There was little doubt of what the result would be. After flipping through her office calendar earlier in the evening, she'd counted days, surprised to find she was well over a month and a half late. With everything going on, time had gotten away from her. "Well, here goes nothing."

She followed the instructions, peed on the stick, capped it, and set it on the counter. She wouldn't have to wait three agonizing minutes for an answer. Two bright blue lines filled the small screen instantly. Stunned, despite the fact that she had known in her heart, she picked up the white plastic and gaped. "Oh, God." She covered her mouth with her free hand, never taking her eyes off the positive result. "Oh, God."

Legs weak, she leaned against the counter, still staring. Here it was. There was no more denying the truth. She could officially say she was pregnant. What was she going to do? She closed the door, turned on the shower and sat on the floor, wrapping her arms tight around her knees, weeping.

~~~~

Weary and minutes from the house, Ethan craved his bed. The thirteen-hour flight home had been hell. He'd done little but worry and think of Sarah. She was making herself sick over the stalking situation and photo shoot, no doubt. The stress and pressure of the swimsuit edition weighed heavily on her every year. The hours were long, the weather hot, and the models weren't always easy to work with. Throwing a murdering psychopath into the deal didn't exactly add up to a recipe for serenity.

It probably didn't help that he hadn't called, but he'd

needed the time and tried not to feel guilty for taking it. He'd been right to give himself the extra two weeks. After thinking over his conversations with both his father and Hunter, he'd been able to come to the realization that Ethan Cooke just wasn't meant to belong to one woman, especially not Sarah. She was puppy dogs, white picket fences, and commitment. He wasn't—never would be. They'd been caught up in a delusion, a cozy rendition of house, but it was time to end that.

Hopefully they could find their way back to being friends again, the way they always had been. He needed that connection with her, but there couldn't be anything more. It would hurt her for a little while, but she would be fine. Pain filled his heart as he thought of the conversation they would have to have, but in the end they would both be okay. He never should have pursued Sarah. It had been selfish. There was a wrong to right, and he would take care of it the first moment he got.

Ethan pulled up to the gate and punched in his code. He drove down his long drive, staring at the ramble of wood and glass he called home. It was good to be here. He let himself into his house, meeting an excited Bear and Reece in the entryway. Tails whipped back and forth while tongues licked his face. "Hey, fellas, I missed you. Yes I did." Both dogs fell to the floor, and he gave them thorough rubdowns. He looked up as Hunter and Austin stood in the doorway, groggy and well muscled in gym shorts.

"Don't let us interrupt," Hunter said, scrubbing his hands over his face.

"Welcome home, boss," Austin said on a huge yawn.

Ethan stood. "What a welcoming committee. Go back to bed, Sleeping Beauties. I'm planning on heading that way myself." He glanced down at his watch, wincing.

"Three-thirty. That's gonna hurt in a couple hours. What time does Sarah have to be on location?"

"Don't worry about it, boss. Hunter and I'll cover her. She scheduled a doctor's appointment when we got home. It's at eight-thirty. We'll go with her before we go on location. You rest. You look like shit."

He had to see her himself and be sure she was okay. "Take the morning off, Austin. I'll bring her to her appointment."

"Uh, if that's what you want. I'm going back to bed."

"Right behind you," Hunter said. "Oh, by the way, Sarah and Kylee are in your room. You'll probably want to bunk somewhere else."

As quickly as they'd appeared, they were gone, leaving him in the darkened silence. He climbed the stairs, longing for sleep, heading for the guest bedroom farthest down the hall. The door to his room was cracked, and he stopped. Hesitating, he poked his head in, breathing in the scent of his aftershave mixed with Sarah's flowery perfume.

When neither Sarah nor Kylee stirred, he walked over to the bed. The light from the bathroom washed over Sarah's face, and her beauty staggered him. He had to touch her. He brushed his fingers through her soft, silky hair and pulled away as he stared at Kylee sleeping with her hand tucked under her cheek, the mirror image of her mother.

He stepped away and emptiness filled him. They weren't his. They never would be.

Moving back down the hall, he collapsed on the guest bed, still fully clothed, and fell asleep.

CHAPTER TWENTY

SARAH OPENED HER EYES, BLINKING AGAINST THE SUN. NAUSEA roiled in her belly, but it wasn't as bad as it had been yesterday—thank God. Settling into her new routine, she sat up and blew out several breaths, waiting for the bile to head back in the direction it belonged. When she was sure her stomach would behave, she got to her feet and made her way to the bathroom.

She twisted the shower to life and untied her robe as she walked to the mirror, scrutinizing her naked body. Turning to her side, she ran a hand over her barely bloated lower stomach. Her tender breasts were heavier, her nipples a darker shade of pink. Denial still wanted its way, but that couldn't be.

She turned toward the shower again and gasped. The pregnancy test still lay on the counter. She placed the plastic back in the box and looked around, shoving the package among the folded towels on the shelf until she could find someplace else to put it.

Disaster averted, she stepped into the water and began to plan her day. Her schedule was crammed tight with the last-minute doctor's appointment, but they would just have to work around it. If she planned for an early start tomorrow, perhaps she could be home before dinner to swim with Kylee. Lately, by day's end, she was completely depleted of energy, but she would find some, damn it.

Dressed in raspberry-colored capris and a white v-neck tank, she made her way to the kitchen, ready to fight her battle with a piece of toast and a glass of milk. Austin sat at the table with the paper and a cup of coffee. The pungent aroma wreaked havoc on her system, causing her to breathe through her mouth. "Good morning."

Austin set down the paper. "Hey, Sarah."

He scrutinized her face. "You're not quite as pale today. How are you feeling?"

She smiled as she popped a piece of bread in the toaster. "Much better," she lied.

"Well, I'm glad you're going to see the doctor anyway. Hopefully they can give you something to help you out."

Not so much. "Oh, I'm sure they will." She buttered her toast and sat down. She'd have to pick up prenatal vitamins somehow. Perhaps Melanie could make another supply run. "I should be ready to go in about fifteen minutes, if that works for you."

"I'm not—"

"Dood morning, Mama." Kylee, messy haired and rumpled, stepped into the kitchen.

"Hi, sweet girl. How was your sleep?"

"Dood."

She walked over to Austin, and he settled her on his lap. "Is Princess Kylee going to build castles with Hailey today?"

Blue eyes bright, she smiled. "Yes."

Sarah chuckled, bringing the bread to her mouth. "I still can't believe Wren put a sandbox in the playroom. I wonder what Ethan will think of that when he gets home."

"Actually, Sarah—"

"Ethan!" Kylee scrambled down and ran toward the doorway.

"Hey, kiddo." He scooped her up and hugged her tight, never taking his eyes from Sarah's.

Heart pounding, she could only stare as the breath backed up in her lungs. His hair was still damp from the shower. The scent of his aftershave carried on the air. The navy blue polo and khakis he wore showed off his muscled perfection. He was really here. She hadn't had any warning, hadn't had an opportunity to prepare.

"Hey," he said.

Austin cleared his throat. "I was just about to tell you the boss is back."

"So I see. Welcome home, Ethan." She stood, hoping she sounded casual as hurt and longing careened through her system with equal force. She took her uneaten toast to the sink and pushed it into the disposal, needing a moment to compose herself. She washed her plate with precise, exacting strokes, stalling, attempting to steel herself to the shock of meeting his gaze again. "Kylee, we should find Hailey and get you settled in. Austin, I'll be ready after I get my purse and camera bag."

"I'm taking you this morning."

Ethan's words sunk in, and Sarah whirled. "No. You don't have to do that. I'm going with Austin."

"Austin's been reassigned. Now that I'm here, he'll go back to private duty during the day."

"Oh." She glanced at Austin as he gave her a shrug. What could she say to that? She wasn't ready for this, wasn't ready to deal with him being back in her life. "Are you sure you don't want to stay home and rest? You look tired."

Eyes unreadable, he set Kylee on her feet. "I'm fine."

"Let me get my purse and tell Hailey I'm ready to go." She rushed from the room and up the stairs, stopping when she made it to the bedroom. She lowered herself to the bed, resting her face in her hands. Ethan was back, and the timing couldn't be worse. She was still reeling from one shock and now she had to deal with another.

She ran her fingers through her hair and blew out a breath as she glanced at the clock. It was time to go. How was she going to handle this? What was she going to do? She tried to find her calm, remembering her resolve to start a new chapter in her life—surprising new twist and all. Nothing had to be decided right now. She would take the time she needed to sort it out. Steadier, she grabbed her purse, her camera bag and knocked on Hailey's door.

Hailey, pretty in her vivid red t-shirt and jeans, opened the door, smiling. "Morning."

"Hi. I really have to be on my way. I'm going to be late for my doctor's appointment. Are you ready for Kylee?"

"Sure." Hailey closed her door, and they headed downstairs. "I'm so glad you're going to have a checkup. I've been worried about you. All this stress has messed with your immune system."

Guilty that her friends were concerned, she tried a smile. "Don't be worrying about me. I'm just fine." She looked closely at her energetic young friend and frowned. "You know, you should get out of the house one of these evenings. I'm sure we can arrange for Austin to take you. You must be going stir crazy around here."

"Austin? Why should I go out with Austin? I mean he's nice and totally hot and all, but I don't know..."

Wasn't this interesting? Smiling, Sarah pulled on Hailey's arm, stopping her. "I just meant that if you wanted to go shopping, catch a movie, or grab a bite out, we would arrange for someone to take you. It'll be safer that way."

Hailey's cheeks burned bright. "Of course. Yeah, of course. Maybe sometime this week. Although, I'm not bored here. This place is like a resort."

Chuckling, Sarah squeezed Hailey's shoulder. She'd needed this; a brush of normal before she started her long day. She took Hailey's hand. "Have I told you how lucky I am to have you in my life? Thank you for all that you do for Kylee and me. You're such a special friend."

"Sarah, you're going to get me all sniffly. You, me, and Morgan need to get together for a movie night in Ethan's game room. When you're finished with this photo shoot, let's do it."

"I'm hoping this will be over by then. We'll be able to have a movie night at my house."

"That sounds good too, but I like Ethan's TV better. It practically takes up the whole wall."

Sarah laughed. "We'll have to see what we can do."

Ethan stepped into the hallway. "Hi, Hailey."

She smiled. "Hi. Welcome back."

"Thanks. We should get going. Hunter will follow behind and wait outside the doctor's office."

Sarah blew out a breath. "Okay. I just need to say goodbye to Kylee."

~~~~

Buckled into the Rover, Sarah stared out at the Pacific rushing by her window, unsure of what to say. Her steepled fingers bunched and relaxed, bunched and relaxed, until her palms began to cramp. She rested her hands on her thighs, counting down the minutes until she could get out of the SUV.

Ethan cleared his throat. "So, how's the shoot going?"

She made brief eye contact and looked down at her sandaled foot moving double-time against the floor mat. "Great, really great. Super, in fact."

Tense silence filled the space again.

Frayed nerves began to snap. Sarah reached forward and turned on the radio, giving herself something to do. She fiddled from station to station until Ethan placed his hand over hers. She pulled away from the warmth of his skin, gave him an over-bright smile then stared straight ahead.

"Listen, Sarah, I don't know if this is the best time, but I was hoping we could talk this evening."

She glanced at his profile. The regret was there, in his eyes, in his voice; she couldn't stand it. It was easier to figure this out now, before things got even more complicated. Eventually she would have no choice but to tell him about the baby, but she would deliver the news without the tatters of a broken relationship hanging in the air. A clean cut was better. "Why don't I make this easier for both of us? It's pretty clear that what we had between us isn't working for you, so why don't we just leave it at that." Biting her lip, she turned toward the window, willing the tears to stay away as her heart shattered.

"Let's talk about this later, when we have more time."

He didn't deny anything she'd said. "No. There's really nothing to talk about. Let's leave it alone, Ethan."

Ethan turned into the medical complex, pulled into a parking spot.

She got out before the vehicle was fully stopped, needing to get to the bathroom before she crumbled. She rushed for the door, but he caught her before she could get inside.

"Wait a minute, Sarah."

"I'm going to be late." Much to her horror, her voice broke. "Please, let me go."

He held her for another moment, searching her face as she blinked at unshed tears. Ethan released her arm, and she walked into the waiting room, doing her best to give the receptionist a smile.

"Good morning. I have an 8:30 appointment. My name's Sarah Johnson."

"Yes. Hello, Sarah. Go ahead and have a seat. The nurse will be right out to get you."

"Thank you." Turning, she almost slammed into Ethan. Their eyes met before she took a seat.

Just as they sat, the nurse called. Sarah bolted from the chair and walked through the door.

"Will your husband be joining us today?"

She met Ethan's stare. "No, he'll wait for me out here." She turned, leaving him behind.

The nurse showed her to the examining room and immediately got started. She wrapped the blood pressure cuff around Sarah's arm. "You don't look like you're feeling very well. Your color's a little off. Why don't you tell me what's going on so I can put your symptoms in the computer for the doctor."

"I had a positive pregnancy test. I'm here to confirm it."

The nurse beamed. "Oh, well, congratulations. Let's get a urine sample and we'll go from there."

Minutes later, the doctor examined her. "You're about nine weeks, Sarah, almost ten. You can take your legs down."

Sarah pulled her feet from the stirrups and began to sit up.

"Wait just a minute. You're far enough along for us to pick up a heartbeat. Let's make sure baby's off to a good start."

Sarah nodded, lying back again. Even with the professional confirmation, she couldn't truly believe she was pregnant. The doctor squeezed a dab of warm blue fluid on her lower abdomen and switched on the small Doppler machine. A burst of static filtered through the speaker as Dr. Humphrey slid the probe around. The fast and steady rhythm of a tiny heartbeat soon filled the room.

Disillusionment was instantly replaced with wonder and love and Sarah grinned. "That's my baby. Oh, listen to that sound. I don't think there's a better sound." In that moment it didn't matter that Ethan didn't want her, that he didn't love her. He'd given her a child. She would treasure the baby they had made in affection if not in love.

After the goop had been wiped away and she dressed, Sarah went out to the receptionist's desk with her yellow form.

"Why, honey, you look like you're feeling a little better already."

She smiled. "I am."

"We'll see you back here in a month, unless you want to transfer your care to OB."

Wincing, she glanced over her shoulder, hoping Ethan didn't hear. "No. I'll be back next month. This is a busy time of year for me. Can I call you and we'll figure out an appointment when I'm in front of my calendar?"

"Certainly. Congratulations, honey, and don't forget your vitamin."

"Thanks." She walked toward the door, and Ethan got up to follow.

He took her arm. "Wait, Sarah. I go first." He punched a number into his cell. "We all set? Okay, we're coming out."

With the coast clear, Ethan walked Sarah to her side of the vehicle. When she was tucked inside, he shut the door. He got in on his side and stared at her.

She pulled sunglasses from her purse and put them on, wanting the barrier. "We should go. I'm already running late."

"At least tell me you're okay."

"I'm fine."

He looked at her a moment longer then started the car, and they headed for the shoot.

~~~~

Sarah's mood immediately plummeted when they pulled up on location. Nicolette walked from her trailer in little more than black floss. *Damn it.* With everything going on, she'd forgotten she would be photographing the French pain in her ass today. She stepped from the Rover, pulling her camera bag with her and started toward the sand with Ethan walking at her side. "Austin or Hunter usually stays by the trailer. You don't have to come with me."

"I know how to do my job, Sarah."

She glanced at him as she removed her sandals and walked to the center of the beachfront, taking her equipment from the bags Melanie had set up and began to read her light meters.

Melanie rushed forward. "Hi, honey. How are you today?"

"I'm feeling pretty good."

Hugging her, Melanie whispered, "Congratulations."

Concerned she was drawing attention from Ethan, Sarah pulled back. "Thanks. Let's get things going. I want this one over as quickly as possible."

Melanie swiped a honey-toned ringlet back from her forehead and smiled, rolling her eyes. "I can't imagine why. What a pain in the ass. Let's send her back to Paris, fast."

Sarah grinned.

"It is so nice that you could join us today, Sarah," Nicolette said as she sauntered toward them.

"And here we go," Sarah muttered. "Hello, Nicolette. I'm sorry I kept you waiting."

"Perhaps I should wait longer while you finish your conversation with your friend."

Unwilling to rise to the bait, Sarah pulled the camera in front of her face, checking her focus. She followed Nicolette through the lens, watching the dark-haired vixen smile slowly, seductively.

"Well, well, well, Ethan darling, I had no idea you would be here today. Berlin two weeks ago and now the beach."

"Hello, Nicky."

Nicolette's fingers brushed down the front of his shirt, accentuating the outline of his six pack. "Perhaps we will have dinner while I am here and pick up where we left off." Her nail skimmed over his palm as she held it out. "I've missed your hands, Ethan. You have such creative hands."

"That's enough." He pulled back, looking in Sarah's direction. His eyes stared straight into hers through the lens.

Sarah let the camera strap fall around her neck and walked off, pulling lenses at random from her bag. The stab of betrayal was sharp and painful, but it was probably better this way. The in-your-face reality check reminded her that what she'd had with Ethan a month ago no longer existed. He would go on as he always had, dating who he pleased when he pleased. He hadn't wasted any time. This cruel slap only highlighted how foolish she'd been to think they shared something special. As she watched Ethan talk to Nicolette, she realized in a humbling moment that she had been nothing more than one of Ethan Cooke's Flavors of the Month. "Nicolette, we need to get started. You and Ethan can talk about what you'll do with his hands later."

He narrowed his eyes, meeting hers, before she walked off to get the day over with.

~~~~

As the sun set, Sarah shoved her equipment bag in the back seat of the SUV. Ethan opened her door, and she hesitated. "Why don't I ride with Hunter? I've hardly seen Morgan in days with both of our busy schedules. I would love to catch up and find out how she's doing, especially now that they'll be going home tomorrow."

"Get in the car, Sarah. You can catch up at home."

She pulled her seatbelt in place as Ethan slammed her door. He hadn't exactly been friendly since her snide comment on the beach earlier that morning.

He slammed his door as well and shot the key into the ignition, bringing the engine to life then shut it off, staring at her, his eyes blazing. "I saw Nicky at an event I was invited to in Berlin. Nothing—"

Her cellphone rang, and she yanked her purse from her lap, holding it up like a shield. "Phone." She didn't want to talk about what he did with Nicolette. She checked the readout and signaled for one minute. "Sorry. It's my mother. I have to take this."

"No, you don't. I'm trying—"

Ignoring him, Sarah pressed 'talk.' "Mom, how are you?"

Eyes narrowing, Ethan turned over the ignition again, put the Rover in first gear, and shot from the parking lot. "We're going to talk about this, Sarah."

Several minutes later, as they pulled up in front of his house, she squeezed every last drop from her conversation, stalling. She was almost there.

"It was lovely talking to you, Sarah, but I really must go. You've been so chatty, and your father's waiting for me."

"Oh, okay. Love you, Mom."

"You too, honey."

The Rover rolled to a stop as Sarah ended the call. She reached for the door handle, and Ethan snagged her arm. "Let's talk about this. I—"

The front door opened, and Kylee came running to the vehicle with Hailey close behind. Relieved and happy to see her daughter, Sarah smiled and waved as Ethan slammed his hands against the steering wheel.

"God fucking damn it! We're going to have a conversation, Sarah."

"It'll have to wait." She opened the door and grabbed Kylee up in a hug. "Hi, sweet girl. How was your day?"

"Dood. Let's swim!"

"We'll have some dinner, then we can go for a swim." She glanced behind her, into Ethan's smoldering eyes and walked off snuggling her little girl.

~~~~

A knock sounded at Ethan's bedroom door and Sarah tensed.

Morgan stuck her head in. "Mind if I come in?"

She relaxed instantly, smiled, motioning Morgan forward with a wave of her hand. "I just finished reading to Kylee."

Morgan glanced at Kylee asleep, snuggled under the covers. "So I see. Does she ever make it to the end of a story?"

"Not after six-thirty p.m."

"You look like you barely made it through yourself."

"I'm a little tired." She could hardly keep her eyes open.

"Since Hunter and I are going home tomorrow, I thought I'd come by and chat. I feel like I haven't seen you in forever."

Sarah yawned. "It's been awhile."

"Why don't we take a rain check? You need to rest."

"I'm okay. Let's talk." Sarah pulled back the covers she'd cozied herself under. "We're both so busy. Are you settling in at the Bureau?"

Morgan sat on the edge of the bed. "Slowly. There's a lot of transition yet, but I'm managing. If I could put this damn mining investigation behind me, I might make it into the office on a regular basis."

Sarah yawned again, fighting the urge to close her eyes.

"Pull those covers back up, Sarah. I want you to get some sleep. Tell me one thing first. Are you okay? Did everything go all right today?" Morgan's brow rose, mirroring Sarah's. "Kind of a loaded question, huh?"

Sarah shrugged with a casualness she didn't feel. "You could say that."

"Let's start with your health."

Sarah wanted to tell Morgan about the baby, to talk it all through, but she couldn't, not yet. She still needed time to absorb the news herself. "I'm fine—just a little rundown with everything going on."

Morgan folded her in a hug. "You had me worried."

She held on, treasuring the comfort of a friend. "I'll be good to go before you know it. Promise."

Morgan eased back. "Are you and Ethan okay?"

Sarah stared down at the soft, cream-colored covers. "Ethan and I weren't meant to be anything more than friends." Saying it out loud hurt.

Morgan took her hand. "Oh, honey, what happened?"

"It's such a long story. I don't even know where to start. I'll summarize. He changed his mind."

"Is that what he said?"

Her eyes watered as she remembered the awkward drive to the doctors. "He would've, but I told him to leave it alone."

Morgan sat on the edge of the bed, huffing out a breath. "Ethan Cooke, you're an idiot."

Sarah chuckled. Only Morgan could make her laugh at a time like this. She yanked a tissue from the box on the side table and blew her nose. "I'll agree with you, but it doesn't change anything."

"I really thought things were different this time. Maybe you should talk to him."

"Yeah, maybe." She didn't know if she could handle some polite 'It's not you, it's me' conversation.

Morgan stood. "I'm going to let you get some rest." She wrapped Sarah in another long hug. "Do yourself a favor, Sarah: Leave a glimmer of hope in your heart. Everything will work out." She stepped away and smiled. "Goodnight."

"Goodnight."

Morgan shut the door behind her.

Sarah settled back against her pillow, replaying

Morgan's words. As much as she loved Morgan, she wasn't sure she could take her advice. She looked at her daughter and brushed her fingers over the new life growing inside her. She didn't have much time to spend on hope. Her hands were full with reality.

CHAPTER TWENTY-ONE

THE SCENT OF KYLEE'S BABY SHAMPOO FOLLOWED ETHAN down the long upstairs hallway. If she'd had her bath, her bedtime routine was close to an end. It was the perfect time to snag Sarah before she could find a way to avoid him—like she had for the last two days.

Surprised by the lack of happy chatter coming from the room, he peeked in, looking at Hailey as she sat on the bed, legs crossed at the ankles, typing away on her laptop. Kylee lay against her pillow, asleep. "Hailey, where's Sarah?"

Her eyes flew up to meet his. "Um, she's down in her office. She's really busy going through the pictures from the shoot. We should probably let her be tonight. She has a lot of work to do. A lot."

Getting the none-too-subtle hint, Ethan tried a friendly smile. "Thanks for the heads-up. I'll catch her in the morning. Goodnight."

"Night." Hailey looked down and began to type again.

He took the stairs in twos. Like hell he'd wait till morning. This was finally his chance. They had a lot to discuss. He couldn't stop thinking about the ride to the doctor's office two days ago. He'd watched her knuckles whiten as her hands pressed together, had heard her struggle with tears, had seen her shattered eyes when she told him it was better to forget the whole thing. He didn't want to forget the whole thing. It was important she understand why he made the choice he did.

He stopped in her office doorway, and a fist of desire sucker punched him in the gut. Shiny blonde hair piled high on her head exposed her long, smooth neck. Her tank top, cut low, showed off swells of creamy breasts while her left arm hooked around the leg that joined her in her chair. Bright blue eyes glanced up from her monitor, covered in black-framed reading glasses squared at the edges. He'd never been able to resist Sarah in her glasses. She looked like every man's image of a very naughty librarian.

"Is there something you need?"

He stepped in and closed the door. "Yeah, I need to talk to you."

She glanced back at her screen. "This isn't a good time. I'm on a deadline. Lisa needs the first set of proofs by early next week."

"Well, when would be a good time?"

"Let's see... I have more outdoor shots next week, proofs to run the week after that, then Lisa and I get to start running through ideas for the *Celebrity* Bikini Ball. She wants behind-the-scenes pictures for the magazine's month-end edition. So let's pencil something in for..." She ran her finger over the calendar pinned to the wall and stopped on a date. "...a month from now. Will that Tuesday work for you?"

He knew she had a temper, but it had never been directed at him. "I'm not sure. I'll have to check my book, or I can have my people call your people." Out of patience, he pressed his palms to her desk. "Damn it, Sarah, I just want to straighten this out."

She removed her glasses and pinched the bridge of her nose as she blew out a breath. "I'm sorry. I'm tired, stressed out, and I really want nothing more than to go to bed right now, but I have hours of work yet. How about tomorrow night?"

"Fine. You look like you're feeling better tonight."

"Yeah, I'm good. It's usually just in the mornings..." Wide eyed, she met his gaze before she popped her glasses on and directed her attention to her screen. "So we'll talk tomorrow night. I should get back to work."

Confused by the direction of their conversation and her reaction to it, Ethan opened the door and walked to his own office. Hunter and Morgan had called it an early night, so he would wait for Sarah to head upstairs. He sat in his seat and booted up his computer, watching her work across the hall for a long time. Eventually he glanced down at his screen and read an e-mail from Detective Tucker Campbell.

Ethan,
May have something on our guy. It's small, but it's something. Call me at home in the morning.
-Tucker

It was about damn time. Ethan flagged the e-mail and closed his laptop. He took a deep breath and began to attack the mountains of paperwork from his month away, losing track of time.

Later, he rubbed at his tired eyes and looked up. Sarah was gone. Rushing to his feet, he moved forward. Where the hell did she go? He hadn't been *that* captivated by the fifty applicants Austin and Hunter had narrowed down for the new positions.

The light was still on in her office. Brows furrowed, he stepped into the room. She hadn't gone anywhere. She lay asleep at her desk, her head resting against folded arms. The glasses he adored slanted diagonally across her face. The screensaver cycled through a slideshow of

Kylee. He glanced at the red digits on the clock at her elbow and realized why he was so tired. It was after one. He trailed his hand over the smooth skin of her arm, torturing himself. "Sarah."

She didn't move.

He tried again, skimming his knuckles against her cheek. "Sarah, it's time to go to bed."

Still nothing.

He scooped her from her chair, and she nestled her head on his shoulder, never opening her eyes. Breathing her in, feeling her soft skin against his, he stayed where he was for a moment. He didn't foresee himself holding her like this again.

He moved down the hall and up the stairs, using his shoulder to open the bedroom door that had been left ajar. Staring into her sleep-softened face, he pressed a kiss to her forehead as he lay her down on the bed. He covered her and fixed Kylee's blanket before he moved into the bathroom. He was running low on the supplies he had transferred to the guest bath.

He opened the medicine cabinet and pulled out a cartridge of razors. He dropped the case on the hard marble counter, and a blade flew free. In his rush to grab it before it hit the floor, he cut himself against the sharp steel. "Well, shit." He closed the door and turned on the dim light while blood oozed down his finger. He placed his wound under the water and winced at the sting. After several seconds, he shut off the faucet. Blood bloomed again. "That's not working."

He walked over to the towels, grabbing one at random. As he pulled the soft cotton free, a small box fell to the floor. "What the hell?" If he kept this up, he was going to wake Kylee and Sarah for sure. He bent forward and froze as he read the pale purple label. *Be Sure: Home*

Pregnancy Test.

Grabbing the box, he opened the side flap that no longer held a seal and pulled the plastic indicator free, staring at two bright blue lines. The illustration on the packaging showed one line for 'not pregnant' and two lines for... He glanced back at the stick again as his heart thundered. "Oh, my God."

Everything made sense now. Sarah wasn't ill because of her workload and stress. She was ill because she had morning sickness. She was pregnant. Why hadn't he figured it out sooner? He remembered how she had been with Kylee.

He sat down on the toilet lid, unable to take his eyes from the piece of plastic that told him he was going to be a father. How long had she known? He got to his feet, unable to be still as anger and fear surged through his veins. He paced away and back again. How long did she plan to keep him in the dark? This was his child too.

Rubbing his fingers over his forehead, he stopped. Could he really blame her for not jumping into his arms with the news? He had more or less vanished from her life—no calls, no e-mails, nothing. Yeah, he'd taken the time *he* needed to sort everything out, but at what cost? *Damn, Cooke, you're on a fucking roll.*

He sat on the toilet lid again, head in hands. There was no use being angry with Sarah when he could only be angry with himself. Why couldn't he get this right? He thought of Kylee, of the magic and wonder she had brought to his life, and the beginnings of happiness overshadowed his misery. A smile ghosted his mouth. He and Sarah were going to have a baby.

He shoved the box among the towels and walked to the bed, staring down at the woman who had been his friend, his lover, and now carried his child. His mind flashed back to the night they shared in the bed she slept in now. He remembered blue eyes captivating him as he moved with her, inside of her, moments after he'd told her he loved her. He clenched his fists as he thought of the tense car ride to the doctor's office and her devastated eyes blinking back tears as she told him to leave it alone. Had she known then?

Ethan's gaze wandered down her blanket-clad body, stopping at her lower stomach, where his baby grew and slept. Everything he ever wanted lay quiet and resting in his bed, and they were no longer his to have. Love swamped him as despair drained him. He wanted it all back, needed it all back. He walked to the glass doors and stared out into the night. What was he going to do? He sure as hell wasn't going to lose it all. He wasn't going down without a fight.

Ethan glanced at Sarah once more then turned away and left the room, determined to get it all back.

~~~~

Zeke sat at his desk, staring at his 'Wall of Sarah.' Every picture he'd been able to find on Google Images had been printed and framed with cornflower blue matting, the same color as his roses; the same color as her eyes. He'd spent hours cropping the asshole movie stars she usually posed with out of the photographs, but it had been worth the time. When he woke each morning or needed to get himself off, all he had to do was look over and Sarah smiled at him, just for him. Her serene beauty would be even more stunning in death.

He closed his eyes, grinning, shuddering, as he worked himself hard, imagining what it would be like to ram his cock inside of her while she stared up at him in terror—but he would wait to cum until she struggled for her last breath, until her gaze grew dull and lifeless. He hissed out a breath as his imagination sent him over. He had to have his angel soon, his sweet, sweet angel, or he might go mad.

It'd been *weeks* since he'd been able to get close to her. Other than photographing the sluts by the ocean in their whore clothes, she never left Master Cooke's fortress. He couldn't even get close to her at the beach. Fuck knows he'd tried, but the muscle-jacked assholes she surrounded herself with *never* left her alone.

The long-range lens he watched her with wasn't good enough. He needed to touch her, smell her, fuck her, *punish* her for making him wait for so long. Just two more weeks, and they would meet face-to-face, and oh, it was going to be sweet.

He was ready for her now. None of the others would do. With his plan in place, he smiled, sitting in his juices, eager to start his fantasy again, never taking his eyes from Sarah's.

CHAPTER TWENTY-TWO

SARAH SHOT OUT OF BED IN HER RACE FOR THE TOILET. Thankful she hadn't closed the lid an hour ago, she leaned forward and retched, just making it. Yesterday's reprieve from nausea was clearly going to be short lived. Depleted and shaky, she lay on the floor, pressing her cheek to the cool marble tile. Someone walked through the bedroom and stopped in the doorway. She didn't have the energy to turn to see who it was. At this point, she didn't care.

The faucet was turned on and a paper cup filled. Ethan, sweaty in his gym shorts, knelt down beside her. "Here, sip this."

"I can't. I'll just throw it back up." She closed her eyes.

"You have to drink or you're going to get dehydrated."

She struggled to sit up.

Ethan cupped her by the armpits and helped.

Dizzy, Sarah's stomach pitched and she leaned forward, vomiting again. Sighing, she rested her elbow against the seat and settled her forehead in the crook of her arm as water rushed into the sink. Moments later a cool cloth lay around the back of her neck. Ethan's hand moved up and down her back as he sat next to her on the floor. She couldn't count the number of times he had done the same thing when she'd been pregnant with Kylee. "I'll be fine in a few minutes. You don't have to stay."

His callused hand continued to move over her cotton tank top, making contact with the skin of her shoulder blades with each upstroke. His gentleness weakened her, and she longed for something that would never be.

"Really, Ethan, I'm pretty steady again." Sitting up fully, needing to break the contact between them, she gave him a small smile.

He held the paper cup to her lips, and she took a long sip, swished the water around in her mouth, and spat it into the toilet. He held the cup to her mouth again, and she relieved her dry throat.

"Thanks. The worst has definitely passed."

Concerned eyes scrutinized her face. "Are you sure?"

Unable to resist, she placed her hand over his and nodded. "Yeah."

He continued to hold her gaze. "When were you going to tell me, Sarah?"

Her hand tightened on his before she pulled away. "I-I don't know..." She tried again. "What are you..." She stopped any pretense of denial and stared at the floor. There wasn't any point.

"How far along?"

"Almost ten weeks. It must've happened the first time we were together."

He shoved a hand through his hair, blowing out a deep breath. "Damn, Sarah, ten weeks. That's my child you're carrying."

"I just found out a couple of days ago myself. Everything's been so hectic. I lost track of time."

"What did the doctor say? Is everything okay? Are you okay?"

Her eyes filled. This wasn't the way it was supposed to be. They were having a baby, and there was so little joy. "We're both fine. I heard the heartbeat. It sounded perfect."

He looked into her eyes. "What are we going to do?"

Wasn't that the ultimate question? What *were* they going to do? Everything was so different now, so messed up. They weren't a couple in love sharing a family, and there was no easy friendship to depend on. A myriad of emotions flooded her—confusion, regret, and fear mixed together, but it was the deep, unbearable sadness that almost broke her. A tear raced down her cheek and she stood, turning away. "I don't know. I guess we'll hope they catch this guy soon so Kylee and I can go home. It's time to—"

"What do you mean you'll go home?" Ethan rushed to his feet, turning her to him. "We're having a baby."

Tears fell, unstoppable. "What does that have to do with anything?"

"I want you and Kylee to stay here with me. I want us to raise the kids together, to be a family."

She yanked away. "What are you talking about? We can't raise a family on affection, Ethan. We would only be cheating ourselves. You deserve more than that. I deserve more than that."

He stepped closer. "Affection? I love you."

Sarah closed her eyes, breathing out a trembling breath, wishing it were true.

He pulled her against him, her cotton shirt colliding against his bare chest. "I *love* you, Sarah."

She opened her eyes, staring into gray pools teeming with desperation and panic. "I believe you think you do, but what happens when you go away again? You left me for a month and never called. You spoke with Hunter or Austin every day, but you didn't once speak to me. You met Nicolette in Berlin."

His fingers tightened against her arms. "I didn't *meet*

Nicky in Berlin. I *saw* her at a function. We said hello and that was the end of it. I tried to tell you the other night. And I didn't talk to you because I needed time to think. I was so caught up in you, I couldn't think."

She wanted to believe his words, to believe in him, but she couldn't. It hurt too much. "I'm sorry, but I can't do this. Ever since things changed between us, you've teetered back and forth. You hold yourself back. I want it all, Ethan."

"You can have it."

She shook her head vehemently, denying herself what she wanted to take. "No. What happens if in a month from now or six months from now when you decide you don't want me, or this, or us? I can't live like this. I don't want to live like this. So no, Kylee and I won't be staying here with you. When all of this is over, we're going home. I need to put my life back together. I have two children who'll be depending on me." On a sob, she left the room, running on rubbery legs to the downstairs balcony. She wanted the wind on her face and the sound of the sea. As she opened the kitchen door and stepped on smooth wood, Ethan caught her and spun her around.

"This isn't over, Sarah."

"As far as I'm concerned, it is."

He took her chin in his hands. "Do you love me?"

She stared into eyes burning with hurt, but she wouldn't answer. She needed something for herself.

His fingers moved through her hair, pulling her face closer, his gaze never leaving hers. "Do you love me, Sarah?"

Weeping, she could only speak the truth. "Yes, I love you."

"That's all I need to know." He pressed his mouth to

hers and she struggled, fighting the need that left her reeling. She bunched her fists against his chest as he held her in place, as she caved to his familiar taste, losing the battle.

His lips moved over hers, persuading, and she stilled, moaning, surrendering. Ethan's tongue sought hers as his fingers curled in her hair. She unclenched her hands, skimming her palms against the warm skin of his stomach, settling them against the sides of his waist.

He nibbled her lip then traced the spot with his tongue before diving in again, before easing away. He skimmed his knuckle against her cheek as he stared into her eyes. "I want you, Sarah. I want Kylee, and I want this baby. I don't care what I have to do to prove that to you. I'll give you time to think about that, but I won't wait long."

He walked away, turned, met her gaze again then continued through the kitchen.

Heart pounding, stomach fluttering, Sarah sat down on a padded wicker seat and stared out at the ocean waves, not knowing what to do.

~~~~

After a shower, Ethan dressed and settled down at his desk, eager to find out what Detective Campbell had on the case. He dialed Tuckers's home number and waited.

"Hello?"

"Tucker, it's Ethan Cooke."

"Hey, Ethan."

"I got your e-mail last night. What did you find out?"

"Like I said, it isn't much, but we have to start somewhere. He's made his first mistake. The cardstock he's been using is manufactured from rice paper made right here in the city, at a shop in China Town."

"That's great."

"It's a beginning. The shop is fairly small, but the family who owns and runs it does a serious business. They distribute the paper to several stationary and florist stores throughout L.A. We're talking two or three hundred vendors."

Ethan's jaw clenched in frustration. "Well, shit, anyone could've bought it then."

"Not necessarily. The paper isn't sold mass market. It's used by the businesses themselves for bookmaking, card making, etcetera. We have their client lists, so we're going to attack that. We'll start with the floral side of things."

Ethan rubbed his fingers over his forehead. "Makes sense."

"There are about one hundred-fifty, one hundred-seventy-five shops."

"If you slip me the files, I can start crosschecking orders as well—try to find some sort of pattern."

"I'll download the data and send it your way tonight, from home."

"That works. I'll let you know if I find anything."

"Sounds good."

"Tucker, we're going to get this fucker."

"Damn right. I'll talk to you soon."

Ethan hung up and swiveled around, staring out at the deep green of his lawn.

They had a lead. Tucker was right: It was small, but all it took was one domino to send the rest tumbling. He was looking forward to watching them fall.

He heard the front door open and close again. Moments later, Bear and Reece bulleted across the lush grass. The dogs rolled around before trotting off to water the shrubs bordering the long drive. That was going to piss off the gardener. Someday in the not too distant future, his child would toddle after his golden mastiffs just the way Kylee did now. Although she didn't toddle much anymore—she ran. She was getting so big. Where had the time gone? He loved her, had always loved her as if she were his. She *was* his in every way that mattered. The fact that a part of her came from Jake made her all the more special.

When he told Sarah he wanted her here, that he wanted all three of them here, he'd meant it. More than that, though, he *needed* them. Fear settled like bricks in his belly as he thought of what he would lose if he couldn't fix this with Sarah, of what they would all lose.

His memory drifted back to holding Kylee for the first time, of how tiny she had been, and an idea struck him. He'd promised her something he had yet to fulfill. He picked up the phone again and dialed his sister.

"Do you *know* what time it is?"

He smiled at the disgust dripping from Wren's sleepy voice. "Seven a.m., sis. Rise and shine."

"This has to be some sort of crappy attempt at passive aggressive behavior because I'm better looking."

A grin split Ethan's face. Nothing soothed him quite like Wren. "Yeah, but I'm in better shape."

"Bastard. What do you want?"

His smile vanished as he fisted his hand against the desk. "I need your help, Wren."

"Are you okay?" The traces of humor left her voice.

"No." He'd always been able to be honest with his sister.

"What's wrong?"

"It's a long story. Can you meet me later, at my office

downtown?"

"Of course. What time?"

"Seven, if that works for you."

"I'll be there."

"I know." She always had been, just like he'd always been there for her.

He hung up and scrubbed his hands over his face. Hopefully this would be a step in the right direction.

~~~~

The twinkling lights of the city stretched as far as the eye could see. Ethan stared out his office window while he waited for his sister as this morning's conversation with Sarah played through his mind. He turned when Wren knocked on the doorframe.

Pretty in fitted black slacks and a white scoop-neck blouse, she smiled. "Sorry I'm late. I stopped off for sustenance." She held up a large brown bag covered in grease spots. The scent of grilled meat and fried onions filled the air.

Touched that she remembered his favorite comfort food, Ethan walked forward and pulled her into a hug. "You brought us burgers from Malcom's. I can't remember the last time I had one."

"You sounded like you needed one." Easing back, she stared into his eyes. "Tell me what's wrong."

"Let's sit down first."

They sat at the conference table overlooking the city, and Ethan pulled massive cheeseburgers and two large boxes of golden, battered onion rings from the bag. "God, this is great. Thanks."

Brows furrowed, Wren took his hand. "You're really worrying me, Ethan."

Ethan stared into eyes the mirror image of his own and blew out a breath. "Sarah's pregnant."

Brows drawn together, winged up in surprise. "Wow. I didn't know she was seeing anyone."

"The baby's mine, Wren."

The onion ring she picked up fell back into the box. "You and Sarah?"

He stood again, restless, pacing. "Yes, me and Sarah. What's wrong with that?"

"Nothing. Nothing. I'm just a little surprised—a lot, actually. You two've always been so close. I didn't know there was more there than friendship."

"There wasn't, until recently. About nine months ago, things started to change—for me anyway. One night we took Kylee out for pizza. The waitress said we had a beautiful daughter. That wasn't such a big deal; people make comments like that all the time. We always laugh it off. It's a pretty natural assumption—man, woman, child, sitting at a table together, equals a family out for dinner."

"Okay." Wren made a 'go ahead' motion with her hand.

"Anyway, the pizza comes out and Sarah grabs a slice after cutting one up for Kylee. She bites in and this massive string of mozzarella droops down as she pulls the slice farther and farther away. She started to giggle when it stuck to her chin. I pulled the cheese from her chin, plopped it in my mouth, and she grinned at me. I'd never seen anyone so beautiful. I don't know what the hell happened, but she just about knocked me out of my fucking chair. All of a sudden, I'm looking at Sarah, one of my best pals, and I'm not thinking of her like a friend."

He turned back to the window, staring out. "I thought it would go away. I tried to keep my distance, but I couldn't stop thinking about her. I started wondering what it would be like if things were different. So, the night of Morgan and Hunter's wedding, we get into this fight and I kiss her. Things grew from there."

Wren's hand pressed against his shoulder and he turned. "You're in love with her."

"I'm so far past in love with her, and she doesn't believe me."

"That doesn't make any sense. How can she not look at you and see it? She knows you as well as I do."

"Because I fucked everything up—again!" He all but vibrated with frustration. "After I finally convinced her we should give being more than friends a try, I started getting twitchy. All of these what-ifs popped into my head. 'What if I mess it up?' 'What if I let her down?'" He met Wren's gaze, still haunted by the question that continued to eat at him. "What if I'm like Mom and Dad?"

Her eyes filled with sympathy, and she stepped closer, taking his hand, squeezing. "You are *nothing* like our parents, Ethan, in any way. Neither of us is. When we were kids, I used to get pretty upset that Mom and Dad weren't like Jake's parents or Hunter's mom. I just wanted them to pay attention to us, even a little bit, but now that we're older, I look back and thank God they left us alone. We were so lucky to have Ms. Willa all those years."

Ethan thought of their childhood nanny and smiled. "Yeah, we really were."

"I know I tease you about Mom and Dad, but that's only because I don't think I've ever met two people more ridiculous in all my life, and that's saying something in this crazy town we work in."

He chuckled.

"You're a good man, Ethan, the best I know. Sarah

will come around. She's a smart woman. Now, let's eat and you can tell me about my new niece or nephew."

And just like that, his world settled. Ethan followed Wren back to the table and sat down next to her. "Your niece or nephew is ten weeks old. He or she is the size of a strawberry and is looking less like an alien every day. I kept the book I bought when Sarah was pregnant with Kylee."

Grinning, Wren bit into an onion ring. "Aw, I bet he or she is the cutest little alien on the planet. I can't believe this. You're going to be a daddy, Ethan."

"I can hardly believe it myself. This is where you come in. I need your help, oh, master decorator."

"What can I do?"

He swallowed a bite of burger. "I want to surprise Sarah with two rooms for the kids; something special for Kylee and a nursery for the baby. I also need to make good on a promise I forgot about until recently. Kylee needs a kickass swing set for the yard."

"I can help you with all of this."

"I need it done as soon as possible."

"It's going to cost you."

"Good thing I'm a wealthy man. I want the best. It has to be the best for them."

"Leave it to me, brother. Luckily, I know Sarah well enough to know just what she'll like. I'll be by to take measurements Monday morning."

"We'll leave for meetings with Lisa at eight. Oh, and let's keep this quiet. We haven't told anyone yet."

~~~~

The stage was finally set. It was time to begin. Zeke pulled a blue topaz earring from his pocket and snickered. The poor fucker wasn't even going to know what hit him. He glanced over his shoulder as he walked through the shadows, making his way to the car of the man he'd been watching. He shoved a wedge in the door, slid a piece of metal through the small opening and released the lock. This was too easy! He popped the trunk next, pulling back the lip of the carpet, and dropped the earring with his gloved fingers.

Stifling his laughter, he grabbed a baggie from the pocket of his black hoodie, pulling one strand of blonde hair from the plastic at a time, scattering them about, making sure they stuck to the carpet fibers. He tossed in the taser, box of condoms, and wire next. Oh, he couldn't *wait* to watch this unfold.

He stared down at his treasures one last time and closed the trunk, sticking his middle finger up at the darkened windows of the bastard's house. He took out a pre-paid cell phone as he moved further into the shadows and dialed 9-1-1.

"Nine-one-one, what is your emergency?"

He deepened his voice and spoke. "I've got a tip on the 'Blue Chip Rapist.'" Zeke grinned, all but giddy. He *loved* his title. It felt so fucking good to say it out loud.

"Can I have your name please?"

"He lives at 2579 Riker Street, Santa Monica." He hung up as he snorted out a laugh.

Heart pounding with the thrill of it all, Zeke waited in the bushes until the wail of sirens got closer. Chuckling, he ran in the opposite direction, settling himself in his seat and drove away. Tomorrow was bound to be a spectacular day.

CHAPTER TWENTY-THREE

IN A PANIC, SARAH TORE THROUGH HER CLOTHES HANGING IN Ethan's closet. It was after midnight, and she had nothing to wear to her meeting in the morning. Out of nowhere, her belly had grown just enough to make buttoning and zipping her tailored slacks impossible. She snagged a pale purple sundress from a hanger and hurried to the bathroom, pulling her tank top over her head, replacing it with the dress. Staring in the mirror, she huffed out a breath. Her breasts, which had also increased in size, bulged dangerously against the fabric, making her look like a centerfold. "This isn't going to work."

Frustrated, she yanked the dress back off and studied her changing body. She and Ethan would have to stop by her house tomorrow and find her box of maternity clothes. When she'd packed everything up so long ago, she never thought she would need it again, but she hadn't been able to give it away. It was a link to Jake. Now she was happy she'd kept it.

She walked back to the dim bedroom, moving into the closet once more, hoping that by some miracle she could find something that would work until tomorrow afternoon.

Ethan popped his head through the crack in the door. "Sarah, are you okay?"

She tried fruitlessly to cover her skimpy panties and bra. "Yeah, I'm fine."

Despite the fact that she was scantily clad, Ethan

walked in and closed the door. Dressed in his boxers, his brow rose as he scanned the room. "What the hell have you been doing in here? It looks like a bomb went off."

Glancing around at the pants, tops, and dresses scattered about, she sniffled. "My clothes don't fit anymore." Horrified she was becoming emotional over something so silly, she turned for the bathroom. Grabbing a tissue, she blew her nose.

Ethan stood in front of her, brushing his hands down her arms while he smiled. "Go ahead and have your jag, Sarah. You had them with Kylee too."

She plucked up another tissue and dabbed at her eyes. "I'm not having a jag. I'm trying to figure out what I'm supposed to wear to my meeting with Lisa tomorrow. All of a sudden, nothing fits. It took months to show with Kylee; now look at me." *Is this really coming out of my mouth?* She closed her eyes on a wave of disgust. "Okay, I'm having a jag. I'm sorry."

Ethan continued to move his hands along her arms, sending her pulse racing.

"You don't have to apologize to me." He took a step back, his gaze tracking down her body and back up before he met her eyes. "You're absolutely amazing."

Self-conscious, she turned, grabbing for her robe on the back of the door.

Ethan took hold of her hand, stopping her. "Wait a minute." He turned her again until her profile reflected in the mirror and his muscled form moving forward. "Look at your belly, Sarah. You actually have a little bump." When he rested his big hand against her, covering the small curve, she watched his eyes fill with wonder, and her resolve to keep her distance began to crumble.

Her palm covered his and he stepped closer.

Enchanted by the moment, she didn't resist when he pressed his lips to hers. He deepened the kiss and she closed her eyes, savoring the feel of his mouth against hers. He stroked callused fingers over her belly, making her shiver. Her hands rested against his chest, intending to push him away, but they wandered to his shoulders, pulling him to her.

Ethan feathered kisses over her cheeks, her jawbone, down her neck while his fingers journeyed up to move in slow circles over the silk of her bra. His gentle touches left a trail of goose bumps, hardening her nipples. His warm breath heated her sensitized skin, and she gasped as she began to simmer from the inside out. He flicked his tongue against fabric as he tugged at the front clasp, catching her heavy breasts in his palms. "My God, Sarah," he groaned, suckling, tracing circles until she snagged her lip with her teeth on a moan and ran her hands through his hair. "You're so beautiful."

Staring into his eyes, listening to her heart, she met his mouth again in a hungry daze. Her mind protested her mistake, but she didn't care. Reality was for later. Tugging on his arm, she knelt with him, thigh to thigh, on the plush bath mat. She pressed herself against his firm chest, and he closed his eyes, hugging her close, stroking the skin of her sides.

"Let me be with you, Sarah. I miss being with you."

She rested her head on his shoulder and moved her hands over his firm butt, aching to touch him, craving to be touched.

He eased back. "Sarah."

She couldn't take the anticipation anymore. "God, Ethan. Put your hands on me."

Something passed through his eyes, something dark, dangerous and primitive as he stared at her, laying her back against the large rug. A thrill coursed through her and she moaned from the promise alone, knowing he was about to take her exactly where she wanted to go.

He began his journey down, skimming his teeth against her skin, tugging her panties free, leaving her half crazy from the waiting. He rained kisses along her knees, her thighs, and her hips set a rhythm. "Ethan."

His lips barely made contact as his tongue darted out in just the right spot. She shuddered out a breath and sucked one in, on the edge. He nipped next, bringing her pleasure and pain. "Mmm, Ethan."

He spread her legs wider, pulling her into his mouth, suckling. Gasping, she tensed, clenching her fists, raising herself up on her elbows, watching his assault, *feeling* the smooth skin of his inner lips, the coarse tension of his tongue. "God, Ethan, God, Ethan," she panted. She was there, almost over.

His finger plunged in, sweeping, massaging, while his mouth continued, relentless, and she lost her breath on a half cry, half scream, shattering as she never had before. Lost in something indescribable, she shuddered violently in wave after wave of bliss. Bright colors flashed before her eyes, and her head fell back. Before she could recover, he thrust himself into her, and she cried out again as he sent her reeling.

Flesh slapped against sweaty flesh as he slid back and forth. She gripped his hips, unable to do more. Ethan puffed gasps in and out and she stared as his glorious body tensed, as he threw his head back on a feral groan. He collapsed on top of her, his rapid breathing heating her shoulder, before he pulled away and rolled to his side.

They stared at each other, catching their breath. When he smiled at her moments later, she smiled back, not knowing what to say.

He trailed his hand to her lower stomach, resting his palm there. The animal was gone and Ethan was back, touching her tenderly. "I never knew I'd find a pregnant woman so sexy."

"Just give it a few more weeks. We'll see if you change your mind."

His smile vanished. "I won't. You're carrying my baby and I love you."

The truth was in his eyes, but she wasn't ready to give him everything again. Would she ever be? Losing him would wound her as deeply as losing Jake. If he came home one day, deciding he had changed his mind, it wouldn't be any different than the day the soldiers knocked at her door. She wouldn't be able to find her way through the grief this time. She couldn't lose like that again. On muscles still weak, she tried to sit up, needing to break contact.

He held her down with one hand against her shoulder. "I love you, Sarah. I love Kylee and this baby. Why don't you believe me?"

"Love is just a word without the feelings behind it."

Hurt flashed in his eyes as he moved back, pulled on his boxers and stood. "I know I screwed up, Sarah. I know I let you down, but what is it going to take to prove to you I mean exactly what I say? You believed me a month ago. How do we get back there?"

Sitting up, she wrapped her arms around her knees. "I don't know. I really don't. Everything's changed. I don't recognize my life anymore. Right now I need time. Just give me time to figure everything out."

He crouched in front of her, taking her face in his hands. "I won't give up on us, Sarah. I love you. I need you. Make sure you think about that while you're figuring everything out." He stood and walked out.

~~~~

Ethan made his way to the guest room all but vibrating with frustration. He tried to ignore the hurt hovering under the surface but wasn't succeeding. As he shut the door, he had to stop himself from slamming it, from smashing his fist against the wood. Damn it! Why wouldn't she believe him? He'd watched her eyes while they moved together. She'd been with him. They'd been connected, on the same page. Why did everything seem less complicated when they were in bed?

Pacing about, he stopped and stared out the window, focusing on the wild waves of the Pacific, already knowing the answer to his own question. When they were together, lost in the sensations they brought each other, it was all about emotion. Sarah wasn't willing to let her emotions lead her right now.

He'd hurt her, more than he realized. It was going to be a long road back to where they left off. The only thing he could do was keep telling her, keep showing her that he wasn't going anywhere. It would be his goal to spend as much time with her and Kylee as possible. His family *would* be together by the time the baby came. There was no other option.

Bone tired and weary, Ethan rubbed at his eyes, turning toward the bed. He glanced at the clock and winced. It was going to be hell on earth getting up in four hours. He pulled the covers back as the flashing red blip on his phone caught his attention. Whoever had left the message could wait. Lying back against the pillow, he closed his eyes. What if it was Wren? What if she was in trouble?

"Goddamn it." He grabbed the phone, coming to attention when he read Tucker Campbell's number in his missed call box. Pushing a button, he retrieved the message.

"Ethan, it's Tucker. We've made an arrest in the stalker case. It looks like we've got him cold. I'll keep you up to date as things unfold."

He dialed Tucker's number, unable to wait for an update.

"Detective Campbell."

"Tucker, it's Ethan. I know you're busy, but do you have a second?"

"I have about two. Hold on." The racket of the police station quieted when a door closed. "Okay."

"So, you've got him?"

"Yeah, it looks like. An anonymous tip came in at one a.m. yesterday morning. We've been keeping the break under wraps until we can be positive, but it looks pretty tight."

"How can you be sure?"

"For one, this is the first night in weeks we haven't been called out to find a woman dead with piano wire wrapped around her neck, and two, his trunk was loaded with all kinds of evidence. CSI found numerous blonde hairs, the taser, wire, and condoms. The lab is rushing results on the hairs, but at this point we're pretty damn sure."

"How long until they get back to you?"

"About four or five days. I really have to go. I have a date with our man-of-the-hour in interrogation room one."

"Keep me posted."

Ethan hung up, putting his phone back on the side table and stared at the ceiling. A cautious weight lifted from his shoulders. It was over. They caught the bastard. Sarah was no longer in danger. Life could go back to normal. They would wait for the lab results, of course, but by next week, Sarah and Kylee more than likely wouldn't be living with him. The house felt empty already. It would be too quiet without Kylee's chatter and noise, without Sarah's laughter.

Ethan scrubbed his hands over his face, reminding himself they would only be two miles down the road—but they might as well be two hundred. Nothing between Sarah and him would ever be the same. He doubted his open-ended invitation would still exist.

He should be happy. Sarah was safe. He could get back to work at the office and have his bed back. His life would be his own again. God, that sounded awful. Ethan sat up in a panic. What if he couldn't get her back? What if he couldn't fix this?

No, he would. He had to. She loved him. She'd told him so, albeit reluctantly, but she did. They'd all but destroyed each other on the bathroom floor. There was still something between them to salvage. His heart rate settled, and he rested his head against the pillow, waiting for sleep to take him under.

~~~~

Ethan followed the noisy sounds of a Monday morning breakfast to the kitchen. Kylee sat in her booster seat, chewing a mouthful of blueberry pancake. She grinned up at him as syrup dribbled down her chin. "Morning, kiddo. You're making a mess."

"I eating pancakes."

"I see."

She held up her fork, offering him a bite.

Bending forward, he took it and a warm blueberry burst in his mouth as he chewed. "Thank you. It's delicious."

"I made plenty. Help yourself," Sarah said as she walked to the table with a plate of her own.

He stared at her, gauging her mood. Where were they at after last night?

Sarah smiled at Kylee and cut into her pancakes. Apparently they were status quo despite the after-sex tension. "So, I see you found something that fits."

She looked at him and glanced down at the green strapless sundress he'd taken off her the night they'd eaten lobster tail on his upstairs deck. "It's a little tight, but it'll have to do. We have to stop by my house this afternoon. I need to pick up different clothing."

"Okay." Ethan made his way to the platter of pancakes, serving himself half a dozen. He sat next to Sarah at the table, pouring syrup lavishly.

"My God, Ethan. It's a wonder you're as cut as you are. How can you stand to eat all that?"

He grinned as she wrinkled her nose in disgust. "This is just my first helping."

"You've got to be kidding me."

Chuckling, he cut into his breakfast. "Of course I am. This should hold me until lunch."

A smile split her lips. "I certainly hope so."

He took her chin between his thumb and finger, examining her face. Her pale cheeks and dull eyes of late were replaced with a healthy glow and a bright blue sparkle. "You look good this morning."

"I feel good this morning. I'm hoping the sickness has passed." She pulled free from his hold and turned to her pancakes.

He chewed a bite and swallowed. "I have some

news."

She set her fork down. "What is it?"

"I got a call from Detective Campbell last night. They think they've caught him."

"What?" she whispered.

"They're pretty sure they have him."

"I-I can't believe this." She clutched at her napkin. "It's all over."

Ethan scooted his chair closer, skimming a finger against her cheek. "Hey, I thought you would be happy about this."

"I am. It's just hard to take it all in, hard to believe. I've been afraid of my own shadow for weeks. Now I don't have to be." She shrugged. "I imagine that sounds silly."

"Not at all. You've been through hell, Sarah."

She closed her eyes, pressing her cheek against his palm. He wanted to lean forward and feel his lips touching hers, but he stayed where he was. This morning was a step in the right direction; he'd be damned if they would take another step back. He brushed a hand over her hair, and she opened her eyes, smiling, bringing her hand up to rest over his.

"I can't seem to make it sink in. I want to laugh. I want to cry, but mostly I want to *believe* it." Her eyes watered. "We're safe. Kylee and I are safe."

What magic did she possess that undid him so easily? "Yeah."

"When did this happen?"

"Very early Sunday morning. Apparently someone called in a tip."

"So it's over? I think I might ask you a million times."

He grinned and broke their connection. "I think so. I know you're eager to get home, but I want you to wait a couple more days, just to be sure."

She stared down at her plate. "I'm not trying to sprint out of here. When you and the police think it's safe, Kylee and I will go."

"Okay." He cut into his pancake again, fighting the need to pressure her to stay. That wouldn't work with Sarah.

She picked up the remote for the small TV attached to the underhang of the oak cabinets. "Let's see what the news is saying about all of this."

"Tucker said they're keeping it quiet."

She pressed power anyway, and a sleek brunette filled the screen. "...the 'Blue Chip Rapist' has been apprehended. At this point, details are still coming in."

"So much for keeping it quiet," Sarah said, standing, making a grab for Ethan's empty plate.

He blocked her with his shoulder. "I can take care of my own dishes."

"I'm heading to the sink anyway. I need to get a cloth for Miss Messy."

They both glanced at Kylee, still busy with her pancakes. "More pease, Mama."

Sarah smiled. "More? You've had two."

Ethan grinned. "She must be growing. I'll get her another." He took Kylee's plate and walked to the counter, cutting a pancake into small pieces, listening to the news report with half an ear.

"No, that's not right."

He glanced up as Sarah stood close to the television. The snapshot of a man that looked very much like him filled the screen.

"That's not him."

He frowned as he brought Kylee her plate and moved to stand next to Sarah. "What do you mean?"

She turned to look at him. "That isn't him, Ethan. The eyes aren't the same. I'll never forget his eyes and the way they looked at me." She shuddered.

Buds of unease bloomed as he watched distress move over her face. He pulled her rigid body against him, wrapping his arm around her shoulders. "They're pretty sure, Sarah. The evidence is there."

She shook her head and met his gaze, determined. "This is wrong. It's all wrong."

"Okay. I'll put in a call to Tucker. I'll tell him what you just told me."

Nodding, she hugged him to her, holding on tight. She stared back at the screen as they flashed the man's picture again, along with his name: Eric Walker. "He looks so much like you, Ethan."

And it didn't sit right. Something about all of this didn't add up. He ran his hand over her soft hair. "I'll go make that call. Do you still want to keep your meeting with Lisa?"

"Yes, of course. I'm going to clean Kylee up, and we'll go wake Hailey. Let me know what Tucker says."

"We'll talk on the way to the florists." He pressed his lips to her forehead as her hand still resting at his waist tightened against the fabric of his shirt. "We'll figure this out, Sarah."

She gave him a small smile that didn't reach her worried eyes. "I know."

"Get things settled with Kylee and we'll go." He walked over to the sticky toddler and brushed her hair with a kiss. "Have fun with Hailey, squirt." He left the kitchen, making his way to the office and sat at his desk, putting his password into the computer. Within minutes he hacked his way through Los Angeles Police Department's firewall. He pulled up Eric Walker's mug shot and stared back at a face that could have been his own. The short black hair and gray eyes were close. Eric's cheekbones weren't as prominent, his coloring a little lighter, his lips a little thinner, but damn, the resemblance was something else.

Jotting down Eric's social security number and date of birth, he ran a search. Fifteen minutes later, he stared down at the information he'd called up, frowning. The guy was whistle clean. Nothing but a speeding ticket blemished the man's record. His Facebook account showed that he was engaged to a woman named Savannah. Savannah was astoundingly hot and bore no resemblance to nor shared any characteristics with the women he targeted for rape and murder. Her dark golden skin, brown eyes, and black hair were the polar opposite of Sarah. Eric had attended Princeton, graduating at the top of his class. He'd studied cancer research. If this was their guy, he didn't see the connection between UCLA's medical research facilities and rice paper card stock. When he'd gone through the files Tucker sent over, he didn't remember seeing a campus billing address. Ethan picked up the phone and dialed Tucker's number.

"Detective Campbell."

"Tucker, it's Ethan Cooke again."

"Hey, Ethan, what can I do for you?"

"You can answer some questions. I've run your man, and he doesn't fit."

Tucker blew out a breath. "On paper, you're right. He doesn't."

"It's more than that. Sarah saw his mug shot this morning. She's hell bent those aren't the eyes that stared back at her through the window at my parents' house."

"I don't know what to tell you, man. It's wrapping up

pretty solid on this end. Do you remember the earring Sarah received in the mail a few weeks back?"

"Yeah."

"We found the match under the carpeting in his trunk. The lab's working on the hair samples 'round the clock. They should have something for me later today, tomorrow morning at the latest."

The evidence was there, so why wasn't this sitting right? "Will you call me when you know? Sarah's ready to get home and get back to her life. If you've got a positive match, she can put this behind her and move on." He glanced up as she stood in the doorway.

"I'll let you know when I do."

"Thanks." Ethan hung up, his eyes never leaving Sarah's. She'd fixed her hair so it fell in loose curls, accentuating her stunning face. Need for her swamped him, and he clenched his jaw against it. Struggling for casual over the sudden burst of anger, he stood and stared out the window. "They're pretty convinced he's the rapist."

"Did you tell him what I said?"

"Yeah, I did, but the evidence against this guy is solid." He turned to face her, meeting her gaze. "Tucker should be able to wrap this up within the next twenty-four hours at the latest. You should be home by tomorrow night if everything goes the way he thinks it will."

She walked to his desk, her flowery scent filling the space. "That's quick."

"Yeah. We should go. I'll call Hunter during your meeting. He can go by your house and double-check the security system. When we get back this afternoon, we'll pack you and Kylee up."

She wandered around his desk, standing in front of

him, resting her hand on his arm. "I told you before, Kylee and I aren't planning to dash out of here."

If she wouldn't stay, he needed her to go. It would be better to get the transition over with instead of drag out the pain. Unable to hold the helpless frustration back, he gripped his chair. "You want out, we'll get you out. This is the way you want it, Sarah, not me."

Her arm fell away. "I'm sorry, Ethan."

"You're sorry? Don't be *sorry*, Sarah. What the hell good does that do? Your apologies don't change a goddamn thing. Let's just get out of here and get this over with." Despite the hurt he saw in her eyes, he walked off, leaving her standing there.

Chapter Twenty-Four

SARAH NIBBLED AT HER LIP AS ETHAN DROVE IN STONY SILENCE along the Pacific Coast Highway. His cellphone rang, interrupting the uncomfortable quiet. He pulled the phone free of its holder and pressed 'talk.' "Cooke. I take it you saw the news. Can I call you back in ten? Talk to you then." He put the phone back and glanced in her direction before turning his attention to the road.

Guilt swamped her as she thought of their conversation in his office. She'd heard his weary voice when he told Tucker she wanted to go home and move on with her life. He made it sound as if she was leaving him behind. In a way, wasn't she?

She snuck a peak at his handsome profile and was knocked back by a wave of love. No, of course she wasn't leaving him behind. She never could. He was a part of her life and always would be, but she needed to pick up the pieces first before she could move forward. But by protecting her own heart, she had hurt his. She needed to fix that. "Um, I forgot to tell you that next Friday is the baby's first ultrasound. Do you want to come with me?"

Ethan stayed silent for so long she figured he wouldn't answer. "Yeah, I'll be there."

"The appointment's at nine. If you want, Kylee and I can pick you up, or you can drop by and get us. We could go out for breakfast first."

"Next Friday's pretty busy for me. I'll probably just meet you there."

"Okay. If they really have caught the rapist, I was thinking about celebrating by bringing Kylee to the zoo—maybe this Saturday. You're welcome to join us."

He yanked the Rover to the side of the road, and she gasped, gripping the door handle. "Is this the way it's going to be?" he exploded. "Am I going to have to schedule appointments to see Kylee and my own child? Will you call me when he or she takes their first steps? Are we going to do the every-other-weekend deal? And what about the fucking holidays? Do you get Christmas and I'll take Thanksgiving? Fuck this!" He got out of the car, slammed the door, and walked toward the water.

Shaken, Sarah sat stone still, watching Ethan stand by the surf. His hair blew wild in the wind as his shirt and pants molded to the front of his body. In all the years they'd known each other, she had never seen him so angry. She took a deep breath as she pulled the keys from the ignition and walked to where he stood. The breeze rushed up to cool her hot skin while she stared out at the endless blue. "I don't know what to do, Ethan. I don't know how to give us both what we need right now."

He turned to face her. "I fucked things up between us. I know that. I get it, but when do I get to stop paying? What about the kids? Do they have to pay too? I could hate you for this Sarah, I really could."

Sarah felt the blood drain from her face as white hot rage surged to the surface. "Is that what you think this is, some sort of payback for breaking my heart? Has it really come to this between us?" She swiped at the hair blowing in her eyes. "You're *unbelievable!*" Rushing toward the vehicle, she had every intention of taking the Rover and leaving Ethan where he stood. She pressed the button to unlock the driver's side door as he grabbed her arm, spinning her around.

Using the anger and hurt radiating through her, she shoved him back a step. "Stay away from me, you bastard. You don't get to have it all. I gave you everything, and you didn't want it. Now I'm going to do what I need to to take care of myself." She tried to steady her ragged breathing echoing with unshed tears. "I'm late for my meeting. Get in or I swear to God I'll leave you behind." She got in on the driver's side and started the SUV, yanking her seatbelt in place as she joined the flow of traffic and Ethan shut his door.

"Sarah—"

"No. Don't you talk to me. I have absolutely nothing to say to you right now."

Moments later, she pulled up in front of the florists and shut off the engine. She rested her hands against the steering wheel and closed her eyes, taking several cleansing breaths. Steadier, she reached for her purse on the passenger side floor, brushing Ethan's pant leg. He bent forward and their fingers touched. Sarah yanked the bag from his grasp and whipped the visor down, reapplying her gloss and fixing her windblown hair.

She took another deep breath and stepped from the Rover, taking her camera bag from the back seat. How the hell was she supposed to concentrate on taking pictures when she was seething? She opened the door to the small but elegant shop and walked into the scent of flowers and espresso. Lisa and a dark-haired man sat at a table in the corner, chatting with tiny white cups set in front of them. She mustered up a smile. "I'm so sorry I'm late."

Lisa and the man in gray slacks and matching tie stood. Sarah suppressed a shudder as she met his translucent green eyes.

"No problem," Lisa said. "Matthew and I were going over our ideas for the ball. Matthew Denmire, meet my photographer, Sarah Johnson."

She held out her hand, and he gripped her fingers against his smooth, soft skin. "How lovely to meet you, Ms. Johnson."

She wanted to yank her hand back. His gaze met hers with such intensity, it felt as if he invaded her soul. "Please call me Sarah."

"All right, Sarah. Can I get you something to drink? Lisa and I are enjoying an espresso."

"I'll take water if it's no trouble."

"Of course." He finally released her and walked to a small refrigerator in the back office.

The door opened, and she turned as Ethan stepped inside. He wore his professional mask, but Sarah knew anger and resentment bubbled underneath his smile for Lisa. "Hey, Lisa."

Lisa smiled. "Ethan, it's always nice to see you. When am I going to finally convince you to grace the pages of my magazine? Circulation will go up twenty percent. We're doing a segment on 'America's Hottest Bachelors' in two months. Can I count you in?"

His polite smile grew into an arresting grin. "I'm thinking not."

"Well, if you change your mind, you tell Sarah."

He looked at her and his smile dimmed. She was sorry for it.

Matthew came back with her water, and she turned, taking the bottle he held out.

"Thank you," she murmured as Matthew's gaze wandered to Ethan. His eyes changed from friendly to hostile and back so quickly, she was sure she imagined it. "Matthew, this is my...friend, Ethan Cooke. I hope you don't mind, but he'll be joining us today."

"No, not at all. Mr. Cooke, can I get you a drink?"

"No, thanks. Do you mind if I use your office? I have a couple of phone calls to make."

"Help yourself."

Ethan wandered back to the room, dialing his cellphone as he went.

Sarah joined Lisa at the table with Matthew following behind.

"All right," Lisa said, "we should probably get down to business. Sarah, I'm looking for shots of Matthew's shop as well as a shot of Matthew and me together. I'd like to be able to give the business a plug even though it doesn't need one."

Sarah took her camera from the bag and changed lenses. "I'll start inside and work my way out." She framed a clever arrangement of sweeping calla lilies and roses all in white, settled in an ornate glass vase. It should have looked overdone, but the effect was somehow perfect. She moved about, capturing the simple yet chic ambiance of Matthew's shop while his and Lisa's voices carried on with their meeting.

Sarah focused on her next shot of a small fountain flowing into a pool surrounded by lush water plants, and goose bumps skittered along her skin. It felt as if Matthew watched her every move. She slid her gaze to the right, to where he and Lisa sat and met his stare. Ethan's murmurs came from the office to the left and every instinct shouted at her to run to him.

Admonishing herself for being silly, she gave Matthew a smile. When he smiled back, his eyes changed. The stirrings of a memory fought to surface, but she lost it. Chilled to the marrow, she moved toward the door. "I'm...just...going to get a few outside shots."

She stepped into the bright sunshine and crossed her arms, rubbing them, trying to bring the warmth back. She'd seen Matthew before, she was sure of it, but where?

Ethan stepped outside. "You didn't tell me you were leaving." His voice was cool and his eyes unreadable behind the black tint of sunglasses.

"I needed some fresh air."

"Are you okay?" He took a step forward and stopped.

She wanted to tell him that Matthew made her uncomfortable, that there was something about him that made the hair stand up on the back of her neck, but Ethan stood in front of her, jaw clenched and rigid. "Yeah." She stepped back and focused on the sign 'Elegant Expressions.'

A silver Mercedes sports convertible drove up, parallel parking behind the Rover. When Sarah heard Hunter's voice, she turned, frowning.

Ethan moved close, speaking to him before he walked to the Rover, got in and took off without sparing her a second glance.

Sarah let her camera dangle by the strap as she stared after the SUV until it disappeared around the corner of the busy street.

Hunter rocked back on his heels, running his tongue over his teeth. "Looks like you're stuck with me for a while. Ethan has some stuff to do."

"Oh, okay." She glanced down the street again.

"Are you going to tell me what's going on between the two of you?"

"Nothing's going on between the two of us. Absolutely nothing." Speaking the truth as far as she was concerned, she opened the door to the shop, steeling herself against her discomfort and walked in with Hunter following behind.

"What is this, Beefcake Monday?" Lisa said, smiling at Hunter.

Hunter chuckled, shaking his head.

"How's that beautiful wife of yours?"

"Morgan's great—very busy with work, but chaos makes her happy."

Sarah rested her hand against Hunter's well-muscled arm. "Hunter, this is Matthew Denmire. He's handling the flowers for the Bikini Ball."

"Nice to meet you, man."

"Likewise."

Sarah removed her hand from Hunter's arm as Matthew stared at it.

"What do you say we get a couple of good pictures of Matthew and me? That should wrap us up for the day," Lisa said.

"Sure. Matthew, I want to start by getting a couple shots of just you. Why don't you stand over here next to this amazing arrangement. This should be fairly quick and painless." Sarah stood next to him. "Do you mind if I fix your tie first, just a bit?"

"No, that's fine."

She gave a gentle tug to the knot and brushed her hands over his surprisingly firm shoulders, making sure he was wrinkle free. "Perfect." She smiled, stepping back, holding the camera up, tightening her focus on his acne-scarred face. "Give me a smile, Matthew."

When he did, she pressed the button.

"Okay, Lisa, why don't you come on over now." Both Lisa and Matthew smiled, and she took another picture then dropped the camera strap around her neck as the memory that wanted freedom surfaced again, just out of reach.

Eyes amused—as if they laughed at a private joke—stared into hers. "Is something wrong, Sarah?"

Snapping back, she shook her head. "No, I'm sorry. I feel like I've seen you somewhere before."

Matthew's brows furrowed slightly as if pondering. "I don't think so. It would be hard to forget a face like yours."

The chill ran up her spine again, and Hunter stepped forward. "Are we finished, Lisa?"

"Sarah's free to go. Matthew and I plan to meet again next Sunday. Sarah, I'd like for you to be here. He'll have a bunch of mockups ready for us. I want some shots of those."

"What time?"

Lisa looked at Matthew. "What time, Matthew?"

"Does one-thirty work for both of you?" He smiled, looking at Sarah. "I have some great ideas. I can't wait to show you."

Although his smile was pleasant enough, his words felt like a threat. Sarah reached for Hunter's hand as she moved toward her camera bag. "I look forward to it," she lied. "Your arrangements are beautiful."

"I watched you admiring the lilies and roses. Please take them along with you—a small gift from me to you."

There was nothing she wanted less. She just wanted to leave. "Oh, I couldn't possibly. Your customers will miss out."

He walked to the arrangement and picked up the vase, handing it to her. His hand rested on hers as he spoke. "I insist. You wouldn't want to hurt my feelings." The pressure of his fingers increased for the flash of a second.

Hunter's eyes began to heat with warning as he grabbed the vase. "Why don't I carry these for you,

Sarah."

"Thank you, Matthew, for the kind thought. We should go."

Hunter opened the door, and she breathed in the sea. Relieved, she turned back, smiling. "I'll see you both on Sunday."

"Thank you, honey. Hunter, will you or Ethan be joining us too?"

"I'm not sure. Hopefully this whole ordeal will be history by then."

"I heard about the arrest early this morning. My reporters should be sinking their teeth into the story as we speak. I certainly hope they've caught the bastard—sick son of a bitch."

"Now there's an understatement," Hunter said, putting his arm around Sarah as they headed out the door. "See you, Lisa. Matthew."

Sarah sat in the convertible and rested her head against the seat. "That was absolutely exhausting."

Hunter glanced in his rearview mirror as he pulled into traffic. "That guy was obnoxious."

"I didn't like him. He gave me the creeps."

Hunter took his eyes off the road, his brows disappearing under his sunglasses as he frowned. "If we get the all clear tomorrow, I can still go with you on Sunday."

"No, that's okay. I'm sure he's nice enough. He just came on a little strong."

"Yes, he did. He needs a few lessons in subtle flirting. You never get the girl like that."

"Maybe you could teach him. From what I hear, you're pretty sly." The first genuine smile in hours split her face. "Rumor has it you've got great moves."

He squirmed in his seat. "Jesus, Sarah."

She threw her head back and laughed, deep and long. God, she loved to tease him. "Oh, it's too easy. You make me smile, Hunter. You always have."

"What about Ethan? He doesn't seem to make you smile these days, and vice versa."

Her light mood vanished. "It's complicated and I'm not ready to talk about it."

"I'm not going to push, but I hate seeing two of my favorite people so miserable. It took me a little time to get used to it, but I like the idea of you two. I think you're good for each other."

"I'm not so sure. Since the moment things changed between us, it's been one rollercoaster ride after another."

"Isn't that part of the deal? Since when is a relationship supposed to be a smooth ride? I love Morgan more than I ever thought possible; we haven't had a smooth day yet. Quite frankly, I don't want one. Where's the fun in that?"

"But you and Morgan are perfect together. What you have works. Everything's so messy between Ethan and me. I don't remember it being like this with Jake."

"Ethan isn't Jake."

"I know. I'm not comparing them."

"You sure about that?"

Was she? Ethan and Jake were entirely different. Where Jake had always been easygoing and sweet, Ethan was intense and funny. She'd never mistaken that. The only similarity she could draw between the two was her fear of loss. She lost Jake so suddenly, so unexpectedly. In many ways, she'd lost Ethan the same way. He'd left, and that had been the end of it.

She'd had no choice when Jake died, but she could choose not to wait around for Ethan to break her heart again. It was easy for him to say he wanted permanency, that he wanted it all, but living the reality of what that meant was entirely different. "Yes, I'm sure."

Hunter turned into Ethan's drive, stopping at the security gate. He punched in the code and pulled through, waiting for the gate to slide shut as Ethan and Austin always did. "Look, Sarah, you have to do what's best for you. Ethan has to do the same. Just try to remember your history. You two've been through a hell of a lot together. I would hate to see things damaged to the point that you can't fix them."

She closed her eyes. "I'm afraid we're getting to that point. It's time for me to go home. I hope those results come back tomorrow and tell us all what we want to hear. I think we both need some space." She got out of the Mercedes when Hunter pulled up behind the Rover and walked around to his side, giving him a hug as he closed his door. "Thank you, for everything. I love you so much."

He hugged her back. "I love you too. Everything's going to be okay."

She wanted to believe him. It was on the tip of her tongue to tell him about the baby, but she needed a little more time. "I'm going to go make Kylee's day and take her in the pool."

"See you soon. Morgan and I will stop by tomorrow night if you're back at your house."

"That would be great." She kissed his cheek and headed toward Kylee and Hailey's noisy laughter coming from the side lawn.

~~~~

Ethan's gloved fists slammed into the punching bag

over and over in a futile attempt to rid himself of the simmering, helpless anger. Gritty rock pounded out of the stereo system as drops of sweat flew from his body with each blow to the bag. The last three months had finally taken their toll, and he'd had enough. Everything with Sarah was so far past fucked up, he didn't even know where to start to turn it around. Perhaps it was better that she was leaving tomorrow.

Tucker had called with the news an hour ago. The DNA results were in, and it looked like the show was over. Their man was going down big time. It was time to move forward—wherever the hell that was. The music died down to a dull roar, and he swung around.

Hunter stood across the room, staring at him.

"I'm not in the mood for company."

"It's a good thing I'm not company then," Hunter said, walking forward.

He turned again and his fist connected with the bag. "I mean it, man. You're bound to get punched in the face."

"I'll take my chances. And I promise I'll punch back." He sat on the weight bench. "What the fuck crawled up your ass, Ethan?"

"Nothing. Just a shit week."

"We have shit weeks all the time. What makes this one any different?"

"Everything. Everything's different."

"And that means..."

"That means things are pretty much over between Sarah and me, but there's just one problem, one minor complication."

"Again, and that means..."

"That means Sarah's pregnant."

Hunter rushed to his feet and stopped the swaying

bag. "What?"

Ethan's gloved hands rested on his hips as he puffed air in and out. "You heard me."

"You son of a bitch. You better not be backing out."

Ethan surged forward, shoving Hunter up against the wall. "I'm not backing out of anything. I want Sarah and this baby, Kylee too. I want the whole fucking package."

"Well, what's the problem then?"

He backed away from Hunter and began to pace. "Ironically enough, Sarah doesn't. She's leaving tomorrow with my baby, with Kylee, with all of it. And there's nothing I can do." The helpless anger erupted again. Yelling out, he turned, landing a roundhouse kick into the punching bag. The black leather swung back and forth, and he swept his leg around again, connecting once more. He punched, over and over then threw his boxing gloves to the ground. Finally spent and completely defeated, he sat on the weight bench Hunter abandoned. "I don't know what to do, Hunter. I don't know how to fix this mess."

"Do you love her?"

Ethan's gaze snapped up to Hunter's. "What the hell kind of question is that? Of course I love her. I want to marry her, to share my life with her, with our kids. I hurt her when I left. After the conversation you and I had, I saw my dad at the airport and he pretty much confirmed what you said."

"I was wrong. I was absolutely and completely wrong."

"I'm working on believing that. I'd like to think Sarah and I could make this work. I want it to work."

"That's most of the battle. Let her go home tomorrow. You both need a few days. Give her a little time. Sarah's done a hell of a job of pulling her life together. These past couple of years've been hard for her. I can only imagine it must be scary for her to think she could lose it all again. One day she had Jake, the next day she didn't. I'm sure that's something she never wants to live through again."

He hadn't thought of it that way, but he should have. Hunter's words were like a balm, relieving most of the sting of the past few days. "I'll back off a bit and give her some time to sort through everything."

"Not too much time, though." Hunter tossed him a towel.

Ethan wiped the dripping sweat from his face and torso.

"Oh," Hunter continued, "congratulations, man. You're going to make a hell of a father. You already are. I think Jake would be damn proud to know you stepped up to the plate for Sarah and Kylee. He'd be happy to know you love them the way he did."

Honored by Hunter's words, Ethan held out his hand. "Thanks, man." Hunter grabbed hold and pulled him into a quick hug.

~~~~

Zeke closed the store early. How could he go on with his day when she'd been so close? He couldn't stand the thought of making nice with all the rich ho-bags that would come in demanding their flowers.

As soon as Sarah left with the fucking Golden Adonis, and he'd been able to shove the ever-offensive Lisa out the door, he'd locked up, eager to get home, desperate to be in front of his 'Wall of Sarah.' Holding the water bottle she'd left behind, he stared at picture after picture of her bright blue eyes, remembering the way her hands had felt against his skin, the way she'd smelled of wildflowers. She had smiled at him, just as she did in the pictures. Those beautiful eyes of hers had looked straight into his, and it had been magical. It made him surer than ever that this was destiny.

She was looking forward to his plans for her next Sunday. He relished her exact words. Closing his eyes, he thought of pretty pink lips moving over straight white teeth as she said them. He was only days away from feeling those lips against his mouth, against his hard cock. Groaning, he freed himself and moved his hand up and down, imagining how much she was going to love it. She would thrash around in ecstasy, screaming for him as he returned the favor, but that wasn't the best part.

The best part would be watching her eyes fill with fear as he held the wire close to her neck, listening to her beg, as she would in pleasure as he rammed himself into her. The scream before he wrapped the cable tight would be the greatest moment of his life. God, he couldn't wait for her to kick and claw until she stilled. Her beautiful blue eyes would stare into his, blank with death. He moved his hand faster and faster, exploding, thrilled with the power of knowing he would be the last person she would see before it was all over.

After cleaning himself up, he wiggled the mouse on his computer, calling up the local news and began to laugh. He laughed until tears ran in torrents down scarred cheeks. It was just so perfect. The poor bastard was actually taking the fall. Who said there wasn't justice in the world? He'd been exactly right to pick a slick-looking asshole who thought he was better than everyone else, just like fucking Ethan Cooke. He seethed as he thought of the way Master Cooke had waltzed into his shop with his perfect skin and perfect muscles, barely sparing him a look. He thought he was better than Ezekiel Matthew Denmire.

Well, fuck him, because he was about to be replaced. Ethan wasn't going to end up with Sarah; he was. When he was done with Sarah, he looked forward to teaching Master Cooke that the good looking guys were about to start finishing last.

Standing, Zeke made his way to the front door. It was time to peruse Santa Monica Boulevard and find himself a street whore. He needed to take care of his craving for Sarah for the night. No one called the police when they went missing. It was a short-term solution to fulfill his ever-growing need to kill.

Grabbing a fresh box of rubbers, he left. He had a few new moves to try on the lucky bitch he would snag tonight. He could hardly wait. Once he finished with that, he'd head out for a nice dinner, then come home and plan his date with Sarah. It was going to be perfect. It had to be.

CHAPTER TWENTY-FIVE

SARAH FOLDED A SMALL PINK TANK TOP AND PLACED IT IN Kylee's suitcase. She grabbed another shirt from the laundry basket on Ethan's bed, repeating the process. The ever-present ocean winds blew through the open balcony doors, filling the master suite with the scent of late afternoon low tide while Kylee chattered away at Mr. Ruff and smushed bright green Play-Doh against her large play mat. Smiling as she listened to her daughter, Sarah picked up a pair of pajama bottoms and absently put them where they belonged. Her smile faded as she thought of how silent her own room would be when she tried to sleep in it later that night. She was going to miss the rush of waves outside her window and the comfort of knowing Ethan was just down the hall.

She didn't have to leave, but that was the choice she was making. The last few months of hell were finally over. It was time to move forward. Ultimately she wanted to stay and give Ethan everything he wanted, everything they both wanted, but she knew she needed to go. Their situation had become volatile, their emotions too strong. They were teetering on the edge of destroying something that meant too much to both of them. It was better to take some time and sort this mess out and see what they could salvage after everyone had a chance to breathe.

She hadn't seen Ethan since he'd left her at Matthew's shop yesterday. His Rover hadn't left the driveway, but he'd avoided her. Their argument played through her mind like a broken record. Did he really believe she was going home just to punish him, that she would keep him from the children out of spite? She shook her head. No, he'd been frustrated, angry and lashed out. The last thing she ever wanted to do was hurt him. Despite what he thought, she loved him too much for that. This was exactly why they needed their space. Right now, all they were doing was causing each other pain.

More determined than ever that this was the best decision for everyone, Sarah picked up her pace. She couldn't move forward if she didn't begin. *They* couldn't move forward if she didn't go home.

She zipped Kylee's full suitcase as Ethan knocked on the doorframe. Sarah glanced up, giving him a small smile. "Hi."

"Don't lift that. It's too heavy." Casual in jeans, a gray t-shirt, and bare feet, Ethan stepped forward, taking the suitcase handle before she could.

She smiled again as he set the large bag on the floor. "Thanks."

His gaze wandered from her eyes, down her body, settling on the small bulge under her jeans and fitted red camisole top.

Suddenly nervous, she swiped loose strands of hair behind her ear and turned to fold the remaining laundry. "We should be out of the way within the half hour."

"There's no rush."

She went on as if he hadn't spoken, eager to avoid any awkward silence. "I bet it'll be nice to have your bed back. When I'm finished here, I'll put the sheets in the wash before we head out."

Ethan pulled a v-neck maternity top from the basket and folded it. "Don't worry about it."

"The least I can do is throw the sheets in the washing

machine, and you don't have to fold my laundry."

Huffing, he tossed the shirt on top of the pile and sat on the bed. "Is the invitation for breakfast next Friday still open?"

She stopped folding and looked at him, smiling. He was trying to make things right again. "Of course. Do you want to ride together or just meet me at the diner?"

"I'll pick you and Kylee up." He placed his hand on hers as she picked up another top. "I'm sorry about yesterday, Sarah. I said some really asshole things I shouldn't have. As much as I want you and Kylee to stay, I'm going to back off and give you the space you need."

Her fingers tightened against his. "I'm sorry too. I know this is hard. There's no one in the world I want to hurt less than you."

Standing, he wrapped his arms around her, moving his hands up and down her back.

She closed her eyes, holding on tight. She missed this, the easy way they'd always had with each other.

He eased back, staring into her eyes. "I love you, Sarah."

With one declaration, the complications came flooding back. She tried to pull away as her emotions played tug-of-war. She wanted to steel herself to his words, to protect herself from the hurt almost as much as she wanted to hug him close and tell him she would never leave.

He tightened his arms around her, locking her body against his. "Look at me."

The pain radiating in his voice left her no choice.

"I need you to believe me." He skimmed his knuckles along her cheek as his gray eyes pleaded. "I love you, Sarah," firm lips whispered over hers. "I'm so desperately in love with you."

She couldn't help but respond, had no choice but to believe. Closing her eyes, giving into her heart, giving into Ethan's, she moved in, bringing her lips to his. He brushed his hands through her hair, caressing, as her tongue entered his mouth, moving with his, tangling in a gentle dance. There was no urgency, only tenderness.

Ethan eased back, kissing her cheeks, the tip of her nose. "I'm not giving up on us."

"I'm not asking you to give up. I'm asking for time."

"I can give you that." Ethan hugged her once more and stepped back. "Let's get you and the artist home."

Confused, frowning, Sarah glanced over her shoulder at the blobs of dough Kylee busily set about. Her face quickly transformed with her grin. "I definitely see potential there. We may have a famous sculptor on our hands."

~~~~

Ethan walked back to the living room after bringing the last suitcase to Sarah's bedroom. "I think that's it. If you forgot anything, you know where I live."

She smiled, carrying a bag of groceries to the kitchen. "Yeah, I think I'll be able to find you."

Following behind, Ethan took the gallon of milk from the table and put it in the refrigerator. "Do you need any help?"

"No. I think I'm good. I have my helper here."

"I Mama's big helper," Kylee said as she showed him a box of cereal then put it in the cupboard with a flourish and slam of the door.

God, he was going to miss her. "Yes, you are." Glancing around, he saw that everything was under control. "Well, it looks like things are back to normal around here. I guess I'll head out if you're all set." He didn't want to leave them.

Sarah turned from the pantry with a jar of strawberry jam in her hand. "Are you sure? You're welcome to stay. You don't have to rush out."

Unable to go, he leaned against the counter, buying himself a few more minutes. "I have some things to do, but I should tell you we've upgraded your security a bit. I added more motion sensors outside and had security glass put into the panes on the front and back doors. No one's cutting through that stuff."

"Thank you."

"You're welcome." Afraid he would break his promise and beg her to change her mind, he started toward the door. "I'll probably swing by sometime in the next couple of days," he called over his shoulder.

Kylee ran after him. "Bye-bye, Ethan. I miss you."

He swung around and picked her up, hugging her tight. "Bye, kiddo. I'll see you soon."

"O-tay." She squirmed to get down. "I go play in my room. Where's Mr. Ruff?"

"He's on your bed, honey," Sarah said, her eyes fixed on his.

He set Kylee on her feet, and she dashed off. The room was suddenly silent.

Sarah took his hand in hers, gripping it tight. "I'll be working from home a lot over the next couple of weeks. I have dozens of pictures to proof and touch up. I want you to come by as often as you like, just like you always have."

"Maybe we can take Kylee to the park and out for pizza one of these nights."

"I think that sounds great. Call me when your schedule looks good, and we'll make it happen."

He couldn't stand to draw this out any longer. He reached for the doorknob with his free hand.

"So, the security system's all set then?"

He paused with his hand on the knob. "Yeah. Just set the panel like usual, and you should be good to go." With nothing more to say, he opened the door and she dropped his hand.

"Wait." Sarah blew out a breath. "I-are..." Staring into his eyes, she took his hand, placing his palm against the swell of her lower stomach. "This baby is as much yours as mine. Just because I'm here doesn't change that. It doesn't make you any less a part of our lives. Thank you for trying to understand, for giving me time."

Unable to speak, he pulled her into a hug, and they both held on. How was he going to get through this? "I've gotta go, Sarah."

"Okay." Nodding, she pressed her lips against his and stepped back. She closed the door behind him and emptiness consumed him. The last three months of his life had revolved around Sarah and Kylee, more so than the last few years. Lost, he had no idea what to do with himself. Perhaps a walk on the beach and some take-out would be a good way to start. Maybe he would drive into the city afterward and get some work done at the office. He would go over reports until he was too tired to care that he was going home to an empty house. He reached for the door handle on the Rover, stopping when Sarah's front door opened again.

"Ethan?"

"Yeah?" How could he leave and get this over with if she wouldn't let him go?

"I was going to grill a couple of pieces of chicken and make a big salad, maybe warm up some thick slices of whole grain bread. Do you want to stay for dinner?"

He smiled as he realized she didn't want him to go either, that this was as hard on her as it was on him. Hope bloomed bright as he started back toward the house. "That sounds good. Let me start the grill."

~~~~

It had been ten days, ten goddamn days since Sarah had gone back to her own house, and fucking Ethan Cooke was always there! Why was he *always* fucking there? It was like clockwork. Without fail, his rich boy Rover would pull up in her drive sometime after six and stay for hours.

True, he had no plans to take her, not yet, but Master Cooke was screwing everything up. How could he watch her through his binoculars and imagine all the things he would do to her when the cock-sucker was framed in every single shot? He'd had more than enough.

Zeke stared down at his new purchase and picked it up, tempted to get out of his car and put a bullet right between Ethan's eyes. Prince Charming wouldn't be so pretty with half of his face on the pavement, now would he? He dreamed of murdering Ethan Cooke as often as he dreamed of making Sarah cum.

With reluctance, he set the gun back down. If he didn't already have plans for his beautiful Sarah, he would do it, but a moment's satisfaction wasn't worth messing everything up. N*othing* was going to mess up what he had in store for Sarah. Just three more days— three more days that felt like an eternity.

A movement caught his attention, and he glanced up. Ethan and Sarah stepped out her front door. They both gave the twerp—Sarah's mirror image—a kiss and headed for the SUV. The hot little babysitter waved along with the child from the doorway as the Rover pulled out of the driveway. Where in the hell were they going?

Zeke stared at the babysitter as she talked to the kid and shut the door. Hmm, should he follow Fuck Head and Whore Bitch or head for the house? Decisions, decisions. The babysitter wasn't blonde and her eyes were brown, but a good fuck was a good fuck. Her tight little body looked like it could give him a nice, fast ride, *and* he was willing to bet she would fight like hell as he squeezed the life from her. Need throbbed through him and he closed his eyes, breathing through his cravings to take another life.

Moments passed before he found a loose grip on control. Calmer, Zeke glanced up just as Ethan took a right at the stop sign. Sarah's shiny locks blew in the wind as the vehicle accelerated. He needed to follow her. She wanted him to. He started his car, made a u-turn, and trailed at a distance, pulling into a parking spot a hundred yards from Ethan and Sarah as they stopped at the beach. He grabbed his binoculars, watching Sarah, dressed in Capri jeans and a flowing white cotton top, take off her sandals. Master Cooke rolled his slacks past his ankles then took off brown leather Oxfords that cost more than the suit Zeke still wore. Why did some bastards have it all? Ethan pulled off his sage green tie next and threw it in the vehicle along with his and Sarah's shoes.

Zeke clenched his jaw, steaming in and out several deep breaths when Ethan wrapped his arm around Sarah's waist, and she did the same. They ordered ice cream cones and walked along the beach. The surf rushed up to meet their feet, and he flashed back to the glorious moment when he'd fallen for Sarah. The image was now destroyed, was now ruined, as he watched her hold her strawberry cone up to Ethan's mouth for him to taste.

She smiled and swiped her tongue against the vanilla ice cream Ethan held to her lips. When their eyes met, staring into each others, Zeke reached for his gun. "Fuck you, whore! You fucking whore!" He slammed his palms against the steering wheel until bruises bloomed along his palms. Hands shaking, he slipped the magazine into place just as he remembered the blue dress he'd ordered for Sarah. It had arrived in the mail earlier this afternoon. If he didn't calm down, he'd mess it all up. She wouldn't be able to wear it. She would pay on Sunday while she wore just what he'd picked out for her. Oh, she would *pay*.

~~~~

"It's such a beautiful night for this. What a good idea," Sarah said, smiling into Ethan's eyes.

Ethan winked, smiling back. "Stick with me. I'm full of them."

"You're certainly full of something."

He stopped, glancing at her grinning face, then at the waves and back. "I'd be careful. You're treading on dangerous ground."

With a mischievous twinkle, she drilled her finger into his stomach. "Don't even think about it. The water's freezing, and besides, you wouldn't want our baby to hear me scream. It could be very traumatic."

He narrowed his eyes. "Now who's full of shit? I read that the baby won't be able to hear until twenty weeks gestation. We've got eight weeks to go."

She shrugged, diverting her gaze. "I don't know what you're talking about."

A grin split his face. "Christ, Sarah, you're such a bad liar."

She raised her chin and looked down her nose. "Again, I don't know what you're talking about."

Delighted with her and relieved that they were back to where they started, Ethan chuckled and pulled her closer against him as they walked again. "I'll give you a free pass for the next six months, but after that, all bets are off."

"I guess we have a deal, if that's what you want to call it." She chuckled as he kissed the tip of her nose.

They continued down the beach until he stopped abruptly, turning their bodies so that Sarah's back rested against his chest and his chin nestled the top of her hair. The foamy surf rushed up, tickling his toes as the spectacular pinks and purples of the sunset painted the sky. He stared down at the bump as the wind blew against Sarah's shirt. It still amazed him that his child grew inside her. "Let me put my hands on you," he said next to her ear. "I want to feel my baby with you."

Sarah laced their fingers and placed their hands on her stomach. Glancing up, she smiled. "I can't wait to see him or her tomorrow. I pulled rank and asked my dad to request 4D imaging. I think he's as eager to get a peek at his new grandbaby as we are."

"It always helps to have an in with the obstetrician." Ethan moved his palms up and down over the firm swell that now reached Sarah's belly button. "We should start a baby book."

"I bought one the other day."

"So, what do you think, are we having a girl or a boy?"

"My gut tells me we're having another girl, but I could be completely wrong."

Another daughter. Thrilled with the idea, he kissed the top of her head. "I'll take whatever we're given and be more than happy. Just think, little Mildred Cooke will be here before we know it."

Sarah frowned. "Mildred? I don't know about that."

It was so much fun to mess with her. "Mildred was my great-grandmother's name. It has to at least make the list of options." He had no idea what in the hell his great-grandmother's name had been.

"As long as we're in agreement that it will get crossed off the list too."

He stared into her eyes, clutching his chest. "You're breaking my heart here, Sarah."

She searched his face as he bit the inside of his cheek. "Maybe we can use it as a silent middle name that only you and I know about."

He threw back his head, roaring out a laugh. "God, Sarah, I love you."

She gave his arm a smack and turned away. Moments later, he heard her snort of laughter. "Mildred Cooke. That's just awful."

"Yeah, it is." He turned her to him again, holding her face in his hands as he darted a glance at her lips, lips he hadn't touched since she'd moved back to her house. Restraining himself, he took her hand and they started toward the Rover. "Come on, let's get you home. We have an important date in the morning."

"Do you want to stay over?"

He tightened his grip on her fingers, knowing what she offered. Not only was she willing to share her body, but the intimacy of her bed. They were moving in the right direction. He didn't want to ruin it. "Not tonight. Let's take a little more time."

"Okay." She glanced over her shoulder, frowning,

searching, shuddering.

He followed her gaze around the beach and parking lot. "What is it?"

"I don't know. I keep getting a creepy feeling. Sometimes it still feels like I'm being watched. I haven't been able to shake it." She smiled, shaking her head. "I know, silly."

Ethan pulled her closer as he continued to look around. The man accused of the rapes still sat in a jail cell. He'd been refused bail, but something still didn't sit right, something still didn't add up. "Would you feel better if I stayed tonight?"

"You don't have to."

"I know I don't have to, but I will. I'll camp out on the couch. It'll be like old times."

"I wouldn't hate it," she hesitated.

"Then I'm staying. Let's go home and break out the spare pillow and blankets. Maybe we can find a movie on TV."

She rested her head against his shoulder, and he felt her body relax.

After the ultrasound appointment tomorrow, he was going to go home and continue crosschecking the orders for rice paper. After the evidence had come back on the accused, he'd stopped looking. His gut told him there were answers in the rice paper, to keep going, so he would.

Chapter Twenty-Six

THE DIM EXAMINATION ROOM ECHOED WITH THE RAPID heartbeat of his child, and Ethan loved more than he knew he could. Kylee sat in his lap with Mr. Ruff while he gripped Sarah's hand in his. Everything that mattered most in his life was right here.

Enchanted, he couldn't take his eyes off the screen. Their tiny baby's arms and legs moved about at random. Perfect little fingers flexed as the fetus turned, showing off its still elongated rump. "The baby's mooning us," he said, grinning.

Sarah looked away from the monitor, laughing, and smiled at him.

"Mooning us," Kylee repeated with relish.

Snuggling her against him, Ethan stared at the screen as the little body continued to shift about in Sarah's womb. "That's your baby, Kylee, your brother or sister."

"My baby."

"That's right." He kissed the top of her soft blonde hair pulled back in perky side ponytails.

The sonographer continued to mark spots and freeze the frame, pointing out different parts of the anatomy. She stopped on the face with its tiny nose jutting from a profile that still resembled an alien's. Ethan could just make out earlobes still forming and smiled. The sonographer pressed and clicked at random, or so it seemed. "I have everything I need. I'll print out pictures for you to take home. Congratulations." The woman handed Sarah a paper towel and left the room.

Sarah wiped the clear goop from her stomach and fixed her pants. Sitting up, she beamed. "Wasn't that amazing?"

"It really was." Ethan stood with Kylee in his arms and pressed his lips to Sarah's, caught up in the wonder of the miracle they had created together. "You're amazing. I love you."

Bright blue eyes locked on his as her hand moved to his cheek. "I...love you too."

He rested his forehead against hers, happy, relieved. It had been so long since she'd told him.

"I love you too," Kylee chimed in as her small hand rested against Ethan's other cheek, mimicking her mother.

He grinned, looking at Kylee as she pushed her forehead up. Catching on, he rested his forehead against the baby soft skin of hers. "I love you too, Squirt."

The sonographer came back in with a form for Sarah to give to the front desk and pictures in an envelope.

"Thank you. " Sarah smiled. "We'll have to put these in the baby book."

"Little Mildred's first pictures," Ethan said with a wink.

Sarah hopped down from the table, giving him a nudge to the ribs. "You better be careful, Ethan, that name might grow on me."

He opened the door, scoffing. "Like hell."

"Like hell, Mama."

Wincing, Ethan put his hand over Kylee's tiny mouth as he walked down the hall. "You're going to get me in trouble, kid."

Sarah's brow winged up. "You're right about that one. That's just what I need Kylee saying at her Monday morning playgroup."

"Sorry."

"Sorry, Mama."

He grinned as Sarah rolled her eyes.

When they made it out to Sarah's sedan, Ethan buckled Kylee in. "See you tonight, ma'am."

"O-tay."

He shut Kylee's door and pulled Sarah against him before she could get in the car. "Do you mind if I come by later?"

"You know I don't. I have a few errands to run, but we should be home before dinner."

"I'll be at the house for most of the day. I have some things to do." He thought of the files he planned to crosscheck. "I'll be over around six."

"We'll see you then." She kissed him quick and moved back, settling in her seat. "I'll try to have the baby book ready for you."

"I look forward to it."

Sarah started the car and drove away with a wave.

Ethan got in his Rover, eager to get home. He had work to do.

~~~~

"Ethan?" Sarah called out as she climbed the stairs, holding the present she'd thought of while out on her errands. "Ethan?" she called again as she started down the second story hallway. When there was no answer, she continued on, surprised. It was mid-afternoon. She'd expected to find him sitting in his office chair, talking on the phone, or down in his gym, working out the muscles of his glorious body. Lust curled tight in her belly as she thought of Ethan, sweaty and intense, pounding away at his punching bag.

She stuck her head in his bedroom, listening to the shower running in the master bathroom. Not wanting to catch him by surprise and end up with a gun pointed in her face, she walked toward the sound of water slapping against granite as it ran off his body. "Ethan, I'm here. I didn't want to startle you." Along the way she set the wrapped gift on his dresser.

Frowning, she continued forward when he didn't respond. Was he okay in there? Peeking around the corner of the doorframe, she watched him, naked, sculpted, and wonderful as he rinsed the shampoo from his hair. "Knock-knock. I'm here. I didn't want to..." She stopped when he still went on as if he didn't hear her. What was going on? She walked forward, speaking the entire time, expecting him to respond or strike out in reflex. "Are you deaf, Ethan? I'm talking to you, for God's sake." Still nothing as he held his head under the spray, breathing out through his mouth.

Perplexed and concerned, she stepped from her sandals, making her way as far into the massive walk-in shower as she could without getting herself completely soaked. She reached out to tap his back, trying again. "What is wrong with you? Why won't—" Her words were cut off on a stifled scream as he grabbed her wrist, yanking her forward into the stream of warm water.

Instantly soaked, she stared in shock at Ethan's grinning face. "What in the *hell* are you doing?" She swiped at her hair, now plastered to her head then attempted a shove. "Look at me!"

Gray eyes gleamed with mischief as Ethan chuckled and backed her against the granite wall. "I *am* looking at you, baby. You're the best sight I've seen since this morning." He rested his hands on her hips, where navy blue cargo pants met her striped blue and white top.

With as much dignity as she could muster, Sarah raised her chin and glared into eyes that continued to dance with glee. "I can see you're quite proud of yourself. Just how am I supposed to stop by the supermarket when I look like a drowned rat?"

"You're not. You're supposed to stay here with me so I can do things to you that will make us both crazy." He traced the swell of her breasts until her nipples firmed against fabric and she shuddered. "I want to make you crazy, Sarah."

"What if I'm not interested in playing your games?" she asked in a voice gone thick with desire.

His hands snuck under her sopping wet shirt. In seconds he unclasped her bra and molded her sensitive breasts against his callused palms. She whimpered, and he smirked. "Then I'd have to call you a liar."

Heart pounding, already needing him, already wanting, she pulled his mouth down on hers. Lips slippery from the water slid against his before he moved to her neck, sending waves of pleasure dancing along her skin as his teeth grazed her collarbone.

Ethan pulled her shirt over her head and threw it. Blue and white cotton landed on the floor with a soggy slap, followed by her bra. He took her nipple into his mouth, running his tongue around its peak in slow, torturous circles.

Her full breasts tingled and she moaned, grabbing hold of his shoulders, clutching as fierce eyes stared into hers. "You better hold on, Sarah, because I'm just getting started." He unsnapped her pants and unzipped them, yanking them down, taking her panties with them, sending a thrill up her spine.

She remembered the night on the bathroom rug

when he'd been rough and demanding. She'd liked it, wanted more.

Ethan pressed her against the wall, fingers and lips trailing down her body as he left open-mouthed kisses along the way, before he stopped at her rounded belly. He molded the swell with his big hands, kissing tenderly.

She ran her fingers through his wet hair, touched by the gentleness overshadowing need.

His busy hands began to wander again, palms skimming her skin, tracing slow, sensual circles over her hips, moving to her butt, cupping her, bringing her closer to the warmth of his breath puffing against her upper thighs, promising her what she needed. He kissed and nibbled just shy of where she wanted him.

She moaned, waiting for release. All he had to do was touch her.

He tortured her with teasing flicks of the tongue, brushing here, there, always shy of the mark.

"Ethan, please." She pressed palms to his head, urging him forward.

Looking up, he spoke against her skin, only adding more skittering sensations. "Not yet. I'm not ready yet."

He continued, and she gasped, legs trembling, when his tongue feathered her lightly, bringing her further up.

Tensed, she teetered on the peak. "Ethan."

He journeyed up slowly, tracing his fingers against her, and she sucked in a breath, expecting him to send her over.

"Not yet, Sarah." He twisted off the jets, and she groaned in frustration, aching and desperate as he pulled her mouth to his, walking with her still in his embrace, grabbing a towel as they moved past the rack. He attempted to dry her as his tongue dove deep and he guided her to the bed. He dropped the towel and they fell to the mattress, still soaked.

Sarah straddled him at the waist as she stared into his eyes, eager to give. Her fingers journeyed down firm pectorals, skimming the lines of his muscled stomach. She moved down, taking him into her hand, and she smiled when he shuddered, enjoying the power of making him weak. "I'm just getting started, Ethan," she repeated, giving him back his own words as her hand continued its busy work and her mouth followed the same journey her fingers had taken, kissing, licking. She stopped at his trembling lower stomach, meeting his gaze as she touched him with her lips, setting a slow pace, until he gasped, until he closed his eyes and his jaw clenched.

Ethan tugged her up, and they were eye-to-eye.

She continued to work him with her palm until he rolled on top of her, trapping her hand against both of their bodies, making it impossible for her to continue. "You're going to end things if you keep that up. I don't think either of us is ready for that."

"I could live with it," she said, smiling.

"I couldn't. It's my turn."

Before the smile left her face, he pulled her legs up, knees meeting shoulders, and sent her flying high with his tongue. His mouth and fingers played her until she could hardly catch her breath, until she screamed out for him, fisting her hands in the sheets. Wave after wave careened through her system until she was dizzy and her legs shook with fatigue.

Breath tearing in and out, she clawed at his shoulder in defense against his continued assault to her system. "Ethan, Ethan, I'm going to pass out."

Triumphant eyes stared into hers as he flicked his tongue against her, making her body jump and tremble before he moved back up. "I guess we should stop then."

"No, I didn't say that." She gripped his firm butt, yanking him down, reveling in his weight settled against her. "I just need a second."

"A second's about all I can give you." He kissed her again. "I need to be inside you."

Shuddering, she spread her legs wider, inviting him in. She brushed his hair back from his sweaty forehead. "I think I'm fully recovered."

"We'll have to do something about that." Pushing himself into her, thrusting deep, he pumped hard and fast.

She built again, feeling him slide against her smooth skin, until her muscles tensed, her breath rushing out, and she pulsed around him. Crying out, she wrapped her legs around him, pulling him deeper.

Ethan nestled himself against her neck, breath rushing in and out, groaning loud and deep close to her ear as he stiffened and pressed her into the mattress with all of his weight. He panted and played with her hair as she concentrated on leveling her heartbeat.

After another deep breath and a nibble at her earlobe, he adjusted himself, propping himself up on his forearms. "I know I need to move. I'm crushing you and the baby."

Sarah caressed her fingers over his back. "We're both okay. You worked hard. Go ahead and take a minute."

He grinned and kissed the tip of her nose. "You're a real trooper, Sarah. I appreciate it."

Chuckling, she looked toward the bathroom. "I need a serious drink of water."

"Let me get it. I could use one too." He pulled himself free of her and walked to the bathroom. He stopped at the dresser on his way back. "What's this?"

"Something for you. That's the reason I came by, although this was a great addition to my afternoon plans."

He smiled. "You got me a present?"

"Just something small." She patted the bed next to her. "Come sit down and open it."

Settling himself next to her, he handed her the water and tore at the pale yellow paper. He said nothing when he pulled the wooden picture frame free.

Frowning, she put her hand on his and looked down at the picture. "You don't like it."

He met her gaze. "It's our baby. I love it. How could I not?"

Sarah smiled at the soft look that came into his eyes and kissed his cheek. "I thought maybe you might want to put it in your office or right here by the bed."

He brushed his knuckles against her jaw. "You have no idea how much this means to me." He pulled her forward, pressing his lips to hers. "Thank you."

"You're welcome."

He moved his fingers through her hair, playing with it. "I love you."

It was easier to say this time. There was no question he meant it. "I love you too."

"I know I said I would give you time and I will, but I want you to know I'm so ready for this, for you and Kylee, for this baby. I want my family, Sarah. I won't bring it up again, and I'm not pressuring you, but when you think it's time, I'll be waiting right here." He pressed her back against the comforter, running his hands along her belly, kissing her stomach. "I can't even tell you what it was like seeing our child growing inside of you today. I didn't know I could love like this, all three of you."

He stroked small circles against the baby within her

and sat up, looking in her eyes. "I've been so afraid I would screw everything up and disappoint you, that we would somehow end up like my parents, but when I watched our child move around while I held Kylee, while I held your hand, I knew I would never do to you what they've done to each other."

He took her chin in his hand, and her heart pounded at the unwavering look in his eyes. "I want you to look at me. I want you to see it in my eyes. This is me promising you, Sarah, that I will love you for the rest of my life. When you're ready, I want you to marry me. I want to raise our children together, make more babies, if that's what you want. I just have to be with you."

Overwhelmed by his words, consumed by love, she hugged him close, knowing he meant everything he said. "I love you, Ethan, so much, but I still need a little more time." She took his face in her hands, needing him to understand. "I want you to know I want everything you do. I still have some feelings I need to work through, to be fair to you, to be fair to all of us. I just need you to be patient for a little bit longer."

He blew out a breath and nodded before resting his forehead against hers. Frustration all but vibrated from him.

She kissed him again. "I love you, Ethan. I want you to remember that."

"I do." His cell phone rang on the side table. "I really have to get that. I've been waiting on this call."

He kissed her again then moved forward.

"I'm going to go throw my clothes in the dryer and head out. I'll see you for dinner tonight."

"Okay."

CHAPTER TWENTY-SEVEN

"I WOULD LIKE TO THINK I WON'T BE ANY LATER THAN THREE, maybe three-thirty. I'll give you a call on my way home," Sarah said to Hailey as she walked out the front door.

Hailey followed. "I know you're not looking forward to this."

Sarah blew out a long breath as she opened the door to her sedan and placed her camera bag on the backseat. "No, not particularly, but by this evening I'll be able to say it's over."

Hailey smiled. "That's a good way to look at it."

She smiled back. "That's me, the eternal optimist. I'll see you two later. Oh, we're going over to swim at Ethan's later. He's planning on firing up the grill. You're welcome to join us if you want. Morgan and Hunter are coming over too."

"I don't want to intrude."

"Don't be silly. You wouldn't be." She slid into her seat. "I'm pretty sure Austin will be there too."

"Austin?"

Sarah bit her cheek, preventing a grin as she looked at Hailey and closed her door. Poor Hailey hadn't been able to resist Austin's good looks and sweet, quiet nature. She started the car and rolled down the window. "I'll leave it up to you. You're probably sick of all of us anyway."

"I might tag along," Hailey said quickly. "Besides, I can help you with Kylee and stare at your cute little baby belly."

She doubted Hailey would remember her baby belly if Austin walked around without a shirt on. "Sounds like it's all set then. I'll call on the way home. We'll head over when I get back. Make sure you tell Kylee I gave her a kiss before I left."

"I will. I want a happy girl after her nap. Hurry back. Maybe you'll score another killer arrangement from the creepy florist." Winking, Hailey turned and walked back toward the house.

"That would be the highlight of my day." Sarah tossed a wave out the window as she buckled up and pulled out of her driveway. She blew out a weary breath, attempting to muster up at least a glimmer of enthusiasm for her meeting with Matthew and Lisa, reminding herself of what she'd told Hailey. The sooner she went, the sooner it would be over. How bad could one afternoon with Matthew really be? If she thought about it, she actually felt a little sorry for him. He was clearly looking for companionship, but went about it the wrong way.

Perhaps she could think of someone to set him up with. He wasn't particularly attractive, but the kindness underneath was what counted. She remembered his soulless green eyes and shuddered. What was it about him that made her want to run away? No, on second thought, she wouldn't be setting him up with anyone she considered a friend. She just had to make it through a couple of hours, then she wouldn't have to see him again.

As Sarah parallel parked in front of Matthew's shop, her mind wandered to happier things—to Ethan—and she smiled. He wanted to marry her, to be a family. She never thought she'd have this again, this opportunity to forge a life with a partner who would stand with her and raise her child—children, she amended as she ran a hand over her stomach. He wanted to make more babies and be Kylee's daddy.

She absently reached for the wedding ring that no longer rested against her chest, and a small slice of grief overshadowed her joy as she thought of Jake. Would he be okay with this? She thought back to her last moments with Jake via Skype as Ethan cut Kylee's umbilical cord. "This is for you, man. I wish you could be here doing this yourself," Ethan said as he snipped through the thick cord.

"Since I can't be, there's no one else I could want in my place. Take care of them, Cooke, until I get home. I love you, Sarah. I love you, Kylee. I have to go."

But he never came home, and Ethan was still here. He loved them, of that she had no doubt. He'd told her he was ready. Was she? Sarah closed her eyes and smiled as she moved her hand over her small belly again. Yes, she was. Tonight, after everyone went home, she'd talk to him. She would tell him it was time to begin their lives together.

Finally at peace with her choices, knowing she was making the right decisions for Kylee, for her baby, for herself and Ethan, she stepped from the car, grabbing her bag. With a new enthusiasm she didn't have to fake, she walked into Matthew's store.

Matthew stood by the large picture window and greeted her. "Hello, Sarah."

"Hello, Matthew." It was worse than she remembered. A wave of unease washed over her, and she stepped back automatically as he approached.

"You're a minute or two early. Lisa isn't here yet."

"Oh, okay. I guess I'll set up while we wait." She glanced around but didn't see any mockups to photograph. Frowning, she met his piercing gaze. "Um, we're photographing the mockups today, right?"

He grinned. "There's been a change in plans."

Gauging the distance to the door, Sarah took a step forward as Lisa walked in. Relieved, she wiped her damp palm against her pale pink tunic top, wanting to hug the older woman to her. "Hi, Lisa."

"Hi, Sarah, Matthew, I'm sorry I'm late. I got caught in traffic."

"Not a problem," Matthew said, taking a step closer to Sarah.

Sarah moved next to Lisa, wanting more space. "Lisa, I guess there's been a change in plans?"

"Oh?" Lisa looked to Matthew.

"Yes. I've arranged for us to drive over to the flower warehouse off of Wilshire. I thought it would give Sarah more photo opportunities, and you'll have literally hundreds of flowers to browse. We'll make mockups on the fly."

Lisa beamed. "Now that sounds like fun. What a great idea."

Matthew glanced at Sarah, and she nodded, smiling. Something moved through his eyes that told her to agree with Lisa. "I should be able to get some great shots. Where is the warehouse exactly? I've heard of it, but I'll need directions."

Matthew rested his hand on her shoulder. "We can all ride together. It's about eight miles from here. It doesn't make sense for all three of us to take our cars."

"I agree. Let's get going. I have a five o'clock meeting back at *Celebrity*," Lisa said.

Sarah pulled out her phone, wanting to tell Hailey where she was going. "I'm just going to call and check on Kylee."

"Oh, for heaven's sake, Sarah, Kylee's fine or Hailey

would've called you. Let's get a move on, here."

"Yes, Sarah. We really should be going. This is going to be very special." Matthew turned to Lisa. "I'm happy to drive."

"Lead the way."

Stuck, Sarah had no choice but to follow. She pulled out her sunglasses as they walked out of Matthew's shop into the warm afternoon sun. Matthew opened the passenger side door of his blue Cadillac STS, motioning her forward.

"Lisa, I know you get carsick; do you want the front seat?"

"You know what, I think I'd better." She smiled and slid into the seat. "Thanks, Matthew."

Sarah reached for the door handle of the backseat, pausing when Matthew slammed Lisa's door and moved around to the driver's side.

He glanced over the roof of the vehicle. "We must be going, Sarah. We have a schedule to keep."

She got in and stared out the window as Matthew pulled into traffic and Lisa chattered away to Matthew. Sarah listened with half an ear, rubbing her hand over her ever-growing belly, wishing she were home with Kylee and Ethan. Hopefully his meeting would be over and the grill would be going by the time she, Hailey, and Kylee got over to his house, soon to be her house too. She glanced at her watch, wondering how long this unexpected trip would take.

"Are you in a hurry, Sarah?"

Snapping to attention, she met Matthew's eyes in the rearview mirror. "Huh?" She shook her head and tried a smile. "I'm sorry?"

"I asked if you were in a hurry. You keep looking at your watch."

340

Hopefully he was paying as much attention to the road as he seemed to be her. "Not particularly."

"We'll try to make quick work of the warehouse. I'll have you home before you know it."

"Please don't feel we have to rush on my account."

Grinning, he pulled his sunglasses down, his translucent green eyes gleaming into hers. "Oh, I plan to rush for my own. I don't know about you, but I have afternoon plans I've been looking forward to for months."

She fought against a shudder and gave him a polite smile as she averted her gaze just below the mirror. "That sounds very exciting. What will you do?"

"I have a date."

Sarah relaxed a degree, and her smile warmed. He was interested in someone else. "She's a very lucky woman. We'll hurry with the photos and flowers. We don't want you to be late. Isn't that right, Lisa?"

"Who am I to stand in the way of true love?" Chuckling, she turned and winked at Sarah.

Moments later, Matthew pulled into the vacant parking lot of the flower warehouse. The massive building, usually bustling from Monday to Saturday, stood empty. He stopped next to the large metal door. "Door to door service."

Sarah stepped from the backseat, surveying the metal structure devoid of any windows. "Wow, look at this place. It's huge."

"It's the biggest warehouse on the west coast. This company distributes flowers to most of the western half of the United States," Matthew said, walking over to where Sarah stood.

Lisa joined them as she put her cell phone back in her purse. "Had to check my messages. My meeting's been pushed back a bit, so we have a little more time, unless it's going to interfere with your plans, Matthew." She patted his arm and cackled.

"We'll just take it a step at a time." He extended an arm to both Sarah and Lisa. "Shall we go have some fun?"

Sarah locked her arm through his as Lisa did the same. She might as well try to enjoy herself. It didn't appear as though this was going to be a quick shoot. "I'm ready if you are."

He dropped their arms when they approached the door and stuck the key in the deadbolt. He ushered Lisa through, Sarah next. The cool air of the refrigerated space chilled her skin as the scent of flowers engulfed her senses. The snap of several light switches filled the silence, and within seconds, Sarah was surrounded by every color she could have ever imagined. Gasping in delight, she stepped forward. "Oh my goodness, look at this place." Hundreds of rows of flowers stacked five-high occupied the entire floor.

"It's enchanting, isn't it? Almost like a fairyland."

Delighted, already pulling her camera from her bag, she smiled absently at Matthew. "That it is. Thank you for bringing us here. I don't know how you're going to get me to leave."

"I'm in no hurry. Look around, enjoy yourself. I'm certainly going to. Lisa, why don't you follow me? We'll pull some stems along the way and bring them back to the offices. When we're ready, we'll come get Sarah."

Lisa turned in a circle, craning her head in every direction. "I'm overwhelmed. There's so much to choose from. How will we pick?"

"Oh, I've just the thing in mind for you, Lisa. Don't you worry about that. Remember, I've been planning this event for a very long time." Matthew offered her his arm again, and Sarah smiled as they walked off discussing the Bikini Ball.

The hum of the refrigeration system accompanied Sarah through several aisles. She rubbed at her chilled arms, ignoring the slight discomfort as the vivid colors surrounding her captivated. "Oh my, these are lovely," she murmured to herself. Dark pink hydrangeas, the size of her head, sat in buckets of solution. Kneeling down, she tightened her focus until the texture of a single bloom filled her lens, blurring the rest.

She moved to the next row, and the scent of sweet peas grabbed her. She stepped closer, closing her eyes and breathing deep. She opened her eyes again and forgot about her pictures and her assignment as she thought of Ethan while she stared down at the elegant blooms—one of her very favorite. This would be one of the flowers she would carry in a bouquet trailing elegantly with pale pinks and purples as she walked down the aisle to him. Yes, she could see it. White roses in full bloom would intertwine with the bolder colors of the sweet peas. It would be stunning, but she wouldn't be looking at her bouquet as she made her way to the man she would spend the rest of her life with. No, her eyes would lock on the gray of Ethan's.

Her heartbeat accelerated and flutters filled her stomach from the intensity she knew she would find there. It was the same look she saw when they made love. *Easy, Sarah. You're getting yourself all worked up in a warehouse.* Chuckling to herself, she glanced up and gasped. "Oh Matthew, you startled me. I didn't hear you come up."

"Sorry about that. You seemed lost in your own thoughts. I didn't want to interrupt when they were clearly so pleasant."

How long had she been daydreaming? How long had he been watching her? "Where's Lisa?"

"She's using the restroom. I imagine she'll be along in a minute."

She peeked at her watch, realizing it was well after three. "Wow, I really lost track of time. You must be ready for those pictures."

"We have time yet." He took her arm as he spoke, pulling her forward. "While we wait for Lisa, I would like to show you some of my favorite flowers, some I think you'll enjoy."

Sarah glanced over her shoulder, looking back at the darkened office area before she returned her attention to Matthew. Why were the lights off in the office? Uneasy, she tried to remove her arm from Matthew's grip by reaching into her camera bag. "Let me change lenses so I can take a few pictures of you." Because it soothed her to talk, she continued. "As a florist, I imagine it must be hard to have just one favorite flower."

"No. When I find something I like, something I must have, it's all I want. Do you understand?" His voice changed, intensifying as he stared at her.

"I'm not sure I do." She gripped icy fingers together as unease ripened to fear. "I should go check on Lisa. She's been gone awhile."

"Lisa no longer warrants your concern, Sarah."

Her heart shuddered in her chest with the finality of his words. "What do you mean?"

They stopped in front of a shelf, and she could only stare. Blue roses. Shelf after shelf of blue roses. Her mind flashed to her front porch, to the night she found the first blooms; to her kitchen table, where she put them in a pretty glass vase, thinking they were from Hailey and Kylee; to the vile newspaper clippings and dead petals she'd pulled from the envelope with *Celebrity*'s insignia in the top left corner.

He sent her a sadistic grin, and her breath shuddered in and out as terror flooded her body. She knew where she'd seen his eyes before. Those same mad eyes had smiled into hers through the window in a thunderstorm. Trembling, she stepped back and ran for the front door. She only made it halfway before Matthew grabbed a handful of her hair, yanking her back against him, and she cried out in pain.

"You're not going anywhere."

Hot breath fluttered against her cheek before she elbowed him in the stomach, just like Ethan had showed her how to do. Matthew's grip loosened as he gasped, and she broke free. In her panic, she slammed into a shelf full of sunny yellow pansies, knocking the entire cart over in her attempt to escape. Somehow, she made it to the metal door. She was almost there, almost free. Her heartbeat throbbed in her head. Her hands shook as she shoved against the door that wouldn't budge. "Damn it, damn it. Come *on*." She used her shoulder next, but froze when she heard the distinct click of Matthew releasing the safety on his weapon next to her ear.

"You'll want to turn around right about now. You're ruining *everything*, whore bitch!"

With no other options, she put her hands higher in the air and did what he said. "Don't shoot me, Matthew, please. Where's Lisa? What did you do to her? I want to help her."

"Lisa doesn't need any help, I can promise you that, but you do."

"What did you do to her?" She was afraid she already knew.

"I did what I had to." He shook his head on a

chuckle. "Actually, I did what I wanted to, but that's enough about dear Lisa. You have bigger problems to worry about." He pointed the gun at her forehead. "Don't make me use this, Sarah. If you try to run again, I will."

Bile rose in her throat, and she fought to keep it down. He'd killed Lisa while she snapped pictures and fantasized about her wedding. She clenched her jaw and muscles, attempting to keep her trembling at bay. She had to calm down so she could *think* and survive. Thoughts of Lisa tried to enter her mind, but she blocked them. She couldn't do anything to help poor Lisa. She had to think of her babies. They were depending on her. "I won't try to run again. Just don't hurt me, please."

Smirking, Matthew stuffed the gun in the waist of his beige slacks. "I'm not a big fan of making promises, especially when I don't plan to keep them. Don't piss me off and you should be fine... For now."

A scream clawed at her throat, but she battled it back. There was no one here to help her. Despite her efforts, Sarah thought of Lisa, dead somewhere in an office in the back, and fought against tears of sorrow, tears of fear and helplessness. Something told her Matthew would find satisfaction if she broke down, so she wouldn't. "What are you going to do to me?"

"Oh, all kinds of things, but first we're going home. I have a surprise for you. If you try to run when we get outside, if you even blink the wrong way and draw attention to yourself, I'll have to kill you."

"I told you I wouldn't."

"You're a woman. You're word doesn't mean dick to me. You're all liars, every last one of you." His eyes widened, his pupils dilated, and the madman was back.

Disgust, mixed with fear, skittered along her skin like spiders. Shuddering, she looked away.

"Let's go. You're screwing it all up. We're late."

Late for what, she wondered as they stepped into the sun and noise of a busy Sunday. Cars drove past, people rode by on bikes. Help was only a shout away, but she didn't dare, not when he could shoot her and kill the baby or both of them. She had to get a call out to Ethan, but how?

Matthew stood behind her as they approached his vehicle. "Remember what I said. Now get in the car so I don't have to hurt you." He pressed his nose to her hair and inhaled deeply. "You smell so good."

Slamming her eyes shut, trying not to gag, she opened the door, got in, and put her purse down at her side. If she could reach in and dial Ethan's number, he would be able to hear what was going on.

Matthew shut his door and yanked her purse away. "You won't need that."

Now what? She glanced at her watch as he pulled into the busy traffic, heading back toward the Palisades. It was four-thirty. Hailey would be expecting her; so would Ethan.

"Go ahead and keep looking at your watch, bitch." He began to laugh. "Do you think by some miracle Master Cooke is going to come and save you, Sarah? Not this time. By the time anyone realizes you're gone, we'll have moved on to our more exciting plans for the evening."

Sarah wanted to spit in his face and try to grab the butt of the gun resting at his waist, even jump from the car. If she didn't have the baby, she would've done all three, but she did. She wouldn't risk her child. Instead she stared out the window, desperately trying to think of a way out of this.

It wasn't long before Matthew turned off the Pacific

Coast Highway and headed into the quiet neighborhoods. He pulled into a drive four blocks from her house. The pretty, two-story house, painted a glistening white with black shutters, surprised her. It looked so...normal, even cozy. When she spotted the blue roses, wrapping around the trellis, she remembered there was nothing normal about Matthew Denmire.

He blew out a deep breath teeming with satisfaction as he leaned back, relaxing his hands on the wheel. "Well, this is it. What do you think?"

She stared straight ahead, not daring to look at him "It's lovely."

"It's your new home until I decide otherwise. Let's get you settled in."

Sarah stepped from the car with no choice but to follow.

CHAPTER TWENTY-EIGHT

DEEP BLACK FADED TO GRAY AS SHE MOANED, BLINKING, trying to focus. Stabs of sharp, excruciating pain sliced through Lisa's skull, and she whimpered. Where was she? Why did she *hurt* like this? She turned her head and cried out against the unbearable ache. Tears coursed down her cheeks, and she retched in agony.

Lying still, breath sobbing in and out, she stared at the pool of blood and vomit puddled on dirty concrete. Where was that coming from? Her eyes darted about the dim room. Everything was so blurry. A white calla lily dangled from the table above and it clicked—the flower warehouse. "Matthew," she croaked. Where had he gone? Where was Sarah?

Dull and listless, her mind clicked off again. For several minutes she listened to the hum of the pipes above, fighting to find the will to think over the confusion. It was so hard to think over the drumbeat in her brain. "Sarah?" Why weren't they coming for her?

And then she remembered. Where was he? She had to hide, to get away from the monster with the dead green eyes. He'd smiled at her, holding the heavy crystal vase she'd chosen from the shelf in the next room.

"Who knew a crude broad like you actually had taste, Lisa? Do you know what I'm going to do with your lovely selection? I'm going to smash it over your head."

She stepped back, trying to make it to the door, and he laughed. "Although I do love a good game of hide-and-go-seek, I just don't have time today. It's your day to die, Lisa. I'm very much looking forward to killing you." He pulled a gun from his pocket. When he pressed the trigger, a hot current screamed through her body and she fell to the ground in pain, unable move. He waited until she made it to her hands and knees before she heard him say, "Night-night, Lisa." And then she felt the crushing blow before she felt nothing at all.

Had he done the same thing to Sarah? What if she was out on the floor, unconscious? She had to get to her phone. Her purse lay feet away, leaning against the chair she'd pulled out to sit in before Matthew had gone mad.

Lisa scooted forward, inch by agonizing inch as black and red spots danced in front of her eyes. She closed them, taking several deep breaths, before she opened them again. Her purse looked farther away than it had when she started.

Sweat dripped into her eyes, and she brushed her arm over her forehead, gasping as she pulled back, watching deep red drops dribble down to her wrist. Would she bleed to death before she could call for help? Her heart pounded in utter terror as she imagined dying alone on the filthy office floor. Her head throbbed with the tempo, only increasing the mind-numbing pain. She had to get a grip or she *would* die here.

Like hell she would. That bastard wasn't going to win. This wasn't how she was going out. Determined to live, determined to pay Matthew Denmire back, Lisa pulled herself forward, far enough to reach the strap of her bag. She tugged her purse toward her and reached in, feeling around until her fingers clamped against the cool plastic of her phone. Her vision grayed, wavering and she bit her lip. She pressed 9-1-1 against the pad and moved it closer to her ear.

"Nine-one-one, what's your emergency?"

"I need...help..." The gray grew darker, circling up, and grabbed her.

~~~~

Ethan sat in front of his computer, cross-referencing the rice paper orders for the third time in two days. Nothing was adding up to Eric Walker being the buyer. Two names stuck out due to the large number of orders they had placed in the last six months, and the man accused of being 'The Blue Chip Rapist' wasn't one of them.

Terrance Ward, over in Bel Air, had ordered hundreds of extra sheets, as well as an Ezekiel M. Denmire. Ethan kept hovering his mouse over that name. Why the hell did it sound so familiar? And why was Ezekiel having paper delivered to a personal address instead of a place of business? That was certainly worth looking into.

The phone rang. He picked it up without glancing at the readout. "Cooke."

"Ethan, it's Hailey."

He instantly picked up on the tension in her voice. "Is everything okay?"

"Well, I'm not sure. Sarah isn't back yet."

He darted a glance at the clock on his computer screen—five-twenty. "Her appointment was at one, right?"

"Yeah, and she said she thought she wouldn't be any later than three-thirty. I've tried her cell several times, but she isn't picking up."

He didn't like it. "Keep trying her phone. I'll call Lisa." He hung up and searched through his numbers until he found Lisa's assistant. He punched in her number, waited impatiently, tapping his fingers against the wood of his desk. Sarah always answered her phone, especially when it was Hailey.

"Good afternoon, *Celebrity* Magazine. This is—"

"Dana, right?"

"Yes. Who's this?"

"Dana, this is Ethan Cooke. I'm a good friend of Sarah Johnson's. She and Lisa were supposed to have a meeting this afternoon."

"Yes, we've been unable to reach Lisa for the last couple of hours. If—"

He hung up and stood. Something was wrong. He punched in Hunter's number on his way out the door.

"We're on our way over, man."

"I can't find Sarah."

"What do you mean?"

"Hailey just called. Sarah was supposed to be home an hour and a half ago. She's not answering her phone. I just called the magazine. Lisa hasn't answered hers either."

"I *knew* I should've gone with her. That guy was a fucking creep."

Remembering the day clearly enough, he knew he hadn't paid a damn bit of attention. He'd been too caught up in the fight he and Sarah had had on the beach to focus on the florist. He couldn't even remember what the guy looked like. "I'm heading over there now to see if I can find out what's going on."

"I'll call Austin and drop Morgan off at Sarah's. We'll start canvassing the area between the shop and her house. Maybe she stopped off somewhere, broke down, and locked her purse in the car."

As Ethan yanked the Rover door open, he knew Hunter didn't believe that anymore than he did. "Yeah, maybe. I'll call you when I get there."

Ethan drove well over the speed limit on his way to the florists. He cut off a Lexus as he changed lanes. The driver honked, waving his arms about madly. "Get over it, asshole." He took the left leading down the side street, passed "Elegant Expressions." The storefront was dark, yet Sarah's blue sedan sat parallel parked close by, along with Lisa's snappy black Porsche. Something was definitely wrong.

He continued searching for a parking space with no luck. The bistros and chic little restaurant across from the shop did a steady business. People wandered about; there wasn't an empty spot to be found. "Fuck." Unwilling to waste another second, he jerked the wheel to the right and pulled into an alley, reaching under his seat, pulling his gun from the reinforced box. He placed the Glock in the belt holster he grabbed next and stepped from the SUV, walking at a fast clip as he dialed Tucker's number.

"Detective Campbell."

"Tucker, this is Ethan Cooke."

"Hey, what can I do for you?"

"Sarah's missing."

"What do you mean?"

"What do you mean, what do I mean?" he spat out. "Sarah's *missing.*"

"Just calm down."

Ethan approached the shop, cupping his hand against the window, peering in. "Don't tell me to calm down, Tucker. I've been crosschecking your paper orders for two days and there isn't one, not *one* fucking link to the man you have in jail right now. Sarah left for a meeting five hours ago, and she's not answering her phone. Neither is her boss."

"Maybe they're somewhere they can't get a signal."

"Don't give me that shit." He stepped from the curb and looked in Sarah's car, spotting nothing but Kylee's car seat. He moved to Lisa's next. "I'm standing next to both of their vehicles. The florist shop where they were supposed to meet is dark."

"Let me..." Voices entered Tucker's office, cutting him off. "Hold on, Ethan."

Ethan jogged to his Rover, knowing in his heart Sarah wasn't there. Where the hell was she? Fear threatened to cloud his brain, but he pushed it back. He needed to keep a cool head. "Tucker?"

"I'm going to have to call you back."

"No, wait—"

"Right back, Ethan."

He heard the click. "You've got to be fucking kidding me." He sat in his seat, dialing Hailey again.

"Hello?"

"It's Ethan. Have you heard anything?"

"No, nothing."

"Keep trying." He swung a u-turn on the busy street, waving his hand in thank-you at the car that let him out. He drove past the shop again, stopping as a couple stepped into the crosswalk. Waiting, he scanned the darkened picture window and Sarah's car, pressed on the accelerator, planning to head home, then slammed on his brakes, stopping traffic, as he zeroed in on the small squiggle of a name under the bold, fancy scroll of 'Elegant Expressions.' He yanked his door open and ran closer, reading *Proprietor: E.M. Denmire.*

Everything clicked. Ezekiel M. Denmire. The florist who had paper sent to his home instead of his business. The florist, who in Hunter's words, was 'a fucking creep.' Running back among the honks and shouts from disgruntled drivers, he moved again, punching in Hunter's number.

"Phillips."

"He's got her. The fucking rapist has her. I can feel it."

"I'll call the police."

"No. Listen to me. I've already tried that. I have his information at my house. It should still be up on the computer."

"Austin's there. He went over to see if Sarah might end up there."

"I'll call him for the address. You and Austin meet me. LAPD had their chance." He hung up and dialed again, reaching Austin on the second ring.

"Yeah, boss."

"I need the address on my computer for an Ezekiel M. Denmire. He has Sarah."

Ethan heard the tap of keys, waiting. "Shit. That's close. He lives at 2019 Dearborn Avenue. It's four blocks west of Sarah's."

"Meet me there."

He was close, minutes away. He sped down the Pacific Coast Highway, praying he wasn't too late.

Chapter Twenty-nine

Sarah stood, arms wrapped tight around herself, in the small room Matthew shoved her in an hour ago. Blue roses decorated the side table next to a queen-sized bed. The wedding ring quilt, adorned with different hues of blue and yellow, had been pulled back, hotel style. There were even fancy chocolates placed in the center of the pillows. She stared at the bed again, realizing what he would expect from her later, and clutched her arms tighter.

Moments after he'd slammed the door and locked it, Sarah rushed into the bathroom, looking for escape. The setting sun had blazed bright through the small window high above the toilet, but it was too far up and the window too small for her to fit through anyway. When she knew she was officially stuck, that there was nothing more she could do, she sat on the spotless tile, rested her back against the cabinet and wept until she'd been able to think through the fear.

Resolved to find a way through this, to survive for her children, for Ethan and the life they planned to make, she'd stood and started to plan. At some point, Matthew would come for her. When she found the right moment, she would do whatever she had to to get out of there.

Matthew knocked on her door as if he wasn't in charge of the sick game he played and entered. "Why aren't you relaxing, Sarah? We have a very special night ahead. I'm fixing your favorite meal as we speak. Who knows, this might be your last supper. We'll have to see, though. If I like your style—" his gaze wandered to the bed as he smiled "—I might keep you around a little longer."

"How am I supposed to relax when you say things like that to me?"

"Death is just another part of life. Don't worry, I'll try to make it quick." He walked over to the closet, leaving the door ajar. She took a step forward, and he turned. "Don't try it. You're going to make me have to punish you. Besides, I bought you something. Here, put it on." Smiling, he pulled the flowing blue dress from the closet and handed it to her. The fabric matched the roses and her eyes exactly. "I put some cosmetics and hair pieces in the bathroom for you, along with your favorite shampoo and soaps. I'll be back in half an hour. I expect you to look your best." He walked to her and lifted his fingers, skimming them along her cheekbones.

Sarah cringed at the touch of his soft skin and stepped back.

He grabbed her arm, squeezing, yanking her forward, his face going pink with rage as his breath blew out in puffs against her skin. "What, am I not good enough for you, Sarah? Am I not pretty enough for you like your stud boyfriend?" Spit flew as he talked, landing on her face.

She desperately wanted to wipe it away. The grip on her arm tightened until her fingers tingled from lack of circulation, but she didn't struggle, didn't speak. That was what he wanted.

His hand flew up, cracking her across her face. She stumbled back in surprise as pain radiated along her cheek and the metallic taste of blood filled her mouth. Whimpering, she threw her arms up in defense as he came forward again.

"That's what I thought, you little bitch. When I ask you a question, you answer. Now, get your ass dressed." He walked toward the door and stopped. "I have a better idea. Maybe I'll help you undress. I think I'd like to watch you shower. Yes, indeed, I think I would. I'll wash your back." He groaned and touched himself. "Do you want to feel what you do to me, Sarah?"

Her stomach churned with nausea. "No, I don't."

The distant buzz of a timer sounded. "Well, saved by the soufflé. I can't have it falling. What would we have for dessert? I'll be back in thirty minutes. Oh, and try to relax. You're looking a little stressed out." Chuckling, he shut the door, locking her in.

She walked to the bed on trembling legs and sat down, fighting to steady her breathing. "Oh, God," she whispered. There was no doubt in her mind he would rape her after they ate and more than likely kill her. She tried to stand, but her knees buckled. She couldn't stop trembling. Her cheek stung and throbbed with every heartbeat. Hopelessness consumed her, and she closed her eyes. Lying back, she rested her hands on her belly. The echo of her baby's heartbeat mixed with Kylee's laughter as Ethan's grinning face flashed through her mind. She couldn't give up. Her family needed her to live.

Determined to make it through this, Sarah sat up and walked to the bathroom. She closed the door and locked it, turned on the shower and undressed, stepping in. Washing quickly with one eye on the door and her ears tuned for footsteps, she tried to absorb the warmth and steam. She was chilled to the bone.

Moments later, she turned off the faucet and toweled herself dry then opened the small medicine cabinet and slammed it closed as she took a step back. The products were identical and arranged just the way she had them at home. How could he have known what she bought and the way she arranged them? Resting her palms against the counter, she stared at the swirls in the marble, trying to digest the gravity of his obsession. Despite the fact that she was standing in Matthew's bathroom, held against her will, the medicine cabinet shook her to the core. He'd been in her home again, but when? How?

A loud bang downstairs startled her back to the moment, and she checked her watch. She was running out of time. Matthew would be back in fifteen minutes. It was almost six o'clock. Surely Ethan knew something was wrong by now. Lisa would have missed her meeting. "Find me, Ethan, please find me," she whispered.

Determined to look her best for the meal, she opened the cabinet again, pulling out the cosmetics she would need. The happier Matthew was, the less likely he was to hurt her. She shut the glass-paneled front and stared at the purple bruise covering her cheekbone, touching it gently, wincing from the deep pain. There would only be more if she wasn't ready.

She twisted her hair in an elegant up-do then tried her best to hide the mark on her face with concealer. After adding eyeliner and mascara to play up her eyes, she stepped into the bedroom, staring at her outfit for the evening. The fitted, spaghetti-strap dress with a full skirt reminded her of something from a Disney movie. She took it from the hanger and pulled it over her head, adjusting the skirt in place. She reached behind her for the zipper and tugged, but the fabric gaped in the back from the fullness of her belly. She sucked in and tried again, but it was no use. What was she going to do?

She rushed to the bathroom and looked at herself.

Panicked, she held her breath and sucked in yet again. The zipper soared up, stopping at her full breasts. Yank after yank proved useless. Her stomach stuck out like a beacon, announcing her pregnancy.

Matthew knocked on the door and she braced herself, glancing down at the counter, searching for any weapon she could find. There was nothing. She opened a drawer and found a pair of cuticle scissors and a file with a sharp point. "Um, just give me one more second please." Where would she put them? She looked in the mirror and inspiration struck. She pulled her hair from the twist and refastened it, replacing one of the chopsticks she'd used with the file, pushing the metal piece deep into her mass of hair until only the small handle showed. Hopefully he wouldn't notice the difference.

"Your time's up, Sarah. I'm coming in."

She turned from the bathroom and walked into the bedroom as the door opened. Matthew's smile faded quickly as his gaze traveled down her body. He stopped on her stomach and rushed forward. "You fucking whore." He grabbed her, and she lost her balance as he threw her to the bed, straddling her. She could do little but try to protect her face as his fist rammed forward. "You slutty little cunt!" Matthew connected with her other cheek, and she saw stars.

He yanked at her arms, shaking her until her vision blurred. "You let him fuck you. Now you're full with his bastard." He slapped her again, and her lip puffed immediately. "Maybe I'll take my turn now too." He jumped from the bed and pulled up her full skirt. "You've ruined it all. You've ruined everything." He paced away from her, grabbed the vase and threw it. Glass, water, and blue blooms fell to the floor with a loud crash.

Sobbing quietly, Sarah didn't dare move as Matthew swore at her and trashed the room. He yanked her up by the hand, and blood dribbled warm down her chin from her wounded lip. "We're going to have our date, Sarah. Then I'll fuck you until I get sick of it. After that, I'm going to kill you. I'm going to strangle the life from you and get a bonus when I kill the bastard's kid. It's a two-for-one deal."

She struggled to keep her footing as Matthew yanked her down the stairs, pulling her forward until they stopped in the dining room glowing with candlelight, decorated with masses of blue roses. The elegant space would have been beautiful if it wasn't for the crazy man standing next to her. The table, set for two, with fine china and silver, somehow didn't seem real. How could a man so full of violence and hatred create something like this? Violin music played quietly in the background, making her want to weep as her gaze settled on the window open to the cool breeze. The familiar smell of the ocean scented the air, along with the perfume of hundreds of blooms. She wanted nothing more than to dive through the screen and run screaming until someone came to help her.

"Take your seat." Matthew shoved her into her chair.

Her knee cracked against the walnut table leg, and she closed her eyes against the pain, refusing to cry in front of him again. Most of her body ached. Her head throbbed, but all that mattered was keeping her baby safe.

He smiled at her pleasantly. "Now, where were we? Ah, yes, dinner. Let me get our first course, and we can begin."

~~~~

Ethan pulled up to the curb three houses down from Ezekiel's as the sun sank low, reflecting against the windows of the homes up and down the street. The neighborhood was quiet except for the children laughing and playing, riding their bikes along the sidewalks, passing him by. What would their parents think when they found out they lived next to a monster?

His phone rang again and he hoped, as he did every time, that it would be Sarah calling to tell him she was okay, but the readout showed him it wasn't and he ignored it. He did an initial scan of the house through the windshield while he waited for Austin and Hunter. Lights were ablaze throughout the first and second story. He had to fight the urge to knock down the door and get Sarah.

This was too important to rush. They would take every possible precaution. Her life was on the line—if the fucker hadn't killed her already. Ethan closed his eyes, shaking his head. Sarah was alive. She had to be.

Battling through rage, Ethan glanced down when the phone rang again. He was tempted to let it ring. He didn't have much to say to Detective Campbell at this point. He already knew how this conversation would go.

Hunter and Austin pulled up on the other side of the street, further down from the house they would all be watching. Ethan threw them a stop signal with his hand and held up his phone. They both nodded.

"Detective Campbell, what can I do for you?"

"Have you found Sarah yet?"

"No, but I know where she is."

"We do too. We just left Lisa Turnington's hospital room. She's been in and out of consciousness with a pretty serious head wound. Apparently Matthew

Denmire hit her with a large crystal vase several hours ago at some flower warehouse. The last time she saw Sarah was at the warehouse."

"This is all fascinating, but how the hell is that going to get her back?"

"We're on our way with a team to his house."

"I'm already here with Hunter and Austin."

"Don't get stupid, Ethan. Wait for us."

"No, I've waited long enough. I'm not going to let you bring some negotiator on scene so they can try to bargain with Sarah's life. He'll kill her, and we both know it."

He hung up and drove forward, stopping in front of Austin's vehicle. They had less time than he wanted with the cops on the way. He stepped from the Rover, careful not to slam his door as Austin and Hunter did the same. "We have to move. I just got off the phone with Tucker. They're on their way, but we're not waiting."

"No, we're not," Hunter said. "Here's my thought. You can tell me if you agree."

Ethan was surrounded by the best: Hunter, a former Recon Marine; Austin, a former Navy SEAL. This was their area of expertise—reconnaissance and rescue. He would do whatever they told him to.

"We'll do a very quick up-close-and-personal and locate Sarah's exact whereabouts within the house. Once we know, we'll go from there."

Austin handed out earpieces as Hunter continued.

"Austin, I want you to go in around back. It looks like the bastard has several windows open. Ethan, you go in around the side. I'll gain access through the second story."

Ethan took over. "We'll use two taps against our microphones when we're all in place. If you've got a shot on him, three taps and take it. Otherwise, surround and we'll go from there. If possible, two-man tackle with the other pulling the principal from the scene. Be careful with her. I don't want the baby hurt."

"We'll get her, boss."

He had to believe they would.

CHAPTER THIRTY

MATTHEW SET A DELICATE CUP OF STEAMING LOBSTER BISQUE in front of Sarah. The longer it took her to eat, the longer she knew she would live. She smiled as Matthew took his seat. "This looks lovely, Matthew, and smells wonderful."

He brightened. "I made it from scratch. I scoured the internet for just the right recipe."

Sarah lifted her spoon, gesturing toward her dish. "May I?"

"Please."

She dipped the silverware into the cup and brought it to her lips. The heat against her wound stung, but she didn't dare flinch. She sampled the cream-based broth, a little heavy on the salt, and smiled again. "Very nice. It's delicious."

Preening, he tasted himself. "I watched you eat it at the party Master Cooke's parents had."

The spoon paused halfway to her mouth before she brought it to her lips again. He'd been in the Cooke's home. Of course he had. She remembered feeling as if someone watched her all night. "Were you a guest? You should've introduced yourself."

"I wasn't important enough to receive an invite. You have to gross at least five million to make those parties." He looked at her, his temper brewing. "Or be fucking their son. That'll get you in the door too."

She didn't want him to hit her again. Desperate to change the subject, Sarah zeroed in on the dishes. "Where did you buy your china? The pattern has a bit of a European flair."

He stared at her for several seconds as she gripped her hand against the napkin resting on her lap, bracing herself for another blow. "I ordered them while I was over in England two years ago."

She relaxed when he began to eat. "Do you travel to Europe often?"

"When it suits me. My business has become very successful, so I don't have a lot of time for traveling anymore."

She glanced toward the window as a vehicle drove by. The dark gray of what she swore was a Range Rover caused her to look again, but it was gone. Maybe it was Ethan, or maybe she was desperate to believe he had come for her.

Would she ever see him again? Would she ever snuggle with Kylee and read until she fell asleep? Her eyes watered and tears threatened. Fighting to hold them back, she took another bite of bisque. Matthew seemed calmer. She wanted to keep him that way. "If you don't mind, I'm going to save a little of this to enjoy with my salad. We are having salad, right?"

"Yes. A house salad with a warm honey mustard drizzle. Like I said, we're sampling your favorites tonight. I'll go get the second course."

Sarah wanted to ask him how he knew her favorites but stopped herself. The answer would probably be more than she could handle, much like the medicine cabinet full of cosmetics.

Matthew took his dish away, and she turned, watching him disappear into the kitchen. When she heard the refrigerator door open and dishes clatter against the marble countertop, she inched her chair to the left, craning her neck to see if she could catch another glimpse of the Rover she prayed she hadn't imagined. Hope began to fade—Ethan wasn't there.

"What are you doing?"

She jumped, whirling around in her seat, her heart pounding. "Nothing. I was enjoying the breeze coming in from the window. Most people hate the smell of low tide, but there's something so...earthy about it."

Matthew studied her face, his eyes narrowing, as he moved forward with their plates. He set an elegantly prepared salad down. The presentation was excellent, with vivid colors from the deep greens of the lettuce, red of tomatoes, orange from shredded carrots.

"I think you have two callings, Matthew—flowers and food." Afraid she'd overdone the compliments, she glanced at him, gauging his reaction. She let out a long, quiet breath when he only appeared pleased.

Sarah took a bite, chewing, listening to Matthew talk about himself with half an ear while she planned. If she could convince him to open the window just a bit further, she would dive through the screen when he went in to prepare the next course. No one was coming for her, and time was almost up. Lights had come on in the homes across the street. If she dove and screamed as soon as she hit the ground, she'd draw someone's attention before he could get outside and take her back in. She took another bite and swallowed. "Matthew, would you be willing to slide the window up just a touch more? I really do love the breeze. It would make this the perfect evening."

He paused with a cherry tomato on his fork, refusal on his tongue.

She gave him an encouraging smile, regretting it instantly as pain radiated through her lip, but he set his fork down.

"Just a little more," he said, standing, pushing the frame as far as it could go.

"Thank you." She had no doubt she would fit through. She brought another bite of salad to her mouth, ready to move things along. It was time to save her own life.

~~~~

Ethan crouched back against the thick bushes, using the shadows dusk provided, listening to Sarah's voice carry through the window screen. If he didn't know her as well as he did, he would've believed she was enjoying herself, but the tension was there, in every careful word she spoke. Rage choked him as he inched his way forward and saw her face in the candlelight. He watched her wince ever so slightly as she brought a spoon to her swollen, split lip. A deep purple bruise bloomed over her cheekbone and another along her jaw. He had to get her out of there.

He looked for a shot on Denmire right then, but the bastard sat too close to Sarah in the elegant dining room. He hesitated, not wanting to lose sight of Sarah, but moved to the side of the house, making it to the unlit room beyond the kitchen. The window he would use to gain entry was open six inches. He slit a hole in the screen and tugged on the frame, removing it. Pushing up on the windowsill next, wincing, praying it wouldn't make a noise, he boosted himself up, glancing back just in time to see S.W.A.T pull up down the street. Men and women dressed in black carried sniper rifles and moved in different directions through the neighborhood, preparing to execute their crisis response. They were going to fuck everything up.

Breaking silence, Ethan spoke as quietly as he could. "S.W.A.T's here. Move."

Two taps echoed in his ear, followed by two more, and he took a deep breath. They were all inside now. One of them had to get to Sarah before S.W.A.T initiated their first phone call. That would be the end. Ezekiel would kill her right then. He would have nothing left to lose.

Ethan took the Glock from his holster and released the safety, holding the gun in both hands, arms braced against his chest, ready to fire. He walked down the hall, silently, keeping his back to the wall, concentrating on the sound of Sarah's voice getting closer with every step. He made his way to the living room, just steps away from Sarah, and Austin appeared from a door on the opposite side of the room, mirroring his stance with his own pistol. "Optimal position upstairs," echoed in his earpiece when Hunter whispered.

"I have to use the bathroom, Matthew."

"We just sat down. Is this some sort of game, bitch?"

"No. The baby sits on my bladder and—"

"I don't want to hear about your little bastard," Matthew hollered, making Ethan's finger dance on the trigger. That asshole wouldn't hit Sarah again. He would die first.

"I'm sorry, but I really do have to go. You can stand outside the door if you like. I thought it best to use the restroom now before you bring out the main dish, which smells amazing, by the way."

"Master Cooke's little bastard's fucking it all up," he muttered, enraged. "Fine, but don't try anything. I'll have to punch you again, which I thoroughly enjoyed." Two dining room chairs slid over wood.

Ethan met Austin's gaze as Austin eased back into

the dark of the room he'd come from, disappearing from sight. Ethan glanced around. There was nowhere for him to hide. He backtracked toward the office, but it was too late. Sarah stepped into the living room and glanced to her right, pausing, her eyes locking on his before she looked straight ahead and kept going.

A million thoughts passed between them in that second. There was nothing he wanted more than to grab her up and take her away from this nightmare, but he couldn't. He stayed where he was, watching her eyes fill and her lips tremble as she continued forward, as if she hadn't seen him while she wore the blue dress that pressed snug against her body, accentuating her pregnancy, gaping open in the back, exposing her white bra and smooth skin. *Good job, Sarah. Keep going and we'll end this.*

She'd only taken two steps into the room when Matthew, or Ezekiel, or whatever the hell his name was, yanked her back against him. "What are you sniveling about?"

"Nothing. I'm just a little tired."

"Yeah, well by the time I'm done with you, you'll be way past that." He grazed his mouth against her ear. "Maybe I should give you something worth crying about."

"No, please don't."

"You said you had to piss, so get on with it. The haddock's going to dry out, then I really will have to punish you. I'm beginning to think you like it." Matthew shoved her with such force, she almost fell.

A red haze of fury all but blinded Ethan as he stepped forward. Enough was enough. He pointed his gun, surging toward her.

Matthew's eyes widened in surprise. "What the

fuck?" He stepped back, dragging Sarah as he grabbed a butcher's knife from the antique woodblock decorating his buffet table. "Get out of my house before I kill her."

Tears streamed down Sarah's ghostly pale cheeks as she stood trembling with the knife pressed to her throat.

"I'll put down the gun, but I'm not leaving." Ethan placed the weapon at his feet, never taking his eyes from hers.

"I say you are." He skimmed the knife against her skin, and she whimpered, tightening her grip on the arm Matthew wrapped around her waist as a small trickle of blood dribbled down her neck.

Hunter's voice sounded in his ear again. "Get him to move a little more to the left. Austin should be able to get a shot on him."

"Confirm that," Austin said.

Ethan put his hands in the air and took a step forward, toward the door. "Okay, I'll go. Just don't hurt her anymore."

Matthew's eyes gleamed bright as he began to laugh. "You're not so tough now are you, pretty boy? All those muscles aren't doing you a damn bit of good. Zeke Denmire's in charge now, and don't you forget it."

Sarah choked out a breath. "Take care of Kylee, Ethan."

"You shut *up*," Matthew said, skimming the knife against her again, and she gasped as pain and terror radiated across her face.

"That's enough! Stop it! " He couldn't take it anymore. "I said I would go."

Matthew stepped to the left as Hunter had wanted, blocking Ethan's path to the door.

Hunter spoke again. "No good. He needs to move further into the room."

Ethan wanted to punch and rage with the helplessness he felt, but he took another step forward, mindful not to get too far from his gun. "I'm going. See? I'm going."

"You know what? I don't think that'll work for me anymore. I had other plans for Sarah tonight, but I just thought of something even better. You're going to watch her die, Master Cooke. You're going to watch them both die."

A thousand waves of fear washed through him as Matthew moved the knife, pointing the tip straight at Sarah's belly.

"I'm going to gut her like a pig and take your fucking kid along with her." He raised the knife, ready to plunge.

Sarah's eyes widened and she sobbed. "I love you, Ethan."

"No shot. No shot," Austin yelled as he stormed from the room directly behind Matthew and Sarah. Hunter ran down the stairs, vaulting over the banister halfway down the staircase.

Matthew turned, staring, before gripping the knife high again. "You can all watch her die!"

Ethan grabbed his gun, saw his shot as the knife descended in Matthew's grip, and without hesitation, took it. The bullet exploded, along with the left side of Matthew's face. Spatter covered Sarah as Matthew fell sideways to the floor.

Ragged breathing filled the sudden silence, and Sarah dropped to her knees, weeping. Ethan ran forward on trembling legs and scooped her up, turning away from the mess pooling on the floor. "It's okay, Sarah. It's over. I've got you."

S.W.A.T rushed in and chaos reigned while Ethan gripped her tight, unwilling to let her go.

Tucker Campbell came through the door, gun raised, meeting Ethan's glinty stare. He holstered his weapon. "Get her out of here, Cooke. There's an ambulance outside."

"Thanks for nothing, Campbell."

Hunter touched his shoulder, and all four left Matthew Denmire's home.

"I'll have questions for you," Campbell called out the door.

"It was self-defense. You see the knife on the floor. You can ask your questions later," Austin said as they continued forward.

Ethan walked to the ambulance and tried to set Sarah on the waiting stretcher. She wrapped her arms tighter around his neck. "Please, no. I'm not ready to let you go."

Drops of blood covered her hair and face. Tears dripped down her swollen cheek as she trembled against his grip. "I'm not going anywhere."

"Ma'am, we need to put you on the stretcher," the paramedic said.

"You'll have to put us both on."

The man opened his mouth to argue, met Ethan's stare and stopped, nodding. "Okay."

Ethan sat down with Sarah, swinging his legs up to the bed, resting his weary body against the cushion, clutching Sarah as tightly as she clutched him. He stared at Hunter and Austin as the doors closed and the ambulance drove off.

CHAPTER THIRTY-ONE

HOURS LATER, AS DAWN BROKE, SARAH LAY IN ETHAN'S BED, clean, bandaged and sleeping. She clung to him, her arms wrapped around his waist, as she had since he'd picked her up off of Denmire's wooden floor. He stared down at her battered face and lip that had required two stitches, simmering with a rage he hadn't been able to leave behind as easily as he'd left Denmire's house. The bastard had almost taken her away, had almost killed her and their child. He moved his hand to rest against the baby and closed his eyes. The vision of a butcher knife traveling toward Sarah's belly flashed through his mind, and he sat up, nauseated, unable to handle what might have been.

Sarah stirred and opened her eyes, still pale but smiling. "Hi there."

"Hey."

She brushed her fingers through his hair. "You don't look like you've gotten any sleep."

He smiled back and kissed the tip of her nose. "I was too busy looking at you."

"That's what you said an hour ago, and two hours before that. I'm not that interesting, especially when my eyes are closed and I'm not moving."

He skimmed his knuckles against her temple, unable to stop touching her. "We'll have to disagree there."

"Why don't I make us some breakfast? I'm starving." She started to sit up, but he held her down by the shoulder.

"I'll get it. You stay here and rest." He shifted out of her arms and stood.

"You heard the doctor, Ethan. I should take it easy, but I'm fine." She glanced down at her bulging lower stomach and snagged his hand, resting his palm against it, smiling. "We're both fine. I don't want to dwell on what happened. It's over."

Sighing, he sat on the edge of the bed. "It's not that easy. I keep seeing it, Sarah. I keep seeing the knife coming toward you."

She sat up and hugged him. "But you saved me—my own knight in shining armor."

He closed his eyes and held on, mindful of the bandages against her neck and bruises on her arms. "How can you take this lightly?"

"I can't if I think about it too much, but that's the thing: I don't want to. I don't want to give him another minute of power over us, because that's what he wanted."

She eased back and kissed him, wincing as she pressed her fingers to her lip. "Ow."

"We should probably get you some ice." He moved to stand, she pulled him back down.

"In a second." Her brows furrowed as a snap of temper filled her voice. "I'm not finished."

Ethan grinned for the first time in twenty-four hours. "All right, bossy, finish what you have to say."

"Thank you. I will." Her voice softened as she brushed her fingers over his cheek. "You saved me, Ethan—you, Hunter, and Austin. If you hadn't come when you did..." She shook her head. "No, I'm not going there." She glanced down, taking a deep breath then met his gaze again. "Several women's families will now be able to find closure. An innocent man has been set free. Lisa will make a full recovery. Let's concentrate on that.

We have too many good things coming our way."

He kissed her forehead, amazed by her strength. "I'll certainly give it a try. Now, make me happy and let me pamper you a bit. Let me make you some breakfast. I'll bring up a tray. Kylee should be awake soon. We can eat out on the deck."

"That sounds nice."

By the time he'd pulled on his jeans and headed back up with a bag of ice for her lip, she was asleep again. Kylee stirred on the air mattress, and he scooped her up before she could wake Sarah. He held a finger to his lips, and she gave him a sleepy smile. He walked downstairs, grabbed two bananas from the counter for their impromptu breakfast, and headed outside with Bear and Reece in tow. "I have a surprise for you, ma'am."

Kylee clapped. "Ooh, a surprise."

"Yup, I think you're gonna like it."

Ethan watched her eyes go huge when they turned the corner toward the side of the house. A massive cedar structure with a bridge attached two princess-style turrets. Swings hung from the bridge while the turrets offered two slides—one twisty, the other tall and bumpy. A jungle gym Kylee wouldn't yet be able to climb leaned off the back. He and Wren had gotten a little carried away, but as Kylee squirmed down and ran forward, squealing her delight, he didn't care.

He laughed as she made a bee-line for the two-person swing shaped like a horse. Someday soon her brother or sister would join her. He couldn't wait. "Do you love it, Kylee girl?"

She held on to the pale pink handles and beamed. "Yes!"

"Should I give you a push?"

"Yes!"

"Hold on tight."

Her small fingers gripped the handles tighter, and Ethan sent her soaring. Her laughter rang out, mixing with his.

~~~~

Sarah woke, blinking. She'd dozed off again. The sun had risen higher in the sky and she was still in bed. Determined to go on as if nothing had happened, she stood. The cuts on her neck stung and her bruises throbbed while every muscle in her body ached. Giving in, she walked to the bathroom and pulled one low-dose Tylenol from the bottle Ethan had picked up on their way home from the hospital.

She stared in the mirror, wincing. "Good heavens, look at me." She brushed her fingers against the bandages on her neck and purple welts on her face then took a step closer, zeroing in on her lip. The doctor told her the stitching wouldn't leave a scar, but the sutured gash sure as hell looked ugly now. It could've been worse though, much worse.

Her mind flashed back to Matthew's living room and the knife coming toward her. Her heartbeat accelerated as her breath backed up in her throat. She walked to the bathtub on unsteady legs and sat down on the wide edge. "It's over. It's really over," she repeated, gripping her hands together. She would never have to see Matthew again, ever.

She closed her eyes, trying to relax and thought of Ethan and the way he'd held her tight while the ER doctor had given them another ultrasound to check on the baby. The tiny heart had beaten loud and strong as Ethan's breath shuddered in and out against her hair.

"Oh, thank God, Sarah. Thank God."

When Hailey dropped Kylee off, Sarah had carried her sleeping child, at her own insistence, to the air mattress Ethan had set up, breathing in deep, comforted by the smell of baby shampoo and her daughter's soft hair pressed against her cheek. There was so much to look forward to, a whole new life to make. Matthew Denmire would never have another moment of her time, not one, because he couldn't touch what she had. He could never touch what she and Ethan would make together.

Standing, steady and strong, Sarah walked to the balcony, listening as Kylee's peals of laughter and Ethan's deep voice echoed on the ocean breeze. Puzzled, she made her way through the house and outside, following the sounds that brought joy to her heart. She turned the corner and stopped, gaping. "Wow, Ethan, look at this swing set."

His gaze met hers across the lawn and he grinned. "It's pretty crazy, huh?"

"Yes, but it's beautiful." She walked closer, watching Kylee run about, giggling on her way down the twisty slide.

Sarah slid up next to Ethan and snaked her arm around his waist, enjoying the simple pleasure of holding him close.

"I figured both of our children would enjoy playing on this."

Both of their children. Yes, *their* children. Warmth radiated in Sarah's smile. "I think you're absolutely right."

Kylee stepped from the slide and ran toward them, eyes sparkling. "Look, Mama."

"I know. Go ahead, have fun and play."

Ethan snagged Kylee up, throwing her high and catching her. "We have one more surprise."

"You're going to spoil her, Ethan. This is certainly plenty."

"It's for both of you."

They wandered back to the house and up to the second story. Ethan set Kylee on her feet. "Kylee, go open that closed door for me."

"O-tay." Kylee moved like a bullet, stopped and twisted the doorknob. "Ooh, pretty."

"What have you done?" Sarah took the hand Ethan offered and walked to the door, stopping short. "Oh, Ethan, look at this room." Her eyes watered as she took it all in. Pastel purple dots—large and small—decorated pale pink walls. Smiling butterflies and caterpillars adorned a light quilt, covering a beautiful pine bed. Lamps in the same theme sat on matching dressers. Big, bold letters, all pastel, spelled out KYLEE. Stuffed animals piled high filled a corner of the room. It was perfect. Then she saw the picture—Jake's smiling face adorned a frame on her dresser. Sarah walked forward and picked up the photograph, staring at the man who had given her Kylee.

Ethan took her hand, and she turned, brushing her fingers against his cheek. He loved Kylee enough to share. Kylee would never have to choose, would never have to feel guilt for loving both of her fathers. "You are the most amazing man, Ethan Cooke."

"He would've been so proud of her, Sarah, so proud of both of you." Ethan kissed the tip of her nose and wrapped his arms around her waist as Kylee rolled on the plush, pink ladybug rug.

She set Jake's picture down, saying her final goodbye. So many emotions raced to the surface, but there was no room for sadness when she'd been blessed with so many gifts. Today was a day for the present, for the future. "You and Wren have been very busy."

"We didn't stop here."

She met his gray eyes. "What do you mean?"

He caught the tear running down her cheek and took her hand, stopping at the closed door next to Kylee's room and across from the master suite. "Open the door, Sarah."

"I don't know if I can take any more surprises."

Ethan kissed her forehead and placed her hand on the knob. "Give it your best shot."

She took a deep, unsteady breath and walked into the most beautiful nursery she'd ever seen. Light yellows and greens filled the space. Sweet-faced chicks accented the bedding and mobile hanging from the crib. She brushed her fingers along the soft fabric of towels, blankets, and burp cloths in the same baby duck theme, all tucked neatly away in pine furniture that matched Kylee's. She sat in the rocking chair and closed her eyes, imagining what it would be like to nurse their baby while she rocked him or her to sleep.

"Wren isn't finished in here," Ethan said, still holding her hand. "When we know what we're having, she wants to add some pink or blue touches."

"I can't imagine it being any better than this." Tears tracked down her cheeks as she stared at his handsome face. "Oh, Ethan."

"Did you see the view from the window seat? I like to imagine our child sitting there one day, thinking their thoughts, daydreaming."

She couldn't remember ever being so happy. She walked to the window, staring out at lush green trees and the Pacific tossing waves far in the distance. "It's so wonderful—all of it. I don't know what to say."

"Say yes."

She turned as Ethan stood in the center of the room, holding a square-cut, two-carat diamond ring. "Say you're ready to be my wife, that you're ready for us to be a family. I fell for you one night when you grinned at me with pizza cheese stuck to your chin, but you're all I've ever wanted. I love you, Sarah. Marry me."

Kylee came running into the room, wrapping her arms around Ethan's leg. Sarah walked forward, staring into gray pools, seeing her future, their future. She smiled, caressing her fingers against his cheek. "I love you too, Ethan. I'll marry you. I'm ready. I'm ready for everything."

He slipped the ring on her finger as he brushed her lips with a gentle kiss, took her hand, and swooped down for Kylee.

Sarah rested her head against Ethan's shoulder as the two of them walked from the nursery, each carrying one of their children.

On that bright sunny morning, with the ocean breeze blowing, life was truly perfect. And it had only just begun.

ABOUT THE AUTHOR

Cate Beauman is the author of the best selling series, The Bodyguards of L.A. County. She currently lives in Tennessee with her husband, two boys, and their St. Bernards, Bear and Jack.

www.catebeauman.com
www.facebook.com/CateBeauman
www.goodreads.com/catebeauman
Follow Cate on Twitter: @CateBeauman

OTHER TITLES BY CATE BEAUMAN

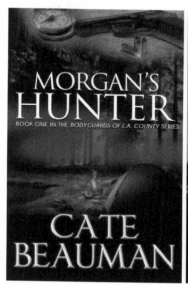

Printed in Great Britain
by Amazon.co.uk, Ltd.,
Marston Gate.